Up at
Butternut Lake

Up at
Butternut Lake

Mary McNear

WILLIAM MORROW
An Imprint of HarperCollins*Publishers*

P.S.™ is a trademark of HarperCollins Publishers.

UP AT BUTTERNUT LAKE. Copyright © 2014 by Mary McNear. All rights reserved. Printed in the United States of America. No part of this book may be used or reproduced in any manner whatsoever without written permission except in the case of brief quotations embodied in critical articles and reviews. For information address HarperCollins Publishers, 10 East 53rd Street, New York, NY 10022.

HarperCollins books may be purchased for educational, business, or sales promotional use. For information please e-mail the Special Markets Department at SPsales@harpercollins.com.

FIRST EDITION

Designed by Diahann Sturge

Library of Congress Cataloging-in-Publication Data has been applied for.

ISBN 978-0-06-228314-6

14 15 16 17 18   OV/RRD   10 9 8 7 6 5 4 3 2 1

To Harry and Rose, my bright, shining stars

Up at
Butternut Lake

CHAPTER 1

O kay, sleepyhead, time to wake up," Allie said, reaching into the backseat of the car and giving her five-year-old son, Wyatt, a gentle prod. "We're here. We're at the cabin." Wyatt stirred but didn't wake up. She didn't blame him. It had been a long day. Make that a long *week*, she corrected herself. And, if she were really counting, it had been a long two years. But she tried, whenever possible, not to count. It didn't make the time go any faster, or the loss any easier to bear.

She exhaled slowly and resisted the urge to put her head down on the steering wheel. She was exhausted—beyond exhausted, really—and it occurred to her, in that instant, that they could just sleep in the car that night. God knows, they were tired enough.

But no sooner had she considered the idea than she rejected it. This was supposed to be a fresh start. A new beginning. For both of them. It wouldn't do to wake up in the car tomorrow morning, wearing wrinkled clothes and stretching stiff limbs. They would spend the night in the cabin. The cabin that would hereafter be known as their home.

The only problem with that, she thought, studying the cabin

by the light of the car's headlights, was that it didn't look very home*like*. And that was putting it mildly. Several shingles had fallen off the roof. Knee-high grass was growing right up to the front porch. And the porch itself was listing dangerously to one side.

But it was still standing, she told herself. And *that* was something, wasn't it?

It had been over ten years since she'd last seen it. Part of her had thought it might have vanished altogether, swallowed up by the forest around it. But of course that hadn't happened. This wasn't a fairy tale. This was real life. She, of all people, knew that. She'd learned it the hard way.

She turned off the car's headlights, and the cabin all but disappeared into the darkness. She shivered unconsciously. Living on a suburban cul-de-sac these last several years, she'd forgotten how dark the darkness could be.

Maybe she should just keep driving. If memory served her correctly, there was a motel on Highway 169. They could be there in fifteen minutes. But then what? They'd still have to come back here in the morning. And the cabin wouldn't look any better by daylight. It might, in fact, look worse.

"Mommy?" Wyatt's voice broke into her thoughts. "Are we there?"

"Yes, we're here," she said, in her best imitation of cheerfulness. She turned to smile at him. "We're at the cabin."

"The cabin?" Wyatt asked, struggling to get out of his car seat.

"That's right," Allie said. "I'll show you." She reached for the flashlight in the glove compartment and turned it on. But as soon as she got out of the car, she could see the flashlight was no match for the night's darkness. Its weak beam barely cut through the blackness. She glanced up at the sky. No moon that she could see, no stars, either.

She shivered again and tried to ignore the sensation that the darkness itself was somehow palpable, like a weight pressing down on her. Even the air, she realized, seemed to have a cottony thickness to it.

She opened the car's back door, unfastened Wyatt's seat belt, and lifted him out of his car seat. She settled him on her hip and shone the flashlight in the direction of the cabin.

"There it is," she said. She hoped her voice sounded reassuring. Especially since she was feeling in need of some reassurance herself. Wyatt frowned in the direction of the cabin.

"I can't really see it," he whispered. "*It's so dark.*"

"It *is* dark," Allie agreed, and her heart sank a little more. But she caught herself. *Stop it. This is what you wanted, isn't it? Peace. Quiet. Solitude. And now you're unnerved by a little darkness?*

She reached for the canvas tote bag she'd placed on the backseat beside Wyatt. She'd filled it with everything they might need their first night here. She'd unload their other belongings in the morning. Right now, the important thing was to get Wyatt inside and into bed.

Poor kid, she thought, slamming the car door and walking up the cracked, overgrown flagstone path to the front porch. She'd woken him up at dawn that morning, when the movers had come to put the contents of their house into storage, and, except for a few well-timed rest stops, he'd spent the whole afternoon and evening in the car. But he hadn't complained. He almost never did that anymore. And it worried Allie. Complaining, after all, was one of childhood's God-given rights.

She stepped gingerly onto the cabin's front steps, testing them for stability. They held. So, too, did the warped and slanting front porch. She fished the front door key out of her tote bag and opened the rusted lock. And as she pushed the door open, she said a silent prayer. Something like, *Please don't let there be three generations of raccoons living here now.* But when she turned on the lights, the cabin looked exactly as it had the last time she'd seen it. Relief flooded through her.

Wyatt, though, didn't like what he saw. After a quick look around, he buried his face in the nape of her neck.

"Hey, what's wrong?" Allie asked, lugging him and the tote bag inside and locking the door behind them.

But Wyatt refused to lift his head. He just burrowed it deeper into her neck.

She frowned, looking around the cabin's living room. It looked fine to her. Homey, even. She could see there was a layer of dust on the furniture, and a few spider webs in the corners of the room. And it was stuffy, after being shut up for so long. But for the most part, it had stood the test of time remarkably well. There was nothing wrong with it that a little elbow grease wouldn't set right.

Still, she tried to see it from Wyatt's perspective. After all, he'd lived his whole life in a three-bedroom ranch house replete with all of life's modern conveniences. By his standards, this cabin wouldn't just look rustic. It would look downright primitive. But scary? She didn't think so.

"Wyatt," she said softly. "What's wrong, honey? I know it's not like our old house. But it's fine, really. It's just a little dusty, that's all. And the furniture is a little old. But it's nothing you and I can't fix up together."

But he shook his head violently and whispered something she couldn't understand.

"What did you say?" she asked, positioning her right ear against his mouth.

"I said 'he's looking at us,'" he whispered back.

Allie felt her body stiffen involuntarily. "*Who's* looking at us?" she asked, feeling a little unnerved. Okay, *a lot* unnerved. The movie about the boy who could see dead people came to mind, but Wyatt had never exhibited any such gift. At least, not to her knowledge. She fought down a little shiver of dread.

"Wyatt, *who's* looking at us?" she asked again. But he only shook his head and wrapped his arms more tightly around her.

She willed herself to be calm. *Nobody is looking at us,* she told herself. *We're all alone here. In more ways than one.*

So she forced herself to look at the cabin's living room again. *Really* look at it. And this time her eyes came to rest, almost immediately, on the antlered buck's head hanging above the fireplace. *Of course,* she thought, with a shaky exhale. Wyatt had never seen anything like that before. It *would* be frightening to him.

"Wyatt," she asked softly. "Are you afraid of the buck's head over the fireplace?" He nodded his head emphatically but still didn't look up.

"Oh, honey, don't be afraid," Allie said, snuggling him closer. "It's not real. I mean, it *was* real. But it's not alive anymore. My grandfather, your great-grandfather, brought it back from a hunting trip," she explained. "It's been hanging there since before you were born. Since before *I* was born." She admitted, "I didn't really notice it when I was a child. I guess because I was used to it. But I can see why it might be a little frightening to you."

Unlike her, of course, Wyatt hadn't been raised in a family of hunters and fishermen. His exposure to wildlife, in fact, had been limited to the fireflies and frogs he'd caught in their backyard in suburban Minneapolis.

With some effort, Wyatt lifted his head up. He shot the buck's head a quick look. But once again he squeezed his eyes shut and buried his face in her neck.

She tried a different tack. "Wyatt, it's like a stuffed animal," she explained. "Only bigger. But it's nothing to be afraid of. I promise you. It can't hurt you."

Wyatt cupped his hands around her right ear and whispered directly into it. "But he's staring at us."

Allie glanced at the buck's head again. Maybe it was the angle she was looking at it from. Or a trick of the light. But it did, in fact, appear to be staring at them. She sighed inwardly. This was one difficulty she hadn't anticipated.

She felt a flash of annoyance. Not at Wyatt. At the taxidermist responsible for the buck's head. Did he have to make the buck look so realistic? And so . . . so *fierce*? That buck did not look at all pleased to be hanging up there. In fact, he looked downright angry. *No question about it,* she thought. *He will have to go.*

"Wyatt, I'll take him down tomorrow," Allie announced decisively. "But until then, can you just not look at him?"

Wyatt lifted his head again and looked at her doubtfully. "I'll try," he said. "But, Mom," he whispered, stealing a sideways glance at him, "where's the rest of him? That's just his head."

All at once, Allie felt exhausted. "The rest of his body . . . isn't here," she said finally, opting to skip the gory details. "And after tomorrow, his head won't be here either, okay?"

Wyatt nodded, apparently satisfied. At least for the time being. As he snuggled back down into her arms again, Allie felt a surge of sympathy for him. She'd taken him away from everything that was familiar to him: his home, his extended family, his friends. And all she had to offer him in exchange was this creaky old cabin. *Make that this* creepy *old cabin,* she corrected herself, taking another look at the buck's head.

She tried to push any negative thoughts out of her mind. Maybe she *had* made a mistake bringing them here. But that didn't change the fact that she needed to get Wyatt to bed. And the sooner the better.

But first she looked around for something, *anything,* that would reassure him. Something that would help him understand, even a little, what it was about this place she had loved as a child.

She settled on the leather couch in the living room. It was old and worn with age. But she knew from experience that it felt deliciously buttery and smooth to the touch. She walked over to it, lowered Wyatt onto it and sat down beside him.

"This couch was my favorite place to read when I was a child," she said, patting one of its arms. "Especially on rainy days."

Wyatt frowned, a tiny line creasing his adorable brow. "I don't know how to read," he reminded Allie.

"I know that," she said, tousling his hair. "But you'll *learn* how to read. You'll start kindergarten here this fall."

But Wyatt shook his head. "There are no kindergartens here," he said, sadly.

"Of course there are," Allie said, smiling. "There are kinder-gartens everywhere."

Wyatt gave her a pitying look, almost as if he thought she'd lost her mind. "There's nothing here but trees," he said, twisting his little body around and looking out one of the cabin's many windows.

Allie resisted the urge to smile. "It's true. There *are* a lot of trees here. And you're right that there aren't any kindergartens in these woods. But," she said, pulling him into her arms and kissing the top of his head, "there *is* a kindergarten in Butternut. I've already told you all about Butternut, the town this lake is named after. It's only fifteen minutes away from here by car. We'll drive there tomorrow morning, and I'll take you to Pearl's, the little coffee shop there. And if it's still open—and I hope it is—I'll order you the best blueberry pancakes this side of the Mississippi. What do you say?"

Wyatt didn't say anything. He just sighed wearily.

"Time for bed," Allie said brightly. Maybe a little *too* brightly. She was fighting that by now familiar sense of guilt. The feeling that she'd failed Wyatt, that she'd somehow been less than the mother he needed her to be. But what was done was done, she reminded herself. They were here now and she needed to make the best of it.

So she helped him change into his pajamas. And she watched while he brushed his teeth. She had another tense moment when she turned on the faucet in the bathroom. There was an alarming gurgling sound before dirty brown water came sputtering out. But after a few seconds, the water ran clear. And Wyatt, fortunately, was too tired to have noticed anything amiss.

Of course, she was working hard to distract him. She kept up a steady, one-sided conversation about all the things they'd do that summer: fish off the pier, swim in the lake, and paddle around in the canoe.

By the time she delivered Wyatt to his bedroom, he seemed reasonably content. The room had been Allie's room, too, during her childhood summers at the lake. And she was pleased to see that, like the rest of the cabin's interior, it seemed remarkably well preserved. It was a tiny room, with a steeply sloped ceiling, and knotty pine furniture. There was a colorful braided rag rug on the floor, cheerful red-and-white-checked bedspreads with matching curtains, and an oilskin-shaded lamp that threw a soft glow over everything its light touched.

Being in this room again, Allie felt a wave of nostalgia. But none of this meant anything to Wyatt, she reminded herself. As far as he was concerned, they might as well be spending the night in a motel room. So now he watched, with solemn detachment, while she opened the windows, made up the bed with fresh sheets, and plugged in the night-light she'd remembered to pack in the tote bag.

As she tucked him in, she tried to reassure him. Tried to make an unfamiliar place seem more familiar. "Wyatt, did you know this is the same room I stayed in as a child?" she asked, sitting down on the edge of his bed.

He shook his head.

"Well, it is. And do you know what the best part of staying in this room is?"

Again he shook his head.

"I'll tell you," she said. "It's that when you wake up in the morning, you can see the lake from your window. You can't see it now because there's no moonlight tonight. But tomorrow morning, when you look out your window, the lake will feel close enough to touch. And, if it's a nice day, the water will be the bluest blue you've ever seen."

He stared skeptically at the black square of window above his bed.

"It's there," Allie reassured him. "And you're going to love it."

She reached over now and tried to smooth his hopelessly tangled brown curls, but she quickly gave up. It was impossible. The gesture, though, seemed to soothe him. He sighed and his eyes blinked closed. She waited as he hovered on the edge of sleep.

A moment later, though, he opened his eyes. He seemed suddenly wide-awake again. "Mom?" he asked, a worried expression on his face.

"Yes," she said, reaching out to stroke his hair again.

"What if Dad can't see me here?" he asked softly. So softly that Allie had to lean closer to hear him.

At the word *Dad* she felt the familiar tightening in her chest. But she forced herself to look directly at him. "What do you mean by 'see you here'?" she asked.

He squirmed a little under the covers. "Well, you said he would always be watching over me. Only now we're not at home anymore. We're here instead. So how will he know where to look for me?"

Allie felt her eyes fill with tears. She blinked them back. She was determined not to cry. Not in front of Wyatt, anyway. There'd be plenty of time for that later, after he'd fallen asleep.

"Wyatt, he'll always know where you are, wherever you go," Allie explained. "You don't need to worry about that."

"And he'll always be watching over me?" Wyatt prompted.

"Always," Allie said with a smile.

He squirmed again. "Even if I'm getting into trouble?" he asked.

Now it was Allie's turn to frown. "What do you mean by 'trouble'?"

"Well, remember when Teddy came over, and we caught that frog?" he asked, suddenly animated. "And we put him in the sink in the laundry room? To live there. Only I didn't tell you about it. Because I didn't think you'd let me keep him there. And then you found him anyway. And you got mad. Was he watching me then? Because if he was, he might have been mad at me, too." He collapsed back on his pillow, slightly out of breath.

Allie shook her head vehemently, still fighting back the tears. "No, Wyatt. He wasn't mad at you. Not at all. And neither was I. Not really. I was just a little . . . *surprised* when I found the frog, that's all."

Then she smiled, remembering something. "You know, Wyatt, your dad did much more mischievous things than that when he was a little boy. I'll tell you about them sometime, okay?"

He nodded, obviously relieved.

"And Wyatt? From now on, why don't we say that your dad is only looking down on you when you need him to, all right? I mean, he'll always be there for you. But he doesn't have to watch you every minute of every day. He knows you're a big boy now. He knows that most of the time you can take care of yourself."

Wyatt nodded again, this time sleepily. And Allie made a mental note to be more careful of how she phrased things in the future, given how literal Wyatt's thinking still was.

Now, he snuggled deeper under the covers and Allie looked out the window. She found the break in the trees that denoted the lake. It was too dark to see the water, but her eyes followed what she knew to be the shoreline. About half a mile away, across the bay, she saw a lighted dock. She frowned. A dock meant a house, and a house meant a neighbor. There hadn't been any neighbors the last time she was here. Her family's cabin had had the whole bay to itself.

She sighed. She should have known there would be changes here, too. Even in Butternut, Minnesota, time didn't stand still.

But a neighbor? That hadn't been part of her plan. Her plan had been to come to a place where there were no neighbors. At least not any close by.

She thought of their neighbors back home in Eden Prairie. They'd tried to be helpful. They'd brought her and Wyatt an endless procession of casseroles. They'd raked their leaves, shoveled snow out of their driveway, and mowed their lawn. All without asking.

She knew she should have been grateful. And she was, to a point. But she couldn't help but wonder if it would have been easier to grieve privately. Without feeling that you'd somehow become a curiosity. Someone to stare at, surreptitiously, at the grocery store, or speak to, a little self-consciously, at the playground.

Of course, the novelty of her widowhood had eventually worn off, but what had replaced it was worse. Because what came next were the suggestions, sometimes from family and friends, sometimes from only casual acquaintances, that it might be time to move on, to pick up the pieces. She was still young, they'd pointed out. There was no reason to think there wouldn't be another husband someday. Maybe even another child.

These conversations, it turned out, and not the pitying glances, had been Allie's breaking point. When they'd started, she'd known it was time to leave.

Now, sitting on the edge of Wyatt's bed, she gave herself a little shake, trying to throw off some of the exhaustion that had settled over her. She listened, for a moment, to Wyatt's breathing. It had settled into the regular rhythm of sleep. He was down for the count, she knew. He rarely woke up after he'd fallen asleep for the night. She turned off the lights and left the room, careful to leave the door open. She would be able to hear him, from her bedroom across the hall, if he needed her for any reason.

Then she made up the bed in her room, changed into a tank top and pajama bottoms, and brushed her teeth. It wasn't until she'd gotten into bed and turned off the bedside table lamp that she let herself contemplate the enormity of what she'd done. She'd sold their house, the only home Wyatt had ever known. She'd put most of their belongings in storage. And she'd bought out her brother's share of the lakeside cabin they'd been given by their parents, who now lived full-time in a retirement community in South Florida.

And now she'd returned to a place she hadn't been in years. A place she hadn't even spent a whole summer in since childhood. She had no relatives here. And no friends to speak of. The few friends she'd once had here had probably long since moved away. There was nothing here for her now, she knew. Nothing for either of them. Which begged the question of why, exactly, she'd decided to come back.

She heard a faraway sound, haunting but familiar. It had been a long time since she'd heard it, but if you heard it even once, you never forgot it again. It was the sound of coyotes howling. Not an uncommon sound in the woods of northern Minnesota, but not exactly comforting, either. She felt a tremor of fear. Even knowing they were safe inside the cabin it was unnerving. Tiredness, however, quickly overcame her, even if it didn't completely obliterate her anxiety. *I must be crazy,* she thought as she fell into a troubled sleep. *Why else would I have thought moving here was a good idea?*

CHAPTER 2

By eleven o'clock that night, when Walker's cell phone rang, his mood had gone from bad to worse. He glanced at the caller ID. It was his brother, Reid, the last person he wanted to talk to right now. But in addition to being his brother, Reid was also his business partner. And a demanding one at that. Walker ignored phone calls from him at his own peril.

He picked up his cell phone and hit the talk button. "What is it?" he growled, by way of a greeting.

"Jeez, Walk, is that the way you answer your phone now?" Reid asked mildly.

"It's eleven o'clock at night," Walker pointed out, leaning back in his leather desk chair. "We've been through this before, Reid," he said, massaging his temples, feeling the beginnings of a headache coming on. "Remember? You may work twenty-four hours a day, but I'm more of an eight-to-eight man myself."

"Well, that may be," Reid said, sounding faintly disapproving. And despite his bad mood, Walker felt a corner of his mouth lift in amusement. Only a workaholic like Reid would find evidence of laziness in a twelve-hour workday. "But your character defects aside," Reid continued, "I finished running the numbers on the Butternut Boatyard tonight." He paused for effect.

"And?" Walker asked, wishing Reid would hurry up. He wasn't in the mood to talk about business right now.

"And you did it," Reid said simply. "You said you needed five years to turn the boatyard around. You did it in three. Congratulations."

There was a long pause while he waited for Walker to answer. Walker didn't answer.

"Hey, Walk, I thought this was good news."

"It is," Walker said finally. "Of course it is. I'm just in a lousy mood."

"Yeah, I figured that out all by myself," Reid said. "And you know what? I don't blame you. If I lived in Butternut, Minnesota, population twelve hundred, I'd be in a bad mood, too. Seriously, Walk, what do you do with your free time up there?"

"What free time?" Walker asked, only half jokingly.

"Walk, even I have a *little* free time," Reid pointed out. *And we both know how you spend it,* Walker thought. Chasing women. And, more often than not, catching them.

"If you must know, Reid, I fish," Walker said. "It's very therapeutic. You should try it sometime. God knows you could use a little therapy."

Reid chose to ignore that remark. "Listen, Walk, I didn't just call to congratulate you on the boatyard. I wanted to discuss something else with you, too."

Walker tensed. They both knew what that something else was.

"I think you should move back to Minneapolis," Reid said, without waiting for Walker to give him an opening. "I need you back here at headquarters. We agreed you'd live in Butternut for as long as it took you to turn the boatyard around. Well, you've done that. You've done that and more. That boatyard's gone from being a cash drain to being one of the most profitable we own. Now I need you to do that again with another boatyard. And another. Because nobody's better at day-to-day operations than you, Walk. Not even me."

That was high praise, indeed. And they both knew it. But still, Walker didn't answer.

Reid tried a different tack. "Seriously, Walk, I don't know how you live up there year-round. I mean, it's beautiful, I'll grant you that. And you have every right to be proud of the cabin you've built. But you're single. You're in the prime of your life. And you've chosen to live in a place where the hottest game in town is Friday night bingo at the American Legion. Besides, you've told me yourself how competent your general manager is. So put him in charge and move back to the Twin Cities. You can still go up to Butternut on weekends. And fish to your heart's content. Maybe even play a game of bingo or two."

Walker sighed. The promise of a headache had materialized, throbbing steadily at his temples. "Reid, can we talk about this later?"

"No, we can't. We can't because I've been meaning to talk to you about this for a long time. I've tried to be supportive, Walk, even during your little . . . domestic experiment—"

Walker interrupted him. "Is that how we're referring to my marriage now? As *a domestic experiment*?"

"Look, call it what you want," Reid said. "It didn't work out. And it's not surprising, really, when you consider that our first exposure to the concept of marriage was our parents' marriage."

Walker winced. That was true enough. Their parents' marriage had been a train wreck, and witnessing it had been more than enough to instill a lifelong fear of the institution of marriage in both of them. It was, they knew, something to be avoided at all costs. Walker's brief, and unsuccessful, stab at it had done nothing to convince them otherwise.

"Listen, Reid, I'll call you in the morning," Walker said.

"Walk, I need an answer from you."

"Later."

"*Now*," Reid insisted.

"I think you're breaking up," Walker lied. "There's a storm moving in."

"I'm not breaking up—" Reid started to argue.

But it was too late. Walker pressed end on his cell phone and flipped it shut, dropping it on the desk. Reid would be annoyed, but he'd get over it. It wasn't the first time Walker had hung up on him. And it most likely wouldn't be the last time either.

He left his study and went to the kitchen, grabbing a cold beer from the refrigerator. Then he cut through the living room and pushed open the sliding glass door that led onto the deck. It was pitch-dark outside. He glanced up at the sky. What moon there was was covered by a gauzy layer of clouds. He reached back inside the cabin and flipped on the outdoor lights. Then he walked out to the edge of the deck, found the black sheet of lake below, and twisted off his beer top. He sat down on an Adirondack chair and drank his beer slowly, setting the empty bottle down on the deck when he was done. He thought about getting another one, but stopped himself. No point in drowning his aggravations in beer. Especially when it wasn't even Reid who'd aggravated him. In fact, he felt a little guilty now for hanging up on him.

No, even before Reid's phone call, he'd been in a bad mood.

And all because of an otherwise innocuous little shred of fabric he'd found that afternoon.

He'd been taking down a fishing tackle box from the top shelf of the hall closet when he'd felt something else up there, too. Something improbably silky and soft. He couldn't see what it was until he'd yanked it down, and by then it was too late. He'd stared at the object in his hands, simultaneously fascinated and repelled by it. It was a lacy little nightgown. His ex-wife Caitlin's lacy little nightgown, to be exact.

Once he'd realized what it was, he'd tried to hold it with only his fingertips. As if it would burn him if he touched any more of the fabric than was absolutely necessary. Which was ridiculous, he knew. It was a piece of material, not some talisman with supernatural powers. But still, it was all he could do to force himself to hold it up, gingerly, for inspection.

He hadn't remembered this particular piece of lingerie. But then again, Caitlin had owned so many of these frothy little concoctions. Never mind how impractical it was to wear them during northern Minnesota's long winters. She would have done better to invest in a high-necked, long-sleeved flannel nightgown. But no. Practicality had never been her strong suit. Still, how this one—a white slip of a nightgown, with a lacy trim at the neckline and hem—had gotten left behind, he had no idea.

And it had occurred to him, for a second, that she might have left it there on purpose. In a place where he'd least expect to find it. But he decided that hadn't been the case. Caitlin was many things, but she wasn't devious. Or malicious. Besides, by the time she'd left, she'd been so furious at him the last thing she would have wanted to do was leave anything behind.

No, he decided. Maggie, the woman who came out from town

to clean once a week, had probably found it after Caitlin had left. Tactful as ever, she'd put it somewhere where she thought he wouldn't find it. At least not for a while.

But now that he had found it, he had no idea what to do with it. He thought about throwing it away, but that seemed somehow disrespectful to Caitlin. Even if things had ended badly between them, he didn't bear her any ill will. He thought about sending it to her, but he quickly dismissed that idea, too. He didn't have her address. And even if he did, how exactly did someone mail his ex-wife her nightgown? In an otherwise empty envelope, with no return address on it? Or wrapped in tissue paper, with a friendly note? Something like, *I guess you forgot to pack this when you were screaming hysterically at me and throwing all your clothes into suitcases in the middle of the night*?

In the end, he'd put the nightgown back where he'd found it, on the top shelf of the hall closet. When he had enough clothes to donate to a local charity, he reasoned, he'd bundle the nightgown in with them. But for now, there was nothing else to be done. The nightgown would be out of sight, but not out of mind.

A breeze blew off the lake now, stirring the branches of the great northern pines that towered above his deck, and Walker exhaled slowly. He felt his headache ease a little. He knew Reid didn't understand why he lived here. Not full-time, anyway. And Reid was right. It wasn't entirely necessary for him to do so. He could easily split his time between Butternut and Minneapolis. He also hadn't needed to build a cabin here. He could have lived in the apartment above the boatyard office. It would have been as comfortable, and maybe even more comfortable, than many of the places he'd lived in over the last several years.

But what Reid didn't understand was that where Reid found

escape in casual hookups and one-night stands, Walker found escape here. In this town, this lake, and this cabin.

The town was gossipy, it was true. Most small towns were. Even without trying, Walker already knew more about its residents than he wanted to know. But he had been careful, after his wife left, not to get personally involved with any of them.

And when he wasn't working at the boatyard, he was here, in a cabin he'd designed and built himself on one of northern Minnesota's most pristine lakes. Living out here, he'd been able to avoid any more complications in his life. Because here was untrammeled wilderness, and wildlife galore. There were miles of trails to hike around the lake; and on the lake, which was over twelve miles long and one hundred and twenty feet deep, there were dozens of pine-crested islands to explore. But in all this natural beauty, there were no messy entanglements, no senseless misunderstandings, no heated arguments. In short, there were no relationships, and that suited him just fine.

Not that he was a monk. He wasn't. He kept an apartment in Minneapolis, and when he was there on business, he'd get together with a woman he'd known since college. Like him, she put her job first. And also like him, she was uninterested in a long-term relationship. The time they spent together was brief, fun, and uncomplicated. In short, it was just about perfect.

As he reached down to pick up his empty beer bottle, his eyes scanned the opposite shore of the lake. They stopped on an unfamiliar light, faint but still visible, through the trees. He tried, from memory, to picture what was there. He knew this bay now like he knew the back of his hand.

But there was nothing there. Not really. Just a derelict old cabin he'd assumed was abandoned. That and a falling-down dock and boathouse. Certainly he'd never known anyone to actually stay on that property. Not since he'd built his own cabin. Maybe, he thought, the place had been discovered by local teenagers, looking for somewhere to drink beer and make out out of sight of watchful parents. *That's probably it,* he thought, heading back inside the cabin. No one would be crazy enough, or brave enough, to actually live there.

CHAPTER 3

"Wyatt, look, it's still here," Allie said excitedly, tugging on her son's hand as they crossed Butternut's Main Street the next morning. For the first time since they'd arrived at the cabin, she felt a small surge of optimism. *This* was a good sign, she decided. Pearl's was still here. Still open for business. And, as far as she could tell, still exactly the same as it had been when she was a child. The same red-and-white-striped awning, she noted with satisfaction. The same hand-lettered sign, advertising THE BEST PIE IN TOWN. And, she saw through the windows, the same Formica-topped counter and red swivel stools.

But when they reached the sidewalk outside of Pearl's, Wyatt hesitated. Allie squeezed his hand encouragingly.

"Hungry?" she asked, smiling down at him. He nodded. "Good. Because I'm starving. And it's either Pearl's, or that can of baked beans I found in the back of the kitchen cupboard this morning." She waited for a response. He glanced anxiously through the glass door. *This* was new, she realized, with a little jolt of anxiety. This reluctance to go into unfamiliar places.

"So, what's it going to be?" she prompted, letting go of his hand long enough to tousle his hair.

"This place," he said, resignedly. *Too* resignedly for a five-year-old, Allie thought.

But she pushed open the swinging glass door and gently pulled Wyatt in behind her.

Once inside, though, Allie felt an unexpected shyness herself. She nodded politely to the customers who looked up from their conversations or their newspapers, but her cheeks burned. It had been a long time since she'd been a stranger anywhere.

She led Wyatt over to the counter and boosted him up onto one of the empty stools. Behind the counter, a pretty, blue-eyed, strawberry blond woman of about forty was shoveling coffee grounds into an industrial-sized coffeemaker.

"I'll be right with you," she said, glancing up with a smile.

"No hurry," Allie said, picking up a menu. She offered to read it to Wyatt, but he had discovered that the top of his stool rotated three hundred and sixty degrees, and with a rare glimmer of excitement in his eyes, he was using both hands to push off the countertop and spin himself around.

Allie smiled nervously at the woman behind the counter. "He was cooped up in a car for the better part of the day yesterday," she explained. But the woman, looking over at Wyatt, only smiled.

"Three generations of children have spun on those stools," she commented, flipping a switch on the coffeemaker. "And with any luck, three more generations will spin on those stools, too."

Allie started to say something, then stopped. The woman was frowning at her in concentration. "Don't tell me," she muttered. "It's right on the tip of my tongue . . . Allie Cooper," she an-

nounced, finally. Triumphantly. "Your family has a cabin on Butternut Lake."

"That's right," Allie said, flushing with surprise. "How did you
know?"

"I never forget a face," the woman said, taking out a pencil and
a check pad. "Although truthfully, sometimes, I wish I could. My
ex-husband's, for instance. Now *there's* a face worth forgetting."
She didn't sound bitter, though. Just matter-of-fact.

"I *do* forget faces," Allie confessed. "And names, too."

"Well, I don't expect you to remember me," the woman said
with a shrug. "You were just a little girl when your father used to
bring you in here for breakfast. I was a teenager. And this was the
last place I wanted to be on a summer day. Busing tables when
my friends were all out at the lake."

Of course, Allie thought, with an internal sigh of relief. She
did remember her. Caroline, she thought her name was. Her
grandmother Pearl had worked the register. Her mother, Alice,
had taken orders, and her father, Ralph, had worked the grill.
Allie had to subtract the years from her face, and replace her
middle-aged warmth with adolescent sulkiness, but she could
see her now as she had been then. Busing tables with a bored,
slightly exasperated expression on her face.

"You're Caroline. Caroline Bell," Allie said.

"I was. I'm Caroline Keegan now. I didn't keep my husband,"
she said, with a smile. "But I did keep his last name."

"Well, I'm not Allie Cooper anymore, either," Allie explained.
"My last name now is Beckett. And this is Wyatt," she added,
gesturing to Wyatt, who continued to spin furiously.

"That's right," Caroline said. "I heard you'd gotten married.
Your brother was up here fishing with friends some years ago,
and he brought me up to date on all your lives."

"I *did* get married," Allie said, quickly, checking to see that Wyatt was still absorbed in spinning on his stool. "But . . ." She paused. This was the hardest part, telling people who didn't already know. Oh, who was she kidding? *All of it was the hardest part.*

"But my husband was in the Minnesota National Guard," she said, finally. "He was sent to Afghanistan with them two years ago this summer and . . ." She stopped again. She couldn't go on.

"And he didn't come back," Caroline finished for her, speaking softly. "I'm so sorry, honey."

Allie shook her head, fighting back the tears.

Wordlessly, Caroline flipped over the empty coffee cup on the counter in front of Allie and filled it up from a steaming pot of coffee. Then she pushed it, along with cream and sugar, over to her.

"Now, I'll take your orders," Caroline said, companionably. "But I can't get them started right away. The grill's on hold while Frankie, my fry cook, tinkers with the air-conditioning. It's on the blink right now. And I don't need to tell you how bad the timing is, what with the weather reports calling for a heat wave."

Allie nodded, sipping her coffee. She was grateful to Caroline for changing the subject. It was an art form, she'd decided, that few people had mastered.

"Oh, here's Frankie now," Caroline said, as a massive man maneuvered his way behind the counter. Wyatt caught a glimpse of him and abruptly stopped spinning. Then he stared, wide-eyed, as Frankie scrubbed his hands at a deep sink, dried them off, and took an enormous apron down from a hook on the wall and tied it around his huge waist.

"Frankie, the griddle cakes are up for table three, and table seven needs the breakfast special, sunny-side up," Caroline said, cheerfully.

Frankie nodded and turned to face the grill, but Wyatt continued to stare at his back. Caroline noticed him staring and smiled. She leaned on the counter and said, quietly, to Allie and Wyatt, "Frankie is six feet six inches tall and three hundred and fifty pounds of pure muscle. But he is the gentlest man I've ever known." She added, "I have never, *ever*, seen him lose his temper. He doesn't need to. One look from him and an unwanted customer clears right out of here."

I'll bet they do, Allie thought with amusement. Coming up against him would be like colliding with a solid wall of rock.

"Now, for those orders," Caroline said.

"Wyatt and I will both have the blueberry pancakes," Allie answered.

"And I'll have a chocolate milk shake," Wyatt chimed in.

"Not for breakfast," Allie corrected him.

"But you said I could have one yesterday," Wyatt said, determinedly.

"I did?"

He nodded. "When we were driving in the car yesterday, you told me about Pearl's. And I said, 'Do they have chocolate milk shakes?' And you said, 'Yes, they do.' And I said, 'Could I have one when we go there?' And you said, 'Yes.'"

"Oh," Allie said, momentarily at a loss for words.

"I'll tell you what," Caroline said. "How about if I bring you an extrasmall milk shake as a compromise? After all, it is breakfast time. And a growing boy like you needs food that'll stick to his ribs."

Wyatt thought about it. "Okay," he said finally. "But not *too* small."

Caroline winked at Allie, scribbled their orders down, and ripped the sheet off the check pad. She stuck it to a clip above the grill, at eye level with Frankie. A customer came up to the counter to pay then, and she moved down to the cash register.

"Your cabin is on Otter Bay, isn't it?" she called down to Allie.

Allie nodded in surprise. As far she knew, Caroline had never been to her family's cabin. But she'd forgotten how much people in a small town knew about each other's lives. Even, it turned out, the location of an otherwise remote little cabin.

"You have a new neighbor out that way," Caroline said, handing her customer his change.

"I know," Allie said, a frown playing around her lips.

She'd taken Wyatt down to the dock first thing that morning, and they'd seen the cabin across the bay. It was built on a bluff, perched over the lake, and it had been designed in such a way as to make it look as if it were hovering there, over the water. It was sleek and contemporary, all clean lines, pale wood, and glass.

Below the cabin, on the lakefront, was an enormous boathouse, with at least half a dozen slips in it, and a seemingly endless dock, jutting far out into the water.

Allie's ramshackle boathouse and dock, on the other hand, presented an almost comical contrast to their luxurious counterparts across the bay. The boathouse roof had partially fallen in, and so many birds were nesting in its exposed rafters that it looked like a rookery. The dock, unfortunately, hadn't fared much better. It was in the process of collapsing into the lake, with only part of it visible above the waterline.

"Your neighbor's name is Walker Ford," Caroline said, coming back down the counter to stand in front of them. "He bought the local boatyard a few years back."

"Really?" Allie asked, with more politeness than enthusiasm.

She wasn't thrilled about having a neighbor, especially one as seemingly ostentatious as this man. His owning the boatyard, though, did explain why he had so many boats.

Caroline put place settings, pats of butter, and pitchers of syrup in front of them. "It'll be nice to have a neighbor all the way out there," she said. "And I think you have at least one old friend from town who's still around."

"Really?" Allie asked, puzzled.

"That's right," Caroline said. "You remember Jax Lindsey, don't you? You two used to be inseparable, didn't you?"

Of course Allie remembered Jax. The two of them had met the summer they were sixteen. They'd bonded over the makeup counter at the local drugstore. But it had never occurred to her that Jax, of all people, would still be living here. Her family life had been troubled, to say the least, and Allie had always assumed that when Jax left home, she'd put as much distance between herself and her parents as possible.

"I can't believe she's still here," Allie murmured.

"Well, she is," Caroline said. "She stayed in Butternut. Although, honestly, if she hadn't met a nice local boy—Jeremy Johnson—she might have moved on. Anyway, they got married, took over the local hardware store from Jeremy's parents, and had three daughters. With a fourth on the way."

"*Four* children?" Allie breathed. She'd often felt she was barely holding her own with one.

"That's right," Caroline said. "And she makes it look easy, too." She sighed and shook her head. "I have one daughter. Daisy. But four? I'm frankly in awe of Jax."

"How old is Daisy?" Allie asked.

"Eighteen," Caroline said. "She's starting college in September. She has a full scholarship to the University of Minnesota. But she moved down to Minneapolis after school ended a few weeks ago. She wants to work and save money before school starts."

"Sounds like a good idea," Allie said.

"It *is* a good idea," Caroline agreed. "But that doesn't mean I don't miss her," she said, a little wistfully, reaching behind her, to the counter beside the grill, and sliding two plates of blueberry pancakes in front of them. Then she presented Wyatt with his chocolate milk shake. It was in a small juice glass, but it had a hefty dollop of whipped cream on it, with chocolate syrup drizzled over it. Needless to say, Wyatt didn't complain. He picked it up immediately and took several large gulps. When he set the cup back down, empty, he had a little glob of whipped cream on his nose. Allie laughed and wiped it off with a napkin.

"Not bad, huh?" Caroline asked, smiling. "I've got to take a few orders," she said, coming out from behind the counter. "You two enjoy your breakfasts."

"Thank you," Allie answered. She reached for Wyatt's plate of blueberry pancakes and started to cut them for him. Otherwise, she was afraid he'd swallow them whole. Her own stomach was rumbling hungrily. Often, over the last two years, she'd had to force herself to eat. This morning, though, that wouldn't be necessary. Perfect blueberry pancakes might not be able to solve the world's problems. They might not be able to solve *her* problems, either. But right now, it was almost possible to believe that they could.

CHAPTER 4

Walker was still in a bad mood the next morning as he slid onto a stool at Pearl's and signaled Caroline for a cup of coffee. She was taking an order at one of the tables, but she looked up long enough to give Walker a quick nod that said she, and a fresh pot of coffee, would be right with him. He glanced at his watch. He was late for a meeting with one of the boatyard's biggest suppliers, and last night's headache, despite the aspirin he'd swallowed before leaving the cabin, continued to throb dully at his temples.

At least he'd managed to get to the counter without being drawn into a conversation with any of the regulars, he thought. Because this morning, he had neither the energy nor the patience for Butternut's particular brand of folksiness. Instead, as he waited for his coffee, he watched Frankie, the gargantuan fry cook, crack several eggs in rapid succession onto the sizzling grill. It never ceased to amaze him how a man that large managed to maneuver so gracefully in a space that small. But Walker had never seen him make a single false move. It was rumored, he knew, that Frankie had done time. Hard time. Which might explain why he obviously felt so at home in such close quarters.

But as much as Walker was enjoying watching Frankie, something to the right of him caught his eye. Three stools away, a woman was sitting with a little boy. A mother and a son, obviously. Walker knew immediately they weren't from Butternut. He would have recognized them if they were. He sighed. Was it possible that he knew, at least by sight, every single one of Butternut's twelve hundred residents? Maybe Reid was right. Maybe it was time to move on.

He tried, out of politeness, to look away from his counter mates. But he couldn't. Probably because, even in profile, he could see how pretty the woman was. She must have sensed his eyes on her, too, because she turned and met his gaze, head-on.

He hadn't been wrong about her, he saw. She was pretty. Exceptionally pretty. But in a totally unselfconscious way. As if she didn't know that she was pretty. Or didn't care. Though neither scenario, Walker thought, seemed likely. In his experience, women both knew about, and cared about, their relative attractiveness.

This woman had long, honey-colored brown hair that fell in a straight curtain down to her shoulders, and hazel eyes that were striking against a golden complexion. She smiled at Walker, now, a polite but disinterested smile. Walker recognized that smile. It was the smile he smiled when he didn't want to appear unfriendly but didn't want to be drawn into a conversation either. After the smile, she turned back to cutting her son's pancakes.

Walker felt a little jolt of surprise. *That* was unusual. Not that mothers of young children were in the habit of throwing themselves at him. They weren't. Not usually, anyway. But they also weren't completely immune to him either. His eyes skated, almost unconsciously, to her ring finger. There was a thin gold band on it. No surprise there. Young, single women were in short supply this far north. Not much excitement up here. Unless, of course, you were an avid fisherman.

He watched, as discreetly as possible, while she finished cutting her son's pancakes and slid the plate back in front of him. He was a cute little boy, Walker thought. He wasn't good at guessing ages, but he thought this kid looked like he was somewhere between four and six years old. He had a mop of curly brown hair, and a sweet but serious expression on his face.

Now, he wolfed down his pancakes hungrily, ignoring his mother's mild protestations. Walker suppressed a smile. He couldn't blame the kid. He'd had the blueberry pancakes before. They were beyond good.

"You look like you could use an extrastrong cup of coffee," Caroline said, materializing in front of him with the coffeepot.

"That sounds good," he said, tearing his eyes off the woman and her son.

"For here or to go?"

"To go," Walker said, glancing down at his watch again.

"No breakfast?" Caroline asked, reaching for one of the paper cups stacked behind the counter, filling it up to the rim, and snapping a plastic lid on it.

"No breakfast," Walker confirmed.

Caroline frowned a disapproving frown, but otherwise said nothing. In her own, no-nonsense way, Walker thought, she was as maternal with her customers as the woman down the counter from him was with her son. Caroline didn't like it when one of her regulars left without a hearty breakfast under his or her belt. But after almost three years, she knew Walker well enough to know he couldn't be browbeaten into ordering food he wasn't in the mood to eat.

Walker laid a five-dollar bill on the counter and stood up to go.

"Not so fast," Caroline said, sliding the cup over to him. "I want you to meet your new neighbors. It just so happens that they're here this morning, too."

"My new neighbors?" Walker repeated, blankly. "I don't have any neighbors."

"You do now," Caroline said. She gestured to the mother and son sitting a few seats away from him.

"Allie, Wyatt," she said, loudly enough to get their attention. "This is Walker Ford. Your closest neighbor. Unless, of course, you count the black bears. And I'm not counting them," she added, winking at Wyatt.

Walker's counter mate turned to look at him again. She didn't look happy. In fact, she looked distinctly *unhappy*. Which was strange, Walker thought. He hadn't given her a reason to dislike him yet, had he? He frowned. He wasn't used to people, especially women, finding him uninteresting *or* unlikable.

But her good manners obviously won out. She slid off her stool and, gently pulling her son after her, came over to shake Walker's hand. Her hand felt soft and smooth in his own work-roughened hand, and for a second, he felt at a loss for words. It didn't help that she was standing so close to him, either, though it was no closer than was absolutely necessary to shake his hand. She made her son shake his hand, too.

"I'm Allie Beckett," she said, smiling that noncommittal smile again. "And this is Wyatt. We just moved in last night, actually."

"I saw the light on in your cabin," Walker said, mesmerized by her hazel eyes. He saw, up close, that they were actually light brown with darker flecks of green in them.

"You must have been surprised," Allie said. "It's been a long time since anyone's been there."

"I *was* surprised," Walker confessed. "To be perfectly honest, I didn't know that cabin was actually habitable."

Allie frowned, and he knew he'd said the wrong thing. Pink color rushed onto the gold of her cheeks, although whether from anger or embarrassment, he couldn't tell. And he didn't really care, either. Because the change in coloring only made her look more ridiculously pretty than she already looked.

"Well, it *is* habitable," she said. "But it *does* need some work," she agreed. "Which is where Wyatt and I come in. Right, kiddo?" she said, pulling the boy closer. He nodded solemnly. "Fortunately, we're not afraid to get our hands dirty," she added.

"Are you sure it wouldn't be easier to just tear it down?" Walker asked, without thinking. He was having trouble thinking. Thinking clearly, anyway.

"Tear it down?" she repeated, aghast. More pinkness flooded her tawny cheeks. Even he could see that she was angry now. Very angry.

"My grandfather built that cabin himself," she said. "And it was built to last. It's not ostentatious, like some of the later cabins on the lake," she added, pointedly. "But it's not meant to be, either."

Ouch, thought Walker. It was impossible to miss that dig. He felt the tiniest flicker of embarrassment. Maybe because when he'd built his cabin he'd wondered himself if it was perhaps just a *tiny* bit pretentious to build something that big on that lake.

But he was reluctant to end the conversation on a sour note. They were, after all, neighbors now.

"Is your husband a fisherman?" he asked, changing the subject.

"My husband?" she asked, startled.

Walker checked her ring finger again. It was definitely a wedding ring. She followed his eyes to it and looked at it as if she were seeing it for the first time. Maybe he'd been wrong about it being a wedding ring, he thought. But if it wasn't a wedding ring, she probably wouldn't have worn it on the ring finger of her left hand.

"My husband's not here," she said, looking back up at him. And there was something about the way she said it that led him to believe their separation was permanent. He could relate to that, although, in his case, there hadn't been a young child involved. That was bound to make things more complicated. He wondered if she wore the ring for her son's sake. Maybe she thought taking it off would upset him.

"It was nice meeting you, Mr. Ford," she said now, and Walker almost winced. She'd said it was nice meeting him the same way she might have said it was nice going to the dentist. He watched while she led her son back to his seat at the counter. Then he picked up his cup of coffee and headed out the door.

"*That* went well," he muttered to himself, as he drove his pickup truck to the boatyard outside of town. He reminded himself that it didn't matter whether the two of them liked each other or not. In fact, it was probably better if they didn't. He didn't want a neighbor, and, apparently, neither did she.

So why, he wondered, did their meeting only add to his irritability? He had no idea. But it did. And not only that, but for the rest of the day, when he should have been thinking about work, he found himself thinking instead about Allie Beckett and her son. There was something strangely unsettling about his meeting with them.

Maybe Reid was right. Maybe he did have cabin fever. He needed to get away from Butternut, he decided. He'd go to Minneapolis on Friday. A couple of days in the city would do him good. Clear his head. And, with any luck, help him forget about the nightgown he'd found in the closet. Because, as ridiculous as it seemed, Walker couldn't help thinking that his finding it was a bad omen, a harbinger of more trouble to come.

CHAPTER 5

By five o'clock that evening, Allie's earlier optimism had completely evaporated. She and Wyatt were sitting on the cabin's lopsided front steps. Wyatt was playing with his Hot Wheels, and she was swatting listlessly at the mosquitoes and wondering what on earth had possessed her to move here. She was already nostalgic for the snug ranch house they'd left behind, especially when another shingle fell, unceremoniously, off the roof of the cabin, barely missing the front steps they were sitting on.

It brought to mind what her new neighbor, Walker Ford, had said about the cabin that morning. *Wouldn't it be easier to just tear it down?* She'd bristled at that remark, but the man had a point. Because while the cabin had a certain ramshackle charm, it was beginning to dawn on her that when it came to actually living with it, charm might be an overrated commodity.

Wyatt, at least, seemed content. He was propelling a bright red car along one of the cabin's warped front steps, supplying the sound effects for it whenever he thought it necessary.

Soon, she knew, it would be time to make his dinner. Run his bath. Read him a bedtime story. And otherwise pretend that it was business as usual, and that she hadn't made a terrible mistake in uprooting their suburban lives and bringing them here, to what suddenly felt like the end of the earth.

Wyatt stopped playing now and looked up. Something had caught his attention. In the next moment, Allie realized what it was. It was the sound of a truck, coming up the long gravel driveway to the cabin.

She couldn't imagine who it might be. She didn't know anyone here. And the few people she did know now—Caroline Keegan and Walker Ford—seemed unlikely candidates for a visit. But in the next moment, a red pickup truck coasted into view and stopped, and a petite woman swung open the driver's-side door and jumped lightly out.

"Jax?" Allie said in astonishment, standing up and going to meet her halfway. She hadn't seen Jax since the summer they were sixteen years old, but as far as Allie could tell, she still looked exactly the same. She'd been tiny then, and she was tiny now. Barely five feet tall and just a shade under a hundred pounds, as Allie recalled. She still wore her jet black hair in a ponytail, and her eyes, fringed by dark lashes, were still a vivid blue. She even had the same spray of freckles across her cheeks and the bridge of her nose that she'd had when they were teenagers.

But when Jax came over to hug her, Allie saw, and then felt, that there was one difference between the Jax then and the Jax now. This Jax was pregnant. *Quite* pregnant.

"It is so good to see you," Allie said, hugging her. And when the firm roundness of Jax's belly intruded between them, Allie laughed and held her at arm's length to look at her. "When are you due?" she asked.

"Not for three more months, if you can believe it," Jax said with a sigh. "It's because I'm so small," she explained. "The pregnancy weight doesn't have anywhere else to go, so it all goes right here," she added, pointing to her swollen belly.

"Well, that may be," Allie said, "but other than being pregnant, you don't look any different than the last time I saw you."

Jax shrugged. "I'm thirty now, the same as you, Allie. But I know how young I look. I know because whenever I take the kids to the Kmart out on Highway 53, all the grandmothers there give me dirty looks. You know, 'children having children.' That kind of thing."

Allie laughed. Those grandmothers must have been shocked to see a woman who looked barely old enough to drive a car with three children in tow, and a fourth on the way.

"Speaking of children," Jax said, approaching Wyatt, "this must be Wyatt. Caroline told me you are a world-class pancake eater." Her blue eyes were dancing.

Wyatt looked shyly down, but he didn't say anything, and Allie felt her heart contract. She remembered Wyatt as a toddler. He'd been positively gregarious. When had he started to change? But that was a silly question. She knew exactly when he'd started to change.

Jax, though, was undaunted by his shyness. "You know, Wyatt," she said, lowering herself onto the step beside him, "I have three daughters at home. Joy is twelve, Josie is nine, and Jade is six."

Wyatt frowned. "That's a lot of girls," he said softly. He looked worried.

Jax laughed, but then her expression turned serious. "That *is* a lot of girls," she agreed. "And, just between you and me, there's going to be at least one more," she said, running a hand over her belly. "Because this baby is going to be a girl, too."

Wyatt had nothing to say to that, but the worry lines on his forehead deepened.

"I should tell you though, Wyatt," Jax said, her tone still serious, "the three girls we already have are no ordinary girls. Their father has taught each one of them how to hit a fastball." That got Wyatt's attention. He looked up, interested.

Jax leaned closer and lowered her voice. "And if the truth be told, Wyatt, I think their father would like to keep going until we have enough daughters for our own baseball team. That would be nine in all." She smiled and brushed his cheek lightly with her fingertips, and Allie was relieved to see that Wyatt didn't recoil under her touch. Instead, he stared expectantly at her, waiting to hear what she would say next.

"Oh, I almost forgot," she said, jumping up. "I brought you two something." She went back to her truck and reached into the backseat. Then she lifted out a whole flat of strawberries, six quarts in all.

"Let me help you," Allie said, coming over to her, but Jax waved her away.

"I picked these from our garden this morning," she explained. "You'll probably want them in the refrigerator," she added, heading up the front steps of the cabin.

"Careful on the steps," Allie called, rushing to keep up with her. Pregnant or not, Jax was remarkably agile.

Jax opened the door to the cabin and Allie followed her inside. Wyatt, still looking interested, trailed behind them. But no sooner had she gotten over the threshold than Jax stopped.

"It looks exactly the same," she said, her eyes traveling around the room. Allie smiled. She'd felt the same way when they'd arrived last night. Entering the cabin, for her, had been like entering a time capsule. She imagined that Jax was feeling the same way now.

"I feel like I'm sixteen again," Jax said softly. "Remember that summer? I think we spent most of it French braiding each other's hair."

Allie smiled, remembering.

"But I don't remember *that*," Jax said with a frown, pointing at the buck's head. Allie had tried to take it down that morning, but it had proved too difficult. Instead she'd covered it with a blanket.

"Oh that," Allie said, leading Jax into the kitchen. "That's that old buck's head my grandfather put up. Wyatt doesn't like it, but I couldn't get it down."

"I don't like them much myself," Jax admitted, setting the strawberries down on the kitchen counter. "But Wyatt had better get used to them. People in these parts take their hunting very seriously."

Allie opened the refrigerator door and started putting the strawberries in. But then she paused. "Jax, Wyatt and I can't eat all these strawberries."

"Oh, you don't have to eat all of them now. You can use whatever you don't eat to make strawberry jam."

"I don't know how to make jam," Allie admitted, arranging strawberries.

"Well, that's going to have to change if you're planning on living up here," Jax said, an amused expression on her face. "Canning is practically a sport in Butternut. Second only to hunting, really."

Allie smiled. "Well, maybe you can teach me how to can sometime. But until then, are you sure you don't want to take some of these back with you?"

Jax shook her head.

"Well, thank you then. They're beautiful. Can I least offer you an iced tea before you leave?"

"I'd love an iced tea," Jax said, sitting down at the kitchen table.

Allie poured them both a glass of iced tea and poured Wyatt, who'd followed them into the kitchen, a glass of milk. He took it into the living room with him and started playing with a train set he and Allie had set up that afternoon.

"How are your parents and your brother?" Jax asked, as Allie joined her at the table.

"They're fine. My parents live in a retirement community in Florida. They wanted Wyatt and me to move down there too. But I couldn't see us joining them for the early bird special every night. And my brother, Cal, lives in Seattle with his wife. They're both total workaholics, but otherwise, they're fine. What about your parents?" she asked, then immediately regretted asking it. She didn't know a lot about Jax's family. But she knew enough to know it had not been a happy one.

But Jax only shrugged. "My parents are both gone now. A diet rich in bourbon whiskey, apparently, doesn't lend itself to old age," she said, with a sigh.

Allie flushed. She was sorry she'd brought them up.

But Jax reached over and patted her arm. "Hey, it's okay," she said. "Because twelve years ago I met Jeremy. And things started to turn around for me."

"Caroline said the two of you own the hardware store. And that you make having three children look easy."

Jax smiled. "I don't know about *easy,*" she said. But then her expression clouded over. "Caroline told me about your husband. I'm so sorry."

Allie's throat tightened. "He was a specialist in the Minnesota National Guard and his unit was deployed to Afghanistan," she said, forcing herself to speak evenly, and to maintain eye contact with Jax. "They were resupplying mobile combat units in the field when the Humvee Gregg was riding in drove over an IED." She paused. "He didn't survive."

"Oh, Allie. You must miss him so much," Jax said, gently.

"I *do* miss him. He was my best friend." And had been, really, since the moment she'd met him. It was on her first day of college, in her Introduction to Psychology class. Gregg had walked over to her row and asked, with a shy smile, brushing his sandy brown hair out of his eyes, "Is this seat taken?"

"No," she'd said, a little flustered, and he'd sat down next to her. The next time they'd been apart—*really* apart—was ten years later, when he'd left for Afghanistan.

Jax reached over now and took Allie's hand and held it in her own small, almost childlike hand.

"Allie? I'm glad you moved up here," she said. "I really am."

"Well, that makes one of us," Allie said, only half joking.

"You're not sorry, are you?"

"I don't know if I am or not," Allie confessed. "But it's occurred to me it might have been a selfish decision on my part. I mean, I moved here because *I* wanted to get away. But what about Wyatt? He didn't get to vote or even weigh in with an opinion."

Jax considered this, then said, "You don't strike me as a selfish person, Allie. Besides, making decisions is part of a parent's job. And usually, what's best for us is what's best for them, too." She paused, looking thoughtful. "But, at the risk of prying into your personal life, why *did* you decide to move up here?"

"Too many memories at home," Allie said, deciding to keep her answer simple. After all, that was *part* of the reason she'd decided to leave. "Gregg and I never had time to come up here when we were together," she explained. "We were so busy, and it always seemed so far away. Besides, Gregg hated fishing. He said it was less exciting than watching grass grow. And you know what, Jax?"

"What?"

"Now I'm glad we never came up here together. There are no memories of him here. Except, of course, the ones that I brought with me," she added, with a little sigh.

"Won't you be homesick, though?" Jax asked, concerned.

"I don't know. Maybe. But I got so tired of everyone feeling sorry for me. It's exhausting to be the object of so much pity. And so much well-meaning advice."

Jax considered that. "Well, you won't have that problem here," she said finally, with a sad little smile. "People up here have plenty of troubles of their own. I mean, you remember Walter Starr, don't you? He owns the bait and tackle shop. He's got advanced prostate cancer. And Don and Liz Weber, remember them? They used to own the gas station? Last spring they lost everything—*everything*—in a house fire. And Caroline, from Pearl's? Her daughter left for college this summer. That child is everything to her, and Caroline misses her so much that sometimes, I swear, I'm afraid her heart will break in two. I could go on"—Jax shrugged—"but I won't."

Allie felt her eyes glazing over with tears. She knew Jax hadn't meant to make her feel like a jerk, but she felt like one anyway. "I know how selfish I must sound," she confessed now. "But one of the worst parts of losing someone you love is that it makes you so self-absorbed. Sometimes I forget that Wyatt and I aren't the only people in the world who have a reason to grieve."

"You have *every* reason to grieve," Jax said, staunchly. "I didn't mean to imply that you didn't. But the people of this town aren't strangers to hardship, either. So you don't need to feel like your misfortune will make you some kind of curiosity to them. It won't." She added, with a rueful smile, "Although I should probably warn you, like most people who live in small towns, they're not immune to a little gossiping, either."

"And speaking of gossip," Jax continued, refilling her glass from the pitcher of iced tea on the table, "have you met your new neighbor?"

Allie nodded. "Walker Ford, right? I met him this morning at Pearl's. We didn't get off to a very good start with each other," she admitted.

"No?" Jax asked. "Well, he can be a little aloof."

"Aloof? I was going to say arrogant."

"Arrogant? Well, *maybe* a little," Jax conceded. "But he's done a lot for Butternut. I mean, when he took over that boatyard a few years ago, it was barely limping along. Now, after the lumber mill, it's the biggest employer in town. Besides," she continued, a mischievous gleam in her eye, "that's not the only public service he's provided around here."

Allie raised her eyebrows, curious in spite of herself.

"Well, as I said," Jax continued, "people up here do *occasionally* gossip. And he's given us all plenty to gossip about."

"Really?" Allie was intrigued.

"Well, you've seen him, haven't you?" Jax asked. "The man looks like a movie star, for God's sake."

Allie reviewed their meeting. Walker *was* tall and athletically built, with close-cropped, dark hair, a summer-tanned complexion, and dark blue eyes. He wasn't bad-looking, she supposed. But she couldn't say he was good-looking, either. She simply didn't see men in that way anymore.

But Jax brushed off her ambivalence. "Well, whatever you think of him, he's found many admirers up here," she continued.

"I mean, his looks aside, he's under forty, successful, and single."
She ticked off these attributes on the fingers of one hand. "In
other words, he's in a small minority of the population in a town
the size of Butternut. But he was also married—briefly—which
only added to the intrigue. Everyone loves to speculate about
what went wrong in that marriage."

"Who was he married to?" Allie asked.

"She wasn't from up here," Jax said, with a shrug. "And she
wasn't very well liked, either. I mean, she was beautiful. But
she was cold, too. They got married in the fall, and that winter,
less than six months later, she left. That was it. Nobody really
knows what happened. Nobody except Walker, that is. And he's
not talking."

I could hazard a guess as to what went wrong, Allie thought,
remembering how off-putting she'd found Walker that morning.
But she didn't say anything about that to Jax.

And Jax, sipping her iced tea, moved on to a different topic.
"Allie," she asked, "are you still interested in art?"

"Art?" Allie echoed, uncertainly.

Jax nodded. "I remember you used to bring those enormous
art books up here with you. And study them, too. Just for fun.
You told me once you wanted to major in art history in college
and get a job in the art world afterward."

"Oh, *that,*" Allie said, slightly embarrassed. "Yes, I used to
fantasize about moving to New York after college and working
in a gallery in SoHo. But that didn't exactly pan out the way I'd
planned."

"Why not?" Jax asked.

"Well, because reality intruded, I guess," Allie said. "I did
minor in art history in college, and I might have majored in it,
too, except by then I knew that Gregg and his brother, Travis,

were going to take over their family's landscaping service, and I thought a degree in business might be more useful." She'd been right. Together, the three of them had built what had been a small lawn-mowing business into a full-service landscaping company.

"Did you like having a landscaping business?"

Allie hesitated. "I *liked* it," she said. "I don't know if it was my *dream*. But it was exciting building something from the ground up." Besides, she'd still snuck away to museums and galleries in Minneapolis whenever she could find the time.

"Do you still own part of the business?" Jax asked.

"No," Allie said, "I sold out our half to Gregg's brother. And I sold our house, too. So hopefully, I've bought myself some time to figure out what I want to do next. I mean, the money won't last forever. I'll have to earn a living again at some point."

"Well, then you'll be just like the rest of us," Jax said, breezily.

"I guess I will," Allie agreed. It was funny how Jax could be so direct without ever being unkind, she thought. Probably because she didn't have an unkind bone in her body.

Jax stood up from the table. "I should get going," she said, a little reluctantly. "I need to be starting dinner."

"Of course," Allie said, feeling like she'd already taken up too much of Jax's time. "Wyatt and I will walk you out to your truck." Wyatt had just wandered back into the kitchen and had opened the refrigerator. Now he was staring longingly at the strawberries inside. They'd have some for dessert, Allie decided. Over the vanilla ice cream she'd bought at the grocery store that day.

As they started to leave the cabin, though, Jax turned back. She was looking at the buck's head with the blanket draped over it.

"I know someone who can help you with that," she said. "And

do any other work you need done around here, too." She doubled back to the kitchen, where Allie had left a notepad and pencil on the counter, and scribbled down a name and phone number. She tore the sheet off and handed it to Allie.

"His name's Johnny Miller," she said. "He's a carpenter and a handyman. He's pretty old, but his work is first-rate, and I think you'll find his prices are reasonable."

"Thank you," Allie said, studying the paper. "We can use all the help we can get."

She and Wyatt walked Jax out to her pickup and stood in the driveway until she'd driven out of sight. Then they went back inside. Wyatt seemed a little forlorn, and Allie didn't blame him. The cabin had seemed somehow brighter, and lighter, with Jax inside of it.

"Come on, kid, you can help me with dinner," Allie said, feigning cheerfulness. But even to herself, her voice sounded a little hollow.

CHAPTER 6

Caroline knew she'd been sitting at her desk for too long when she felt the familiar knot of pain between her shoulder blades. She sat up straight, clasped her hands behind her head, and arched her back, trying to stretch her cramped muscles. *Who would have thought that owning a coffee shop would require so much paperwork?* she thought, closing the folder in front of her and filing it under "payroll taxes" in the file cabinet beside the desk.

There was a light tap at the office door, and Frankie, the fry cook, opened it.

"Miss Caroline, I'm going to leave now," he said, his massive frame filling the entire doorway.

Caroline glanced at the clock on her desk. "Frankie, it's five o'clock," she said in surprise. "Why are you still here?"

He shrugged his gigantic shoulders. "I fixed the air-conditioning," he said. "It's been on the blink again. Then I cleaned the deep fryers. By then the floor needed another mopping, so I did that, too."

"Frankie, your shift ended at three o'clock," Caroline protested.

"I don't mind working late."

"I know you don't," she said, motioning him into the room. "But that's not what concerns me."

Frankie came into her office. It wasn't easy for him. The room was low ceilinged, and he had to be careful not to let the top of his head scrape against the fluorescent lighting. But he couldn't very well sit down, either. The only other chair in the room, besides the one Caroline was sitting in, was a rickety-looking folding chair. And both of them knew it wouldn't support his weight.

"What concerns me, Frankie," Caroline said, "is that you're working late because you feel you owe it to me to work late."

"That's not it," he said. "I just like working here."

"And I *like* that you like working here," Caroline assured him. "But, Frankie, you only get paid to work until three o'clock. I wish I could pay you to work beyond then. But I can't, Frankie. I can't afford it. So you should stop work at three o'clock, and go home and do . . . well, whatever it is you like to do." Here, her imagination failed her. Frankie had been working for her for three years, but she still had no idea how he spent his free time.

"But what I like to do is work here," he said, bringing the conversation full circle. "And," he added, "while I don't feel like I *owe* it to you, exactly, maybe I should feel that way. You took a chance on me, Miss Caroline, when no one else would. It's not easy for an ex-con to find work."

"I know that, Frankie," she said, gently. "But it was the right decision. You have more than justified my faith in you. And it hasn't been a one-way street, either. You may have gotten a job, but I got the best fry cook I've ever had. Not to mention an air-conditioning repairman to boot."

Frankie smiled one of his rare smiles. "Well, I guess I'll be going now, Miss Caroline."

"That's fine. And Frankie?"

"Yes?"

"I don't suppose there's anything I can do to persuade you to stop calling me *Miss* Caroline?" she asked, hopefully.

Frankie thought about it, then shook his head. "No, ma'am," he said. "It just wouldn't seem respectful to call you anything else."

"Well, I thought it was worth a try." Caroline sighed as Frankie turned to leave the office. This was no simple matter. He had to practically pivot in place to turn his gigantic body in such a small space, and then he had to more or less launch himself through the narrow doorway.

When he'd left, closing the door behind him, Caroline stood up from her desk, stretched again, and left the office, too.

Then she walked down the narrow hallway behind the coffee shop and up the flight of stairs to her apartment above it. She paused at the front door and took longer than necessary taking her keys out of her apron pocket and fitting one of them into the lock. She dreaded this moment every single day. Had dreaded it, in fact, ever since her daughter, Daisy, had moved to Minneapolis two weeks earlier.

She turned the key in the lock, pushed open the door, and went straight to the kitchen, where she turned on the radio. It was still tuned to the classic rock station that she and Daisy liked, and she turned the volume all the way up, trying to drown out the silence. But she was only partially successful. The music was loud. There was no doubt about that. But music had been only one of the many sounds ricocheting off the walls of their apartment when Daisy had lived there.

Now, as Bob Seger's "Night Moves" played, Caroline left the kitchen and walked over to the bathroom. She undressed and stepped into the shower, trying not to think about the silence that lay below the lyrics to the song. She shampooed her hair and lathered her body, washing away the odor of bacon grease that clung to her like a second skin by the end of every workday. Then she turned off the shower and stepped out of it, dripping on the bathmat. She toweled herself off, put on a bathrobe, and brushed out her wet hair, twisting it into a knot on top of her head.

Then, and only then, did she let herself do what she *really* wanted to do, which was to flop down on her double bed and bury her face in the pillows. But she didn't cry. She wasn't big on crying. Maybe because if life had taught her anything, it had taught her that crying was a waste of time. She'd had many opportunities to learn this firsthand. She'd lost both her parents, for instance, when she was still a young woman. She'd lost her husband, too, not to death but to serial infidelity on his part. She'd also raised a daughter alone and run a business by herself. If she'd let herself get into the habit of crying, she reasoned, it wouldn't have left much time for her to do anything else.

But Daisy's leaving . . . *That* had hit her hard. The phone rang then, interrupting her thoughts. She reached over to the bedside table and answered it, hoping it would be Daisy. It was.

"Hi, Mom," Daisy said, sounding so much like herself that Caroline felt a catch in her throat.

"Hi, sweetheart," Caroline said, with studied casualness. "How've you been?"

"Other than worried about you?" Daisy asked.

"*You're* worried about *me*?" Caroline said. "I think it's supposed to be the other way around, sweetie."

"But I don't give you anything to worry about, do I?" Daisy asked. And it was true. She'd been born responsible, as far as Caroline could tell.

"You don't *usually* give me anything to worry about," Caroline qualified. "But you've never lived on your own before. Even you might have a learning curve."

"Speaking of learning, guess what Giovanni said today?" Daisy asked. Giovanni was the Italian man who owned the coffee bar that Daisy was working at for the summer.

"What?"

"He said I made a perfect cappuccino."

"Well, of course you did," Caroline said, loyally. Cappuccino, though, was out of her depth. She served two kinds of coffee at Pearl's: regular and decaf.

"Trust me, it's not easy to make one," Daisy said.

"Well, it should be for you," Caroline said. "You've got coffee in your veins, honey."

"That's true," Daisy laughed, and then she chatted with Caroline about her apartment, her roommates, and a boy who came into the coffee bar to flirt but hadn't asked for her phone number yet. Caroline listened and made what she thought were all the appropriate remarks. But Daisy wasn't fooled by her performance.

"Mom, what's wrong?" she asked, when there was a lull in the conversation.

"Nothing," Caroline said, a little too quickly.

"Mom," Daisy said, sighing, "I know you so well." And she did. But if Caroline told her how much she missed her, it would only make Daisy feel guilty. So instead she told her about Frankie's long hours, and about Allie Beckett, and her son Wyatt's, terrible loss.

"Mom, I know Frankie works too hard. And I'm sorry about that woman and her son. But I want to talk about *you*. Do you remember that conversation we had before I left?"

"Which one?" Caroline asked, being deliberately vague.

"The one where we talked about how you're always worrying about everyone else, and never worrying about yourself?"

"Well, I'm not worried about myself because I don't have anything to worry about," Caroline said. "I mean, beyond the usual things everyone worries about."

"Okay, forget I used the word 'worry' then. I don't mean that, exactly. I mean, when is it going to be *your* turn to think about *you*?"

Caroline frowned. "Wasn't that an episode of Dr. Phil?"

"I don't know, maybe," Daisy said, exasperated. "But again, Mom, you're getting away from the point."

"Which is?"

"Which is that it's *your* turn now. Your turn to concentrate on your own life. You took care of Grandpa and Grandma. You took care of me. Now you need to take care of yourself."

"I *do* take care of myself," Caroline objected.

"Mom, I'm not talking about taking vitamins, okay? I'm talking about doing things for yourself. Taking a class. Or taking a trip. Or joining a book club. Something like that."

"But I don't want to join a book club," Caroline said, a little irritably.

"Mom, you like to read," Daisy pointed out.

"I *do* like to read," Caroline conceded. "But I don't want to be *told* what to read."

"Oh, Mom," Daisy scolded. "You don't even have to read the books if you don't want to. Just think of it as an opportunity to socialize."

Caroline was silent. It was her opinion that she did plenty of socializing at the coffee shop as it was, but she didn't want to hurt Daisy's feelings.

"Well, I give up for tonight," Daisy said, with a sigh. "But I'll call you tomorrow."

"Bye, sweetie," Caroline said, and she hung up the phone slowly. Then she lay very still, listening. Was it her imagination, or was it even quieter now in the apartment than it had been before Daisy called?

CHAPTER 7

I wish you'd let me buy you a dishwasher," Jeremy said to Jax, coming up behind her at the kitchen sink that night. He slid his arms around her waist—or what had, until recently, been her waist—and brushed his lips along the edge of her right ear.

"I *like* doing dishes," Jax said, her body responding instantaneously to Jeremy's touch. Even after twelve years of marriage, she marveled, he still had that effect on her.

"All right, I won't buy you a dishwasher," he said, tightening his arms around her. "But at least let me and the girls help you wash them."

"Maybe," Jax mused. But she knew she wouldn't. The truth was, she liked washing the dishes by herself. It was relaxing to her to be up to her elbows in warm, soapy water. And it allowed her time to think without being interrupted, something that was a precious commodity for a mother of three.

Usually, she used the time to think about her daughters, and the things they'd said or done that day. She didn't believe in chronicling every moment of their lives, the way so many of her friends did with their own children. She didn't take videos, or keep scrapbooks, or write in baby journals. Instead, as she washed the dishes every night, while Jeremy said good night to the girls, she tried to commit their lives to memory. The big moments and the little moments. But mostly, the little moments.

Tonight, though, her usually pleasurable dishwashing was tinged with sadness. It seemed wrong, somehow, to be happy when Allie and Wyatt were so sad. Her visit with them, only a few hours old, was still fresh in her mind. She'd told Jeremy about it before dinner.

Now, cradling her in his arms at the sink, Jeremy asked, "Are you thinking about your friend and her son?"

Jax nodded, somberly.

"She was really special to you, wasn't she?" Jeremy asked, gently.

She nodded again. "That summer we were sixteen, we spent so much time together. I loved being with her family at their cabin. They were so, so . . ." She struggled for the right word. "So *normal*," she said, finally.

"Jax, everyone's family was normal compared to yours."

"That's true," she mused.

"Honey, you know there's nothing you can do about what happened to them, don't you?" Jeremy asked, after a long silence.

Jax nodded. But then, thinking of something, she brightened a little. "I can't do anything about what happened to them, but I might be able to make things a *little* easier for them now. I mean, Wyatt doesn't know any children here. And we have three of them. One of whom is practically the same age."

"Are you suggesting we adopt him?" Jeremy asked, nuzzling her neck. "Because his mother may not want to give him up that easily."

"I'm suggesting we include him in our lives," Jax said, ignoring his teasing as she emptied the soapy water out of the sink and started to rinse the dishes. Jeremy reluctantly released her, picked up a dish towel, and started drying the dishes as she handed them to him. "I mean, I told the girls I'd take them blueberry picking next week," Jax continued. "I'm going to ask Wyatt to come, too. And then, in July, we're having our annual barbecue. Half the town will be there. We can have it be a 'welcome to Butternut' evening for the two of them."

"All right," Jeremy said, drying another dish. "I'll tell our social secretary to put them on the guest list."

"Very funny," Jax said, but she stopped what she was doing and kissed him anyway. And when they were done with the dishes, Jeremy took her into his arms again and kissed her, with a sense of urgency that was unusual even for him. *It's like he's knows there's something wrong*, Jax thought, uncomfortably. *Something I'm not telling him about.*

And, as if on cue, he stopped kissing her long enough to murmur, "Before we go upstairs, there's something we need to discuss."

"What is it?" Jax asked, her body tensing involuntarily.

"It's Joy," he said, drawing her closer and saying the words into the hollow of her neck. "She's reading under her covers with a flashlight again. And I'm wondering how I'm going to have my way with my very beautiful, very sexy wife, if our daughter won't go to sleep when she's supposed to."

Jax relaxed. "Honestly, Jeremy, do you ever think about anything else?" she said.

"Not if I can possibly help it," he answered her, pulling her closer. "It doesn't help, of course, that you look so goddamned beautiful when you're pregnant."

She rolled her eyes. "Jeremy, I look like the side of a barn. And I'm barely into my third trimester."

"More time for me to appreciate you this way, then," he said, his eyes lingering with appreciation on the new fullness of her breasts. He cupped one of them now, and Jax felt the warmth of his fingers through the thin cotton fabric of her maternity blouse and shivered with anticipation. But there was something she needed to do now. And she needed to do it alone.

"Jeremy," she said, "if you don't let me finish cleaning up down here, we're going to end up having sex on the kitchen floor."

"And that would be a bad thing?" Jeremy asked, kissing her again.

"Yes," Jax said. But she couldn't quite hide her smile. "Now go upstairs and tell Joy to stop reading under the covers and go to sleep. I'll be up as soon as I've wiped down the counters."

"Okay, but hurry," Jeremy pleaded, giving her one final kiss before he headed up the stairs.

Jax waited a minute, then opened one of the kitchen cupboards and reached into the back of it. She took out a recipe box and set it on the counter. Then she flipped the box open and removed an envelope from the back of it.

The envelope had already been opened. She slid the letter out and unfolded it carefully, squinting at the nearly illegible handwriting. Penmanship had never been Bobby's strong suit, and a stint in state prison, apparently, had done nothing to improve it. She was still able to read it, though. She'd already read it, in fact, a dozen times. And it always made her feel exactly the same way. Sick to her stomach, with a racing heartbeat, and sweaty palms. Tonight, unfortunately, was no exception.

After studying it for a few minutes, she refolded it, put it back into the envelope, and tucked it back into the recipe box—the one place where she knew Jeremy would never look. Then she put the box back into the cupboard. It looked perfectly innocent there, but the letter inside of it, she knew, was a time bomb. And it was ticking so loudly she could hear it in every room of the house.

CHAPTER 8

Hey, Walker, are you still here?" Cliff Donahue, the boatyard's general manager asked, poking his head into the
break room on his way out of work on Friday evening.

"I'm still here," Walker said, pouring himself a cup of coffee
from a decrepit coffeepot.

"I thought you were going to Minneapolis this weekend."

"I was," Walker said. "But I changed my mind."

Cliff raised his eyebrows. "Any problems here I need to know
about?"

"Not a one," Walker said, taking a sip of coffee. He winced. It
had the taste, and texture, of sludge.

"Actually, there is *one* problem," he amended. "This coffeepot.
Seriously, how long's it been here? Since the Great Depression?"

"Maybe." Cliff shrugged. "The old-timers don't seem to mind
it. Of course, unlike you, they might not have been spoiled by
Caroline's coffee."

"That's true," Walker conceded. Caroline brewed the best cup
of coffee he'd ever tasted. And that included some very high-
priced cups at some very upscale coffeehouses in Minneapolis.

"Well, I'll be heading out then. You can reach me on my cell, though, if you need me for any reason."

"Thanks," Walker said, and he went back to his office. But he didn't go back to work right away. Instead, he sat back in his desk chair, put his feet up on his desk, and sipped his lousy coffee. He was thinking that not only were there no problems at the boatyard, but Cliff was doing such a good job as GM that Walker might not be able to justify his presence here much longer. And then he frowned, remembering something. Because the day he'd interviewed Cliff for the general manager's job, three years ago, was also the day Caitlin had come to the boatyard to see him.

His interview with Cliff was winding down when there'd been a light rap on his closed office door.

"Who is it?" Walker called out, with barely concealed annoyance. The few employees who worked at the boatyard then knew better than to disturb him when his office door was closed.

"It's Caitlin," a voice answered. *Caitlin?* he thought. *Here?*

"Come in," he said, trying to sound nonchalant. But his mind was racing. Caitlin was the woman he was dating on his weekend trips to Minneapolis, but she'd never been to Butternut before. She'd never been there for the simple reason that he'd never invited her. They weren't at that point in their relationship yet. And it wasn't clear to him that they ever would be. The more time they spent together, in fact, the less they appeared to have in common. Recently, it had occurred to him that the initial physical attraction they'd felt for each other might not be strong enough to sustain their relationship much longer.

Which was probably why she was here, he realized, with relief, as she hesitantly opened the door to the office. She was here to break up with him. Though why she thought it was necessary to drive all the way up here on a weekday to do it was beyond him. She could have done it, much more conveniently, over the phone. Most people, he knew, would have considered that rude, but he wasn't one of them. It would have spared them both the awkwardness of her doing it in person.

He stood up then and gave her a perfunctory kiss on the cheek. He started to introduce her to Cliff but saw that Cliff was in no condition for introductions. He was staring, dumbstruck, at Caitlin. And Walker couldn't blame him. Not entirely. Because the first time he'd met Caitlin, at a bar in Minneapolis, he'd had a similar response.

She had long blond hair, wide cornflower blue eyes, and skin so pale it was almost translucent. She was a beautiful girl. There was no question about it. But like a lot of beautiful people, Walker had come to suspect that she'd never been called upon to develop the rest of herself. Because either she didn't have a personality, or she hid it behind her quietness. Still waters might run deep, or, in her case, he thought, they might just run *still*.

"Cliff," Walker said, turning to his interviewee, who had partially recovered himself, "I'm going to have to cut this short. But I'll be getting back to you soon."

They shook hands and Cliff left. Walker gestured for Caitlin to sit down on the chair Cliff had just vacated. She sat down, uneasily, and Walker sat down, too.

"Would you like a cup of really terrible coffee?" he asked.

"No, thanks," she said.

He smiled at her, and said, casually, "I think I know what brings you up here."

She looked surprised. "You do?"

He nodded. He tried to choose his words carefully. "Our relationship has hit some kind of a wall. It's not your fault, and I hope it's not mine. But it doesn't seem to have any real momentum left . . ." His voice trailed off uneasily. Something about the way she was looking at him made him stop.

"What are you saying, Walker?" she asked.

"I'm saying what I thought you came up here to say."

"Which is . . ." she prompted him.

"Which is that you want to break things off with me." *There*, he thought. He'd said it. Now that it was out in the open, they could get this over with.

"You think I came up here to break up with you?" she asked, incredulously. And a bright red spot suddenly appeared on each of her pale cheeks.

"Didn't you?" he asked. So much for this not being awkward.

She shook her head. "Not even close, Walker."

He frowned. What was not even close to breaking up? But she didn't give him time to contemplate that question.

"I came to tell you that I'm pregnant," she said bluntly.

He didn't say anything. He *couldn't* say anything. He was too shocked to put a whole sentence together. And when he finally did, he didn't choose his words carefully. He said the first thing that came into his mind.

"How did this happen?" he asked.

Whatever Caitlin had hoped to hear from him, this wasn't it. She rolled her eyes. "How do you *think* it happened, Walker? You took sex education in high school, didn't you? Or were you absent the day they covered the part about the sperm fertilizing the egg?"

Sarcasm, Walker thought. He'd never known Caitlin to be sarcastic before. But who was he kidding? He'd never really known her *at all* before. He knew enough about her now, though, to know she was annoyed by his apparent stupidity. So he rephrased the question.

"I know *how* it happened. What I meant was, you told me you were using birth control, so I assumed it *couldn't* happen."

"I *was* using birth control," she said, defensively. "But even the most effective birth control isn't one hundred percent effective."

He nodded, dumbly. They'd covered that in sex education, too. Then a thought occurred to him. Actually, it was more of a hope. A tiny hope. Like reaching for a life vest right before you're engulfed in a tidal wave.

"Are you sure it's . . ." He stopped. He knew he was crossing a minefield here. But there was really no tactful way to phrase this question. "Are you sure it's mine? Could it be somebody else's?" He braced himself for her response.

But when she answered him, it was with more hurt than anger. "Of course not," she said. And then, "How many people do you think I'm having intimate relationships with right now, Walker?"

"I, I don't know . . ." he said, honestly. It was the wrong thing to say.

"Walker, for God's sake," she snapped. "I hope you know me well enough to know that you're the only one."

Walker didn't answer. He couldn't. His brain was going into shut-down mode again. So they lapsed into another silence. An intensely uncomfortable silence.

"Look," she said finally, her tone softening. "I'm as surprised as you are. I almost fainted when I saw the results of the pregnancy test. But I'm not here to discuss how it happened. I'm here to discuss something else. I'm here to discuss what we're going to do about it."

"Okay," Walker said. His brain still wasn't working very well. But it was working well enough to realize that Caitlin had just said more at one time than he'd ever heard her say before. "Go on, Caitlin."

She took a deep breath, and Walker had the feeling that she'd rehearsed whatever she was going to say next. "I'm going to have the baby, Walker. And I'm going to raise it—I mean him, or her—by myself. But I'm going to need your help. Financially, I mean. As you know, right now I'm a receptionist. I can't do this by myself. Not on my salary. If anything changes for me, well, then, obviously, whatever financial arrangement we make would change, too. I mean, I don't want to be a receptionist forever. And I still want to get married some day, even though this"—here she gestured at her still perfectly flat stomach—"might make it more difficult. And Walker?" she continued. "I know I was irritated when you asked if it was yours. But I agree that we should have a paternity test done when the baby's born. If only for your peace of mind."

Peace of mind, Walker thought. It already sounded like a foreign concept to him. He didn't think he would ever have peace of mind again.

Caitlin stood up. She'd obviously accepted the fact that he was either unable, or unwilling, to say anything more.

"My lawyer will be in touch with you," she said, starting to leave. Walker almost let her. But something occurred to him.

"Caitlin," he said. His brain was working again.

She turned back from the door.

"Where do I fit in all this, other than helping you financially? Which I'll do, obviously. But what would my relationship with our child be?"

She hesitated. "I guess that depends."

"On what?"

"On you," she said. "On what kind of relationship you want to have with our child. You don't have to have *any* relationship with him or her if you don't want to. I'm not going to force you to be someone you're not."

"What is that supposed to mean?"

She sighed, a little sadly, he thought, and sat back down on the chair. "It means I don't exactly think you're father material, Walker. At least not yet."

He thought about it. "No, you're right," he admitted. My life is pretty . . . *commitment adverse,* I guess you'd say. I haven't given any real thought to marriage before. Or fatherhood, for that matter." *Liar,* he told himself. *You've given plenty of thought to both of them. And you've decided you didn't want any part of either one of them.*

"And that's fine," Caitlin said. "I'm not asking you to change overnight. Or change at all. You don't have to be a part of this. Not if you don't want to be. I mean, beyond providing financial support, that is."

Walker didn't say anything. He was thinking about his own childhood. And about his own relationship with his father.

His parents had gotten divorced when he was seven. For a while, his father had seen Walker and his older brother, Reid, every weekend. Then, gradually, the visits had tapered off. It hadn't helped that his parents fought as much when they were divorced as they had when they were married. It also hadn't helped that Walker's father got remarried to a woman who resented the time he spent with his sons. When she and Walker's father had a daughter of their own, she resented it even more.

By the time Walker entered adolescence, his father had more or less dropped out of his life. He sent the occasional birthday card or Christmas present. He sent alimony and child support payments, too, but eventually those became less frequent as well.

When Walker's mother took him to court to enforce those payments, the deal was pretty well sealed. Their father started sending the checks again, but he didn't send anything else.

Walker had seen him one more time, though. It was at a Minnesota Twins baseball game several years ago. Walker had recognized him, and when he'd approached him, his father had been friendly enough. They'd had a brief, awkward conversation, but they'd had almost nothing to say to each other.

"No," Walker said, suddenly. His voice sounded loud in the quiet room.

"No, what?" Caitlin asked, surprised.

"No, I don't want to be that kind of father."

"What kind of father?" She frowned.

"I don't want to be a stranger to my own child. To *our* own child," he corrected himself. "That's the kind of dad my dad was. I was the kid on the Little League team checking the bleachers every sixty seconds to see if he was there yet." He paused. "He was never there yet. He was never there at all. If I'm going to do this, I want to be there, Caitlin. I want to be in the bleachers for that Little League game."

"It might be a girl, you know," Caitlin said. "In which case, it might not be a Little League game. It might be a soccer game, or a volleyball game." But the hint of a smile played around her lips.

"It doesn't matter," Walker said. "I want to be there."

"You *can* be there," Caitlin assured him. "We don't have to work out all the details today, but if you want visitation rights, you can have them."

"Visitation rights?" Walker repeated. The phrase left a bad taste in his mouth.

Caitlin shrugged. "I think that's the correct legal term."

"Well, that's not what I want."

She sighed and he noticed, for the first time, how tired she looked. "Well, what *do* you want?" she asked, with a trace of exasperation.

What he said next couldn't have shocked Caitlin as much as it shocked him.

"I want us to be a real family."

"A real family?" she echoed, skeptically.

"Yes," he said, with conviction. "A real family. Marriage, a house, a baby. Everything."

Now it was Caitlin's turn to be speechless. "Walker, are you proposing to me?" she asked, finally, after a long silence.

"I guess I am," he said.

She shook her head in wonderment. "Where is this coming from? We've never discussed marriage before."

"Well, maybe it's time we did."

"I, I don't know what to say," Caitlin admitted. "Of all the outcomes I considered for today, this wasn't one of them."

"I'm a little surprised myself," Walker said. And then, because he felt something more was called for, he said, "Come here."

She stood up and came over to him. He took her hand and pulled her, a little awkwardly, onto his lap.

"I'm sorry that wasn't a very romantic proposal," he said, putting his arms around her waist.

"That's okay," she said, almost shyly.

"So are you going to accept it?" he asked.

She smiled, a little shakily. "Why not?" she said.

"Exactly," Walker said. "I mean, how difficult can this whole marriage thing be?"

Plenty difficult, it turned out. But they hadn't known that then. They hadn't known *anything* then, as far as Walker could tell. Now, three years later, sitting in his office at the boatyard, he could only feel regret. Regret and guilt.

But something else tugged at his consciousness now: Allie, the woman he'd met at the coffee shop last weekend, and her little boy, Wyatt. Strangely enough, he'd been thinking about them lately, too. He had no idea why. Probably because Caroline had told him about Allie's late husband. It had made sense to him, somehow. Somewhere beneath her prickly defensiveness, he'd guessed there was a deep sadness. And a soft vulnerability.

He should have gone to Minneapolis today, he thought. Because here he was worrying about two people he didn't even know. Didn't even *want* to know, really. He forced them out of his mind and drained the last of the coffee from his cup. It was like drinking mud. If he did nothing else tomorrow, he decided, he'd buy a new coffeepot at the hardware store. Then he'd have something, however small, to show for staying here this weekend.

CHAPTER 9

Allie and Wyatt were already sitting on the front steps of the cabin when they heard the crunch of Jax's tires coming up the gravel driveway.

"Wyatt, there's something you need to know before you go blueberry picking this morning," Allie said, putting his Minnesota Twins baseball cap on him and adjusting the visor to a jaunty angle.

"What?" he asked.

"Eating blueberries from the pail is a time-honored tradition," she said, playfully. "So is eating them directly off the blueberry bush. So don't worry about filling up your pail. I don't care how many blueberries you bring home. I just want you to have fun. Okay?" She waited for a response. There was none. "Okay?" she said again, lifting up his visor and looking into his chocolate brown eyes.

Wyatt didn't say anything. He didn't need to say anything. His trembling lower lip said it for him. He didn't want to go blueberry picking without Allie. *Oh God, please don't cry*, she thought desperately. *Because if you cry, my resolve will crumble. And I'll come with you. Or I'll let you stay home. And you're already with me twenty-four hours a day, seven days a week. It can't be healthy, and it can't be fun, being with someone who's always pretending that everything's all right, when it's so obviously not all right.*

But Allie didn't know how to say any of this to him. So instead she handed him a slightly battered tin pail, and said, "You have to trust me on this one, okay? You're going to have a good time blueberry picking with Jax and her daughters. And I'm going to get a lot of work done here by myself cleaning out this old cabin."

"Oh, look, here they are," she added, brightly, as Jax's pickup rolled into view. "Let's go, buddy," she added, standing up and brushing off the seat of her blue jean cutoffs. Wyatt sighed, and stood up, slowly. Wearily. *Just like a little old man,* Allie thought sadly.

But in the next moment, Jax and her daughters came tumbling out of the truck, creating a welcome distraction. And Allie was amused to see that Jax's three daughters were all scaled-down, but otherwise identical, versions of Jax. They each had jet black hair, vivid blue eyes, and creamy white complexions sprinkled liberally with freckles. Soon, the three of them had surrounded her and Wyatt and were all talking at the same time.

When the introductions had been made, Jax said, cheerfully, "All right, everybody into the truck. Let's pick blueberries before it gets too hot, and then we can have our picnic in the shade."

Allie watched as Jade, Jax's youngest daughter, took Wyatt firmly by the hand and led him over to the truck. Wyatt looked surprised, but he didn't object.

Jax glanced over at them and then back at Allie. "Could this be the beginning of a beautiful friendship?" she asked.

"God, I hope so," Allie said, visibly relieved. "I was afraid there'd be a scene," she confessed. "You know, one that ended with you peeling a hysterical Wyatt away from me."

"He looks fine," Jax said, glancing over at Wyatt and Jade. Jade was speaking animatedly to him, and Allie thought she heard her say something to him about a rock collection. Then, a moment later, she watched as Jade took a rock out of her pocket and handed it to Wyatt. He examined it politely.

"I hope Wyatt likes rocks," Jax said, wryly.

Allie smiled and turned back to her. Then she *really* smiled. "Jax, I swear," she said, studying her. "You look so adorable." And it was true. Jax's hair was braided in twin braids, and she was wearing a checked maternity blouse under a pair of faded denim overalls. A battered straw hat, strung on a ribbon, hung down her back.

"I don't *feel* adorable." Jax sighed. "Just big."

"Oh, I almost forgot," Allie said, climbing back up the front porch steps and retrieving a Tupperware container she'd left there. "This is my contribution to the picnic."

"Chocolate chip cookies?" Jax asked, hopefully.

Allie nodded.

"The same recipe we used that summer?"

"The very same." Allie smiled.

They started walking toward Jax's truck and Jax asked, "How's everything going? It's been, what, two weeks now? Are you two settling in?"

"More or less," Allie said. "Sometimes more, sometimes less. But I wanted to thank you, Jax, for giving me Johnny Miller's phone number. He's been a lifesaver. He's already replaced the rotted-out parts of the porch and the steps." She gestured at

the new pine planks that were now interspersed with the older,
darker ones. "And now he's moved onto the boathouse and the
dock."

"I'm so glad it's worked out," Jax said. "I can't say enough about
his work."

They reached the truck, and Allie watched while Jax boosted
Jade and Wyatt into the backseat and fastened their seat belts.
She fidgeted, resisting the urge to give Wyatt another hug and
kiss before Jax slammed the truck's back door.

Then she followed Jax around to the driver's side and watched
in astonishment as she lightly hoisted herself up behind the
wheel. How anyone that small could drive a pickup truck that big
was a mystery to her. She lingered for a moment, feeling the first
stirrings of anxiety. Wyatt wasn't the only one who was nervous
about their separation today, she realized.

"Are you sure this isn't too much trouble?" she asked Jax.

"No trouble at all. Trust me. Any day I spend away from the
house and the hardware store is like a vacation for me. Besides,
you must have a lot you need to get done around here."

Allie nodded and stepped back to let Jax close the truck's door.
Then she smiled and waved as they drove away. But she felt a
little bereft as she went back into the cabin.

She went to the kitchen, where she'd planned to spend the
morning cleaning out the cupboards, but she didn't start work
right away. Instead, she walked over to the window and looked
out at the lake. It was a breathtaking shade of deep blue today,
and its smooth surface, sparkling in the morning sun, was only
occasionally broken by the ripples of a soft breeze. One of those
warm breezes stirred the kitchen curtains now, and it brought
with it the dry, piney smell of the trees, and the clean, almost
tangy smell of the lake. And then she remembered something

she'd seen in the storage shed that morning when she'd been searching for a blueberry pail for Wyatt.

That's it, she thought. *I'm not spending another second inside. The kitchen cupboards will have to wait.* She left the cabin, walked around behind it to the storage shed, and, swinging the door open on its rusty hinges, maneuvered carefully around the junk inside until she came to a canoe in the corner. It dated from her grandparents' time at the lake and was, she knew, at least fifty years old. She turned it over now, gingerly, and looked inside of it. It was lined with leaves, dirt, and spider webs, but she wasn't ready to give up on it yet.

So she took one end of it and dragged it out of the shed and over to the garden hose at the back of the cabin. She turned the hose on full throttle and rinsed the debris out. Then she had another look at it. It just might be lakeworthy, she decided. She could see that the wood was rotting, slightly, in the bottom of the canoe. But there were no actual holes in it. She went back to the shed for some other items she'd seen there: a canoe paddle, a battered life vest, and a sawed-off plastic milk jug used for bailing out boats. She hosed those off, too. Then she threw them all in the canoe and pulled it down to the lake.

And as she did so, she felt her spirits lift. She needed to get away from this cabin, if only for an hour. Since she and Wyatt had gotten here they'd left it only a few times, to go to the grocery store, or the hardware store, or Pearl's.

She wouldn't go far, she told herself, as she slid the canoe down the gently sloping lake bank. No more than a few hundred yards from the dock. And she'd stay close to shore, too, in no deeper than shoulder-deep water. If the canoe started to leak, she'd come straight back. And if it didn't, well, then taking it out would be a nice diversion.

When she reached the lake, she pushed the canoe, bow first, into the water, and walking out on the dock, pulled the canoe out alongside her until it was in water deep enough to paddle. Then she sat down on the edge of the dock, climbed carefully into the canoe's stern, and sat down on the seat. Using the paddle to push off the lake bottom, she maneuvered out away from the dock. Then she started paddling and, after a few clumsy strokes, settled into a comfortable rhythm. She was surprised at how natural it felt after all these years. How right.

She'd gone about a hundred yards, parallel to the shore, when she realized she was heading in the direction of Walker Ford's dock. Even from this distance, though, she could see that no one was on it. *Good,* she thought, since for reasons she didn't entirely understand, their meeting at Pearl's continued to rankle her. She made a conscious effort now not to think about him, and she kept paddling until she noticed that a few inches of water had accumulated in the bottom of the canoe. She stopped paddling, then, and drifted for a few minutes while she bailed the water out. She should probably turn back now, she thought. But if she did, it would be the end of her little adventure. And she wasn't ready for it to end yet.

So she kept going, staying close to the shoreline, in water only deep enough to paddle comfortably in. The canoe, she knew, wasn't going to sink like a lead weight. Not if she kept bailing it out every few hundred yards. Which she did, alternately paddling and bailing, until she realized her arm was getting tired, and the back of her neck was getting sunburned. The weather, which had seemed so delightfully pleasant when she'd started out, now just seemed hot. Besides, she was almost at Walker Ford's dock, and even if he wasn't down there now, she didn't want to take any chances by lingering too long. It was time to turn around. Or it would be, as soon as she could get some more water out of the canoe's bottom.

But as she stopped to bail again it occurred to her that the canoe might be taking on water a little faster. She bailed furiously for a few minutes before she realized with dismay that the water level in the canoe wasn't falling anymore. It was rising. She bailed faster, but the water only rose faster. She stopped, exhausted, to catch her breath, and saw with alarm that lake water was rushing into the bottom now, covering first her feet, and then her ankles.

She looked back at her own dock, shocked by how far away it suddenly seemed. There was no way she was getting back there now, not in this canoe. She looked around the bay. It was deserted. Even if she could have swallowed her pride long enough to ask for help, there was nobody there to help her. Walker Ford's dock, on the other hand, was only about a hundred yards away.

She sat in the canoe, watching it fill with water, knowing what she had to do, and not wanting to do it. But right before the water reached her knees, she made her escape. She dove out, taking the paddle, the life cushion, and the plastic milk jug with her. Then she stood up, in shoulder-deep water, and watched the canoe sink. It wasn't very dramatic. When it had come to rest, forlornly, on the lake bottom, she swam awkwardly over to Walker's dock, tossed everything she was holding on to it, and dragged herself up after them.

Then she stood up and looked around, feeling utterly ridiculous. Lake water dripped off the hem of her cutoffs, trickled down her legs, and pooled in her sneakers. Thank God Walker Ford hadn't chosen this moment to go for a swim, she thought. She glanced up at his cabin, perched on a bluff above the lake. There was no sign of him up there, either. Good. She was going to have to tell him about the sunken canoe eventually. But at least she could skulk back to her cabin now with her dignity intact. Well, *partially* intact.

Still, there was the question of *how* to get back to her cabin. She looked back at her own dock again. Across the open lake, it was less than half a mile away. She was a good swimmer and could cover that distance easily. But as tempting as it was to do that, it would break one of her cardinal rules as Wyatt's only surviving parent. Never take an unnecessary risk, no matter how small. Because the thought of leaving Wyatt without any parent at all, was, well . . . *unthinkable.*

That meant her only option was walking back to her cabin on the main road. She groaned, inwardly. She'd have to skirt around Walker's cabin to get to his driveway and to Butternut Lake Drive beyond it. If he was home, there was a chance he'd see her, and the ridiculous situation she was in. She briefly considered bypassing his cabin and bushwhacking through the woods to the road, but she dismissed the idea. Too many mosquitoes, too much poison ivy.

So she started walking up the dock, towing her gear along with her. The lake water squelched in the bottom of her sneakers, as her fury at herself settled into a slow burn. *Stupid, stupid, stupid,* she said to herself, every time a sneaker slapped against the dock. *What were you thinking?*

She reached the end of the dock and walked right past the boathouse, not bothering to look inside of it. She already knew it housed at least half a dozen boats. All of them, she imagined, in pristine condition. She felt a fresh wave of irritation at Walker Ford.

And when she started climbing up the stone steps to his cabin, that irritation only intensified. *Was it necessary to have so many steps*, she thought, the backs of her calves aching, and her breath coming faster. But when she reached the top of the steps and turned around, breathing hard, even she had to admit that the view of the lake from there was spectacular. Then again, she thought, as she turned back around, the cabin wasn't too shabby, either. It managed to be both contemporary and traditional at the same time, its simple A-frame shape enhanced by field-stone trim and an entire wall of glass that opened onto the back deck. Whatever else you could say about the man, she admitted, grudgingly, he obviously had good taste. Better than good, really. Everything about this place—the dock, the deck, the cabin— was impeccably designed and beautifully built. It managed to be both luxurious and harmonious at the same time, blending in effortlessly with its natural setting.

She glanced now at the stone path that skirted around to the right of the cabin. That was the way to the driveway and the road beyond. But she hesitated, her curiosity about this place getting the best of her. There was obviously no one around, she thought, and if she just took a quick peek through the glass wall, no one would ever be the wiser. She edged out onto the deck, and over to the glass wall, and, stopping at a sliding glass door, pressed her face against it. The inside of the cabin, she saw, was as spectacular as the outside. The room she was looking into—the living room, obviously—had a cathedral-style ceiling with exposed wooden beams and an enormous fieldstone fireplace embedded in one wall. Two vast, cognac leather couches faced each other on either side of that fireplace. And on one of them, she realized, with a little jolt of surprise, was Walker Ford. Though why she was sur-prised to see him inside his own cabin, she couldn't exactly say.

The good news though, if there *was* any good news, was that he was flipping through a magazine and, as far as she could tell, hadn't seen her yet. She stood there, perfectly still, trying to formulate a plan of action, but her options were limited. If she moved now, she might attract his attention. And if she stood there long enough, he'd eventually look up from his magazine and see her standing there. Looking like an idiot. A total idiot. Which was exactly what she was, when you considered the long list of mistakes she'd already made today.

And it was while she was considering this that Walker Ford looked up from his magazine and stared straight at her. Oddly enough, he didn't look surprised. Not exactly. *Disturbed* was a better word. And who could blame him? She could only imagine what she looked like. The creature from the black lagoon, probably.

As he set down his magazine, stood up, and walked toward the sliding glass door, Allie made a last-ditch effort to make herself look a little more presentable, peeling her sodden T-shirt away from her wet skin. She tried to ring some of the lake water out of it, too, but it still stuck to her like glue. She tugged, too, at the hem of her dripping cutoffs but couldn't seem to make them any longer than they were, which right now seemed to be about two inches long. She sighed and gave up. She looked like a horror show. And a scantily clad one at that.

As Walker reached the glass door and slid it open, she wondered what else could possibly go wrong today. She had a feeling she was about to find out.

CHAPTER 10

It was the strangest thing. One minute, Walker was sitting on his couch, flipping through an issue of *American Fisherman* magazine, trying not to think about his new neighbor, and thinking about her anyway. And the next minute, he was looking up and seeing her, standing there on his deck, holding, of all things, a canoe paddle.

That's when it occurred to him that he might actually be losing his mind. That he might be hallucinating. But when he shut his eyes and opened them again, she was still standing there, still holding a canoe paddle.

He stood up, crossed the room, and opened the sliding glass door. And that was when he realized that she was dripping wet. His first thought, obviously, should have been, *What the hell was she doing here?* And, more important, *What the hell was she doing before she got here?*

But his first thought, instead, was that she looked amazing. Like some kind of freshwater mermaid who'd just washed up on his deck.

"I'm sorry to bother you," she said, a little sheepishly, "but my canoe sank and—"

"Where's your son?" Walker interrupted, his brain kick-starting itself.

"Oh, no, he's not with me," she said quickly, reading the expression of alarm on his face. "He's picking blueberries with Jax and her daughters—"

"Wait," he said, interrupting her again. "Did you say your canoe *sank*?" He looked out at the lake. The water was as smooth as glass.

"Yes. I know, it sounds strange, but—"

"*Sank* or *capsized*?" he clarified. An inexperienced canoer could capsize a canoe, but canoes did not, as a general rule, sink. Not on a day like today, under weather conditions like these. If he'd special ordered a summer day from a catalog, it could not have been more perfect than this one.

"I know the difference between capsizing and sinking," she said, a frown line forming between her hazel eyes. "Believe it or not, I'm an experienced canoer."

Walker didn't believe it. And her tone, when she spoke again, told him she *knew* he didn't believe it.

"Look," she said, "I took out my grandfather's wooden canoe. It's at least fifty years old, maybe older. It was taking on a little water when I started out. But I thought I could handle it." She indicated the plastic bailing jug she was holding. "It turned out to be more than a little leak, though. It turned out to be—"

"A big leak?" he interrupted, again. Somehow, the spell had been broken. She still looked irresistibly lovely standing there, her wet clothes clingingly appealingly to her slender body. But he was beginning, belatedly, to see the humor in the situation.

Her jaw tightened. "Yeah, okay. A *big* leak. Anyway, long story short, taking that canoe out was probably a mistake."

"Probably?" Walker repeated, one corner of his mouth lifting a quarter of an inch.

"I'm glad you're finding this so amusing," she said, obviously exasperated. "But the only reason I'm even telling you this is because I need to cut across your property to the road. If it's all right with you, I'll be on my way now."

"Be my guest," Walker said, with a shrug. But then his curiosity got the best of him. "Where'd your canoe sink?" he asked.

"About a hundred yards to the right of your dock. In about five feet of water."

"It was that close, huh?" he asked, the corner of his mouth lifting again.

She flushed, and he watched, fascinated, as a warm pinkness collided with the pale gold of her complexion.

"I wasn't spying on you," she said, "if that's what you're implying."

"I'm not implying anything," he said innocently.

"Anyway, if it's okay with you, I'll come back for it as soon as I'm able to. I don't want it to be a hazard to other boaters."

"I'll take care of it," he said. He loved a salvage project, big or small. "But in the meantime, why don't I run you home? You can't be comfortable in those wet clothes." *Even if you look amazing in them*, he thought. But he immediately regretted thinking it. It seemed disrespectful, somehow, now that he knew more about her personal circumstances.

"Thanks for the offer," she said. "But I'm going to walk back on the road." He watched, fascinated, as a tiny rivulet of water ran down her neck and disappeared beneath her cotton T-shirt. She frowned, again, and crossed her arms self-consciously.

"Look, at least let me get you a towel," he said, in as close to a business-like tone as he could muster.

"A towel would be nice," she admitted. "And then I'll get going."

He slid the door open farther and gestured for her to come inside. "Why don't you wait in here?"

She shook her head. "I don't want to drip on the floor."

"The floor is made from reclaimed wood from a barn," he said, motioning her inside. "It's already withstood a hundred years of exposure from the elements. I think it can handle a few drops of water."

"It's beautiful," she said, examining the floor as she stepped inside.

"Thanks," he said. "I put it in myself. I'll be right back." He brought her a towel, then looked discreetly away while she dried herself off. He thought about offering her some dry clothes, too, but decided that that might be going too far. Besides, he had nothing that would even come close to fitting her. Well, nothing that belonged to him. He pushed the image of his ex-wife's nightgown out of his mind.

"Thanks. That's much better," she said, holding on to the damp towel. "Why don't I bring this back to you after I've washed it."

"That's not necessary," he said. "I can wash it myself." He added, confidentially, "You know, they actually put the instructions on the inside lid of the washing machine."

She didn't smile. But she did hand the towel back to him. And when she did, he caught the faintest scent of coconut suntan lotion and clean lake water radiating off her skin. To him, it was the perfect distillation of summer. If he could have bottled it, he would have.

"Mind if I cut through your house to the driveway?" she asked now, glancing around.

"Of course not. But why don't you just let me run you home in my truck? It'll take five minutes. Less, probably."

"No, you've done enough. I don't want to disrupt your day any more than I already have."

He smiled. "I was reading a fishing magazine," he said. *And thinking about you,* he added silently. "The title of the article was 'Best New Lures for Summer.' Pretty important stuff, obviously. But I can probably tear myself away from it."

She bit her lower lip, weighing his offer. "Okay," she said finally. "If you don't mind, a ride home would be great. I don't want Jax to try to reach me and have me not be home. I was only planning on being gone for a little while."

"Let's go then," he said. He led her through the cabin and out the front door. She murmured appreciatively at the rest of the interior, and he was tempted to remind her she'd used the word *ostentatious* to describe it when he'd met her at the coffee shop. But he didn't say anything. Not about that, anyway. He was thinking about something else he wanted to say to her. *Needed* to say to her.

They climbed into his pickup truck and drove in silence to her cabin. She looked studiously out the window, as if she was trying to memorize each variety of tree they passed. And he tried to look at the road, instead of at her knees. He had a thing about women's knees. Usually, though, they were too bony and sharp. Or too dimpled and ill-defined. Her knees, he saw with a side-long glance, were absolutely perfect.

Too soon, he turned into her driveway and stopped in front of her cabin.

"Hey, you've gotten a lot of work done on this place," Walker said, approvingly. *It doesn't look like it's going to fall down anymore,* he thought, but didn't say.

But Allie only shrugged and started to get out of the truck.

"Hey, before you go," he said, quickly. "I wanted to apologize."

"For what?" she asked, turning to face him.

"For asking you about your husband when we met at Pearl's. That was rude. It was none of my business."

She looked away from him, out the passenger-side window, but otherwise said nothing. He got the sense that she was trying, somehow, to compose herself. A breeze blew outside, stirring the trees and changing the dappled shadings of the sun that played over both of them in the truck.

Finally, he heard her exhale. "It's not your fault," she said. "You couldn't have known." And then, turning to him with a rueful little sigh, she said, "I knew I was right about how quickly gossip traveled in Butternut."

"It wasn't like that," Walker said, frowning. "Caroline told me about it because she thought you and Wyatt might need help."

"What kind of help?" she asked him, warily, not taking her eyes off him. And her eyes were beautiful, he thought. Like mosaics, with little chips of light brown and green intermingled in them.

"I think what Caroline meant," he said, carefully, "is that the two of you might need a neighbor some time. A *real* neighbor. Why she thought I could be that person, I don't know. I don't have any practice at it." *Unless, of course, you counted the fling he'd had with the flight attendant who lived next door to him in his condominium complex in Minneapolis. And he didn't count it.*

"I appreciate Caroline's concern," she said now. "I really do.

But I didn't move here for the whole 'small town experience.' I moved here for the privacy."

"I can understand that," he said. Nobody valued privacy more than he did. But she and her son's circumstances were different from his own.

"But what about your son, Wyatt?" he asked, gently. "Does he need privacy, too?"

She flushed. And there was an edge of anger in her voice when she spoke again. "Wyatt is doing just fine, thank you. And I think I'm probably the best judge of what he does or doesn't need." She paused, then asked, coolly, "Do you have any children?"

"No," he said, feeling a twist of pain in his gut. Its sharpness surprised him. "No, I'm not a father," he heard himself say.

"Then you probably don't know a lot about raising children."

That was harsh, he thought. *Harsh, but fair.*

"You're right. I don't know anything about kids," he said, abruptly. Then he leaned over her and opened the passenger-side door. He knew it was a rude thing to do, but he didn't really care.

Allie didn't move, though. And when she spoke again, her tone was gentler. "Look, I know you mean well. Everybody *means* well. But nobody really understands. I mean, don't get me wrong. I'm not the first person to lose a husband to a war. And I won't be the last. There are plenty of military widows out there. But they're not usually the people giving me advice. Or claiming to understand how I feel. Or trying to be 'helpful.'"

"You say helpful like it's a dirty word," he observed.

She smiled another one of her *almost* smiles. "No, 'helpful' is all right," she said. "Assuming that you want to be helped."

"Instead of just being left alone?" he supplied.

She looked thoughtful. "Sometimes, yes."

He thought about what she'd said. He didn't know why, but

it bothered him. Which was strange, when you considered how much *he'd* wanted to be left alone over the last couple of years.

"Look," he said, "I can't speak for everyone in Butternut. But I can speak for myself. And I'll try to leave you alone. Usually, it's something I'm very good at doing. Leaving people alone, I mean. You might even say it's a specialty of mine."

She bit her lower lip. "I didn't mean I want people to ignore us," she clarified. "I just meant I don't want people to try to help us. Not when I can take care of both of us."

Walker was silent. He didn't think now was the time to mention that she'd taken care of herself so well today that her canoe was sitting on the bottom of the lake.

"Thanks for the ride," she said, favoring him with one of her rare smiles. And then she gathered her gear together and slid out of the truck, slamming the door behind her. He didn't wait for her to walk all the way up to her cabin. When she was a safe distance away, he gunned the engine, turned the truck around, and sped, too fast, up her driveway.

You've met your match, Walker, he thought, turning onto the road and making a conscious effort to slow down. *You've finally found someone who's even more obsessed with her independence, and her privacy, than you are. You two should be perfect neighbors.* But if that were the case, he wondered, why was he suddenly in such a lousy mood?

CHAPTER 11

Jade, *please* hold still," Jax said, with uncharacteristic impatience.

"I'm sorry, Mommy, but you're pulling too tight," Jade said. "I don't see why you have to braid my hair, anyway," she added, in an injured tone.

"Sweetie, you know the rule," Jax said, trying, but failing, to hide her exasperation. "If you want to grow your hair long, you have to wear it braided. Not all the time. But most of the time. And definitely at day camp, all right? Otherwise, it gets all tangled. And Mommy doesn't have the energy right now to get the tangles out every night before bedtime. So try to hold still and I'll get it over with as quickly as possible. I promise."

But a moment later, Jade objected again. "*Ouch!* Mommy, that hurts." She squirmed on the high stool she was sitting on, her back to Jax. They were on the screened-in porch off the back of their house, where Jax's daughters liked to sleep on warm summer nights.

"I'm sorry, baby," Jax said, letting go of one of Jade's braids. She knew she'd pulled too hard. Under ordinary circumstances, she was an excellent braider. But this morning, she was having difficulty making her hands do what she wanted them to do. It was nerves, plain and simple. Her hands had been shaking, for instance, when she'd ironed Jeremy's shirt that morning. And her stomach had churned uneasily when she'd swallowed her prenatal vitamin.

"What's wrong, Mommy?" Jade asked, swiveling around on her stool.

"Nothing's wrong, honey. I'm just pregnant. And tired. And *hot*," she said, reaching over to turn up a nearby fan that felt as if it was barely stirring the already humid morning air.

"But, Mommy," Jade reminded her, "you said you like being pregnant. You said it's easy for you, 'cause you don't feel sick or throw up or anything."

"I did say that, didn't I?" Jax smiled at Jade's upturned face, all wide blue eyes and riotous freckles. "Thank you for reminding me about that, Jade. And do you know what I've decided about today?"

"What?"

"I've decided that today should be a ponytail day for you. What do you say to that idea, sweet pea?"

Jade nodded, relieved.

So Jax started over, brushing out Jade's hair, being careful not to pull too hard on it, and being careful, too, not to complain when Jade started squirming again. It wasn't Jade's fault, after all, that she had trouble sitting still. She was six years old. And for her, today was an ordinary day, like any other day, except better, of course, because it was a summer day. But for Jax, today was a day she'd been dreading for weeks. It wasn't marked on the family calendar that hung in the kitchen. But if it had been, it would have been marked with a big, black X. It was the day Bobby said he'd be calling her from prison.

The doorbell rang then, interrupting her thoughts.

"That's Allie and Wyatt," she said, gathering Jade's hair into a ponytail and twisting elastic around it.

"They're here now?" Jade asked, excitedly.

"Yep," Jax said, reaching under Jade's arms and lifting her down from the stool. "Why don't you let them in?"

Jade raced excitedly to the front door, and Jax smiled, pleased that Jade liked Wyatt so much. He'd been very quiet the day he'd come blueberry picking with them. But far from being disappointed, Jade had simply adjusted her conversational strategy and talked enough for both of them.

By the time Jax got to the front door, Jade had already flung it open and was talking a blue streak to Wyatt.

Jax laughed. "Jade, honey, can you at least say hello to Allie and Wyatt first?"

"Oh, hello," Jade said, a little breathlessly. And, without missing a beat, "Now do you want to come upstairs to my room and see my rock collection? I have like a gazillion rocks. More than anyone else I know. And I'm not even done collecting them."

Wyatt hesitated, but he let Jade take him by the hand and drag him away.

"Make it quick, Jade, okay?" Jax called after her, closing the front door. "Your dad's going to be here soon to take you and your sisters to day camp."

Allie smiled, gratefully, at Jax. "She is exactly what Wyatt needs right now," she said.

"A bossy six-year-old girl telling him what to do all the time?"

Allie shook her head. "No. A friend," she said simply. And

Jax smiled, even though something caught in her throat at the thought of what Wyatt and Allie had been through.

"How about a cup of coffee?" she asked Allie, leading her to the kitchen. "Or on second thought, how about an iced tea? It's way too hot for coffee this morning."

"An iced tea would be nice," Allie said, sitting down at the kitchen table.

Jax busied herself, taking a pitcher of iced tea out of the refrigerator and two glasses out of the cupboard. "By the way," she said, "did you get a lot done at the cabin on Saturday? I forgot to ask you when we brought Wyatt home."

"Oh," Allie said, looking a little vague, "I didn't get as much done as I thought I would. But thanks for taking Wyatt, anyway. It was so good for him. He doesn't spend as much time with other children as he should."

"Have you thought about sending him to day camp?" Jax asked, carefully, setting the glasses of iced tea on the table. She sensed this would be a sensitive subject for Allie. Wyatt, she knew, wasn't the only one having difficulty separating.

"The one your daughters go to?"

"Uh-huh. It's at the little nature museum, right outside of town. They call the campers there 'junior naturalists.' And there's a different theme there every week. The girls love it," she added.

"That sounds like fun," Allie said, a little wistfully. "I'll ask Wyatt about it."

Just then, they heard a car's engine backfire down the street, and Jax's hand jerked, spilling iced tea on the table.

"Jax," Allie said, gently. "Do you think maybe you should cut down on the caffeine? You seem a little . . . tightly wound this morning."

"Oh, this is decaffeinated," Jax assured her, wiping up the spill with a dish towel. "Really, I'm fine. I just couldn't sleep last night. And this morning I feel a little tense." *A little?* She felt like the proverbial live wire, her body practically humming with anxiety.

"Anyway," she said, changing the subject, "in case you're wondering why I asked you to stop by this morning, it's because I wanted to invite you to a party."

"A party?" Allie echoed. She looked horrified, like Jax had said *electric chair* or *plane crash* instead of *party*.

"Yes, party," Jax said. "Parties are supposed to be fun, remember?"

"Not really," Allie confessed. "It's been a while since I've been to one. I've tried to avoid them, I guess, over the last couple of years."

Jax hesitated. She couldn't blame Allie, really, for not feeling as if she had any reason to celebrate. Still, Jax thought, she couldn't avoid parties forever, could she?

"Look, you don't have to come," she said. "But I hope you will. Our third of July party has become something of a Butternut tradition."

"A *third* of July party?"

"Uh-huh. To celebrate the day Jeremy and I met. Well, not met for the first time, because we lived in the same town all our lives. But the day we met again, after Jeremy came home from college." She added, "And making things more complicated is that we can't actually celebrate on that day, which was the Fourth of July, because nobody would come. Everyone in Butternut goes to the fairgrounds for the fireworks. So instead, we have it the day before. We buy the burgers and beer, and we hire a band, and everyone else brings a side dish or a salad or a dessert. And it's fun." She concluded, "Or at least, that's the plan," seeing the same apprehensive expression on Allie's face.

"Jax, I'm sure it is fun," Allie said, with a determined smile. "And Wyatt and I wouldn't miss it for the world."

"Really?" Jax asked, hopefully.

"Really," Allie said. "Now, what can I bring?"

"Can you can bring your chocolate chip cookies?" Jax asked.

"Of course. How many?"

"Well, let's see, They'll be about two hundred people there—"

"*Two hundred?*" Allie said, in astonishment. "Jax, how do you even *know* two hundred people?"

"Easy. In a town the size of Butternut, you know *everyone,*" Jax explained. "Whether you want to or not. But I'll tell you what, I'll settle for a couple dozen cookies. We can just let our guests fight it out for them."

Their conversation was interrupted by a car horn honking in front of the house.

"Jeremy's here to drive the girls to camp," Jax explained to Allie, and she went to the bottom of the stairs to call up to them.

Jade and Wyatt were the first ones down, Jade still clutching Wyatt by the hand. They were followed by Josie, Jax's nine-year-old, who came dragging down the stairs with a scowl on her face that told Jax she'd been fighting with her older sister, Joy. As Josie reached her, Jax gave her a gentle push in the direction of the kitchen.

"Josie, please get the bag lunches out of the fridge," she told her.

"Why do I have to get them for everyone?" Josie objected.

But Jax ignored her. Instead, she looked up at Joy, her twelve-year-old, coming down the stairs. Unlike her sister, she didn't look angry. Her fight with Josie was already forgotten, and she had a soft, dreamy expression on her face that told Jax she was thinking about Andy Montgomery, the thirteen-year-old boy who lived across the street. Jax groaned inwardly. She'd hoped the whole boy thing might still be a few years away. She should have known better.

When Joy reached the bottom of the stairs, Jax took her by the shoulders and, looking into her pretty, freckled face, said sternly, "And you, you stop fighting with your sister. Is that understood?"

"Uh-huh," Joy said, in a way that let Jax know she hadn't heard a word she'd said.

Jax sighed, but there was a flurry of activity now as she got the girls out the door.

"Are you sure you can't stay a little longer," Jax asked Allie then, not wanting to be alone. Because as hard as it had been to be with people since she'd gotten Bobby's letter, it was harder to be alone. Alone with her fear.

But Allie shook her head. "We'd better be going, too," she said, giving Jax a hug. "We have groceries in the trunk."

And then they were gone, and Jax walked, mechanically, to the kitchen. The morning's breakfast dishes were still stacked in the sink. She put the stopper in the drain, turned on the hot water, and added a squirt of dishwashing liquid. Then she waited for the sink to fill up, staring absently into the cloud of steam that rose from the faucet. This was one time, she thought, as she picked up a sponge and a dish, that her dishwashing ritual wouldn't give her any pleasure.

Then the telephone rang, too loudly in the quiet kitchen, and Jax dropped the dish she was holding. Luckily, it clattered to the bottom of the sink without breaking. She walked over to the cordless phone on the counter and picked it up. It felt strangely heavy as she lifted it to her ear and spoke into it.

"Hello," she croaked, her mouth as dry as sandpaper.

"Jax?" Bobby drawled from the other end. Strange, she thought. It had been so many years since she'd heard Bobby's voice, but it sounded utterly familiar. Familiar in an awful kind of way.

She almost hung up, but she restrained herself. Because if she did hang up, he might get angry. And, insofar as she had a strategy, it involved not making Bobby angry. Or at least not any more angry than was absolutely necessary.

"Bobby?" she croaked in answer, her tongue clumsy and uncooperative in her mouth.

"That's right, baby," he said. And then he added, a little peevishly, "You don't sound very happy to hear from me."

"I'm just surprised," she said, looking up at the kitchen clock. "You weren't supposed to call for another hour."

"Change of plans," he said, carelessly. "Besides, I thought if I called you earlier, *she* might answer the phone. And I've never heard her voice before. I'd like to know what Joy's voice sounds like, Jax. She is my daughter, after all."

It was so quiet in the kitchen that the steady drip of water from the faucet sounded almost painfully loud. Jax groped for a chair at the kitchen table, then sank down on it just as her knees buckled uselessly beneath her.

"She's not your daughter, Bobby," she breathed. "I told you in my letter to you. She's Jeremy's daughter. I was pregnant with her when I married him."

"Oh, you were pregnant all right," Bobby said with a snort. "But it was with my baby, not his."

"And you know this because . . ."

"I know this because a couple of weeks before you were hooking up with Jeremy, you were hooking up with me. You and I conceived that baby together, Jax. I know it. And you know it. And now you know that I know it."

"But—"

"Jax, I don't have time for this now," Bobby snapped. "I've got five minutes on my calling card, and twelve guys standing in line behind me, waiting their turn. You think it's easy to make a phone call in prison? Think again."

Jax took a deep breath. She had to get a handle on herself. *Now.* But she also had to change her strategy. Because her denials weren't going to work. And Bobby, for once, had the truth on his side.

"Look, Bobby. Let's not argue about this, okay?" she said, trying a different tack. "I mean, what difference does it make, in the long run, whose daughter Joy is? Isn't it enough to know that she has a good home here with me and Jeremy?"

"But what about me, baby? What have I got?" Bobby whined, and he sounded so exactly like one of her children that Jax almost laughed. *Almost.*

"What you've got, Bobby, if you really believe Joy is your daughter, is the satisfaction of knowing she's well taken care of," Jax said. She didn't think for a minute this gambit would work. But she was hoping, somehow, to increase her negotiating power by appealing to his conscience. Assuming, of course, that he *had* a conscience. And she was not at all sure that he did.

"Look, now you're just wasting my time again," Bobby muttered. "My time *and* the minutes on my calling card. I told you all this in my letter, Jax. Joy's my daughter. And when I get out this summer, I want to be part of her life. I've got rights. Don't think I don't know about them. The library here's got a legal section in it, and I've done my homework. So you and I can either work something out now, or after I'm released, in another six weeks, I can swing by the hardware store and talk to Jeremy about it. Because I'm willing to bet, sweetheart, that the subject of who Joy's real father is doesn't come up very often at the dinner table. Am I right?"

Jax didn't answer. She didn't need to.

"Okay, good. We understand each other," Bobby said. "I'm glad. Because I'm not entirely unsympathetic to your little, um . . . *predicament* here. And, as much as I want to see our daughter, if you think it might be.too much of a shock to her if I did, well, then we might be able to work something out."

"Keep talking," Jax said, a tiny hope stirring inside her.

"Well, here's the thing. When I leave here, it's with nothing but a couple of homemade tattoos. And those aren't going to pay the bills. I've got to start over now. From scratch. And that takes money."

Jax's head cleared instantly. *Money.* She'd hoped it would come to this. She could pay Bobby off, she knew, if the price wasn't too high. "Fine," she said. "How much are we talking about? I don't have a lot, obviously, but I might be able to arrange a small loan to get you started somewhere." *Somewhere far away from here.*

"Uh, I wasn't thinking of a loan, baby. I was thinking more of a *gift.* And I was thinking, maybe, fifty thousand dollars of seed money ought to be enough to get me started in some business. Some *legal* business," he added.

Fifty thousand dollars? Are you crazy? Jax almost blurted out. But then she reminded herself that this was a negotiation. And that fifty thousand dollars was only Bobby's opening offer.

"Look," she said, "there is no way I can get my hands on fifty thousand dollars. But I can offer you twenty-five *hundred* dollars." She added, sternly, "And that's a lot of money for me."

"Sorry, baby, that's not going to do it," Bobby said flatly.

"Five thousand then," Jax said. She knew she was giving in too quickly, but she couldn't help it. She wanted to get this over with.

"I'll come down to twenty," Bobby said, just as quickly.

"Ten is my final offer," Jax said. "You can take it or leave it. But I'm not going any higher."

Bobby was silent for a long time. "All right," he said finally, in a sulky tone of voice.

"And in exchange, Bobby, you stay away from her. And the rest of my family. And another thing, Bobby. You stay away from Butternut, too. Is that clear?"

"You can't tell me where to live," he grumbled.

"I can if you want the money," she shot back.

He was silent. "Yeah, okay," he said, finally. "I don't want to start over in your stupid little town, anyway. But I do need to come there, for a couple of days, after I get out. I've got some loose ends that need tying up. I can get the money from you then, Jax."

"No, Bobby. I'll mail you a check. Just give me a few days to get the money together."

"Oh no, babe, you're not getting off that easily. Besides, I prefer to conduct my business in person."

"Bobby, no. I can't see you in person. It's too big a risk."

"Yeah, well, life is full of risks," he said, darkly. "I learned that the hard way. So I'll see you in Butternut on, uh, August fifteenth. I should be there by then. Why don't we say nine P.M. at the Mosquito Inn."

The Mosquito Inn? Jax thought, appalled. The place was a dive bar on Highway 169 that catered mainly to motorcycle gang members and ex-cons. The thought of her going there, when she'd be nearly eight and a half months pregnant, was ludicrous, and she almost said so. But then something occurred to her. Her chances of seeing someone she actually knew there, someone other than Bobby, were almost nonexistent.

"Okay," she said. "I'll be there."

"Good," Bobby growled, and he hung up the phone.

Jax put down the phone, too, and it was only then that she realized she was shaking all over. *This can't be good for the baby,* she thought, putting her hands protectively over her belly.

"I'm sorry," she whispered, in the quiet kitchen. And, as if in response, she felt the baby move. It was a gentle, fluttering movement, almost like a tiny pair of wings beating. And it comforted her somehow.

She crossed her arms on the table then and put her head down on them. And she remembered the afternoon, thirteen years ago, that Bobby Lewis had walked into the Butternut drugstore and changed her life forever.

Jax had just graduated from high school that June, and she was living at home, working part time at Butternut Drugs. She'd had no idea, at the time, what the future held for her. But she had a feeling that whatever it was, it probably wasn't worth getting excited about.

She wasn't going to college. That much was clear. Her math teacher, Mrs. Martin, had been impressed by her quickness with numbers and had encouraged her to apply to the state university. But she hadn't done it. She didn't believe in herself. And, with the exception of Mrs. Martin, no one else seemed to believe in her either. Besides, even if she could have gotten into the University of Minnesota, there was no money to pay for her to go there.

So instead, she stood behind the makeup counter at Butternut Drugs, rearranging lipsticks and waiting for something, *anything,* to happen. And then, one day, it did. Bobby Lewis came in to buy a bottle of aftershave. And he stayed to flirt with Jax.

"Is that all you do all day? Arrange those little tubes?" he asked, watching her.

"They're called lipsticks," Jax said, unnerved by his proximity to her. "And the middle-school girls who come in here to look at them get them all out of order," she explained. In spite of the drugstore's air-conditioning, her face felt suddenly warm.

"Do you ever get bored working here?" Bobby asked, leaning on the counter.

"All the time," Jax murmured, glancing over to see if Mr. Coats, who owned the drugstore, was within earshot. He wasn't.

"Then why don't you put that little tube down, and you and I will walk out that door and get into my pickup," Bobby said. "We'll buy a six-pack of beer, go for a drive, and have some fun. What do you say?"

"I say no," Jax practically whispered. Her face was burning now. She'd never even been kissed before. And the way Bobby was looking at her, and talking to her, made her think he wanted to do a lot more than kiss her.

"Oh, come on," Bobby coaxed. "It's too nice a day to be stuck inside."

She shook her head. "I'd get fired," she said, putting a coral-colored lipstick back in its proper slot.

"Then I'll come back at closing," Bobby said. "We can drive down to the lake and watch the sunset."

"I don't think so," Jax said, pretending now to be absorbed in dusting the eye shadow display. There was no way she was going out with him. She didn't know him personally, but she knew him by his reputation. And his reputation was bad.

He was a liar, she'd heard, and a cheat and a thief. At twenty, he already had a rap sheet as long as her arm. And he was supposed to be mean, too. Even Jax's father, no saint himself, had once said that Bobby Lewis was the kind of guy who couldn't walk by a dog without kicking it.

But unfortunately for Jax, Bobby did have a few things going for him. He was good-looking, for one thing. And he practically oozed sex appeal, for another. And, as Jax was about to discover, he could also be very persuasive when he made up his mind that he wanted something. And right then, what he wanted was Jax.

"I'm not leaving until you say yes," he said. "And I've got all afternoon."

Jax looked up. Mr. Coats was coming over. And he didn't look happy.

"Fine, I'll go out with you tonight. But you have to go now," she pleaded.

"See you at six," he said. Then he gave her a long, slow smile and left the store.

In later years, Jax often thought that getting fired that day would have been a small price to pay for not getting involved with Bobby Lewis. But the truth was, she wasn't entirely blameless. Because if he had to twist her arm to go with him that time, she went out with him willingly enough the next time. And the time after that.

Why, she couldn't really say. She knew he was trouble, knew it would end badly. But she was bored. And lonely. And flattered by his attention. And deep down, she didn't really believe she deserved anyone or anything better than Bobby Lewis.

But whatever the reason, it ended exactly the way they'd both known it would end, with Bobby sweet-talking Jax out of her clothes, and her virginity, in the backseat of his pickup one night. After that, he dropped the pretense of being charming and alternated between being mean to Jax and just ignoring her.

But soon, he lost interest in her altogether. And one day, when she was at work, rearranging the lipsticks again, Jax realized she hadn't seen him in over a week. *Good riddance,* she told herself.

But at that moment, a tube of lipstick slipped through her fingers and rolled under the counter, and as she knelt to retrieve it, she realized, in a moment like a thunderclap, that she was pregnant. She didn't know how she knew it. She hadn't experienced any physical changes yet. It was too early for her to have even missed a period. But she knew, with absolute certainty, that she was going to have a baby.

Amazingly enough, she didn't panic. She didn't panic because in the same moment she knew she was pregnant, she knew something else, too. She knew that whatever happened, she was not going to let Bobby Lewis have anything to do with this child. And knowing that gave her a sense of purpose. She reached for the lipstick under the counter, stood up, and calmly put it back in its slot on the display shelf.

But one week, and one positive pregnancy test, later, Jax still had no idea how she would keep her promise to herself. She was at Butternut's annual Fourth of July picnic, nibbling on a slice of watermelon and contemplating the enormity of her problem, when Jeremy Johnson bumped into her and spilled some punch on her sundress. He apologized profusely and went to get some napkins for her, but he stayed to talk. And her life changed again, for the second time in one month.

She could still remember every detail of that night.

"How is it that we've never even spoken to each other before tonight?" Jeremy asked her later, toward sunrise the next morning, as they lay on a blanket under an overturned rowboat at the town beach.

"You left for college the summer before my freshman year in high school," Jax pointed out.

"I never should have left," Jeremy said, kissing her. "I should have just stayed here and waited for you to grow up."

"I wish you had," Jax said, kissing him back. "But the truth is, you never would have looked twice at me."

"Why do you say that?" he asked, frowning.

"Because it's true. You and I are from two different worlds," she said. *Your family lives in a clapboard house on Main Street. Mine lives in a trailer in the woods. Your parents own the hardware store. My parents are the town drunks. You went to college. I got pregnant.*

"Look, I don't know about different worlds," Jeremy said, raising himself up on one elbow. "But I do know one thing. Spilling that drink on you tonight was the smartest thing I've ever done."

"You did that on purpose?"

"Of course."

"Why?" She was fascinated.

"Because I was watching you. And I knew I had to talk to you."

Jax was skeptical.

"It's true," Jeremy said. "I saw you, and I thought there was something so . . . so beautiful about you. Complicated, but beautiful. You seemed like this weird combination of fragile and strong. It's hard to put into words. But I knew I needed to find out more about you. Everything about you, really."

Jax thought about what he'd said. She didn't really believe she was beautiful. Or interesting, for that matter. But talking to Jeremy tonight, she could *almost* believe she was both of those things.

"When I did start talking to you," Jeremy said, "I wasn't disappointed. I felt like I could talk to you all night."

Jax smiled then. "Okay. But no more talking now. At least not for a little while." And she pulled him down beside her.

Several minutes later, Jeremy untangled himself from her. By this time, they were both partially undressed. Jeremy in his blue jeans, and Jax in a polka-dot bra and underwear.

"Jax," Jeremy said, breathing hard. "Look, I'm sorry. I wasn't expecting this to happen. I don't have any, um . . . protection with me. So I think we should stop. Or at least slow down." But as he said this his eyes traveled over her body, and he swallowed, hard.

"Or we could just take off the rest of our clothes," Jax said, surprised by her own boldness. She wriggled out of her bra and underwear.

It was almost cavelike under the overturned rowboat, but Jax's bare, creamy skin glowed softly in what little light there was.

Jeremy couldn't take his eyes off her. "Jax," he said, shaking his head. But he kissed her again. And again. They made love right as the sun rose over Butternut Lake.

In later years, Jax often replayed this scene in her head, and she had to admit it didn't reflect very well on her. But at the time, her actions hadn't been deliberately calculating or dishonest. Lying there beside Jeremy that night, her attraction to him was real. So was her impatience for their lovemaking to begin. She couldn't have faked that, even if she'd wanted to. She didn't know how to. What's more, the lovemaking that followed was as intense, and as pleasurable, as anything Jax could have imagined possible. That part, at least, wasn't a lie.

And there was never a moment that night when she'd said to herself, *I'll spend the night with Jeremy. And then I'll tell him I'm pregnant with his child.* But she couldn't deny, either, that she'd known that Jeremy would make an infinitely better husband and father than Bobby ever would have, and that that knowledge may have played an unconscious role in her actions that night.

In any case, a couple of weeks later, Jax told Jeremy she was pregnant. And he proposed to her immediately, without any hesitation. By this time, they were spending every waking minute together, and Jax loved him like crazy. She was pretty sure he loved her the same way, too.

So they got married, bought a house with a small down payment borrowed from Jeremy's parents, and took over the hardware store. And when Joy was born, looking blessedly like Jax, everything fell into place so perfectly that Jax had to believe that this was the way it was meant to be.

Which wasn't to say that she didn't feel guilty about the lie at the center of their lives. She did. She knew what she'd done was wrong. And she knew if Jeremy ever found out about it, it would destroy their life together. But as the years passed and their family grew, the stakes got higher.

So Jax did the only thing she could do. She loved Jeremy and her daughters in the best way she knew how to. And she told herself that it was better for her to live with her lie than for all of them to live with the truth. And most of the time, she believed this. It was the days she didn't believe it that were the hardest.

And Bobby? She never even told him she was pregnant. She didn't need to. That summer, before she even started to show, he was arrested for robbing a liquor store and sent to state prison. And Jax, secretly relieved, had thought that was the end of it. Until she'd gotten his letter that spring, telling her he was getting out of prison and he wanted to meet his daughter. How he knew that Joy was his, Jax had no idea. He'd probably heard that she'd had a baby, done the math, and made a lucky guess. And he'd waited to get in touch with her until he'd known he was getting out. After all, there was nothing she could do for him while he was inside.

Jax sighed now, sitting in her quiet kitchen, and she thought about Joy at the breakfast table that morning. She'd been impossible. Complaining about having to clean her room. Provoking her sisters. Ignoring her mother's pleas for peace. But Jax had caught her, between bites of her French toast, with a soft, wistful expression on her face that told Jax that even as Joy was sitting at the kitchen table with her family, in her mind, she was a million miles away. Daydreaming, probably, of something less ordinary than her ordinary life.

But the funny thing was that it was this ordinary life, in an ordinary house, with an ordinary family, that Jax was determined to protect. Because for Jax, ordinariness was a privilege she'd been denied as a child. And now, she would do anything to keep Bobby from taking it away from Joy. And not just taking it away from Joy, either. But taking it away from all five of them. No, make that all *six* of them, Jax thought, as the baby moved again.

CHAPTER 12

Caroline was flipping the sign on the front door of Pearl's from Open to Closed when she saw a man standing on the sidewalk, reading the menu posted in the window. He wasn't from Butternut, obviously. If he was, he'd already know her menu by heart.

"Can I help you?" she asked, opening the door and shading her eyes against the still-scorching afternoon sun.

He looked up from the menu and smiled. "Oh, I was just looking for a place to get something cold to drink. And maybe a sandwich to go with it."

"We close at three," Caroline said matter-of-factly.

He glanced at his watch. "Is it three fifteen already?" he asked, surprised. "I completely lost track of time. Do you know anyplace else I could get lunch at this time of day?"

Caroline hesitated. The Corner Bar was right down the block, and, in a pinch, you could get a decent hamburger there. But it was the kind of establishment that catered mainly to drinkers, and even on a bright, sunny day like today, it was apt to be dark and gloomy inside. Then there was the gas station on the outskirts of town, which sold the usual selection of rubbery hot dogs and shrink-wrapped burritos. But she couldn't, in good conscience, send him to either of these places.

She gave the man a quick once-over. He was middle-aged, maybe fifty or fifty-five, clean-cut, and neatly dressed in a polo shirt and khaki pants. And if she wasn't mistaken, he was military or ex-military. His ramrod straight posture told her that. So did his only slightly longer than regulation salt-and-pepper crew cut.

He wouldn't give her any trouble, she decided. He might even provide some pleasant conversation. And he'd leave a decent tip. Men like him always did.

Besides, staying open late was better than going back to her apartment, which these days had all the personality and excitement of a mausoleum.

"There are a few places I could send you," she told him now, still shielding her eyes against the sun. "But I couldn't live with myself afterward. So come on in. I can stay open an extra fifteen minutes for you."

"Are you sure?" he asked, politely. "I don't want to inconvenience you."

"No worries," she said, opening the door wider and gesturing him inside. "There's plenty of work I can be doing while you're having your lunch."

"Thanks a lot. I really appreciate it," he said, coming inside.

"My cook went off duty at three," she explained, locking the door behind him. "The grill's already turned off, so you can't have anything hot. Not that you'd necessarily *want* anything hot, the weather being what it is. But I made some fresh lemonade this afternoon, and I can make you a cold sandwich."

"Thank you. That's the best offer I've had all day," he said, bypassing the tables for one of the swivel stools at the Formica-topped counter.

"Now, what can I get you?" Caroline asked, ducking behind the counter and reflexively tying her apron back on.

"What's good?" he asked, looking up from a menu.

"Everything," she said, automatically. Which, in her not-so-humble opinion, was true.

"Well, what'd you have for lunch?"

"A chicken salad sandwich."

"Then I'll have one of those."

"And a lemonade?"

"And a lemonade," he smiled.

Caroline nodded and reached for a glass and a pitcher of lemonade. She liked his smile, she thought, liked the way it made his blue eyes crinkle pleasantly at the corners. He wasn't a bad-looking man. Far from it. His suntanned skin, for instance, was pleasantly weather-beaten, and his nose, which had obviously been broken a few times, lent him a rough-and-ready masculinity.

She poured him a glass of lemonade, put an extra sprig of mint in it, and set it down on the counter in front of him. Then she started to assemble his sandwich.

He took a sip of lemonade, then said, appreciatively, "I can't remember the last time I had lemonade from freshly squeezed lemons. And the mint is a nice touch, too."

Caroline smiled, slicing his sandwich in two and putting it in front of him. "Oh, I've learned a few tricks," she said. "We're not a complete culinary backwater here in Butternut."

"That's good to know," he said, "seeing as how I just put in an offer on a cabin here."

"Really?" Caroline asked. "A vacation home?"

"No, I'm planning on living up here full-time. As of now, I'm officially retired."

"From the military?"

He nodded. "Very observant," he said, taking a bite of his sandwich.

"Did you see any . . . action?" she asked, thinking with a pang of Allie's late husband.

He shrugged. "Sure. I saw some. I was a pilot. But not a fighter pilot. A transport pilot."

"Did you like it? Being a pilot, I mean."

"I loved it," he said.

"But you retired?"

"I did. I was ready for a change. Besides, I'm still a pilot. Only I have my own plane now, a Cessna, and I'm hoping to start a business with it."

"How so?" Caroline asked.

He took his wallet out, took a business card out of it, and slid it across the counter to Caroline.

She picked it up and read it.

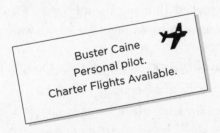

Buster Caine
Personal pilot.
Charter Flights Available.

At the bottom of the card was his cell-phone number and e-mail address.

"What do you think?" he asked, leaning forward on his elbows.

"Honestly?" Caroline asked.

"Of course."

"I think most people in Butternut prefer to drive," she said bluntly, and then immediately regretted her bluntness. She hadn't meant to be rude.

But he only laughed, seemingly unperturbed. "Well, that may be. It was just a thought. I don't need the money—I have my military pension—but I am hoping to stay busy. And I thought working, at least a little, might help me do that."

"Nothing wrong with staying busy," Caroline said, with a smile. Right now staying busy was the only thing keeping her sane.

"What about you?" he asked. "Do you ever fly anywhere?"

"Oh no," Caroline said, suppressing a little shudder. "I've never flown anywhere. But I imagine for you and your family, it's the preferred method of transportation."

"Actually, I'm widowed," he said.

"I'm sorry," Caroline murmured.

"So am I," he said, smiling sadly. "But I have two beautiful daughters," he added, brightening. "They both live in the Twin Cities. Of course, they're all grown up now. They have lives of their own."

Caroline frowned, thinking about his words.

"Did I say something wrong?" he asked, watching her carefully.

"No, of course not," Caroline said quickly. She busied herself with refilling his glass of lemonade. "I was just thinking about my own daughter. She has a life of her own now, too."

"How old is she?" he asked, with interest.

"She's eighteen. She just left this summer for the university."

He smiled, gently. "I imagine that's been hard," he said, finishing his sandwich.

Caroline sighed. "You have no idea. I mean, it's just been the two of us all these years. My ex-husband, Daisy's father, left when she was three." She paused, surprised that she'd revealed so much to a man who was still, for all intents and purposes, a stranger.

And now it was Buster's turn to say, quietly, "I'm sorry."

Caroline shrugged. "No need to be. I've had plenty of time to adjust to single motherhood. It's the empty nest I'm struggling with now. And do you know what the worst part is?"

He raised his eyebrows.

"How quiet our apartment is. I had no idea how much noise she made, all those years."

"Some people get to like the quiet," he mused.

She sighed. "I don't think I'll ever be one of those people."

"Maybe not," he said. "In which case, you can learn how to play the drums. That'll definitely raise the noise level."

Caroline laughed and was still laughing when the back door to the coffee shop opened and Frankie came in. She'd been leaning, companionably, on the counter, but now she instinctively straightened up and took a step back. Which was silly, she realized too late. She wasn't doing anything wrong.

"Are you still here, Frankie?" she asked, a little self-consciously.

He nodded. "I was scrubbing out the trash bins."

"And I was talking to Mr. Caine," she said, recalling his name from his business card. "And by the way, Mr. Caine, I'm Caroline. Caroline Keegan," she said, holding out her hand for him to shake. "And this is Frankie. Frankie Ambrose."

But Frankie was in no mood to be social. He stared at their guest, unsmiling. It was a look Caroline knew well. Calculating. Ruthless. And unforgiving. He generally saved it for unruly customers or rowdy teenagers. But she'd never seen him level it at someone before who she didn't think deserved it.

She glanced at Buster Caine, half expecting him to put a handful of money on the counter and hightail it out of there. It wouldn't be the first time a single look from Frankie had accomplished as much. But Buster met Frankie's look head-on, without blinking. And he didn't so much as budge on his stool, either.

"Well, then," Caroline said, a little too loudly. "Frankie should probably be getting home." She looked at him pointedly. "And you, Mr. Caine," she said, turning back to Buster, "you'd probably like your check."

Frankie said nothing, but he turned away, slowly, and started to scrub up at the sink.

"I'll take the check, if you don't mind," Buster said pleasantly. He seemed completely unfazed by his encounter with Frankie.

Caroline exhaled. The tension had been broken. But she needed to speak to Frankie about his behavior. Because there was protective. And then there was *overly* protective. She didn't want him scaring customers away.

As she was writing up the check, Frankie let himself out the back.

Buster Caine gave a low whistle. "That is one big man," he said.

"I know it," she agreed. "But the truth is, he wouldn't hurt a fly."

"I don't know about that," he said, skeptically, picking up the check and sliding his wallet out of his back pocket. "Those tattoos are prison tattoos."

"I know that," Caroline said, a little defensively. "But Frankie's a gentle giant, really. Besides, I'm a big believer in second chances."

He smiled. "Well, that's good. Because we all need them sometimes, don't we?" he said, standing up and leaving a bill on the counter. "By the way," he added, "it was a pleasure meeting you, Ms. Keegan."

"Caroline," she corrected.

"Caroline," he repeated. "And you can call me Buster. Thank you again for staying open late and for making me the best chicken salad sandwich I've ever had."

"Anytime," she said lightly, and she was glad she hadn't sent him to the gas station for lunch.

She watched him leave, then went over to clear his plate away. He'd left a crisp twenty-dollar bill on top of the check. She'd been right about him being a good tipper, she thought, slipping the bill into her apron pocket. She felt something else in that pocket, too, and fished it out. It was his business card. She started to throw it away, then stopped herself. It seemed a shame, somehow, to just toss it away. So instead she opened the cash register, lifted up the bill drawer, and placed the business card beneath it. The chance she'd ever need it was slim to none, she knew. But for some strange reason, she liked knowing it was there.

CHAPTER 13

When Allie saw how many cars were parked on the street outside Jax and Jeremy's house the evening of their third of July party, she almost kept driving.

"What's wrong, Mommy?" Wyatt asked, noticing her expression in the rearview mirror.

"Nothing, honey. Why?" Allie asked, slowing the car.

"You look frowny," Wyatt said.

Allie sighed. She still forgot, occasionally, how observant Wyatt was.

"I'm not *frowny*," she corrected him, gently. "I'm just looking for a place to park. I didn't realize there'd be so many people here."

She ended up parking two blocks away. As they walked back to Jax and Jeremy's house, she forced herself to be positive for Wyatt's sake. After all, she reminded herself, Jax was right. Parties *were* supposed to be fun, weren't they? She'd certainly believed that herself at one time. Now, of course, she viewed every social occasion with a mixture of fear and dread. The problem was, if she wasn't careful, Wyatt would, too.

"This is going to be fun," she said brightly, squeezing his hand with her free hand. The other hand was holding a Tupperware container full of chocolate chip cookies.

Wyatt looked unconvinced. And now that they could hear the party—the voices, the laughter, and the music—she could feel him slowing down. Resistance was setting in. She gave him a tug and kept going.

"You know who's going to be here tonight?" she asked, as they followed the flagstone path that led around the side of Jax and Jeremy's house to their backyard.

Wyatt shook his head.

"Frankie," she said smiling, glad she'd saved her ace in the hole.

"Frankie is going to be here?" he asked, his eyes widening. He was fascinated by Frankie.

"Absolutely," Allie said. "Who do you think is in charge of grilling the hamburgers and hot dogs and chicken? All your favorite foods, I might add."

"Do you think he'll need help?" Wyatt asked, hurrying to keep up with her now.

"Maybe," she smiled, cocking an eyebrow at him.

They came around the corner of the house then and Wyatt let out a little gasp of surprise. Allie, surveying the scene, understood.

The backyard was awash in lights. Brightly colored Chinese lanterns hung from the trees, tiny white lights were strung on all the bushes and shrubs, and votive candles flickered on the tables scattered around on the dark, velvety grass.

"So pretty," Wyatt breathed.

So much work, Allie thought. But when her eyes scanned the crowd of partygoers and found Jax and Jeremy, encircled by a group of friends, neither one of them looked tired. Far from it. They looked relaxed, serene, and positively aglow with affection for each other. Jeremy, boyishly handsome, had his arm around Jax's waist, and Jax, in an adorable maternity sundress, was gazing tenderly up at him.

Watching them, Allie felt a stab of jealousy. She looked away, guiltily. *It's official, Allie,* she thought. *You've become a terrible person. You know how unhappy Jax's childhood was, and you know, too, that she deserves every good thing that's happened to her since, and then some.*

But she still avoided looking at them again as she studied the scene before her. Jax hadn't been kidding when she'd said it was the social event of the season. All of Butternut appeared to have turned out for the occasion, and Allie was surprised at how many people she recognized. There was Frankie, as promised, manning an enormous grill on the patio, and across from him, one of the clerks from the hardware store was tending a makeshift bar. And there, playing the banjo in the bluegrass band entertaining guests at one end of the yard, was the man from the gas station who'd changed the oil in Allie's engine that morning.

But suddenly, in the midst of all this familiarity, she felt shy. Shy and something else . . . overwhelmed. She'd forgotten how to do this, she realized, tightening her grip on Wyatt's hand. And what's more, she didn't *want* to remember how to do it. It was a part of her old life, her life before Gregg had died. But now, all of it—the crowd, the music, the dancing—all of it seemed wrong somehow. Loud. Jarring. Off-key. And, as if to drive this point home, there was a sudden burst of laughter from a nearby group.

That's it, we're going, she thought. She'd make up an excuse to tell Wyatt on the way back to the car. But as she started to leave, she bumped right into Caroline Keegan.

"Well, hello you two," Caroline greeted them, smiling.

Allie nodded, uncertainly, but Wyatt smiled shyly at her.

"Well, you probably want to leave those on the dessert table," she said to Allie, nodding at the chocolate chip cookies. "And you, because you're growing so fast, probably need something to eat," she said, winking at Wyatt.

They followed Caroline over to a long picnic table that was practically groaning under the weight of the food on it, and Allie set the container of cookies down on the dessert end of it, and popped the lid off. She watched as Wyatt looked up and down the length of the table, practically salivating. There were deviled eggs and baked beans. Rhubarb pie and angel food cake. Slices of watermelon and mounds of coleslaw. And a tin plate piled high with buttermilk biscuits that Wyatt was staring at hungrily.

Caroline noticed him staring at them, plucked one off the plate, and gave it to him. He bit into it eagerly. "Honey, you can have as many of those as you'd like," she said to him. "Seeing as how I'm the one who baked them." And then she asked Allie, in a quieter voice that Wyatt couldn't hear, "Were you leaving when you bumped into me?"

"No," Allie said, automatically. And then, a little sheepishly, "Yes."

"I thought so. No hard feelings, I hope, for interfering with your escape plan?"

"None," Allie said, with a little smile.

"Good, I'm glad. But, Allie," she asked, frowning, "is it still hard? Things like this, I mean?"

"Honestly, Caroline, there are days when *everything* is still hard. But, yes, this kind of thing is especially hard. Too many happy people, I guess," she said, looking Caroline right in the eye. No point, she decided, in trying to hide her selfishness from her.

But Caroline didn't look disapproving, only sad. "Happy people," she said softly, looking around her. "Oh, Allie, you wouldn't believe the things I could tell you about some of the people here tonight. I mean, don't get me wrong, they're good people. But to say their lives aren't perfect, well, for some of them, that's an understatement. But they're here. Trying, I guess, to squeeze a little joy out of life." She sighed, watching Wyatt help himself to a second buttermilk biscuit. "And, honestly, I think they might be onto something."

"Maybe," Allie said, considering this. She usually found it irritating when people tried to dispense advice to her. But for some reason, Caroline's words didn't grate on her. Maybe it was the gentle, no-nonsense approach Caroline adopted with friends and customers alike. Or maybe it was because she didn't pretend to have all the answers. Didn't pretend, either, she wasn't still trying to find those answers herself.

And Allie knew she was right about this when Caroline asked, suddenly, "Do you think you ever get used to it? The being without somebody, I mean?"

"I don't know," Allie said, simply, but in that moment Jade and Jax came rushing over to them, interrupting them.

"Wyatt," Jade said, her blue eyes shining. "You're here!" She didn't wait for him to answer. "Come on," she said. "Let's go. Frankie said he'd save the best hot dogs for you and me. My dad turned up the grill too high, and some of them got burned. But we don't have to have the black ones. Even though the black part doesn't hurt you. I mean, you could eat like one hundred of them and not even get a stomachache." She stopped talking, but only long enough to catch her breath. Then she asked again, "Are you coming, Wyatt?"

"Of course he is," Allie said, giving him a little push forward.

And she smiled encouragingly at Wyatt's backward glance as Jade dragged him away in the direction of the grill.

"I'm so glad you're here," Jax said, hugging Allie with such genuine warmth that Allie felt a fresh prick of guilt at her earlier resentment of Jax. "And don't worry about Wyatt and Jade," Jax said. "Frankie will keep an eye on them. Not only is he an expert at the grill, but he is amazingly patient with children. Besides, if Caroline will let me steal you away, there's someone I'd like you to meet."

"Of course," Caroline said.

But Allie was wary.

"Come on, it'll be painless," Jax cajoled, seeing her expression, and she led Allie over to the bar where an attractive blond woman of about sixty was sipping a glass of white wine, and, apparently, waiting for them.

"Sara," Jax said, "this is my friend, Allie Beckett. Allie, this is Sara Gage."

They shook hands with each other and then Jax said, meaningfully, "Why don't you two talk while I get Allie something to drink."

Allie started to object that Jax must have better things to do at her own party than get Allie a drink, but Jax seemed intent on leaving them alone, so Allie called after her, "Thanks, Jax. I'll just have a Coke."

Then she turned back to Sara Gage, who said to her, without preamble, "So Jax tells me you're interested in art."

"I am," Allie said politely, wondering where the conversation was going.

"I don't know if Jax mentioned me to you or not," she said. "But I own the Pine Cone Gallery on Main Street. Are you familiar with it?"

"Of course," Allie said. "It's right across the street from Pearl's." She'd looked in its windows many times before, but she'd never felt comfortable taking Wyatt into a store that obviously had so many breakable objects in it. "It looks beautiful," she said to Sara. "How long have you owned it?"

"I opened it about ten years ago," Sara said, sipping her wine. "My husband and I had retired up here, and he was perfectly happy doing nothing, but I was bored to death. And I realized, too, that making the four-and-a-half-hour trek to Minneapolis every time I needed a culture fix was going to get old really fast. But that first fall we were here, I saw an ad for an art show sponsored by a local artist's co-op. I was skeptical, to say the least. But I went, and I was absolutely stunned. Not just by the number of artists exhibiting there, but by the quality of their work."

"Really? I had no idea Butternut had such an art scene," Allie confessed.

"Well, I don't know about an art *scene*," Sara clarified, amused by Allie's choice of words. "Still, if you thought, as I did, that there weren't many artists living up here, you'd be wrong. Some of them are originally from up here, and others, like my husband and me, are originally from the Twin Cities but decided to retire up here. But they all have one thing in common. They need a place to sell their work year-round. So that's where I come in."

"And you've made a success of it, obviously."

"I have," Sara said, with satisfaction. "I mean, I'll never get rich doing it. But I proved all the people wrong who said that Butternut wouldn't support a gallery. It turns out that locals, and tourists, want a different kind of place to shop here. You know, a place that doesn't just sell Christmas tree ornaments, or scented candles and potpourri."

"Oh, judging from your windows, you've gone way beyond

those," Allie said, admiringly. "Your things look beautiful." And they did. She'd seen watercolor and oil paintings through the gallery windows, but also ceramics, handblown glass, and jewelry.

"Thank you," Sara said. "We showcase some very talented artists. And I'd like to find even more of them to represent, but that kind of legwork takes me out of the gallery. I need someone reliable to be there when I can't be. Which is why Jax wanted me to meet you."

"Me?" Allie repeated, not understanding.

Sara nodded. "That's right. Jax stopped by the gallery last week, and when I mentioned I was looking for someone to work there part-time, she suggested you. She said you know a lot about art, and you have sales experience from running a business."

"I . . . I don't know what Jax told you," Allie said, flustered. "I minored in art history in college, and my husband and I owned a landscaping company, but I'm not sure either of those things qualify me to work in a gallery."

But Sara Gage seemed unfazed. "Look, there's no special qualifications for the job, beyond interest and willingness. So why don't you just come in and have a look around, and we can talk some more."

"You mean, like an interview?"

"A very informal interview," Sara assured her. "And now, if you'll excuse me," she added, frowning and looking away. "I see my husband sidling up to the buffet table, and I don't think his cardiologist would approve of him having any more of those deviled eggs than he's already had."

No sooner had she left, though, than Jax was back, beaming at Allie as she handed her a Coke.

"Did she tell you about the job?" she asked, her blue eyes dancing with excitement.

"She told me," Allie said. "But I wish *you* had told me about it before you introduced me to her."

"Oh," Jax said, her face falling. "I'm sorry. I didn't mean to spring it on you. But I know you love art. And you said you'd need to work, eventually." She added, a little self-reproachfully, "I guess I just forgot that it's much easier to solve other people's problems than it is to solve your own."

"What problems?" Allie chided her. "Because from where I stand, your life looks pretty perfect."

"I wish that were true," Jax said, wistfully, and her expression, in that instant, struck Allie as almost unbearably sad. But the moment passed, and Jax looked like herself again. Her pregnant, radiant self—leaving Allie to wonder if she'd imagined Jax's sadness. Or maybe just projected her own sadness onto Jax.

"Jax," she said, giving her hand a squeeze. "Thank you for thinking of me. You're right about my needing to work, sometime in the not-so-distant future. And working at the Pine Cone Gallery isn't a bad idea; it's just . . ." *Just what*, she wondered. But she couldn't articulate it. Not to Jax. Not even to herself. She just knew she wasn't ready to do all the things everyone expected her to do now. Work. Socialize. Even date. And she didn't know why she wasn't ready. Maybe it was because two years after Gregg's death she still wanted to be left alone with Wyatt and her grief. Or maybe it was because keeping Gregg's memory alive, in her head, and in her heart, was turning out to be a full-time job in and of itself.

Her eyes now instinctively found Wyatt in the crowd of partygoers. He and Jade were in front of the bluegrass band, holding hands and twirling in circles. Jade, as usual, appeared to be the instigator, but Wyatt looked like a more than willing partner. And as Allie watched, he flashed Jade one of his rare but unmistakable smiles.

Allie started to say something about it to Jax, but Jax was frowning, distractedly, at a nearby group of guests. "That's odd," she murmured.

"What?" Allie asked. Her eyes followed Jax's own and settled, almost immediately, on Walker Ford. He was standing about ten yards away, drinking a beer, and talking to another guest. Allie felt an inexplicable twinge of irritation. She hadn't counted on seeing him here. And, after their too-personal conversation when he'd driven her home, she hadn't wanted to, either.

Walker saw Allie and Jax staring at him, and he smiled and lifted his beer bottle in a salute to them. Allie's irritation deepened.

"Does he come to all your parties?" she asked Jax, deliberately looking away from him.

"No," Jax said. "That's why I was surprised he's here. He's never come to *any* of them before."

"So why do you invite him?"

Jax shrugged. "It's a business thing, I guess. He's a good customer at the hardware store. And Jeremy likes him."

"And you don't?" Allie probed.

"I don't know him very well," Jax admitted, glancing in his direction again. "I could count on one hand the number of conversations I've had with him. But I think after tonight I may need the other hand."

"Why?" Allie asked.

"Because he's headed straight for us."

Allie tensed involuntarily. Which was silly, she knew. He was her neighbor, after all. She'd have to get used to seeing the man, at least occasionally.

"Hi," Walker said, coming up to them. "Nice party."

"Glad you could make it," Jax said, but something else had

obviously caught her attention. "It looks like we're out of ice," she said, looking in the direction of the bar. "I'm sorry, I have to leave you two."

"That's okay," Allie said, without much conviction.

"Can I help?" Walker asked.

Jax shook her head. "No, thanks. I've got it." And then she was gone.

Walker looked at Allie, an amused expression on his face.

"Do you know what my first thought was when I saw you here tonight?" he asked.

"No," she said, honestly, surprised at his directness. It wasn't the polite banter she'd expected. But then again, he didn't really strike her as a man who had the patience, or the knack, for polite banter.

"My first thought was that you looked like someone waiting in line at the DMV. You know, like someone who's absolutely dreading everything about the experience they're about to have."

Allie didn't bother to argue the point. "Is it that obvious?" she asked, sipping her Coke.

He nodded. "Uh-huh. But I wouldn't worry about other people noticing. The only reason I noticed is that you reminded me of myself at an event like this. I tend to think of them as necessary evils. Like dental appointments. You don't want to go, but you go anyway."

"Do you, though? Because I heard you don't go to any of these things. That you're something of a recluse, actually."

"A recluse?" he repeated, a corner of his mouth lifting in an almost smile. "That makes me sound a lot more interesting than I am. The truth is actually pretty boring. I just work a lot."

"What is it, exactly, you do at the boatyard?" Allie asked now.

He shrugged. "We build boats, repair boats, store boats, buy and sell boats. Right now, actually, we're restoring a very special boat. A canoe, actually. Vintage. Interestingly enough, I found it at the bottom of the lake. But I think if we replace the rotted-out bottom, it might actually be worth something. They literally don't make them like that anymore."

Allie felt her cheeks flush in recognition. "You're restoring my canoe?"

He nodded.

"Why?"

"Why not?" he shrugged. "I couldn't resist at least taking a look at it. And once I got it out of the water, I realized how beautifully made it was."

"But it doesn't even float anymore," she protested.

"Well, I love a challenge. And when it comes to restoring a boat, the bigger the challenge, the more fun it is."

"It doesn't sound fun." Allie frowned. "It sounds expensive."

"Well, it's fun for *me*," Walker said, smiling. "Probably not for most people. And don't worry about the expense. I'm not charging you anything for it. I have everything I need at the boatyard. Or I can get it from our suppliers wholesale."

But Allie shook her head. She didn't like the sound of this. She didn't want to be beholden to Walker Ford. Not for any reason. They were neighbors. She couldn't change that. But they weren't going to be friends. Not when he made her feel like this every time she saw him. Ill at ease. Tense. And defensive.

"You know what?" she said, suddenly. "Why don't you keep it when you're done restoring it? It's the least I can do, since you went to the trouble of hauling it out of the lake. Besides, I promised Wyatt we'd get something with a motor. Even at five, he's old enough to not be impressed by any boat you have to paddle or row."

"Oh, well, that I *know* I can help you with," Walker said, extracting his wallet from his pocket and taking out a business card. He handed it to Allie and she took it reluctantly. "Cliff Donahue," he explained, as she examined it. "He's the general manager at the boatyard. Come see him, anytime. He can get you a good deal on a new or used boat."

Allie examined the card, then looked back up at Walker and saw him, *really* saw him, for the first time that night. Maybe the first time ever. *The man was ridiculously good-looking,* she thought. And the little extra effort he'd made tonight with his appearance had paid off in spades. His short, dark hair was combed neatly down, and his suntanned jawline looked freshly shaved. Not only that, but he was wearing a blue button-down shirt that brought out the intense blueness of his eyes. She wondered, vaguely, if he'd chosen the shirt for that reason, but decided he hadn't. He didn't look like a man who spent a lot of time looking in the mirror. Or fretting about what to wear.

As Allie was looking at him, it got suddenly darker outside, the way it sometimes did on summer evenings. She took a nervous sip of her Coke and met his eyes above the rim of her glass. But his eyes didn't look back at her. Not exactly. Instead, they sort of brushed over her—*all of her*—in a way that was both hard and soft at the same time. As if they were simultaneously holding her tightly and caressing her softly.

Allie shivered, inexplicably, in the sultry summer evening and tugged self-consciously at the neckline of her sundress. It wasn't an especially revealing dress, but there was something about the way he was looking at her now that made her feel as if she was underdressed. *Undressed,* actually.

She held on to his look for a long moment, held on to it until something inside of her stretched tight, as if it was about to snap.

When she couldn't stand it anymore, she looked away. "I need to find Wyatt," she murmured, almost breathless, and, without looking back, she disappeared into the crowd. She moved past people, not seeing them, and fighting a sudden light-headedness. *I need to get something to eat,* she thought, once she'd thoroughly lost herself in the crowd, and she headed for the buffet table.

Much to her relief, she didn't see Walker again that night.

Later, on the drive home, stopped at an intersection, Allie looked at Wyatt in the rearview mirror just as the headlights from a passing car briefly illuminated him. He had a smudge of dirt on his face and a ketchup stain on his T-shirt. As she watched him, he yawned, sleepily. She turned around and smiled at him.

"Did you have fun tonight?" she asked.

He nodded and looked out the window, contentedly. *He looks different,* Allie thought, as she turned around and drove through the intersection. *He looks happy.*

CHAPTER 14

When Walker opened the door to his office at the boatyard one afternoon in mid-July, he found his brother, Reid, sitting in Walker's swivel chair, his feet propped up on Walker's desk. As Walker came through the door, Reid smiled at him and, by way of a greeting, shot a rubber band in his direction.

"Hi, Reid," Walker said, mildly, fending off the rubber band with a raised hand. He sat down in the office's other chair. "Do you mind telling me what you're doing here?"

"Is that any way to greet your older brother?" Reid asked, feigning disapproval.

"Well, you might have given me a little warning," Walker pointed out.

"I didn't *want* to give you any warning," Reid said, taking his feet off Walker's desk. "It's much more fun to surprise you. Besides, if I'd given you warning, I wouldn't have seen *that*," he added, gesturing to the window of Walker's second-story office, which offered a view of the entire boatyard.

"Seen *what*?" Walker asked, warily.

"Seen you with your new friend."

Walker frowned. "That's not a new friend. It's a new neighbor. And her son. They're here because they want to buy a boat."

"That looked like more than a straightforward sale to me," Reid said, amused.

Walker shrugged, feigning disinterest. "Well, I just said hello to them. Then I turned them over to Cliff." He could have shown them the sale models himself, of course, but he hadn't wanted to. It was important to him, for some reason, to keep his and Allie's personal relationship—if you could even call it that—separate from their business relationship. But that hadn't stopped him from telling Cliff to take 25 percent off the price of any boat Allie was interested in.

Reid didn't say anything now, but he'd sensed Walker's defensiveness. And he was enjoying it immensely.

"Look, Reid," Walker said, with an exasperated sigh. "Don't try to make this into more than it is, okay? It's very simple. They want to buy a boat. I want to sell them a boat. I mean, that is what we do here, isn't it? Sell boats?"

"It is," Reid agreed. "But, Walk, seriously, I wouldn't make a habit of doing business that way. The way you were looking at her, it didn't look very professional to me."

"How was I looking at her?" Walker asked, not really wanting to hear the answer.

Reid pretended to think about it. "Like she was a cupcake you were waiting to eat," he said, finally. "You know, the kind with a lot of frosting on it? And those little sprinkles all over it and—"

"Okay, Reid, I get it," Walker broke in, chagrined that his attraction to Allie had been so obvious. With any luck, though, she wasn't as perceptive as Reid. His brother, after all, had had a thirty-five-year head start getting to know him.

"Hey, Walk, don't worry about it," Reid said, with a shrug. "It's not a problem. At least not as far as I'm concerned. Unless she's married. And then, of course, it's a *big* problem."

Walker shook his head, a little glumly. "No, she's not married. But she's not available, either."

Reid raised his eyebrows, wordlessly asking for an explanation.

"She's widowed," Walker said, after a pause. "Her husband was sent to Afghanistan and . . ." His voice trailed off.

"How long ago?" Reid asked, quietly.

"How long ago was he deployed?"

Reid shook his head. "How long ago did he die?"

"A couple of years ago, I think."

"So this isn't brand-new?" Reid clarified. "For her and the kid?"

Walker shook his head. "No. Her son was three then. He's five now."

"Well, then I don't see a problem," Reid said. "I mean, I don't mean to sound callous. Or disrespectful to her husband's memory. After all, he gave the ultimate sacrifice for his country. But, Walk, his life ended. Her life's gone on."

"That's just it, though," Walker said. "I don't think her life *has* gone on. I mean, superficially it may have. But emotionally, at least, I think she's still kind of shut down." *Kind of, but maybe not all the way,* Walker thought. Unless he'd imagined that moment at the third of July party. That moment when they'd looked at each other and he'd felt something pass between them. Something buzzing and sharp, like a current of electricity.

"Well, if she is shut down," Reid said, "maybe that's where you come in."

"Meaning what?"

"Meaning, at the risk of sounding cliché, that you give her a reason to open up again. To start living again."

But Walker shook his head. "I don't think I'm that person, Reid. Let's face it. Not with my track record."

"Are you referring to your divorce?"

Walker's jaw tightened. "Obviously."

"Well, you two never should have gotten married in the first place," Reid said, dismissively.

"But that's not the point," Walker objected. "Once we did get married . . ."

"Oh, for God's sake, Walker," Reid said, impatiently. "You're not still blaming yourself for her losing the baby, are you?"

Walker flinched. "Reid, I've told you before. I don't want to talk about that."

"Look, I'm sorry," Reid said, holding up both hands in a gesture of surrender. "I'm not minimizing your loss, Walker. Yours or Caitlin's. But, Walker, you've got to let it go. Put it behind you. It's been a couple of years now. That woman"—he gestured at the window—"isn't the only one who needs to move on. You need to move on, too."

Walker said nothing.

"Okay, fine, don't move on," Reid said, with a sigh. "But at least ask her out for a cup of coffee? How difficult can that be?"

Maybe too difficult for me, Walker thought, pushing up from his chair and wandering over to the window. Allie's car was still in the guest parking lot.

"Are they still here?" Reid asked.

But Walker ignored the question. He had one of his own for his brother. "Reid, since when are you so interested in my personal life?"

"Since I realized that neither one of us *has* any personal life to speak of."

"I thought you liked it that way. You know, all work and no play for both of us."

"Not for both of us," Reid qualified. He got up and came over to the window. "I like it for me, but I don't think I like it for you anymore. Because for all your bluster, Walk, I think you want marriage and children. I think you want the whole nine yards."

"Well, then you don't know me as well as you think you do," Walker said, honestly.

Reid put a hand on his shoulder, surprising Walker. His brother, as a general rule, wasn't very demonstrative. Now, though, he left his hand there for a long moment, then squeezed his shoulder and let go. "I've got to push off," he said, heading for the office door.

"You didn't come all this way just to dispense brotherly wisdom, did you?" Walker asked, over his shoulder.

"Of course not," Reid said. "I was looking at a boatyard for sale near Ely. It has definite potential. I'll be in touch with you about it."

"If you want to stick around while I finish up some paperwork, we can grab dinner," Walker offered, leaving the window and sitting down at his desk.

"Another time," Reid said. "I've got to be getting back to the city."

Reid started to leave the office, then turned back.

"One more thing, Walk."

"What?" Walker asked, distractedly, looking up from the stack of papers on his desk.

"Think about what we talked about. About asking that woman out. Because the brother I grew up with was many things, but he was never a coward." And he left, shutting the door behind him.

It's not going to work, Reid, Walker thought. *I'm not twelve years old anymore, and I don't take the bait every time you offer it to me.*

But he didn't go back to work. Instead, he went back to the window and brooded about what Reid had said. Five minutes later, he was heading down the stairs to the showroom.

When he walked into it, he immediately spotted Allie at the far end. She was holding a sheaf of glossy boat brochures with one hand and shaking hands with Cliff with the other. Wyatt was nearby, playing on one of the boats.

"Hey, Walker," Cliff said, when he joined them. "Ms. Beckett was just leaving."

"I hope you're taking a boat with you," Walker said.

"Not quite," Allie said. "But Cliff has given me plenty to think about."

"Good," Walker said, nodding.

Another customer walked into the showroom and Cliff excused himself to greet them.

"Wyatt, it's time to go," Allie called. Wyatt glanced up briefly, then went back to pretending to drive a powerboat. Allie sighed. "It's amazing how selective his hearing is," she said.

Walker laughed, glad for the opportunity to have her to himself, even for a few minutes.

"How are you two settling in?" he asked.

"We're making progress," she said. "Or at least Johnny Miller, our handyman, is. Thanks to him, our cabin isn't falling down around us anymore. So that's a good sign, I guess."

"How long's it been since you got here?" he asked. He knew exactly how long it'd been since he'd seen a light on in their cabin that night, but he was at a loss for conversational topics. She never failed, it seemed, to have this disorienting effect on him.

She looked especially lovely today, too, in a summery blouse and skirt with flat sandals. Her luxuriant, sun-streaked brown hair was pulled back in a simple ponytail, and her suntanned face was devoid of makeup. Not that she needed it. Her skin already had a soft, golden glow, and her long-lashed hazel eyes had a luminosity that no eye makeup could deliver.

"We've been here for six weeks," she said, bringing him back to reality.

Something about the way she said it made him ask, "Six *long* weeks?"

"Sometimes," she admitted. "But we've gotten into a routine, which is good. It makes the time go faster."

"Do you know what would make it go even faster?" Walker suggested.

She shook her head, suddenly wary.

"A boat."

She smiled. "You're quite the salesman, aren't you?" she remarked

"Maybe," he said. "Or maybe I think if you live on a lake as beautiful as Butternut Lake, you should have a boat to explore it with."

Her hazel eyes were thoughtful as she considered what he'd said, but then she seemed to remember something, and she looked at her watch.

"We need to get going soon," she said, glancing over at her son. "I have to get Wyatt over to Jax's house. Believe it or not, I have a job interview."

His expression must have said he didn't believe it.

"At the Pine Cone Gallery," she explained. "Sara Gage, the woman who owns it, is looking for a part-time salesperson. And Jax has somehow persuaded her that I'm that person. Personally, I think they're both crazy."

"I don't know about that," Walker said. "They both seem like smart women to me. But good luck, anyway. And Allie?"

"Yes?"

Here goes nothing. And forget about asking her out for a cup of coffee. That's starting too small. "I was wondering if you and Wyatt would like to come over some night for dinner. Nothing fancy. I could throw a couple of steaks on the grill. Maybe take you two out for a boat ride after dinner . . ."

Allie frowned. "Well, *Wyatt* would like that . . ." she said, uncertainly.

And you, Walker wanted to ask. *Would you like that?* He waited. But when she didn't say anything, he added, "It's not a big deal. Just a couple of neighbors having dinner together."

"Is that all it is?" Allie asked, leveling her gaze at him.

"Yes," he said, unsettled by her directness.

She waited.

"No," he amended. "I mean, I don't know what it is."

She waited for him to say more.

"Maybe it would just be dinner," he said, shrugging. "Maybe it would be something more. We don't know each other well enough to know that yet. But, Allie, I do know one thing about us."

He paused. This part was awkward. He wasn't quite sure how to phrase it without offending her.

"What's that?" she asked, coolly.

"I know that at Jax and Jeremy's party, I felt something between us. I don't know what you'd call it. A mutual attraction, maybe. But I don't think I imagined it. And I don't think it was one-sided, either. Whatever it was, I think you felt it, too."

Her eyes widened with surprise. "Are you saying you think I'm . . . *attracted* to you?" she clarified.

He nodded. He thought he'd made that pretty clear.

Her gold complexion flushed pink. Embarrassed, he wondered. Or angry? He saw her lovely jaw set in a hard line. Angry, he decided.

"Look, I don't know what *you* felt that night, Walker. But I can tell you right now that whatever it was, *I* didn't feel it. I'm not attracted to you, Walker. Not even a little."

"I don't believe you," Walker said, without thinking.

Her cheeks flushed darker. "Well, then you're even more arrogant than I thought you were."

Ouch, Walker thought. That stung a little. But he still didn't believe her. Not entirely.

"Wyatt, we need to go," she called out to her son. "*Now.*"

And Walker, desperate to repair the damage he'd done, tried to backtrack. "Look, I apologize. Obviously, I read too much into the situation."

But Allie didn't answer him because at that moment Wyatt ran over to her.

"Mommy," he said, his excitement momentarily overcoming his shyness. "I want *that* boat!" He pointed to the boat he'd been playing on. "I already know how to drive it," he said earnestly. "I taught myself."

Allie smiled, tensely. "We'll see about that," she said. "But for now, Wyatt, can you thank Mr. Ford for inviting us here today? And for having Cliff show us all those boats?"

"Thank you," Wyatt said dutifully.

"Anytime," Walker said, still feeling like an idiot. "I'll walk you two out to your car."

"That's not necessary," Allie said, and she handed him back the stack of boat brochures. He watched while they left the showroom, and then he put the brochures back. He'd have to apologize to Cliff. That was one sale they were never going to make.

"Thanks a lot, Reid," Walker muttered, as he went back up to his office.

When he got there, he sat down at his desk again and tried to concentrate on the stack of paperwork in front of him. But when he realized he'd read the same sentence three times and it still didn't mean anything to him, he got up and walked over to the window.

He *knew* he was right. He *knew* he hadn't imagined the attraction they'd felt for each other at the party. So either she'd flat-out lied to him when she said she hadn't felt it, or she was in denial about it. *The second one,* he decided, fiddling with the cord on the window's Venetian blinds. She didn't strike him as a dishonest person. At least not an *intentionally* dishonest person. But it was one thing to be honest with other people. And another thing to be honest with yourself. Being honest with yourself was infinitely harder.

And now, he thought, it was time for him to be honest with himself. For whatever reason, they weren't going to have a relationship with each other. *So give it up, Walker,* he counseled himself, still standing at the window. But the truth was, he couldn't. He'd already tried. Somehow, in the short time he'd known her, she'd gotten under his skin. And now he couldn't get her out from under it.

Part of the problem, of course, was the powerful physical attraction he felt for her. But that wasn't all of it. Because most of the time, when he thought about Allie, he didn't think about her in that way. Instead, he thought about her cutting her son's pancakes, as she had been doing the first morning he'd met her, at Pearl's. He didn't know what it was about that image that stuck with him. God knows, it wasn't sexy. It was the opposite of sexy, actually. *It was maternal.*

He stood very still now. Maybe Reid was right. Maybe he did want marriage and children. The whole nine yards, as Reid had put it. But if that was the case, why, then, had he botched it so badly the first time?

He was still turning this over in his mind when he drove out of the boatyard that night. He had his windows rolled down to the warm summer night, and Bruce Springsteen cranked up on the sound system, but tonight this drive didn't give him any pleasure. Because tonight, he was remembering what it was like living with Caitlin in the months before she'd lost the baby.

It was like living with a stranger, he thought now. Only worse. Because he and a stranger would have eventually gotten to know each other. Whereas he and Caitlin went backward in their relationship, from knowing each other to being strangers. Strangers who were married. Strangers who were planning on raising a child together.

Once, they'd had at least one thing in common: their attraction to each other. But that was the first thing to go. Once they realized they'd never had anything else in common, they started avoiding each other. Something that wasn't that difficult to do in Walker's thirty-five-hundred-square-foot cabin. Walker buried himself in his work. And Caitlin? Walker had no idea what she did. She had no career in Butternut. She'd given that up when she'd moved there. She had no friends, either. The locals, Walker knew, had mistaken her reserve for unfriendliness. And he'd done nothing to help to dispel that misconception.

So how she filled her days was a mystery to him. But he'd suspected at the time, and he knew now, that she'd been lonely—achingly, hopelessly, miserably lonely. And Walker, who'd persuaded her to marry him and to move here, had done nothing to help her.

Why hadn't he helped her? he wondered, as he left the town of Butternut behind him and headed out to the lake. But he knew why. He hadn't helped her because he couldn't admit how unhappy she was. How unhappy they *both* were. If he'd admitted that, then he would have had to admit that he'd made a mistake in persuading her to marry him. And admitting a mistake generally meant taking responsibility for it, not to mention actually *doing* something about it. And he couldn't do either of those things, since doing them, apparently, would have taken more courage than he actually possessed. So instead, he ignored her. And hoped, somehow, she would just . . . *just go away.* Disappear. And the amazing thing was, she almost had.

Why else would he have been surprised to see her that late autumn morning, when she came into his study and tapped him, hesitantly, on his shoulder?

"Caitlin?" he said, looking up with surprise. "What's wrong?"

"I'm sorry to bother you, but . . ."

"But what?" he asked, feeling a trace of impatience. He was rewriting the business plan for the Butternut Boatyard.

"It's probably nothing," she said. But she looked shaken.

"What is it, Caitlin?"

"I haven't felt the baby move since I woke up this morning," she said, finally, looking down at the tiny bump that had only recently appeared on her slender frame.

"Is that unusual?" Walker asked, embarrassed that he didn't already know the answer to that question. He'd meant to at least *look* at the pregnancy and childbirth books Caitlin had brought home with her. But he'd never gotten around to it.

"It is unusual," Caitlin said. "I mean, I'm almost six months pregnant. And I've been feeling the baby move for a couple of weeks now. I was feeling it *more* frequently, not *less* frequently, and then today . . . nothing."

"Not even a little?" he asked, feeling the first knife edge of fear.

"Nothing," she whispered, her white skin so pale it was almost translucent.

"Let's go then," he said, springing into action. "I'll call Dr. Novak's office and tell him I'm bringing you over."

Caitlin nodded, and she looked relieved that Walker was taking charge.

But later that evening, sitting up in her hospital bed, her expression was blank. She didn't look frightened, or relieved. She didn't look *anything*. Her pale blue eyes were empty, and her skin, normally pale, was almost gray.

Walker sat on the chair beside her bed. He was looking out the window at the hospital parking lot, where an early dusting of November snow glowed dully under the floodlights.

Caitlin's doctor, Dr. Novak, came into the room.

"How are you holding up?" he asked Caitlin, picking up her chart from its pocket at the end of the hospital bed and examining it.

Caitlin didn't answer him.

"You're probably still in shock," Dr. Novak said sympathetically, coming around to her side of the bed. "And I don't blame you. It's very unusual to lose a baby at this stage of a pregnancy. But it *does* happen, Caitlin. Even if we don't necessarily know why."

Caitlin still said nothing.

"Can I speak to you, Walker?" Dr. Novak asked, indicating the hospital corridor outside the room.

Walker nodded and followed him.

"Caitlin may not be ready to hear this yet," he told him, in a lowered voice. "But when she is ready, remind her that you're both still young. You didn't have any difficulty conceiving a child this time. And there's no reason to assume you will the next time. You can still have a family. It's just going to take a little longer, that's all."

Walker didn't know what to say. He doubted, very much, that there would be a next time for the two of them. But he thanked Dr. Novak and went back into the hospital room. Caitlin's eyes were closed and he thought, for a moment, that she was asleep. But she opened them and said, quietly, "Walker?"

He nodded and moved closer to the bed.

"I'm going to leave when I get out of here, okay? Go home. To Minneapolis, I mean."

"Don't," he said, feeling a stab of guilt. He couldn't stand the thought of her leaving the hospital alone. She looked so fragile somehow. So vulnerable.

But she shook her head at his word of protest. "Walker, we got married for the baby. The baby's gone now," she said, her voice catching on the word *gone*. "We don't need to stay married anymore."

"Don't leave," he said again. And he meant it. "I'll try harder. I know I haven't been very good at this whole marriage thing. But I'll do better. I promise. Just . . . just come home with me. Please?"

In hindsight, he realized that he should have let her go then. It was selfish of him to persuade her to stay, just to assuage his own guilt. But at the time he couldn't see that. *Wouldn't* see that . . .

Walker looked around then, amazed to discover his pickup was idling in front of his cabin. How he'd gotten here was a mystery to him. Because as real as his memories of Caitlin had been tonight, he had no memory whatsoever of the last five miles of the drive.

CHAPTER 15

A couple of days after their visit to the boatyard, Allie was tucking Wyatt into bed when they heard a distant rumble of thunder.

"Finally," she said, with relief, sitting down on the edge of Wyatt's bed. "I thought that storm would never come."

"You wanted it to come?" Wyatt asked, surprised.

"I *did* want it to come," Allie said. "Because I knew once it came, it would cool off."

All day long, the still air had been heavy and humid, the sky overcast, the lake a glassy oval of dark pewter. She'd waited for it to storm, and when it hadn't, it had set her nerves on edge. Though it was hard to know, honestly, how much of that was the weather, and how much of that was Walker Ford's words to her the last time she'd seen him. She frowned now, smoothing the sheet around Wyatt and thinking about what a colossal ego that man obviously had. How else to explain the fact that he refused to believe her when she said she wasn't attracted to him?

There was another rumble of thunder, this one closer, and Wyatt's body went rigid under the sheets.

"Hey, Wyatt, it's okay," Allie said, brushing an errant curl out of his eyes. "We had thunderstorms in Eden Prairie, remember?"

He nodded. "I was scared of them there, too," he whispered.

"I know that," Allie said, gently. And then, to distract him, she brought up something she'd been meaning to discuss with him all day. "Wyatt, do you think you might like to go to day camp?"

"You mean, the same one Jade and her sisters go to?"

"Uh-huh. Because I spoke to the director today—her name is Kathy—and she said they still have room for someone your age. She sounds really nice, by the way. And when I told her about you, and all the things you like to do, she said she thought you'd really like it there."

Wyatt thought about it. "Would you come, too?" he asked, finally. Hopefully.

"Me? No," Allie said, shaking her head. "It's just for children, ages five to twelve. But I'll drop you off and pick you up, and in between, if you need help, Kathy and the other counselors will be there. And so will Joy, Jade's older sister. She's a junior counselor there this summer."

He nodded, distractedly, and she could tell something was bothering him. He shifted under the covers. "I *think* I'll like day camp," he said. "But what about you? What will you do all day? You'll be here all alone. You might get lonely."

"Wyatt," Allie said, after a moment, both touched and saddened by his words. "You don't need to worry about me, okay? *You* worry about *you*. And I'll worry about *you and me*, okay? That's the way it's supposed to be with parents and children. And another thing, kiddo. I'm not going to have time to be lonely while you're at camp, because, as it turns out, I'm going to be busy. I'm going to be working."

"*Working?* Like at a job?" Wyatt asked, so skeptically that

Allie almost laughed. He was too young to remember her having a life apart from him, working for her and Gregg's landscaping business.

"That's right. I'm going to be working at a place called the Pine Cone Gallery. It's a store on Main Street that sells art made by local artists." There was another roll of thunder now, this one close enough, and loud enough, to make Wyatt tense up again. So Allie went on, quickly, "Anyway, the woman who owns it asked me if I wanted to work for her during the hours you're at day camp, from nine o'clock to three o'clock, and I said yes. I mean, it works out pretty well for both of us, don't you think? This way, we'll both get to do something fun. And afterward, you can tell me about your day at camp, and I can tell you about my day at the gallery. What do you think?" She smiled at him, determined to be positive. This separation, she knew, would be an adjustment for both of them.

But before Wyatt could answer her, there was a brilliant flash of lightning, followed a few seconds later by a boom of thunder so loud it sent Wyatt scrambling into her arms. They listened as the thunder reverberated through the still, evening air and watched as the lights in Wyatt's bedroom flickered, then went out, then flickered back on again.

"Hey, it's okay," she murmured, hugging Wyatt to her and trying to think if there was a storm warning for that day. But she didn't know. They hadn't been into town, so she hadn't listened to the car radio or read the newspaper. Maybe she should turn on the television, she thought, starting to get up. But in the next second, there was a burst of lightning, followed a moment later by an earsplitting crack of thunder that sent Wyatt burrowing deeper into her arms. The cabin's lights flickered off and on again, then went out for good.

"Hey, you know what?" Allie asked, giving Wyatt an extra-hard hug, "It wouldn't be summer in Butternut if we didn't lose power at least once. So let's get the flashlight, okay? Because in a few hours, it'll be dark." But as she led Wyatt to the kitchen, it occurred to her that it was already much darker outside than it should be for this time of the evening. And as she was opening the utility drawer in the kitchen, she glanced out the window and discovered why.

On the far shore of the lake, an entire wall of black clouds was amassing. But unlike an actual wall, this wall wasn't stationary. It was moving. Fast. So fast, in fact, it seemed to be bearing directly down onto the cabin.

Watching it, Allie felt the hairs standing up on her arms. She angled her body between Wyatt and the window, so he couldn't see it, too.

"Found it," she said, pulling a flashlight out of the drawer. But when she turned it on, the beam was weak. Wyatt had been using it to play "camping" under his blanket fort in the living room. She sighed and groped in the drawer for batteries. It might be several hours, she knew, before the electricity came on again.

But there were no batteries in that drawer. Or in any other drawer, for that matter. She'd ransacked the last one when her eyes settled on the phone on the kitchen counter. *That* at least was working. But who would she call? And what would she say to them? Without an answer to either question she picked up the receiver and held it up to her ear. There was no dial tone. *So the phone was out, too?* She thought about her cell phone. Nope. She still hadn't switched to a plan with coverage up here. Then she glanced out the window again. The cloud wall was closer. She felt a cold shiver of fear travel the length of her spine.

And then she remembered what she'd said to Wyatt only a few minutes ago. About how it was her responsibility to take care of him. Well, she wasn't doing a very good job of it right now, was she? She needed to stay calm. She needed to *think*.

"Wyatt, I think I might have seen an old camping lantern in the hall closet," she said, giving him the flashlight. "You can help me look for it." Wyatt followed her over to the closet and directed a wobbly flashlight beam into it as she fumbled around in its mothball-scented depths. Every time there was another peal of thunder, though, she felt him stiffen beside her.

She was standing on her tiptoes, reaching for the closet's top shelf, when Wyatt suddenly walked over to the living room window.

"Somebody's here," he said, turning back to her.

Allie looked at him, blankly, trying to push a sleeping bag she'd accidentally dislodged back up onto the top shelf. *Who in their right mind would be out in this weather?* she wondered. And then she froze. Because what if whoever it was *wasn't* in their right mind? What if they were like the character in the B movie she'd seen once, the homicidal maniac who'd terrorized a family vacationing at their lakeside cabin? Or had it been flesh-eating zombies who'd terrorized that family? She gave the sleeping bag another shove. She'd definitely seen too many movies.

"Wyatt," she said warningly, finding her voice, "do not open that door. Remember what we talked about? If a stranger comes to our front door, you come and get me, okay? You don't let them in."

"But it's not a stranger," Wyatt said, staring out the window. "It's Mr. Ford. From the boatyard."

"Mr. Ford?" Allie said, letting the sleeping bag she was hold-

ing fall to the floor. *Here? Now?* She would have been less surprised if it *had* been flesh-eating zombies.

But a pounding on the door spurred her into action.

"Should I let him in?" Wyatt asked, turning to her.

"No, you stay here," Allie said, pointing to one of the living
room chairs. "I'll see what Mr. Ford wants."

No sooner had she slid the bolt on the front door and pushed
it open against a surprisingly strong gust of wind, then Walker
brushed past her into the cabin.

"Do you have a cellar?" he asked.

"A cellar?" she repeated, startled by his brusqueness. She
closed the front door on another brilliant flash of lightning.

"Yes," he said, quickly. "A cellar, a basement, anything like
that? Anything underground?"

She shook her head. "No, nothing like that," she said, but her
words were lost in a boom of thunder that shook the cabin.

"Where's your son?"

"Over there," Allie said, gesturing to Wyatt. He wobbled the
flashlight beam in their direction.

"Well, grab him and let's go," Walker said, opening the door
again, and Allie saw then that he'd left his pickup truck's engine
running and its headlights turned on.

"Go where?" she asked.

"To my cabin," he said, quietly but urgently, glancing over
at Wyatt. "I don't want to scare your son, but there's a tornado
watch in effect for this whole county until two A.M. tonight. At
least three of them have already touched down in this area. And
you two aren't staying here." He glanced around and added, "Because this pile of twigs looks like it would come down in a stiff
breeze, never mind a tornado."

Allie stared back at him.

"And don't think, for one second," he said, mistaking her hesitation for a refusal, "that this has anything to do with my asking you out when you were at the boatyard the other day. It doesn't. Trust me. I don't have to work this hard to get a date."

But that wasn't what Allie was thinking. She was thinking, *A tornado? Up here?* Living in suburban Minneapolis they'd been a fact of life, but it hadn't occurred to her to worry about them this far north. Tornados, as a general rule, liked wide-open spaces. They were less common in densely wooded places like northern Minnesota. But they weren't unheard of. She remembered one summer, as a child, when her father had taken her to see a cabin on Butternut Lake that had been leveled by a tornado. Fortunately, nobody had been injured. The family who owned the cabin had been away at the time.

"Let's go," she said, suddenly. She hurried over to Wyatt, her heart pounding. But she forced herself to speak calmly as she knelt down beside him.

"Wyatt, Mr. Ford is going to take us back to his cabin with him."

"Why?" Wyatt asked, still holding the flashlight.

"Because . . ." She hesitated, a hundred convenient lies coming to her mind. But she decided to stick with the truth. "Because this is a bad storm," she said. "And Mr. Ford thinks we'll be safer at his cabin."

Wyatt nodded, and she picked him up and carried him to the front door, where Walker was waiting impatiently. Her mind was racing. She was wearing what she'd planned to sleep in that night—a tank top and a pair of pajama bottoms—but there was no time to change now. So she stepped into a pair of flip-flops she'd left beside the door, grabbed the cabin's key off a hook on the wall, and stuffed them into the pocket of her pajama bottoms.

"Ready?" Walker asked. She nodded and followed him out the door, pulling it closed behind her. She was shocked at how dark it had gotten outside. The storm, she could see, was directly over them now, and the sky was as black as midnight, except when it was illuminated by frequent bursts of lightning.

Walker opened the passenger-side door of his pickup for them, and she boosted Wyatt in. As she scrambled in behind him, she felt the first raindrops on her shoulders. Walker started to slam the truck's door behind them, but the wind caught it and almost flung it back open. Walker shut it again, forcefully, then hurried around to the driver's-side door.

Allie fastened the seat belt clumsily around her and Wyatt, and Walker launched himself into the driver's seat and yanked his door closed. He stepped on the gas and the truck lurched. He turned it around and drove, too fast, down the driveway.

But by the time they reached the road, Allie was worried about more than the speed at which Walker was driving. The wind was blowing harder now, so hard, in fact, that it was littering branches and even small trees down on the road's surface. Walker had to swerve around some of them, and Allie tried not to think about the possibility of a car coming from the opposite direction on this narrow road. Meanwhile, the rain, which had started as big drops splashing onto the truck's windows, started coming down faster. Soon, it was sheeting over the front windshield, and the windshield wipers, going full speed, barely put a dent in its deluge.

"*Damn it,*" she heard Walker say, under his breath. She didn't ask him what was wrong. She already knew. Between the wind and the rain, the visibility on the road was practically nil. How Walker was even keeping his truck on it was a mystery to her.

She turned to Wyatt. He was staring, stoically, ahead of him.

She gave him a reassuring squeeze, just as Walker turned sharply into what she assumed was his driveway. As they started down it, there was a sharp, cracking sound as something landed on the roof of the truck. The sound came again, and then again, until it was so close together that it was nearly continuous, and so loud that Allie shielded Wyatt's ears with her hands.

"What is it, Mommy?" he asked, fearfully.

"It's hail," she said, into one of his ears, "And it'll be over soon." They both watched as a flash of lightning illuminated the view through the front windshield, where golf-ball-sized hail was bouncing off the hood of the truck.

Allie squinted ahead and saw, with surprise, the lighted windows of Walker's cabin coming into view. "Didn't you lose power, too?" she called.

"I have a generator," Walker said, pulling into the cabin's carport.

Of course you do, Allie thought. *And you probably have a whole drawer full of flashlight batteries, too.*

"All right, let's go," Walker said, putting on the brakes and cutting the engine. Allie unfastened the seat belt and slid out of the truck, still holding Wyatt in her arms. She slammed the truck's door and prepared to run the short distance between the carport and the cabin's front door.

"Ready?" Walker asked.

"Ready," she said.

She followed him, running full out, the rain soaking her skin, the wind whipping her hair, and the last of the hailstones biting into her skin. Lightning flared overhead, and she heard an ear-splitting crash that even in her near panic she knew was the sound of lightning striking a tree. She held Wyatt tighter, and he buried his head deeper into her chest.

Then Walker was opening the front door and pushing them both through it.

"Are you okay?" he asked, when he'd slammed it behind them and they were standing in the cabin's vestibule.

"I think so," Allie said, breathing hard and shifting a sodden Wyatt from one hip to the other. "Where should we go?" she asked Walker, her adrenaline still spiking. "To your cellar?"

He shook his head. "No, I think we're okay here," he said, leading them into the cabin's living room. "I built this place to withstand winds of up to a hundred and seventy-five miles an hour."

"That's . . . that's very impressive," Allie murmured, feeling some of the tension ebb out of Wyatt's little body. And as her eyes followed his around the living room, she understood. It was ablaze with light, and from the thick wooden beams that crossed the high vaulted ceiling to the enormous fieldstone fireplace that took up most of one wall, it looked incredibly solid. It felt solid, too. Outside, the storm continued to rage, but inside, it seemed somehow far away. Insubstantial.

"I'm going to get you two a couple of towels," Walker said, and he disappeared.

"Mommy, it's so big," Wyatt breathed, looking around.

"It *is* big," Allie agreed. *It's too big,* she wanted to say. But she caught herself. Its bigness was the reason they were safe here. Their cabin might be smaller and cozier, but then again, their cabin might not actually be standing there anymore.

Walker returned now, handing Allie a couple of towels. "I'm going to be in my study," he said. "I'm tracking the storm on Doppler radar."

She frowned. "The thing that meteorologists use?"

He nodded. "Fishermen use it, too. We sell it at the boatyard.

Do you want me to show you how it works? You can see how powerful this storm is."

"No, thanks," Allie said, a little weakly. "I think I already have a pretty good idea of how powerful it is."

"Right," he said, with a quick smile. And then he was gone.

Allie finally put Wyatt down, then rubbed one of the towels over his damp curls. "That's better," she said, after a few minutes, and turned her attention to herself. There wasn't much she could do, though. Her tank top clung to her damply, and her pajama bottoms were positively soggy. She sighed, patting herself ineffectually with the towel.

Why is it that both times I've come here, she wondered, *I've been barely dressed, and sopping wet?* She felt a flicker of irritation at Walker Ford, which she knew was unfair. After all, it wasn't his fault she kept getting into trouble, and he kept getting her out of it. Still, it was annoying. The man was so damned . . . *capable. So prepared.* He had Doppler radar, for God's sake. And she had . . . well, not much, really. Other than Wyatt. And an obviously misplaced faith in her ability to care for their little family by herself.

When she'd done her best to dry them both off, she led Wyatt over to one of Walker's massive couches, and, careful to spread a sheepskin throw over the leather to protect it from their damp clothes, she sat down and settled Wyatt in beside her. Then she pulled another sheepskin throw over the two of them. Wyatt didn't want to talk. She could tell that. He was still alert, and watchful. But gradually, he relaxed, and, as she stroked his forehead gently, he finally drifted off to sleep.

After that, Allie tried to keep herself awake. But it was hard, especially once the storm outside started to subside. There was something soothing about the sounds of its receding fury, the distant thunder, the dying wind, the now only occasional creaking of the cabin's rafters. Finally, she drifted off too, only to jerk awake when, sometime later, Walker touched her shoulder.

"How are you two doing?" he asked.

"We're fine, thanks," Allie said, straightening up and brushing her hair out of her face. She was embarrassed that he'd discovered her sleeping. It seemed like such an intimate thing to have someone see you doing.

But Walker wasn't looking at her. He was looking at Wyatt, asleep in her lap, and, as he did so, she saw something soften in his face. "He's a brave little guy," he said, quietly.

"He *is* brave," Allie agreed. *He's had to be.*

"I thought you should know the tornado watch was lifted," he said. "For now, anyway. But that storm is part of a whole system of storms that's going to be moving across the region over the next several hours."

"There are more like that one?" she asked, appalled.

Walker nodded. "In the meantime, you two will have to spend the night here. I'd take you home, but the roads aren't drivable. I can take you back by boat by tomorrow, though, as soon as there's a break in the weather."

"I think we'll have imposed on you enough by then," Allie said, apologetically.

But he only shrugged. "Let me show you the guest room, okay?"

Allie followed him, a sleeping Wyatt in her arms, to a downstairs bedroom with twin beds. Like the rest of the cabin, it was both impersonal and luxurious at the same time. Not unlike a resort, she decided. As opposed to, say, someone's actual home.

She put Wyatt down on one of the beds, and he barely stirred. She turned back to Walker, who was standing in the doorway.

"Thanks," she said, again. It was the only thing she could think of to say.

But he waved her thanks away. "Do you need anything? A change of clothes?" His dark blue eyes took in her wrinkled tank top and pajama bottoms.

She shook her head, and her face felt warm. But to cover her self-consciousness, she said, "My clothes are fine. They're practically dry now. And, anyway, I'm too tired to care."

He nodded. "There's a bathroom down the hall. And extra blankets in the closet. And, uh, let me know if you need anything else, all right?"

"I will," she lied.

"Well, good night then," he said, turning to go. But just as he was closing the door he paused. "Oh, by the way," he said, "you should call Caroline in the morning. She was worried about you two tonight."

"How do you know that?"

"She called me on my cell phone. She said she'd tried to reach you at your cabin but your phone was out. She was afraid you didn't know about the storm, and she was hoping I'd check on you two."

"Is that why you came over?"

"No. Actually, when she called, I was already on my way out the door. I wasn't going to let you ride out a storm like this alone," he said, and he closed the door.

Allie tucked Wyatt into bed and got into the other bed herself, turning the light off on the bedside table between them. Then she tried to sleep. She really did. But soon another storm rolled in, and then another one. Eventually, she lost track of them, and they all seemed to somehow run together. She dozed off, occasionally, for a few minutes at a time, flashing on images from the night: Walker's hands on the steering wheel of his truck; Walker's face when he looked at Wyatt asleep on the couch. But no sooner would she see these things than she'd jerk awake again, disoriented in the unfamiliar bed.

She told herself it was the storms that were disturbing her, but she knew they weren't the only thing making her restive. Something else was bothering her. Something right on the edge of her consciousness. Something she had to keep pushing away. Because while the storm had been scary, she had a feeling that this thing—this *feeling*—was a whole lot scarier.

CHAPTER 16

W alker was pouring himself a cup of coffee in the sun-drenched kitchen the next morning when he sensed, rather than saw, Allie standing behind him.

"Good morning," she said, lingering in the doorway.

He turned around, and she waved, a halfhearted little wave. She was embarrassed, he realized, and he couldn't really blame her. They didn't know each other well enough to be doing the whole "morning after" thing. Not that anything had happened between them last night—anything intimate, at least—but it was still awkward. He felt it, too.

"Good morning," he said, pouring half-and-half into his coffee. "How'd you sleep last night?"

"Not very well," she admitted, folding her arms protectively across her chest. She was still wearing the clothes she'd been wearing when he'd picked her and Wyatt up at their cabin last night. A tank top, pajama bottoms, and flip-flops. He tried, but failed, not to stare at her almost-bare shoulders. Her arms tightened across her chest.

"Would you like a cup of coffee?" he asked, trying to fill the conversational void.

She nodded. "I'd love one," she said, coming tentatively into the kitchen. He poured her a cup.

"Half-and-half?" he asked.

"I'll get it," she said, standing next to him. He handed her the cup and she took it, then reached for the carton of half-and-half on the counter and sloshed some into the cup. He handed her a spoon, and she smiled appreciatively as she gave her coffee a quick stir.

He drank his own coffee and watched her. Her honey-colored hair, normally trained into a neat ponytail, fell loose and tousled on her shoulders, and her hazel eyes, usually closer to brown, looked strikingly green in the light streaming in through the windows. But it was her mouth he found especially captivating this morning. It was the palest shade of pink, and it looked so soft right now, so vulnerable. He felt an unfamiliar tightness in his chest, a constriction in his breathing.

"Is Wyatt still asleep?" he asked, trying to ignore the strange sensation.

She nodded. "He slept straight through the night."

"That's amazing," Walker said. He hadn't slept at all. But he didn't know how much of that had had to do with the storm.

"It *is* amazing," she agreed, sipping her coffee. "When he was a baby, he used to sleep so soundly, for so long, that a couple of times I woke him up just to make sure he was all right. Then my neighbor, who'd raised four children of her own, told me you never wake up your second child." She smiled, shaking her head at the memory. "I guess I'll never know," she added, more to herself than to him. And then she blushed, hard, and looked away. She obviously felt like she'd said too much.

But Walker was thoughtful. Did she really believe that? That she'd never have a second child? He thought it was probably too soon to know, especially given how young she was. But he didn't say anything. It wasn't exactly his area of expertise. Not by a long shot.

"What about you?" she asked. "How'd you sleep?"

"I didn't sleep at all," he confessed.

"Not even a little?" she asked, surprised.

He shook his head. "No. At some point, I guess, I just realized it wasn't going to happen."

"Were you worried?" she asked, frowning slightly. "About the boatyard, I mean?"

"Worried?" he repeated, dumbly. He was thinking about how pretty her mouth was. Even frowning.

"No," he said, finally understanding her question. "I wasn't worried. I called Cliff, after you and Wyatt went to bed. He was there, and he gave me an update. There was very little damage, actually. We got most of the boats inside yesterday afternoon."

"So you knew about the storm?"

"I thought everyone did," he said. It wasn't a judgment. Just a statement.

She sighed. "I didn't know about it," she said, guiltily. "I was completely oblivious." She added, with a little shudder, "If it hadn't been for you, last night might have ended very differently."

He started to tell her something, but she put her empty coffee cup down on the counter with such force that it startled him.

"I'm such an idiot," she said, her jaw tightening. "Otherwise, I would have had a cell phone. Or a generator. Or—"

"Hey, don't be too hard on yourself," he said, interrupting her.

"Why not?" she asked, her face flushing. "Why shouldn't I be?

I'm the one who had the brilliant idea of moving us up here. Of starting over again. Of having peace, and quiet, and solitude. None of which, by the way, Wyatt ever asked for. And I was so determined that we'd do everything on our own. So determined, and so *completely* unprepared. I mean, last night I realized I didn't even have flashlight batteries, for God's sake.

"You know, I've been thinking about it since I woke up this morning," she continued, her tone softer, but still tinged with anger. "And I've decided that if our cabin is still there—and that's a big 'if'—I should probably just quit while I'm ahead. You know, sell it and head back to the suburbs, where we obviously belong."

"Allie, stop," Walker said, holding up his hand. "You're blowing this way out of proportion. First of all, as I tried to tell you a minute ago, your cabin is fine. There are a few shingles torn off the roof, some trees down on your property, but that's it. I'm sorry that I made that remark last night about it being a pile of twigs. Obviously, I was wrong." He almost said something, too, about the other remark he'd made. The one about not having to work that hard to get a date, but he decided to let it go.

"How do you know how our cabin is?" she asked, perplexed.

"I went over there."

"When?"

"This morning. As soon as the sun came up. I took the boat over there. I tied up at your dock and took a quick look around. You may have some damage I couldn't see. But all in all, it looked pretty good."

"You didn't have to do that, you know," she said, quietly. But it didn't sound like an accusation. It sounded more like an apology.

"I couldn't sleep, remember?" he said, smiling. "And I wanted to make sure you two had someplace to go home to. Unless you're serious about selling your cabin . . ." He trailed off, afraid of the answer.

She bit her lower lip, considering his question. "No," she said, finally. "I don't think so. We can't move back. Eden Prairie isn't our home anymore, but this isn't our home yet, either. We're sort of caught between two places, Wyatt and me."

"That must be hard," he said, and he meant it. But he was relieved, too, that she wasn't serious about leaving. And then he thought of something. "You know, if you're going to stick around, I can help you with the whole emergency preparedness thing. I mean, you can start by investing in an emergency weather radio. It's easy to use, and you can program it to alert you when a storm is coming."

"Let me guess," she said, teasingly. "You sell them at the boat-yard?"

"As a matter of fact, we do," he said, smiling. "But that wasn't a sales pitch." And then he turned serious. There was something else he wanted to talk to her about.

"You know, in retrospect," he began, "coming over and getting you two last night probably wasn't a very good idea."

"Why?"

"Well, for one thing, your cabin turned out to be a lot better built than I gave it credit for being. And, for another, that drive was dangerous. The visibility on the road was zero. I could have easily driven into a tree."

"But you didn't," she pointed out.

"That's true," he said, watching her. Was it his imagination, or had she come a step closer to him?

"But, Walker, why did you come over last night? Why did you really come?" she asked.

He thought of a hundred possible responses, all of them untrue. Instead, he said, "Isn't it obvious?"

She didn't answer him. She put her coffee cup down on the counter and took a step closer to him, closing the distance between them. Then she reached out her hand, slowly, and ran her fingertips, lightly, along his razor-stubbled jawline.

"You look so tired," she said.

Walker stood perfectly still. He knew if he said anything, or did anything, the moment would be over. She was like the doe he'd seen in the woods a few days ago. Alert. Tense. Skittish. One sudden movement, he knew, and she would bolt.

"I'm sorry I left the boatyard in such a huff the other day," she said now, softly, her fingers still tracing his jawline.

"Don't worry about it," he murmured. He didn't want her to stop what she was doing.

She didn't. She leaned closer, stood on her tiptoes, and kissed him on the lips. Softly, and tentatively. As if she was testing out the idea of kissing him, as opposed to actually kissing him. And, without touching any other part of her body, he kissed her back. As gently as he knew how to.

He was so hungry for her, he wanted her so much, that it took all his self-control to hold back now, to *not* do what he wanted to do to her. He wanted to run his fingers through her hair. He wanted to pull her, hard, against him, and feel every inch of her body digging into his. He wanted to kiss her neck, the hollow at the base of her neck, and her almost-bare shoulders. But he didn't do any of these things.

This kiss, though, like most kisses, wouldn't be contained. Her body swayed gently against his, and he felt her breasts against his chest, soft but firm, her nipples, as hard as pebbles, straining slightly against the thin cotton of her tank top.

And when he couldn't hold back anymore, he still moved as slowly, as carefully, as he possibly could. He slid his arms gently around her waist, his hands settling on the small of her back. Then he pulled her, almost imperceptibly, against him.

In response, she opened her lips, welcoming his tongue into her mouth. And when his tongue touched hers, it delivered an electric jolt so powerful he almost went reeling back. But he didn't. He just kept kissing her. Her lips felt so soft under his, and her mouth tasted delicious, too. Not like coffee—which it should, by all rights, have tasted like—but like something sweet and clean.

And as they kissed, she reached up and grasped his shoulders, anchoring herself against his body, and he strained against her, wanting to feel every inch of her softness against him.

And then something happened. He didn't know what triggered it. One moment she was kissing him with all her heart, and the next she was pushing him away. It was a gentle push, but it was still a push.

"I have to leave now," she said, breathlessly. "I have to wake up Wyatt."

"Why?" he asked, mystified.

"Because *this*"—she made a gesture with her hand that included both of them—"*this* is wrong."

"Wrong how?" he challenged, knowing there was no way in hell that something that had felt that right could be wrong.

"Wrong because I . . . I didn't mean for it to happen," she said, taking a step back. "It was just me being tired, or impulsive, or, or . . . *something.*"

"Well, it wasn't just you," he chided her, gently. "Trust me, I was a more than willing participant."

She closed her eyes and shook her head, dismissing his playfulness. "Look, Wyatt and I need to leave now. Just . . . trust me, okay? We can't stay here." She went to put her empty coffee cup in the sink, and he saw, to his astonishment, that her hands were trembling. She was afraid, he realized. Not afraid of him, but afraid of what had happened between them.

"I'll take you two back in my boat now," he said, feeling a wave of sympathy for her. "You wake up Wyatt, and I'll get the keys."

She nodded, wordlessly, and left the kitchen.

He opened a kitchen drawer and took out the boat keys. As he slammed the drawer shut he felt his cell phone vibrate in his front blue jeans pocket. He pulled it out and glanced at the caller ID. It was Reid. He let the call go to voice mail and put the phone back in his pocket. He couldn't think about anything right now but Allie. He could still feel her, resting lightly against him, and he could still taste her lips on his own.

His phone vibrated again almost immediately. This time he answered it. "What is it, Reid?" he asked, without ceremony.

"I need a damage assessment on the Butternut Boatyard," Reid said, curtly.

"I'll call you back in fifteen minutes," Walker said, slipping the boat keys into his pocket and pouring himself a third cup of coffee.

"It can't wait," Reid barked. "We need to file insurance claims as soon as possible. And don't think Butternut was the only boatyard damaged, either. Those storms wreaked havoc with the whole northeastern part of the state."

"I can't talk right now," Walker said, feeling weariness wash over him for the first time that morning. Until this point, he realized, he'd been running on pure adrenaline. "I'll call you back, okay? There's something I need to do first."

"The hell there is," Reid growled, impatiently.

"Good-bye, Reid," Walker said, pressing end, and he walked over to the kitchen door, opened it, and pitched his cell phone into the nearby woods.

CHAPTER 17

W e were lucky that none of those tornados touched down in populated areas," Caroline said, leaning against the counter at Pearl's. It was late afternoon, and she and Allie were sipping iced teas while Wyatt played with his Hot Wheels on the floor nearby.

"*Very* lucky," Allie agreed, toying with the straw in her iced tea. "It could have been much worse."

"I still can't believe it took them three days to clear Butternut Lake Drive, though." Caroline clucked disapprovingly. "You and Wyatt must have been going stir-crazy."

"Actually, Wyatt was in heaven," Allie said. "All I could think about when I saw the downed trees on our property was how much it was going to cost to have them all cut up and hauled away. But all he could think about"—she gave a little laugh— "was all the new fort-building opportunities they presented."

"Still, didn't you need anything when the road was closed?" Caroline asked.

"Not really," Allie said. "We lost power during the storm, so I had to throw the melted ice cream in the freezer away, but we salvaged enough to tide us over. And Walker Ford called, too, to see if we needed anything else." She added quickly, "I told him we were fine, though."

Was it her imagination, Caroline thought, or had Allie colored slightly at the mention of his name?

"And, by the way," Allie continued, "thank you for asking him to check on us the night of the storm."

"He said he was already on his way to your cabin."

"He was. And he didn't just check on us, either," Allie said. "He took us back to spend the night. Then he went out the next morning, before we were even awake, to assess the damage to our cabin. I'd say he went above and beyond being a good neighbor."

"Well, I'm not surprised," Caroline said, staunchly. "I mean, I know some people around here find him a little . . ." She searched for the right word. "Standoffish," she decided. "But he's not. Private, maybe. Reserved, definitely. But he's not uncaring. He cares a lot about this town, and the people in it. He's just prefers to keep to himself, that's all."

Allie nodded, pensively. "There was something else about that night, though, I wanted to talk to you about," she said, looking over her shoulder at Wyatt. He was totally absorbed in his cars. She turned back, sighed, and shook her head. "I kissed him, Caroline," she said simply. "Standing in his kitchen at eight o'clock in the morning, I kissed him. I have no idea why."

"Well, I imagine it was because you wanted to," Caroline said, trying not to smile.

"Well, of course I *wanted* to," Allie agreed. "But why did I *want* to?"

"Because you're attracted to him?" Caroline supplied. She knew Allie was not an unintelligent woman. Far from it. But on this particular subject, Caroline thought, she was being a little slow.

"Oh, I'm attracted to him all right," Allie said, with a rueful smile. "In fact, if Wyatt hadn't been sleeping in the guest room at the time, who knows where it would have ended?"

Caroline said nothing. She had a pretty good idea, though, of where it would have ended.

"Anyway, since then I've been so confused," Allie continued. "I *want* to see him again. I *don't* want to see him again. But either way, I'm terrified." She added quickly, "Not of him. Of the way he made me feel."

Caroline hesitated, choosing her words carefully. "Allie, is it that surprising that you're attracted to him? I mean, he *is* an attractive man."

"I know he is. I mean, I knew it before that night. But I knew it *intellectually*. I didn't know it . . . *physically*. And Caroline?" she said, her eyes widening. "I wasn't prepared for it. I really wasn't."

"Allie?" Caroline asked, gently. "Is Walker the first man you've been attracted to since . . . since losing Gregg?"

Allie lowered her eyes. "Yes," she said.

She's ashamed, Caroline thought, with surprise. *She's ashamed that she's attracted to him.*

"But it must have occurred to you that you might be attracted to someone else again one day," she said, gently.

Allie shrugged. "Maybe if I'd *thought* about it, it would have. But I didn't think about it. When Gregg didn't come back, I stopped thinking about men. Or, at least, I stopped thinking about them *that* way. It was almost like I didn't even really *see* them anymore, if you know what I mean."

Caroline, it turned out, knew exactly what she meant. Something similar had happened to her after her husband, Daisy's father, had left. She didn't mean for it to happen—not exactly, anyway—but she was so exhausted during those early years, raising a child, running a business, that she'd put the idea of men right out of her mind. And later, when she could conceivably have made room in her life again for a man, she discovered she'd gotten out of the habit of thinking about them as potential love interests. Instead, she was apt to think of them only as customers whose empty coffee cups needed refilling, or whose eggs needed to be served over easy with a side of bacon.

But it was one thing for *her* to see men that way, and another thing for *Allie* to see them that way. Allie was still so young—just thirty—and she had a young son, too. Caroline, of course, had raised Daisy without a father, and she'd turned out all right. In fact, she'd turned out just about perfect. But boys were different, Caroline believed. They needed a father, or a father figure, anyway. Someone to throw a baseball around with them.

So she decided to weigh in with an opinion, something she was usually reluctant to do. Most people, she knew from experience, wanted someone to listen to them, but they didn't necessarily want that someone to tell them what to do. In Allie's case, though, she decided to make an exception. There was too much at stake not to.

"Allie, listen," Caroline said, picking up the iced tea pitcher and topping off Allie's glass. "I *do* know what you mean—about forgetting about men, that is—but here's the thing about men. When you remember them again, they're still there. And it turns out they've been there the whole time, whether you realized it or not." She continued, "And as men go, Walker's a good one. You could do a lot worse if you're ready to test the waters again."

"You make it sound so simple." Allie sighed.

"That's because sometimes it *is* so simple."

"But it's not for me," Allie persisted. "Being attracted to Walker makes me feel . . . *disloyal* somehow. Like I'm being unfaithful to Gregg. Or unfaithful to his memory, anyway."

Caroline sighed. This, she knew, was beyond her understanding, and she hated it when people pretended to understand things they didn't. So she reached over and squeezed Allie's hand, which was resting on the counter. "I can't say I know what you're feeling, honey. Not exactly. But I can imagine it must be very confusing. And very hard."

Allie exhaled slowly. "So what do I do?" she asked, looking directly at Caroline.

"What do you want to do?"

"Right now?"

Caroline nodded.

"I want to have him over for dinner. Partly to thank him. And partly because I'm hoping that I imagined that that kiss was as good as it was."

"So you're hoping he's a bad kisser?" Caroline asked, smiling in spite of Allie's serious tone.

"Yes. A terrible kisser. Disgusting, actually. Then I can just put that first kiss out of my mind. Permanently."

"And that would make it what . . . a fluke?"

"A complete fluke," Allie agreed.

Caroline laughed, and even Allie had to chuckle. "I guess my logic is a little flawed," Allie admitted. "But right now, it's the only plan I've got."

"Well, the asking him over for dinner part is a good idea," Caroline said. "But I wouldn't count on him being a bad kisser.

He doesn't seem to me like the kind of man who does anything halfway."

"No, he doesn't," Allie agreed, suddenly serious again. They lapsed into a comfortable silence, punctuated only by the engine noises Wyatt was making for his cars.

"Thank you, Caroline," Allie said, a little while later. "Thank you for listening to me. And not judging me."

"I try not to judge people," Caroline said. And it was true. If she had a philosophy in life, that was probably it. Don't judge people. Not if you could possibly help it.

The jingle of the front door opening interrupted her thoughts. She'd forgotten to flip the Open sign to Closed after Allie and Wyatt had come in at three o'clock. But when she glanced over to see who her customer was, she smiled with pleasure. It was Buster Caine. She hadn't seen him since the first time he'd come in last month, and she'd started to wonder if he'd changed his mind about buying a cabin up here after all.

"Mr. Caine," she said, as he walked up to the counter.

"Please, call me Buster," he said, smiling, his blue eyes crinkling pleasantly, exactly as she'd remembered them doing.

"Buster," Caroline repeated, feeling suddenly shy in a way she seldom, if ever, did. "Buster, this is Allie Beckett," she said. "Allie, this is Buster Caine." Buster and Allie shook hands.

"I hope I'm not interrupting anything," Buster said, glancing politely at Allie, who was looking from Buster to Caroline with interest.

"Not at all," Allie said, sliding off her stool and helping Wyatt gather up his cars. "Wyatt and I have to be getting back to the cabin now anyway."

"Well, you're welcome to stay longer," Caroline said, pointedly.

If Allie was leaving because Buster Caine was here, she thought, she was being ridiculous. There was absolutely no reason why the two of them needed to be alone with each other.

But Allie and Wyatt were already heading for the door. "Thanks for the iced tea," Allie said. "And, Wyatt, please thank Caroline for the milk and cookies." Wyatt dutifully thanked her.

"Wait, when do you start work at the Pine Cone Gallery?" Caroline called after her.

"Monday," Allie called back. "Wish me luck."

"Good luck," Caroline murmured. But they were already gone, the bell jingling as the door swung shut behind them.

"Is this a bad time?" Buster asked, not sitting down at the counter yet. "Because I can always come back. During regular business hours, I mean." He smiled, a little sheepishly, and Caroline realized he'd hoped to find her alone again. Her stomach fluttered, and she found herself reaching for a dishcloth.

"No, you can stay," she said, with studied casualness, rinsing the dishcloth out at the sink and starting to wipe down the counter with it. "I don't know what I can offer you to eat, though. We've had a really busy day. I feel like we ran out of everything at the same time."

"That's all right. I've already had lunch," he said. "I'd love something cold to drink, though. If it's not too much trouble."

"Not at all. What about an iced tea? I've got a freshly brewed pitcher of it right here."

"Sounds good," he said, sitting down on one of the stools.

"And if I'm not mistaken," she said, "there's one more piece of apple pie left, too."

"I don't see how I could say no to that," he said, smiling.

Caroline poured his iced tea and slid the last wedge of apple pie onto a plate. She set them both down in front of him on the counter, along with lemon wedges, sugar, a napkin, and a fork.

"Now *this* was worth a trip into town," Buster said, helping himself to a forkful of pie.

Caroline smiled and poured herself another glass of iced tea. "So how are you settling in?" she asked.

"Pretty well," he said. "I've got everything unpacked now."

"Were you here the night of the storms?" she asked, concerned.

He shook his head, finishing a bite of pie. "I'd gone back down to the Twin Cities to tie up some loose ends, but I'm back now. And I'm not just here, at this fine establishment, for a piece of pie. Although God knows the pie is a bonus."

Caroline raised her eyebrows. "What are you here for?"

He put his fork down. "I'm here to ask you if you'd like to come up in my airplane with me. You said you'd never flown before. Well, here's your chance."

For a moment, Caroline was too surprised to say anything. "Me?" she finally sputtered. "In an airplane?"

"Why not?"

"Well, *why* would be a better question, wouldn't it?"

He shrugged. "Okay, fair enough. Why, because you'll be doing something you've never done before. And you'd be giving me the pleasure of your company. And I hope I'm not being conceited when I say that I'm not bad company myself, as a general rule."

Caroline hesitated. She was having trouble formulating a response.

"Look," he said, "my plane is at the Butternut Municipal Airport. It's a five-minute drive from here. And we don't have to stay up for long, if you don't want to. Thirty minutes, tops."

When she finally spoke, she said the first thing that came to her mind. "But don't those little planes sometimes crash?"

"Well, nothing in life is entirely risk-free," he admitted. "But I'm an excellent pilot, and I've never had any problems with this plane before."

Caroline wavered again. "Look, I don't know what you charge for your charter business, but I probably can't afford to pay it."

"This isn't a sales call, Caroline," he said, surprised. "I'm not expecting you to pay. I'm asking you to come as a friend."

"A friend?" she repeated.

"That's right."

Caroline hedged. "So this wouldn't be a date?"

"A date?" He looked mildly amused. "You know, I haven't been on one of those in a long time, but I think they still call them that. So, yes. I guess this would be a date. Is there a problem with that?"

"Not a problem, exactly," Caroline said. "But we don't know each other very well yet, do we?"

He looked amused again. "That's true. But isn't that the whole point of a date? Two people getting to know each other a little better?"

"I guess so," she said, doubtfully.

"Okay," he said, considering something. "Maybe I shouldn't take you up in my plane. Maybe that's a little . . . *adventurous* for a first date. Why don't we go out for a cup of coffee? That's assuming, of course, that there's somewhere else around here where we can get a decent cup of coffee."

"No, Buster. This is it," she said, looking around.

He sighed. "You're not going to make this easy, are you?"

She shook her head. "I don't mean to make it hard. I just don't date, that's all."

"Not *ever*?" he asked gently.

"Not *recently*," she said. Because of course she had dated in the years since her husband had left her. A shop teacher from the high school. A veterinarian who had a practice in town. And she had liked them both immensely. But not enough, it turned out, to invite them into the life she and Daisy had built together. And now that Daisy had left home? Might that change now? But no . . . She shook her head, a little sadly.

"So, no to the date?" Buster asked, looking at her quizzically.

"No to the date," she repeated, a little uncertainly.

"That's fair," he said. He took his wallet out and left a bill on the counter. "But if you change your mind, remember, it would *just* be a date, Caroline. Not a commitment ceremony." His blue eyes twinkled unmistakably.

"Thanks for the pie," he said, and Caroline nodded and watched him leave.

Then she picked up the bill he'd left on the counter—another twenty—cleared away his dishes and started wiping down the countertop again, with a little more force than was absolutely necessary. She was thinking about something she'd said to Allie, not fifteen minutes ago. About how sometimes, when it came to men, and relationships, things could be simple. Straightforward. And wasn't that, really, what Buster Caine had just said to her, too?

But the coffee shop's phone rang, interrupting her brooding.

"Hello?" she said, answering it.

"Mom?" It was Daisy. And she sounded worried.

"Hi, honey," Caroline said, emotion welling up inside of her.

"Mom, are you all right?"

"Of course," she lied. "Why?"

"Oh, nothing. It's been a couple days since we talked. When you weren't at the apartment, I decided to try you downstairs."

"I know I haven't called," Caroline apologized. "But I don't want you to feel like I'm smothering you, that's all."

"Mom, I never feel that way. You know that. I *want* you to call. I miss you."

Caroline felt her eyes glaze over with tears. *Don't you dare cry*, she told herself. *Don't you dare leave Daisy with that image of you, alone and sad.*

"But, Mom," Daisy was saying, "isn't it a little late for you to still be working?"

"Not really," Caroline said. "A friend of mine stopped by."

"A friend?" Daisy asked, interested.

"A customer," Caroline corrected herself. "He's new up here. Retired military. He wanted to know, if you can believe it, if I'd like to go up in his airplane with him."

There was a pause, and then Daisy whistled softly. "I can see now, Mom," she said, "that when I told you to join a book club, I was aiming way too low."

"Well, I didn't say yes," Caroline said, exasperated.

"Why not?"

"Because . . . because he said it would be a date."

"What's wrong with that?"

"Oh, honey, I don't know," she said, suddenly irritable. "I just thought, at my age, it would be a little ridiculous."

"Oh, that's right," Daisy said, pretending to remember something. "I forgot you were pushing forty. No, you're right, Mom. You're *way* too old to date. Unless . . ." Here she paused for dramatic effect. "*Unless* you think you could fit your walker in the trunk of his car when he comes to pick you up."

Caroline rolled her eyes on her end of the phone. "Look, it's not just my age. It's that I've . . . I've gotten out of the habit of . . ." Her voice trailed off.

"Gotten out of the habit of being anything other than my mother?"

"Something like that," Caroline admitted. Then, "You must think I'm pathetic."

"Not even a little," Daisy said. "You'll figure it out. But I've got to go now."

"Okay, sweetie," Caroline said. "I love you."

"Bye, Mom," Daisy said, cheerfully. And then she was gone, too.

Caroline sighed and leaned against the counter. For once, she didn't feel the need to be busy. She'd gotten it all wrong, she decided, worrying about Daisy going to college. Daisy was fine. It was her she should be worried about. Because in all those years of being a mother and a businesswoman, of trying to do right by Daisy and the coffee shop, she'd forgotten how to do something else. She'd forgotten how to take a risk.

She walked, slowly, over to the cash register. She opened it, lifted the bill drawer up, and took out Buster Caine's business card. She stared at it for a long time, wondering if she had the courage to call him. Finally, she put it back, and slammed the cash register drawer shut.

"You're hopeless," she said out loud, to the empty coffee shop. But it didn't make her feel any better.

CHAPTER 18

Walker took hold of the edge of the dock with both hands and, in one fluid movement, pulled himself up out of the lake. He sat, for a moment, the lake water sluicing down his body, and then he tipped back and lay down on the dock, looking up at the night sky, his chest rising and falling rapidly from the exertion of a three-mile swim.

It was a beautiful night, the sky so black, and the stars so brilliant against it, that it reminded him of the night sky at a planetarium his parents had taken him to once when he was a child. He sighed, remembering that day. Like so many other days in his childhood, it had ended badly. He'd loved the planetarium show, but afterward, as they were leaving, his parents had gotten into an argument about some trivial thing. The fight had escalated, and by the time they reached the natural history museum's parking lot, they were screaming at each other. His father had driven home in stony silence, and his mother had sobbed miserably in the passenger seat beside him.

And Walker? He'd sat hunched in the backseat, knowing he should comfort his mother but not knowing how to. So instead, he'd tried to remember everything he'd learned that day at the planetarium. If he reviewed the whole thing in his mind now, he'd decided, he would be able to reconstruct it for Reid later that night, at bedtime.

Bedtime was the best part of his day during those years. He and Reid lay there, talking across the small space that separated their beds. Often, they had to talk loudly, to be heard over their parents' fighting. Walker couldn't remember now what they'd talked about. Little things, probably. Baseball, and BB guns, and scary movies.

Reid had been a good older brother, he thought now, lying on the dock. Always helpful. Patient. Willing to listen. And if Walker had gotten on his nerves, he'd never let on. Walker made a mental note to remember that the next time Reid drove him crazy. Which was pretty much all the time lately.

He sat up now and looked, reflexively, across the bay to Allie's dock. The dock light had been turned off. So had the boathouse light. But the cabin's lights were still on, each window a solid square of yellow. He glanced at his watch. Nine o'clock. Over the next couple of hours, the cabin's lights would gradually go out. First in one window, then another, until finally there was only one left on. Then that last light would blink off, too, usually around eleven o'clock.

He knew it wasn't normal, spending so much time every night watching the lights in her cabin go out. But he told himself it wasn't technically an invasion of her privacy, since he was too far away to actually see anything inside the cabin. He told himself, too, that there were worse ways to spend these long, empty nights, like rereading fishing magazines or answering Reid's one-hundredth e-mail of the day.

But still. He knew it was a little weird, a little . . . *obsessive,* even, to spend so much time staring across the bay at her cabin. And *obsessive* was not a word that Walker generally associated with himself. Not when it came to women, anyway. Maybe when it came to working or fishing, but never women. He smiled ruefully to himself. He'd always thought, somehow, he was above all that. The insecurity. The jealousy. The craziness. The general messiness of love that, until recently, he'd believed he was immune to.

Not that his relationship with Caitlin hadn't been messy. Because it had been. In the end, anyway. But what they'd had together hadn't been love. It had been something else. What, he didn't know. And, as if in answer to that question, the memory of a winter night came back to him. It was after Caitlin had come back from the hospital, after they'd settled back into their old pattern of politely and assiduously avoiding each other.

Walker had had insomnia, something that had become increasingly common for him during his marriage to Caitlin, and he'd left her sleeping in their bed and gone downstairs to work in his study. But when he'd finally come back up, he'd been surprised to discover Caitlin was awake, too. All the lights in their room were on, and she'd emptied her clothes out of the closet and the dresser and she was throwing them into a collection of suitcases that were open on the bed. Watching her, Walker saw that her complexion, always pale, had a bright, crimson flush overlaying its paleness. It made her look almost feverish.

"What are you doing?" he asked.

"Isn't it obvious?" she said, trying to force a too-full suitcase closed.

"Are you leaving?" Walker asked. He knew it was a ridiculous question, and so did she.

"That's right, Walker, I'm leaving," she said, starting to stuff clothes into another suitcase. "Your powers of observation are truly astounding, by the way."

Walker flinched. Caitlin was rarely angry. Or sarcastic, for that matter. Of course, he later realized, he'd had no way of knowing *how* she'd felt during the time they'd lived together. She hadn't told him, and he hadn't asked her.

"Caitlin," he said, quietly, "I thought we were doing better. Since you . . ." He stumbled here. He couldn't say the words.

"Since I lost the baby?" she finished for him. "And if, by 'doing better' you mean being polite to each other on those rare occasions when we're actually in the same room, then yes, I'd agree, Walker. I'd say we were doing *fantastic*."

"Look, can we talk about this in the morning?" Walker asked, coming over to her and putting one hand, tentatively, on her shoulder.

But she immediately shook it off. "No, Walker, we can't talk about it in the morning. Because I won't be here in the morning. I'm leaving as soon as I'm packed."

"You can't be serious," Walker objected. "It's snowing. They haven't even had time to plow the roads yet."

"I'll take my chances," she said, closing another suitcase.

"Caitlin, no. It's not safe. If you want to leave in the morning, after the roads have been plowed, I won't try to stop you."

"Walker, you *can't* stop me now," she said, angrily. "I won't let you. And while it may not be safe for me on those roads, it's much more dangerous for me in here."

"What is that supposed to mean?" Walker asked, shocked. He'd never even raised his voice at her, let alone raised a hand at her.

"It means that I'm in danger here, Walker. In danger of dying from loneliness. Did you know that was possible? Because it is. And do you know how I know that? I know that because I researched it on the Internet. Just one of the many things I do with all the hours in the day I have to fill."

"I have to work," Walker said, defensively. "I have to earn a living. I can't just entertain you all the time."

"*Entertain me all the time?*" she shot back at him, furiously. "How about taking me out for dinner? Not every night. Just occasionally. *Just once.* Or how about having dinner with me here? Instead of staying at the boatyard from dawn to dusk and then locking yourself in your study when you come home."

"That's not fair," Walker objected. "You knew my job was demanding when you married me. And by the way, I never stopped you from trying to have your own life here."

"*Walker,*" she burst out, her pale blue eyes brimming with tears, "*that's* not fair. I tried to fit in here, but you didn't help me. You didn't introduce me to anyone. And whenever anyone invited us anywhere, you said no. So what was I supposed to do? Go by myself and explain to people that my husband doesn't care enough about me—or about them, for that matter—to come with me?"

"That's not true," Walker muttered. But he didn't argue the point too strenuously. He knew he hadn't helped her build a social life, and he knew how hard it could be to do that in a town where most of the residents had known one another all their lives.

Caitlin finished closing the final suitcase and, dragging it off the bed, started to carry it downstairs.

"This is crazy," he said, trying to take it, gently, away from her.

"Don't touch me," she snapped, so angry now that her whole body was shaking.

He didn't try to help her after that. And he didn't try to stop her either. He just watched, dismayed, while she loaded the trunk of her car and slammed the hood shut.

Then she turned to him. The sky was just starting to lighten, and a fine, wet snow was still falling.

"One last thing, Walker," she said, with a fury so quiet it scared him. "A little parting advice. Don't *ever* get married again. And don't *ever* consider being a father again either. Because you are *way* too selfish to do either of those things. I know when you proposed to me you thought you could have it all. The wife, the baby, the house. Just like that. But it's not like that, Walker. It's not like some pancake mix you just add water to. It's complicated, Walker. And it's hard. It takes commitment. And discipline. And perseverance. And outside of your professional life, Walker, you haven't got any of those qualities. Not a single one.

"So do some unsuspecting woman you meet in the future a favor, okay?" she continued, breathlessly. "*Don't* marry her. Don't even date her, if you can possibly help it. Because it's bound to end in her being hurt. But you, of course, will be just fine. Because life is pretty simple when you only care about yourself, isn't it, Walker?"

With that, she got in her car and drove away. Walker watched as her car disappeared down the driveway. And he worried, miserably, about the slipperiness of the roads. But he let her go. What else could he do? She *hated* him. And worse yet, she was right to hate him. Every single word she'd said to him was true. He was a bastard. A selfish bastard. And while he might point to his parents' divorce, or any number of other factors to explain why he was the way he was, at the end of the day, it didn't really matter why. He was the only one responsible for the person he'd become, and that person, frankly, was someone he didn't even know if he wanted to spend time with, let alone *be*.

Caitlin never called to tell him she'd arrived safely in Minneapolis. She never called, period. Several months later he was served with divorce papers, and all their future communications were through their respective attorneys. Walker agreed to what his attorney told him was an overly generous settlement, but by then he didn't care; he just wanted that chapter in his life to be over. Of course, it wasn't that simple. It never was.

Now he looked back across the bay to Allie's cabin. All but one light had gone out while he was reliving that memory. So he focused on that light, shimmering faintly across the dark water, and as he did so, he felt a desire for her that was so strong it almost knocked him flat on his back again.

But the flipside to that desire, he quickly realized, was frustration. Because while he wanted her, wanted her like he'd never wanted anything in his life before, he couldn't have her. Not now. Maybe not ever.

The worst part was, even if he *could* have her, he didn't know if he deserved to have her. Maybe what Caitlin had said was true. Maybe he shouldn't get involved with another woman. And maybe that went double for Allie. And for her son, too. They'd already experienced so much loss in their lives. So much sadness. The last thing they needed now was someone like him, some selfish bastard who didn't know anything about commitment.

At least that's what he told himself. But it didn't stop him from remembering that kiss in his kitchen the morning after the storms. The way Allie had felt in his arms. The sweetness of her mouth. And the silkiness of her bare shoulders and arms and neck. Sitting here now, though, it was hard to know whether that kiss was the beginning of something. Or the end.

He watched as the last light in her cabin went out, leaving that whole side of the bay in darkness. He started to get up, but he realized he wasn't tired yet. So instead, he slid back into the water, pushed off the dock, and started swimming a powerful front crawl. He figured another couple of miles, and he'd be too tired to think about anything but sleep.

CHAPTER 19

Almost as soon as Allie worked up the courage to invite Walker over for dinner, she regretted it. And the closer it came to the night they'd agreed on, the more she regretted it. By the time that night actually rolled around, she was practically paralyzed with regret. Regret and something else . . . fear.

"Honey, are you okay?" Caroline asked, sitting on the edge of Allie's bed and studying her face carefully.

She'd come to pick Wyatt up for the night, but she'd stayed to help soothe Allie's nerves. "Because from where I'm sitting," she said, "you look a little green around the gills."

"It's probably just the light in here," Allie said distractedly, frowning at the pile of clothes on her bed. "I'm fine, really."

"Good," Caroline said, not sounding entirely convinced. "Then why don't you get dressed? Walker's going to be here soon."

Allie was still in the Minnesota Twins T-shirt and flannel pajama bottoms she'd put on after she'd gotten out of the shower. Her hair, still wet, was pulled back in a ponytail.

"I . . . I can't get dressed." Her voice faltered as she sorted through the clothes on the bed. "Nothing seems quite right."

She'd ransacked her bedroom closet and dragged almost every article of clothing out if it. But nothing had passed her test yet, and she was beginning to think nothing ever would.

"Oh, who am I kidding?" she said suddenly, sweeping some clothes aside and sitting down on the edge of the bed. "I can't do this," she said to Caroline. "I just can't."

"Can't get dressed?" Caroline asked, calmly.

Allie shook her head. "No. Can't go on a date," she said, her shoulders sagging in defeat. "I thought I could, but I can't. I'm just not ready yet."

Caroline studied her thoughtfully. "Well, then don't think of it as a date," she said, finally. "Just think of it as two friends having dinner together."

Allie rolled her eyes. "That's a stretch," she said. "We barely know each other."

"Well, even friends have to start somewhere," Caroline pointed out. "Now choose something to wear," she said, firmly. "Or I'll choose it for you."

When Allie made no move, Caroline reached over and picked up a short, summery dress.

"How about this?" she asked brightly, holding it up for Allie's inspection.

Allie barely glanced at it. "Too revealing," she said.

"Well, then, how about this?" Caroline asked, after a short search. She held up a long-sleeved blouse and a long skirt.

"Too *un*revealing," Allie admitted, coloring a little.

Caroline chuckled. "You know how I used to choose clothes when I was dating my ex-husband, Jack?" she asked.

Allie shook her head.

"I chose them based on how easy they were to take off. And put back on, of course."

"Well, that is *not* happening here," Allie said, blushing harder. "Besides, I thought you said I should imagine we were just two friends having a casual dinner together?"

"I did say that, didn't I?" Caroline said, picking through the clothes again.

"Hey, what about these?" she asked, holding up a pair of blue jeans and a white eyelet blouse. "Blue jeans are always appropriate, and the white will look great with your tan."

Allie looked at them and sighed. "Okay," she said, taking them from Caroline. "But there's another problem, too."

"What's that?"

Allie held up her left hand and wriggled her ring finger, her wedding ring still on it. "I don't know what to do about my ring. I've already taken it off and put it back on three times. But my finger feels so naked without it."

"Then leave it on," Caroline said, "if that feels more comfortable to you. Now, what about dinner?"

"The roast chicken's in the oven. The wild rice is simmering on the back of the stove, and I've already made the salad."

"See, you *are* ready," Caroline said, beaming at her. "And it smells delicious, by the way," she added, gesturing toward the kitchen.

When Allie didn't respond, Caroline said, "Allie, you know, you *can* do this. Just take it one step at a time, all right? Little steps. *Baby* steps."

But Allie didn't answer her. Wyatt had come charging into the room, carrying a backpack and a sleeping bag with him.

"I'm ready, Caroline," he said, proudly. "I packed all by myself."

"Good for you," Caroline said, reaching out to tousle his wayward curls.

"I brought my canteen, my compass, and my flashlight, too," he explained, patting his backpack.

"Well, then you're very well prepared," Caroline said, seriously.

"What about your toothbrush and toothpaste?" Allie prompted.

"Oh," he said, his face falling a little. "I forgot those."

"Well, go pack them too," Allie said.

He trudged out of the room, weighed down by his fully loaded backpack.

"What does he have in there?" Caroline asked, mystified.

"I have no idea." Allie sighed. "Beyond the canteen, compass, and flashlight, that is."

"Allie, he doesn't think we're going camping, does he?" Caroline asked, frowning.

"No, I told him he's sleeping on your foldout couch. He's very excited. He said he's never slept on one before."

"Well, that's something, I guess. I would have put him in Daisy's room. But I was afraid it would be too pink and too ruffled for him."

Allie smiled, distractedly. "Caroline, you know you don't have to have him stay for the whole night. I'd be happy to pick him up after Walker leaves."

"Absolutely not," Caroline said. "It's much easier this way. You can have a glass of wine—or two—without worrying about driving, and Wyatt and I can make milk shakes and hamburgers at Pearl's without having to worry about getting him home by his bedtime."

"Wyatt will be in heaven," Allie said wistfully, half wishing she was going to be there, too, instead of here, on a date she wasn't even sure she wanted to be on.

But the evening rolled inexorably forward. She walked Caroline and Wyatt out to Caroline's car and said good-bye to them, noting with relief that Wyatt seemed more excited than anxious about his sleepover, and then she went back inside the cabin, blow-dried her hair, and dressed in the outfit Caroline had chosen for her. She debated about whether to wear any jewelry or makeup, then settled on a pair of small, gold hoop earrings, and a tiny bit of lipstick.

There, she thought, surveying herself in the bathroom mirror. She looked fine. She looked . . . *nice.* What she didn't look like was someone who was preparing for a big night. Or a hot date.

As she went to the kitchen to check on dinner, she remembered what Caroline had said about approaching the evening as if she were having a friend over for dinner. *I can do that,* she thought, whisking olive oil and vinegar together for the salad dressing. But she had to admit that if she were having a friend over, her hands probably wouldn't have been shaking when she tossed the salad.

Fortunately, it was only a few minutes later that Walker's pickup pulled up in front of the cabin. Allie went out to meet him, trying, and failing, to appear casual.

"Hi," she said. "You're right on time."

"Well, I didn't have far to come," he said, handing her not one but two bottles of wine. "I didn't know what we were having for dinner," he said, apologetically. "So I brought red and white."

"Oh, that's nice," she said, distracted, for a moment, by how close they were standing. He was freshly showered, his damp hair combed neatly down. And he smelled . . . *he smelled great,* she thought. He didn't smell like aftershave or cologne. He just smelled clean and masculine. It made her want to stand even closer to him. She felt her nerves ratchet up a notch.

"Come on inside," she said, walking up the front steps of the cabin.

"Where's Wyatt?" Walker asked, following her.

"He's over at Caroline's," Allie said, with what she hoped was just the right amount of breeziness. She didn't think it was necessary, or wise, to mention that he was spending the whole night there.

As they walked into the cabin Walker paused to look admiringly around the living room while she searched for a corkscrew in the kitchen.

"This place is amazing," he said. "Has anything changed since your grandfather built it?"

"Very little," Allie said, taking two wineglasses out of the cupboard.

"You can't find wood like this anymore," Walker said, examining the knotty pine walls and ceiling, warm and honey colored in the lamplight. "I know you can't, because I tried to when I built my cabin."

"It doesn't look like you did too badly, though," Allie said, carrying two glasses of white wine into the living room with her and handing him one. She took a big sip—a gulp, really—from her own. She didn't know a lot about wine, but she knew this was good. Really good. She took another, smaller sip and reminded herself to go slowly. She hadn't eaten much that day. She'd been too nervous to.

"What happened there?" Walker asked, pointing above the fireplace.

"Oh," Allie said, taking another sip for good measure. "There was a buck's head mounted there, but it scared Wyatt so I had it taken down." She shook her head, remembering how much he'd hated it. "Wyatt thought its eyes were following him everywhere he went."

"Maybe they were," Walker said, amused.

Allie smiled. "I can't joke about things like that with him. He's too impressionable. I have to be the voice of reason in this family. Even though, half the time, I feel like I'm completely unqualified for that job." She paused, afraid she'd somehow ventured into personal territory. "Anyway," she continued, redirecting the conversation, "I'm looking for a painting to put there. I just haven't found the right one."

"You're going to need a big painting," he said. "What are you looking for, exactly?"

She shrugged and said, "Something of Butternut Lake, I think. I'm not sure, really, but I feel like I'll know it when I see it." She added, "Working at the Pine Cone Gallery should help, since I'll see everything that comes through the door."

"So you got the job," he said, smiling.

She nodded.

"I'm not surprised. You told me about the interview the day you and Wyatt came to the boatyard, and I thought then that Sara Gage would be crazy not to hire you. How's it going, by the way?"

"It's been an adjustment," she admitted. "Going from spending the day with a five-year-old to spending it with other adults was more difficult than I'd imagined it would be. I mean, all Wyatt asks of me is that I know how to make macaroni and cheese, remember to buy Popsicles at the grocery store, and read him his bedtime stories. But Sara Gage and her customers set the bar a little higher." She sighed, remembering how exhausted she'd been after the first day of work. All she'd had the energy to make for dinner that night was frozen pizza. Wyatt, of course, had been thrilled.

"It'll get easier," Walker said now. "The important thing is that you like it."

"I *do* like it," Allie said, honestly. And she did. She liked talking to Sara about the pieces displayed in the gallery, liked meeting the artists responsible for them, and especially liked helping customers choose something for themselves or for someone else, "the perfect thing" to take home or to give as a housewarming gift or thank-you present.

She started to tell Walker more about her first week at the gallery, but the oven timer went off, and she went back to the kitchen to check the chicken for doneness. It was ready, the outside of it a crispy, golden brown. She slipped on potholders, lifted the roasting pan out of the oven, and transferred the chicken to a carving board.

"What's Wyatt doing while you work?" Walker asked, watching her carve the chicken.

"He's going to day camp," Allie said, conscious, as always, of his nearness. It was distracting, but she tried to concentrate on what she was doing. She had to. She had a sharp knife in one hand.

"The first morning I dropped him off, there were a few tears," she admitted, placing the slices of chicken onto a platter. "More than a few tears, actually." *And not all of them were his.* "But he did fine. Mainly because that same day they had a forest ranger visit."

"I take it Wyatt was impressed?"

"Well, let's put it this way," Allie said, carrying the chicken to the kitchen table. "Forest ranger has now edged out race car driver for Wyatt's career choice."

Walker smiled. "Can I . . . uh, help you?" he asked, watching her carry the rice and then the salad over to the table.

"Yes," Allie said. "You can pour us both another glass of wine." She didn't know, though, if she *needed* another glass of wine. Her body already felt tingly all over. The problem was, she wasn't sure if it was the wine that was making her feel that way, or Walker.

Walker refilled their glasses and they sat down at the table, which Allie had dressed up, a little, with a blue-and-white-checked cloth and a bunch of handpicked wildflowers in a Mason jar full of water. She'd drawn the line at candles, though, since their presence, she'd decided, would scream *romantic dinner for two*.

For a while, during dinner, they limited themselves to small talk. Walker was very complimentary about her cooking and helped himself to more of everything. Allie, on the other hand, pretended to eat, her stomach feeling fluttery and uncooperative.

"How's business at the boatyard?" she asked, taking another sip from her wineglass. That, at least, she could manage.

"It's good," he said. "So good my business partner, who also happens to be my brother, wants me to leave the day-to-day management of it to Cliff Donahue and move back to Minneapolis."

"Are you going to do that?" Allie asked, feeling a surprising twinge of anxiety.

"I don't know," he said, with a shrug. "I love living here, but I don't know how much longer I can justify doing it full-time."

Allie shifted in her chair and tried not to think about the possibility of Walker living somewhere else. It was strange that it bothered her so much, considering that, until recently, she'd been hell-bent on avoiding him.

"How did you and your brother get started in the boatyard business?" she asked then, genuinely interested. Either she was starting to get a little drunk, or boatyards had suddenly become a source of unbridled fascination for her.

"Oh, that's easy," he said, pouring her a third glass of wine. "Reid and I have always been obsessed with boats, probably because we grew up next door to a boatyard on Lake Minnetonka. When we were kids, the owner used to give us a few bucks to sweep out the place, that kind of thing. By the time we were in high school, we were working there after school, and then in college, we worked there in the summertime. After graduation, we saved enough money to buy our own boatyard. It was a dump, really, and it had almost nothing to recommend it, except that it was cheap." Smiling at the memory, he added, "But we didn't even know enough, at the time, to know how scared we should be."

"I'm guessing it was a success," Allie said, transfixed by what he was saying. Talking about his work, his usual reserve had fallen away. She'd never seen him so animated, so engaged. She remembered something Caroline had said about Walker. That he didn't seem like a man who did anything halfway. That was true of his work, obviously. Was it true of other things, too? She felt a warmth spreading through her. An anticipation. This was not about the wine, she knew. This was about Walker.

"You know what? It was a success," he was saying, when Allie's mind returned to the conversation. "We were young and dumb, but we were also incredibly hardworking. We turned that boatyard around. And the next one. And the one after that."

"How many of them do you own?"

"Twelve," Walker said, draining the last of the wine from his glass. "Twelve and counting."

"A boatyard empire?" Allie asked, only half joking.

"Maybe," Walker answered, with a shrug. "I honestly don't know. My brother, Reid, is completely driven. Our dad left when we were kids, and I think it hit Reid hard—harder than me, even. Now it's like he's got something to prove, except, by all rights, he should feel as if he's proved it already. But he's still not satisfied." He sighed. "I'm not sure he ever will be."

Allie was thoughtful, fiddling with the stem of her wineglass. "So your brother's trying to even some score with your dad. But what about you? What's your motivation?"

Walker thought about it. Then he smiled, almost shyly. "Honestly?"

She nodded.

"You've been out on the water on a perfect day, haven't you?"

"Many times," she said, smiling. Those days were her happiest childhood memories.

"Well, I have a theory," he said. "I don't care who you are or how many problems you have. I defy you to be in a boat out on the water on a perfect day and not be happy. Not just be totally, irrationally happy. At least that's how I always felt." He poured what was left in the wine bottle into her glass.

"So you're in the boat business for purely altruistic reasons?" Allie asked, teasingly.

"No, not quite," he admitted. "It's a business—and a living— but if I can help someone realize the dream of owning a boat, then obviously, that's the icing on the cake."

"About that dream," Allie said now. "I think I may be ready to take you up on your offer of selling us a boat."

"Good, because I think I've found the perfect boat for you two."

"Really?"

He nodded. "It's used, but it's in excellent condition. It's a twenty-foot Chris-Craft, and it's the perfect size and speed for this lake. I'd love for you to come in and see it. Or maybe we could even arrange to have it towed out here so you could take it out on the lake for a test-drive."

"Wyatt would be euphoric," Allie said.

"I can imagine," Walker said, smiling. "And it's a great all-around boat. You could even fish off it, if you wanted to."

Allie frowned.

"You're going to teach him how to fish, aren't you?" he asked, seriously, as if teaching a child how to fish was a moral obligation.

"I don't see anyone else volunteering," she joked. She didn't add that she'd already taught Wyatt how to tie his shoes, ride a bike, and swim. Teaching him to fish wouldn't be any harder than teaching him those things. Except for the part where you took the fish off the hook . . .

"I'll volunteer," Walker said, suddenly. "I don't know why I didn't think of it before. I go every Sunday morning at five thirty. I can pick him up at your dock—if you think he's ready, that is. He has to be able to wake up early. And sit still for long periods of time."

"Oh, I think he's ready," Allie said. She didn't think it. She knew it. "The getting up early won't be a problem, not if he's properly motivated. Same with the sitting still. He can be amazingly patient when the occasion calls for it."

"Good," he said, decisively. "Then let's do it. This Sunday morning."

"Why not?" she said, fighting a feeling of unease. Everything was happening so fast. *Too fast.* Or was it? Because what, exactly, had happened? Walker was taking her son fishing. That wasn't such a big deal, was it?

They lapsed into silence for a moment, and Allie drank the rest of her wine and set the empty glass on the table. When she looked up at Walker again, he was staring at her. No, not staring at her, not exactly. He was touching her, really, with his eyes. Touching her all over with them, the same way he had at the third of July party. And just like on that night, Allie felt something inside her pull tight, like a rubber band that was about to snap. She realized, then, that she'd forgotten to breathe, and she sucked in a little breath and stood up suddenly, almost knocking her chair over.

"I'll make the coffee," she mumbled, hurrying over to the kitchen counter and fumbling with the lid on the tin of coffee grounds. But when she pried it open and took the scoop out, her hands started shaking again, so much so that when she started to pour the grounds into the coffeemaker, she ended up spilling them on the counter.

"Here, let me do that," Walker said, beside her now and reaching for the scoop. His fingers brushed against hers as he took it from her, and Allie felt an almost adolescent thrill at his casual touch.

"Do you really want coffee?" he asked, gently.

She shook her head.

He dropped the scoop back into the coffee can and took her hand in both of his. Then he turned it over, palm up, and, holding her wrist with one hand, used one finger of the other hand to trace an imaginary line up the inside of her forearm, from her wrist up toward her elbow. Allie closed her eyes. Wherever his finger touched her skin, it felt as if it were burning. Which didn't explain why she suddenly shivered.

When his finger reached the hollow of her arm, opposite her elbow, he stopped. Then, still holding her hand, he bent slowly and kissed her lips, so lightly that Allie almost wondered if she were imagining it.

"What are you doing?" she whispered, opening her eyes.

"I'm doing what I should have done as soon as I got here," he said, in a low, throaty voice. "As soon as I saw you standing there in the driveway, looking so ridiculously beautiful." He kissed her again, and again. Maddeningly light kisses that barely left an impression on her lips and that left her whole body aching for more of them.

"Please," she said softly, without even knowing what she meant by it. But Walker knew. Letting go of her hand, his arms slid around her waist, and he backed her up, almost imperceptibly, against the kitchen counter. She thought it was probably a good thing that he'd given her something to lean on for support. Because when he bent to kiss her again, it was a different kiss altogether from the gentle, soft kisses he'd already given her. This kiss was demanding. Hungry and urgent. And when his tongue pushed into her mouth, she felt a hot, liquid sensation slide through her whole body.

Breathe, Allie, she told herself. *Just try to breathe normally.* But it was hard to concentrate on anything other than how this kiss was making her feel. She felt like her whole body was a tuning fork, and Walker's touch was making it sing.

She ran her hands around his waist and then, palms down, slid them up his back, feeling the warmth of his skin through the material of his shirt. She simultaneously pulled him closer and pressed herself harder against him. She wanted—*no, she needed*—to feel more with each passing second.

And she knew, suddenly, what needed to happen. His shirt needed to come off. She needed to feel his bare skin beneath her hands. So she slid her hands up under his shirt, up over his flat stomach and well-built chest, and then she slid her hands back down again, grabbed the hem of his shirt and, in one fluid motion, pulled it up over his head and let it drop to the kitchen floor.

There, she thought, pressing herself against his bare, sun-tanned skin, too absorbed in the moment to be surprised by her own behavior. She ran her hands over his chest again, over his shoulders and back. His skin was smooth and sun warmed, his chest lightly sprinkled with dark hair, and his shoulders were strong and muscular.

Walker, she knew, liked the way she was touching him. His breath came faster now, as his chest rose and fell more rapidly. She let her hands come to rest on his shoulders, tipped her chin up, and invited him to kiss her more deeply. He did, his tongue probing farther into her mouth in a way that made Allie's breath come faster, too.

Far away, though, in some still sane part of her brain, there was a warning straining to be heard. *Slow down, it's going too fast. Put the brakes on.*

But she paid no attention to it. She was too busy thinking about how good it felt. The holding, the kissing, the touching. *I've missed this*, she thought. *I need this.*

But just when she felt like their passion was reaching a tipping point, Walker seemed to pull back. To slow down. His grip on her loosened, and his lips left her mouth and traveled down her neck, coming to rest at the hollow at the base of her throat. It was an exquisitely sensitive place for Allie, and he seemed, intuitively, to know this. He brushed his lips over it, softly, slowly, with such deliberate gentleness that Allie practically squirmed with desire.

And as he was kissing her there, his hands moved to the front of her blouse and felt for the first of its many tiny buttons. He worked at them, patiently, unbuttoning one, then moving on to the next. When he'd unbuttoned several, she heard him give a little sigh of frustration.

"Too many buttons," he murmured, his breath warm against the nape of her neck.

Is this really happening? Allie wondered. Are we actually undressing each other? In my kitchen? And are we going to make love here? On the countertop? On the floor? It seemed incredible. But also, in some crazy way, possible.

She felt, for all the world, as if she was having an out-of-body experience. Not that she couldn't feel her body. God knows she could feel it—every single cell of it—but it was like someone else was temporarily inhabiting it. Someone who cared about one thing and one thing only: how amazing everything Walker was doing to her felt.

He finished unbuttoning her blouse and pulled it open, carefully, exposing her cream-colored, lacy bra and her suntanned cleavage. "Beautiful," he said softly, gazing down at her. He peeled back one side of her blouse and slid it down one shoulder, then started kissing that bare shoulder with exquisite tenderness.

Allie shivered again, violently, even though the night breeze coming in through the open kitchen windows was sultry and warm. She waited for Walker to take off her blouse, but instead he turned his attention back to her lips. The difference now, though, was that Allie could feel his bare chest through the filmy material of her bra. Her nipples hardened, almost painfully sensitive to the touch of him against her, and she pressed into him with a new, almost frantic hunger.

Walker groaned, low in his throat, and Allie knew he was finally losing his grip on control. It scared her a little, but it thrilled her even more. She knew the logical conclusion—or maybe the *illogical* conclusion—to their shared passion would be mind-shatteringly pleasurable. She just needed to let go, she told herself. She just needed to stop listening to that tiny alarm going off somewhere in her brain and relax. Relax and let it happen.

But no sooner had she told herself this, then a memory came to her, seemingly from out of nowhere. A memory that was so fully formed, so minutely rendered in every detail, that it was less like remembering something than being catapulted back to another time in her life. A heart-wrenching time in her life . . .

It was a warm night in late spring, a few nights before Gregg's National Guard Unit was deployed to Afghanistan, and Allie woke up to find his side of their bed empty. She sat up, immediately alert, and called out to him, but he didn't answer. Then she heard the familiar, rhythmic sound of someone dribbling a basketball. She got out of bed, walked over to the window, and looked out in time to see Gregg sink a basketball neatly into the basketball hoop in their driveway.

She left the window and went to check on Wyatt, sleeping soundly in his brand-new, toddler-sized bed. Then she padded, quietly, through the house and came out through the open garage door. She watched, unseen, while Gregg did a few more layups.

When she came out from the shadows and he saw her, he looked a little sheepish.

"I'm sorry," he said, coming over to her. "Did I wake you up?"

"No," she said, taking the basketball away from him. She let it roll off her hands, and then she folded herself into his arms and pressed her cheek against his sweat-dampened T-shirt. "You didn't wake me up. But you might wake up the neighbors."

"I know. I'll stop," he said, hugging her back.

"Are you okay?" she asked, looking up at him now.

"I don't know," he said, quietly. And then, "I've just been

thinking. And that's probably a mistake. I should be trying to *not* think now, right?"

"What were you thinking?" she asked, putting her cheek back on his chest. She was afraid to look at him. Afraid to know, really, what he'd been thinking about.

He didn't answer her right away. She listened to the sound of his breathing, to the sound of the crickets, to the whisper of a breeze in the trees.

"What if I don't come back?" he said, finally. "What if these next couple of nights are all the time we have left together?"

She tensed in his arms. "Of course you'll come back," she said, hugging him to her. "Of course we'll be together again."

She made him come back to bed then, and they made love to each other until the sun rose on their quiet suburban cul-de-sac. But neither of them was able to go back to sleep.

Suddenly, Allie felt Walker jerk away from her and the present come rushing back.

"What's wrong?" she asked, disoriented.

"I don't know what's wrong. You tell me," Walker said, breathing hard.

"Nothing . . . nothing's wrong," she said, feeling confused. It was strange, somehow, to find herself back in this kitchen with him. In her mind she had been so far away.

"One minute you were here. And the next minute, you were gone," he said, running his fingers through his hair.

"I . . . I was distracted," she admitted, her body already aching for his. "I'm sorry. I'm here now."

He hesitated, then shook his head. "You're not ready for this," he said, picking up his shirt from the kitchen floor and putting it back on.

"I *am* ready," Allie corrected him, automatically.

"Maybe physically," he said, reaching over and trying to button her blouse back up. "But not emotionally."

"That's not true," she said, tears springing into her eyes.

"Allie," he said, struggling with the buttons on her blouse. "How can you say you're ready when you're still wearing your wedding ring?"

She looked down at her finger. There it was, glowing softly in the kitchen light. The fact that she wearing it was indisputable. Incontrovertible. She sighed, shakily, and quickly wiped a tear away. She had no idea why she was crying.

Walker buttoned the last button on her blouse, his fingers unsteady, his breath still coming unevenly. Stopping now was hard for him, too, Allie realized. There was a part of him, a big part of him, that wanted to keep going. To see where this would take them.

"Stay," she said softly.

He shook his head, his blue eyes so dark they looked almost black. "God knows, I want to. But I wouldn't feel good about it later. And neither would you."

She nodded, dumbly. She had nothing to say to that. She knew he was right. She also knew she still wanted him so badly right now that she was experiencing the desire almost as a physical pain.

"I'm going to go," he said, almost apologetically. "But I meant what I said about taking Wyatt fishing. I'll pick him up at your dock Sunday morning. Five thirty sharp, okay?"

She nodded. But as he started to leave, something occurred to her.

"Walker?"

He stopped and came back.

"Walker, what about . . . what about us?" she asked, making a gesture that included both of them.

"Us?" he said. "Well, I guess 'us' will have to wait until you're ready."

She thought about this. It sounded straightforward enough. There was just one problem. "How will I know when I'm ready?" she asked, softly.

"I don't know," he said, honestly. "I guess you'll just know."

"And then I'll come to you and say, 'I'm ready'?" she asked, skeptically.

"Something like that," he said, with a half smile. He kissed her quickly on the forehead and then he was gone.

Allie felt suddenly weak. She sank down on the kitchen floor and sat there for a long time, fighting back more tears and considering the absurdity of the situation. She was trapped. Caught between two worlds. One—her marriage to Gregg—had ended. The other—her relationship with Walker—was poised to begin. But she wouldn't—*couldn't*—let it begin. Not now. Maybe not ever.

So much for baby steps, she thought, miserably, remembering Caroline's words.

CHAPTER 20

N eed help, buddy?" Walker asked.

Wyatt shook his head. "No, I got it," he said, frowning in concentration. He was holding a fishing hook in one hand and a wriggly pink worm in the other.

Ordinarily, Walker preferred to fish with lures, but he'd decided that fishing with live bait would be more exciting for someone Wyatt's age. What he hadn't counted on, though, was how hard it could be to get a worm on a hook when your hands were as small as Wyatt's. Not that Wyatt complained. He didn't. He just kept trying.

"It's harder than it looks," Walker said now, encouragingly. He marveled, once again, at Wyatt's determination to do everything by himself.

Wyatt pinched the worm tightly between his thumb and his index finger and guided the end of the hook through its midsection. "There," he said, with satisfaction, getting ready to cast off.

"Now, remember what I told you," Walker said, leaning forward in his seat.

Wyatt nodded, then put his rod over his right shoulder, and, after a slight wobble, cast his line over the water in an almost graceful arc. When his hook hit the water, the red-and-white bobber Walker had attached to the line floated on the surface. If a fish took the bait now, the bobber would bounce and slide on the water, alerting Wyatt to its location.

"And now we wait," Wyatt said solemnly, borrowing a phrase from Walker.

"Hopefully, not too long." Walker said, smiling and thinking, as he had for over a month of Sunday mornings now, what a cute kid Wyatt was.

Wyatt was sitting now in one of the two seats in Walker's fishing boat, dressed in a sweatshirt, blue jeans, a Minnesota Twins baseball cap, and red Converse sneakers. His chin was resting on the voluminous padding of the bright orange life preserver Walker had strapped him into, and his feet, which didn't reach the bottom of the boat, dangled off his seat.

This was one of the things that had surprised Walker the most about Wyatt, he reflected now. How small he was. All young children were small, of course. But it was one thing to observe their smallness from a distance, and another thing to see it up close and personal.

It made Walker feel protective of Wyatt in a way he'd never felt protective of anyone before. It made him take extra care in fastening the straps on Wyatt's life preserver, in helping him in and out of the boat, and in driving him around in the boat, too. Normally, Walker liked to drive fast. But with Wyatt beside him, he steered cautiously around the lake's bays and inlets. *Like an old man*, he thought. *Or like a father.*

But no sooner had he had that thought than he pushed it away.

Wyatt could do better than to have him for a father. Wyatt had *already* done better, he was sure. He wouldn't be such a sweet kid, Walker figured, if his dad hadn't been a nice guy. A guy who knew what Walker couldn't imagine knowing. Namely, how to be somebody's father.

But if Walker didn't have what it took to be a dad, he figured he could at least begin by being something else to a young child. A coach, for instance. Or maybe just a friend.

And that, probably, was what had surprised him the most about Wyatt. How much being with him felt like being with a friend. The kid, it turned out, was surprisingly good company.

For one thing, he never complained. Not about the early hour they went fishing. Not about being tired. (Although Walker had seen him yawn, discreetly, and even rub his eyes when he thought Walker wasn't looking.) And he never complained about being cold, either, despite the frequent early morning chill on the lake. He also didn't complain about having to sit still, something Walker had thought would be the most challenging part of these mornings for him.

Instead, he soaked up everything Walker taught him like a little sponge. He learned quickly. Amazingly quickly. And far from asking questions all the time, something Walker had assumed all children did, he asked them only occasionally. And when he did ask them, they seemed to Walker to be unusually intelligent and perceptive questions. Although here again, Walker was struck by how little he knew about children. Maybe Wyatt was a typical five-year-old boy. But he didn't really believe that. He seemed too exceptional, somehow, to be anything close to ordinary.

"Look!" Wyatt said now, interrupting his thoughts. He was pointing at his bobber, sliding sideways on the water's surface.

"Hey, you got a bite," Walker said. He wanted to help him, but he reminded himself that Wyatt didn't want any help. Still, he couldn't resist the urge to coach him a little.

"Okay, not too fast. No sudden movements. You want to keep him on the line."

Wyatt nodded, resolutely, and started to turn the reel, slowly but steadily.

"He's coming in," Wyatt said, his excitement momentarily breaking through his seriousness. "He's still on the line."

"Nice work," Walker said, as the line tugged the bobber across the water. When it got close enough, both Walker and Wyatt could see the fish's silver scales flashing below the surface of the green water.

"Okay, now for the hard part," Walker said, feeling suddenly tense. He didn't want Wyatt to lose the fish now, not when it was so close. It had happened once before, and while Wyatt had survived, he'd been disappointed.

But Wyatt didn't lose this fish. He finished reeling it in, reached for the line with both hands, and lifted it out of the water.

"You caught a smallmouth bass. That's not easy to do in this lake," Walker said, approvingly. "It looks like it's about six inches long."

Wyatt brought the fish into the boat and beamed at it as it thrashed energetically on the end of the line. But after a moment he looked up at Walker and frowned, understanding dawning on his face. "It's not big enough to keep, is it?"

Walker shook his head. "It's still pretty small for a smallmouth bass. It's got some growing left to do. It'll be about twice that size by the time it's done."

Wyatt looked wistful. But only for a second. "I'll throw him back," he said, then jumped a little when the fish flailed again on the other end of the line he was still holding.

"Okay, this part I am going to help you with," Walker said, reaching for the fish. "Remember, if you hold it the wrong way, the gills are sharp enough to cut your hand. And taking the hook out is tricky, too."

"Watch how I do it, though," Walker said, reaching for the fish with both hands. "Because next time, you're going to do it by yourself." He gripped the fish carefully in one hand, while he eased the hook out of its mouth with the other. Then he tossed the fish back into the water. Wyatt leaned over and watched it, hovering, just below the lake's surface, before it swam swiftly away.

"Do you think he's all right?" he asked Walker, frowning.

"Absolutely," Walker said. "He'll probably live for many more years. Unless, of course, *you* catch him again one day." He winked at Wyatt.

"Do you think he has a family?" Wyatt asked then, his brown eyes questioning.

"I know he does," Walker answered, seriously. "A big family. With lots and lots of siblings. But I don't think they really know each other. At least, not the way we know the people we're related to."

He waited for Wyatt to rebait his hook, but Wyatt instead kept looking out over the water in the same direction the fish had swum in. And he looked so sad, Walker realized, with surprise. His brown eyes were shiny, as if with tears, and his lower lip was jutting out in a way that managed to seem tragic and sweet at the same time. He wondered if Wyatt was going to cry, and, if he did, if he'd know how to comfort him. *Talk about being out of my comfort zone,* Walker thought. Because what could be more terrifying, really, than the prospect of consoling a tearful child?

But Wyatt didn't cry. He just kept looking sad. And Walker,

feeling helpless, tried to think what it was that was making him feel that way. Was he anxious that he'd hurt the fish? Or was he unhappy because, unlike the fish, he didn't have any siblings?

But when Wyatt spoke, finally, it had nothing to do with the fish. "Do you know how to play basketball?" he asked Walker, looking back up at him.

"Basketball?" Walker repeated, surprised. "Um, yeah," he said, after a moment. "I do. I played on a team in high school. Since then, though, it's just been the occasional pickup game. I'm probably not very good at it anymore." Then he asked, conversationally, "How about you? Do you know how to play basketball?"

Wyatt nodded. "Uh-huh," he said. "But I don't get that many chances to play anymore. I'm probably not as good as I used to be, either."

Walker did his best not to smile. "Well, what about watching basketball games on TV?" he asked Wyatt. "Do you ever do that? Not that that's the same as playing, but it can still be pretty exciting."

Wyatt's face brightened momentarily. "We just got cable TV," he said, "so maybe I can watch basketball now." But then another thought occurred to him and his face clouded over. "I have to ask my mom, though. She doesn't let me watch that much TV. She says it's bad for my brain."

"Well, she's probably right about that," Walker said, smiling. "But maybe when basketball season starts, she'll let you come over to my cabin and watch a game with me." He almost added that his television set, unlike the ancient model he'd seen in Wyatt's living room, was a seventy-inch flatscreen. But he was afraid that would qualify as bribery, especially when he'd probably overstepped his boundaries already. Allie had said he could take Wyatt fishing, not invite him over to watch television.

"I'd like to go to your cabin again," Wyatt said, his face alight with anticipation. "Because when we went there that night of the storm, I was mostly asleep. And you know what? I bet my mom wouldn't even say no to my going. She can be kind of strict sometimes, about stuff like brushing teeth. But she's not really mean or anything."

Walker tried, again, not to smile. "No, I don't think she's mean. But I'll still have to ask her about it first, okay? After all, she is the boss."

Wyatt nodded, satisfied, and started to reach for the lid of the Styrofoam cooler that Walker stored the bait in. But then he stopped and turned back to Walker.

"My dad was teaching me how to play basketball when he went away," he said.

"Oh," Walker said, not sure what else to say. The subject of Wyatt's father had never come up before, and now that it had, he felt himself tensing involuntarily. *Coward,* he told himself. Still, he wondered, what did Wyatt know, and not know, about his father's death?

But Wyatt didn't notice his uneasiness. "He didn't have time to teach me everything," he said. "But he showed me how to do a layout."

"A lay*up*?" Walker corrected him, automatically, and then was irritated at himself for correcting him. What difference did it make what Wyatt called it? He knew what he'd been talking about.

But Wyatt was unfazed. He nodded. "He was teaching me how to do a lay*up*," he said.

"And you remember that?" Walker asked, gently.

"Uh-huh," Wyatt said, nodding emphatically.

Was that even possible? Walker wondered. If his father had died over two years ago, then Wyatt would have been three, at most, when he'd shipped out. Maybe even younger. Could he remember back that far? Walker tried to remember how old he'd been at the time of his earliest childhood memory, but he came up empty. Maybe, he thought, that was just as well.

But he realized then that Wyatt was looking at him expectantly. As if he was waiting for Walker to say something. But what? He was definitely out of his depth here. And then Wyatt surprised him again.

"My dad died," he said to Walker, matter-of-factly. "He was in a war."

"I know that," Walker said. "And I'm sorry," he added, realizing, for the first time in his life, how truly inadequate those two words were.

"That's okay," Wyatt said, and then, much to Walker's surprise, Wyatt reached over and patted his hand. He'd never done anything like that before and, for a second, Walker was so surprised he didn't know what to do. Or say. It was such a small gesture, but it spoke volumes about the kind of kid Wyatt was. How gentle he was, and how sweet.

Walker swallowed past something hard in his throat and did the only thing he could think of to do. He reached over and tugged down on the visor of Wyatt's baseball cap until it covered his chocolate brown eyes, and then he pulled it up again until Wyatt's brown eyes came back into view. Wyatt smiled happily at him, and Walker was reminded, suddenly, of the child he and Caitlin might have had together. He felt a dull ache, then, somewhere behind his chest, as he realized, for the first time, that what he'd always considered to be Caitlin's loss had been his loss, too.

In that same instant, though, he felt a decisive tug on the end of his line. "Hey, buddy," he said, to a still-smiling Wyatt, "I think I'm going to need your help."

An hour later, Walker was steering the boat back to Allie and Wyatt's dock. The sun had burned through the early morning mist by now, and the lake's surface, which had been a pale gray when they'd left earlier that morning, was now a deep blue. It was going to be a hot day, but right now it was perfect. Golden and warm, but with a hint of the night's coolness and freshness still left in the air.

"I bet you're hungry," Walker said, as Wyatt's dock came into view.

"I'm starving," Wyatt agreed cheerfully.

Walker squinted across the water. No sign of Allie yet. She didn't usually come out to the dock until she heard his boat pull up. He'd come to savor those moments, when he picked Wyatt up or dropped him off. They were the only times he saw Allie all week, and they were too brief. But he had to be satisfied with them. They were all that he had of her, and they always kept him going for another seven days. He was like an engine running on fumes, but instead of fumes, he was running on hope. Hope that sometime soon they'd have more than these handoffs of Wyatt, more than the few quick words they exchanged about the weather, the fishing conditions, or the thermos of coffee she always made for him.

As he coasted up to the dock now, he saw Allie come out of the cabin, drying her hands on a dish towel. He waved to her, and she waved back. He cut the engine and angled the boat so that it bumped gently against the end of the dock.

"Hi, Mom!" Wyatt called out, as Walker tied up the boat.

"Hi, sweetie," Allie called back, taking the stone path that led down to the dock.

Wyatt scrambled out of the boat now, and, for once, Walker didn't remind him to be careful. He watched as Wyatt ran down the dock, meeting Allie halfway, and he watched as Allie scooped him up into her arms and gave him a big hug. No sooner had she done that, though, then she wrinkled her nose and held him away from her.

"Wyatt," she said, laughing as she set him down, "did you catch fish or did you roll around in them?"

"We caught them," he said, proudly.

"That's wonderful," Allie said, rumpling his hair. "But maybe you should take a shower before you come to the breakfast table. Why don't you go put your clothes in the hamper and I'll come and run the water for you, okay?"

He nodded and, his enthusiasm undiminished, ran up to the cabin.

"Good morning," she said to Walker, coming out to the end of the dock.

"Good morning," Walker said, trying not to gawk at her. It was hard, though. She was wearing a sleeveless blouse and blue jean cutoffs, both of which showed off a delicious amount of bare, suntanned skin. She'd left her honey-gold hair out of its customary ponytail, and it fell, straight and shiny, to her shoulders.

"Wyatt didn't thank you," she said, apologetically, coming to a stop in front of his boat. Her two perfect knees were right at his eye level.

"He thanked me," he assured her.

"Well, I'd like to thank you, too," she said.

"That's not necessary," he said, unhooking his boat. He would have loved to stay and talk, but he knew Wyatt was waiting for her in the cabin.

"It *is* necessary," she corrected him. "And, if you have time this morning, I was hoping you'd let me return the favor and cook breakfast for you."

He held on to the end of the dock. "Are you sure?" he asked.

She smiled down at him. "Absolutely," she said. "It's the least I can do. I heard in town that good fishing guides can charge up to a hundred dollars an hour."

"I never claimed to be a professional," he said, hooking his boat up again. "But I'd love a cup of coffee."

He climbed out of the boat and walked with her up to the cabin.

"Why don't you wash up at the kitchen sink?" she suggested, when they got to the front porch.

"That'd be great," he said, following her into her sunny, delicious-smelling kitchen and scrubbing up at the sink.

"Here," she said, when he'd dried his hands on a dish towel. She handed him a steaming mug of coffee and an enormous blueberry muffin wrapped in a checked napkin. "Why don't you take these out on the porch? They'll tide you over until breakfast is ready, and you can try out the new porch swing I bought at the hardware store. I'd join you, but I have to make sure that Wyatt remembers to use soap in the shower."

"Is it possible he won't?" he asked, amused.

"It's entirely possible," Allie said, and she smiled at him, almost shyly, before she left the kitchen.

Her shyness was adorable, Walker thought, taking his coffee and muffin out on the porch. And oddly enough, it had the opposite effect on him that it should have had. It should have made him feel more reserved around her. Instead, though, it made him want to kiss her. Or, more accurately, ravage her. But Allie, he thought regretfully, wasn't on the breakfast menu this morning.

So he sat on the porch swing and drank his coffee, which was good and strong and laced with half-and-half, and he ate his muffin, which was buttery, warm, and full of fresh blueberries. Had she and Wyatt picked them together? he wondered, lounging on the swing. He imagined them doing it and wished somehow he could have been with them.

He was still sitting there, still thinking about them, when Allie poked her head out of the cabin. "Breakfast is ready," she said. He followed her into the kitchen, carrying his empty coffee cup. Her blouse, he saw, was slightly damp from supervising Wyatt's shower, and it clung to her appealingly. Her hair, too, had gotten a little wet in the humid bathroom, and it curled slightly at the ends.

"You'd probably like more coffee," she said, reaching for his cup and refilling it from the coffeepot. "Cream's on the table," she added, handing it back to him.

"Thanks," he said, glancing over at the kitchen table. It was covered with a faded, flowered tablecloth, and in the center of it was a bunch of white asters in a water-filled Mason jar. The flowers, he noticed, looked fresh enough to have been picked that morning. And they were dappled with the sunlight streaming in through the kitchen windows.

"I hope you're hungry," Allie said, placing a carafe of orange juice on the table, along with a whole basket of blueberry muffins.

"I am," Walker assured her, watching as she picked up a pair of pot holders, opened the oven door, and carefully removed a cast-iron frying pan from it, setting it on a trivet on the table.

"I made a frittata," she explained, as its delicious odor filled the kitchen.

"A free-what?" Wyatt asked, coming into the kitchen. He had a freshly scrubbed look about him, and his normally curly hair was combed wetly down.

"A frittata," Allie said, gesturing for them to sit down at the table.

Wyatt slid into his seat, staring suspiciously at the egg dish in the center of the table.

"Don't worry," Allie said, cutting a wedge of it and putting it on his plate. "You'll like it."

He put a forkful of it into his mouth, chewed, and swallowed. "Oh, it's just eggs," he said, with obvious relief.

Walker and Allie both laughed, as they helped themselves to it, too.

"By the way," Walker said, between bites, "Cliff Donahue told me how much you two liked the boat you test-drove." Earlier in the week, Cliff had towed a boat out to Butternut Lake and met Allie and Wyatt at the boat ramp there. Then he'd taken them out for a ride, giving Allie an opportunity to drive the boat, too. Walker had deliberately left himself out of the equation. He didn't want Allie to feel that there were any strings attached.

"We loved the boat," Allie said, refilling Walker's empty orange juice glass. "It ran beautifully. I just can't believe how reasonably priced it is."

"That it is," Walker agreed, thinking that, if he was lucky, he'd just about break even on that sale.

After that, the two of them ate in silence. Wyatt, on the other hand, chatted merrily away, but without really asking for or needing their input. Walker wasn't really listening to what he was saying anyway. Instead, he was savoring the moment. So ordinary somehow. But so unordinary too. They were like any family, he thought. Except, of course, that they weren't a family. But still, this must be what it was like to be a part of a family. A real family. A *happy* family.

"Can I be excused?" Wyatt asked, when he'd eaten two pieces of frittata and a huge blueberry muffin. Once again, he'd surprised Walker. How could anyone that small eat so much?

"You may be excused," Allie said. "Just take your plate to the sink." Wyatt carried his plate to the sink and went into the living room where he immediately started constructing new track for his train set.

"Can I help you clean up?" Walker asked Allie.

"Sure," she said. Together, they cleared the table and washed the dishes, Allie washing while he dried. It had never occurred to him before that there was anything sensual about washing dishes. But watching her bare, brown arms submerged to the elbows in hot soapy water was making him rethink this. So was the way she accidentally brushed against him when she reached up to put the dry dishes back in the cupboard. He was actually disappointed when they were finished with this chore.

"Well, you've probably got things to do," she said then, almost apologetically.

Just work, Walker thought. *And since I met you that's been a hell of a lot less interesting than it used to be.*

But he shrugged and said, "Not really."

"No?" she said, looking mildly surprised.

And he almost asked her then if he could stay, stay and spend the rest of the day with them. But he stopped himself. She was supposed to tell him when she was ready for more. And that had seemed reasonable to him when they'd agreed to it that night in her kitchen. The only problem was that now he was beginning to wonder when exactly she'd be ready for more. And how much longer he could realistically wait for her to be ready without going out of his mind.

"Well, I think you've given us enough of your time for one day," Allie said, smiling. "Come on, I'll walk you to your boat."

He said good-bye to Wyatt, who was lying on his stomach and pushing a train along the tracks, and followed Allie out onto the porch. Then he did something totally unexpected. Not only from her perspective, but from his, too. He took her in his arms, and leaning her up against the cabin wall, to the right of the door where they'd be out of view of Wyatt, he kissed her.

Softly, at first. Then harder. She tensed, slightly, with surprise, but after a moment, he felt her body relax into his arms, felt her lips start to move against his. Hesitantly, at first, and then with less inhibition.

Be gentle, a voice inside him warned. But he didn't heed it. He couldn't. He'd spent so many hours imagining this. This and more. Much more. So that now that he was actually holding her, and kissing her, and touching her, he couldn't quite control himself. He knew he was holding her a little too tightly and kissing her a little too hard, and he would have apologized, too, if he could have stopped kissing her long enough to do it.

But that was assuming, of course, that she wanted him to stop kissing her. Which she obviously didn't. Because once she recovered from her surprise, she kissed him back as hungrily as he was kissing her. She was full of surprises that way, he knew. Beneath the reticence, and the shyness, was an urgency and a passion he'd barely scratched the surface of. When they did make love—and they *would* make love—it would change both of them forever. It wouldn't be something that either of them would casually dismiss or forget. It would be something that burned itself into both of them, emotionally and physically.

He slid his hands, now, into the back pockets of her denim cutoffs and pulled her against him. Hard. A little groan escaped from her throat, and she broke away from him.

"*What are you doing?*" she asked, breathlessly, her eyes wide with astonishment. But she didn't look angry. She looked like someone who knew she was veering dangerously close to losing control.

"I'm kissing you," he murmured, kissing her again.

But she pushed him, gently but firmly, away.

"That wasn't a kiss," she pointed out, still trying to catch her breath.

He laughed. "What was it then?" he asked, leaning in again and nuzzling her neck.

"That was making love with our clothes on."

Now it was his turn to groan a little. Just hearing her say those words managed to arouse him even more than he was already aroused. "I don't know if that's possible," he murmured, kissing the hollow of her neck. "But I'm willing to try."

She sighed softly, and he pulled back far enough to look at her. Her hair was tousled, her eyes were warm and liquid, and her lips were slightly parted. He imagined picking her up, carrying her into the cabin, laying her down on her bed, and making love to her. Over and over and over again. There was nothing stopping him from doing exactly that, either, except for that little boy inside the cabin, playing with his train set.

He took a step back, putting a safe, or maybe just a *safer,* distance between them. "Sorry about that," he said, running his fingers through his hair. "I got a little carried away."

"That makes two of us," Allie said, and he could tell she was concentrating on breathing normally. He leaned in again and he kissed her, softly, on the lips. Then he went back down to the dock, got into his boat, unhitched it, and drove it back across the bay to his boathouse.

And the whole time, he knew she was still standing there, still leaning against the outside wall of the cabin for support, still wearing that dazed expression on her face. He didn't know how he knew it. He just did. And he would have staked his life on its being true.

CHAPTER 21

On an unseasonably cool Saturday night in mid-August, Allie found herself in an unusual position for the mother of a five-year-old child: She had nothing to do, and no one to do it with.

Wyatt's last sleepover at Caroline's had been such a success that she'd invited him to do it again. Wyatt, of course, had been beside himself with excitement. Allie, though, had been less so. She loved the fact that Wyatt and Caroline had grown so close over the course of the summer. But what she didn't love was having to figure out how to spend a whole evening by herself. Once, she'd been good at being alone. Lately, though, being alone meant only one thing. No, make that two things. Thinking about Walker Ford and trying *not* to think about Walker Ford.

Of course, she didn't just think about him when she was alone. She thought about him all the time. But when she was with other people—with a customer at the Pine Cone Gallery or with Wyatt at the cabin, for instance—it was easier to keep her mind occupied. And that was a good thing, because when her mind was unoccupied, and free to wander, it always wandered right over to Walker.

She shivered now, sitting on a deck chair at the end of the dock and wondering if the chilly night air was just a rare summer cold snap or a harbinger of the fast-approaching autumn. After she'd come back from driving Wyatt to Caroline's, she'd pulled on an oversized wool sweater, poured herself a glass of white wine, and come down to the lake, ostensibly to enjoy the view of the sunset, but, in reality, to watch Walker's cabin across the bay.

It was pathetic, she knew, to act this way. Like a sixteen-year-old girl with an unrequited crush. But she couldn't help herself. Or didn't *want* to help herself. One or the other.

Either way, she often found herself, at odd moments of the day and night, looking across the bay at Walker's dock and boathouse, and at the cabin perched on the bluff above them. Usually, she tried to justify doing this by doing something else at the same time. She'd be hanging wet bathing suits and towels on a clothesline she'd strung behind the cabin, for instance, and she'd be glancing casually over at Walker's dock at the same time. Or she'd be reading a bedtime story to Wyatt and every time she turned a page she'd look out the window at his distant dock light, glowing softly in the dusky twilight.

For all the time she spent looking across the bay at his cabin, though, she'd never been able to see Walker there. It was simply too far away. Even her twenty-twenty vision wasn't that good. Once, she'd thought about getting out the old binoculars she knew were on the top shelf of the hall closet. But she'd decided that would be crossing a line, a line between idle daydreaming and premeditated stalking.

Still, when she watched his cabin at night, she'd wonder if he was there, and what he was doing if he was. And she'd wonder, too, much to her annoyance, if he was alone or if he was with someone else. Someone else who happened to be a woman. Because while Walker had told her he'd wait for her to be ready, he'd stopped short of saying he wouldn't see other women while he waited for her to be ready.

And why shouldn't he see other women? Allie asked herself, during the rare moment she felt capable of considering the question logically. After all, she hadn't asked him *not* to see other women, and she hadn't given him any reason to believe she'd be ready for him anytime soon, either. So what was he supposed to do, take a vow of celibacy?

Yes, a voice inside her answered. An admittedly irrational voice. *That's exactly what he's supposed to do.* If for no other reason than the thought of him with another woman filled her with a white-hot jealousy. And, as an aftertaste of that, an aching sadness. Sadness that she could want something so badly and still not let herself have it.

She shivered again now and thought about getting a blanket from the house. Or maybe just calling it a night and going inside. She'd been sitting here for a couple of hours already. The sun had set, darkness had fallen, and the temperature had gone from pleasantly cool to uncomfortably cold. And she was still sitting here. A sensible person would go back to the cabin now and take a bath, or get in bed with a good book, but she was way beyond sensible. So she stayed put and watched the light at the end of Walker's dock.

Tonight, like most nights, the dock light had come on at nine o'clock. She wondered if he had it set to a timer. It wouldn't surprise her if he did. It was the kind of thing that would never occur to her, but Walker would do it as a matter of course. He was logical. Practical. Organized. But he was also attractive, she mused. Attractive and incredibly, maddeningly, crazily sexy.

She replayed their last kiss, on the front porch of her cabin last Sunday morning, and she felt her desire for him slowly envelop her, like the real, palpable thing it had become. Then she imagined that desire traveling over the black, rippled surface of the nighttime lake and finding Walker, wherever he was and whatever he was doing, and wrapping itself around him, softly at first, and then more tightly.

Now you're really getting crazy, she thought, impatiently. *Now you really need to go inside and go to bed.* But still, she didn't move. And in a little while, it became clear to her why she didn't move. Tonight was going to be different. Tonight she was going to answer the question she kept asking herself. Why didn't she go to him? Just get up and go to him? There was no obvious reason why she shouldn't. They were both adults. Both available. Both free to enter into a relationship with each other. She needed to consider Wyatt, of course, but she *had* considered Wyatt. Wyatt adored Walker. Trusted Walker. And loved being with him.

So why was she still sitting here, shivering, when she could be spending the next twelve hours in Walker's arms, making blissful, uninterrupted love?

She didn't need to look very far for the answer to this question. It was on the ring finger of her left hand. A thin, gold band she'd worn for eight years. Six years during which she and Gregg had been married, and another two years—no, more than two years, two years, four months, and ten days—during which she'd been widowed.

She'd tried taking it off before. Just recently, she'd taken it off several times. But she always ended up putting it back on again.

Without it, her ring finger felt naked. And she felt uncomfortable. Incomplete. Like she was missing a limb, instead of a ring.

Worse yet, if she left it off long enough, she felt the same way she'd felt after she and Walker had kissed each of those times. She felt as if she was being unfaithful to Gregg, or at least to his memory.

Now, she thought about what Gregg would have wanted for her. Would he have wanted her to be alone? she asked herself. But she knew, in a heartbeat, he wouldn't have. He hadn't been selfish. He'd been the opposite of selfish. He would have wanted her life to go on after his ended. And not just go on but be full of love and happiness.

So why couldn't she take the ring off? She twisted it impatiently on her finger, but she didn't take it off. That was going to be hard for her, she knew. To take it off and keep it off. It might even be the hardest thing she'd had to do yet. Not that the other things hadn't been hard, too. Telling Wyatt his father wasn't coming back. Attending Gregg's funeral. Packing up his belongings . . .

She paused now, remembering something. She'd never admitted this to anyone, but even after she'd sold their house, and even after she and Wyatt had moved out of it, she hadn't been able to give Gregg's things away. She'd saved everything, from the trivial—unopened disposable razors—to the mundane—white athletic socks, freshly bleached and neatly rolled into pairs. She'd packed everything with meticulous care, in neatly labeled cardboard boxes, and put it in a rented storage unit. And she'd never really asked herself why. Until tonight.

She bit her lower lip now, concentrating. Why would she do that? Why would she keep all his things unless . . . *unless.* She sat perfectly still. She didn't even breathe. She was right on the edge of something, right at the brink of some discovery. Something so simple but at the same time so difficult for her to understand.

And then it came to her. The reason she'd kept all his things was because, on some level, she didn't really believe he was gone. She didn't really believe he wasn't coming back.

But he is gone, she told herself now. *He isn't coming back.* Not now. Not ever. Their life together was over. Forever. And the only thing she and Wyatt had left of Gregg were their memories of him.

She waited for something to happen. Something dramatic. Cataclysmic, even. She waited for a bolt of lightning to strike a nearby tree or a crack of thunder to rend the night sky. But nothing happened. Or rather, *everything* happened. But it happened in her heart and in her head. And as shocking as her discovery was to her, the rest of the world continued exactly as it had been before.

She didn't know how long she'd been sitting there when she suddenly stood up and walked, unsteadily, back to the cabin. She let herself in, went straight to her bedroom, and took a photo box out of her bottom dresser drawer. This was where she kept the part of her and Gregg's life she couldn't bear to put in storage.

She sat down on the edge of the bed now and forced herself to go through the box, one item at a time. There was a picture of her and Gregg taken during their freshman year of college, looking impossibly young and happy. There was an invitation to their wedding, five years later. There was a letter Gregg had written her after he'd left her and Wyatt at the hospital, the night after Wyatt was born. In it, he told her how much he loved them both, and he promised to be the best father to Wyatt he could possibly be. There was another photograph, this one of a two-and-a-half-year-old Wyatt sitting on Gregg's shoulders right before they left for their first Minnesota Twins game together. Of course, as it turned out, it would also be their last one together.

There was another letter, too, this one from a man in Gregg's National Guard unit, written after Gregg had been killed. In it, he told Allie how brave Gregg had been and how concerned he'd been for the welfare of the other men in his unit. It had been an honor to serve with him, he wrote.

There were many other things in the box, too. Some silly—a cocktail napkin from the pub Gregg had taken Allie to on their first date in college—and some deadly serious—Gregg's National Guard dog tags. But Allie made herself go through the whole box, examining every photograph and reading every letter and document.

When she was done, she felt exhausted. She put the items back in the box and put the box away, minus the photograph of Gregg and Wyatt. That she propped up on her dresser. Tomorrow, she'd buy a frame for it and put it someplace where she and Wyatt would see it often. Just because it hurt her to look at it didn't mean it should be banished to a bottom drawer.

Then, Allie took off her wedding ring. Slipped it right off her ring finger and put it in her jewelry box, where she knew it belonged now. As she did so, she caught sight of herself in the mirror hanging above the dresser and was surprised to see that her face was streaked with tears. She hadn't even been aware that she'd been crying.

She walked to the bathroom, splashed cold water on her face, and patted it dry with a hand towel. Then she ran a hairbrush through her tangled hair. After that, she went straight to her handbag, which was sitting where she'd left it on the kitchen table. It had everything she needed in it. Wallet, keys, and her brand-new cell phone, with local coverage, which she'd given

Caroline the number to tonight. She checked to see that it was fully charged. It was. She turned it to ring, so she'd hear it if Caroline needed to reach her for any reason.

Then she turned the cabin's lights off and locked the front door. She got into the car, turned on the ignition, and started driving. It was surreal how calm she felt. Not a flicker of anxiety. Not a twinge of nervousness. It was only when she turned into Walker's driveway that she felt a little pulse of excitement. She parked next to his pickup, walked up to the cabin's front door, and rang the doorbell.

Silence. Then footsteps. Then, after what seemed an eternity, Walker opened the door.

"Allie?" he said, surprised. He was wearing jeans and a T-shirt. There was rock music playing on a stereo in the background, and she could see a half-empty glass of red wine sitting on a nearby table. He looked like a man planning on spending a relaxing night at home alone. But he didn't look disappointed to see her. Far from it.

"I'm ready," Allie said, simply.

There were, she supposed, a million things he could have done at that moment, but what he did was smile at her, pull her into his arms, and close the door behind her.

CHAPTER 22

Where's Wyatt?" he asked, wrapping his arms around her.
"He's at Caroline's," she said, twining her arms around
his neck and kissing him, full on the lips, without any inhibition.

He kissed her back for a few delicious moments. But then he
reluctantly broke away from her and, holding her at arm's length,
looked at her strangely. As if he'd never seen her before.

"What's wrong?" she asked, feeling a tiny flicker of anxiety.
Her coming here tonight had felt so right to her. But what if it
didn't feel right to him?

"Nothing's wrong," he said, reaching up and gently stroking
her cheek. "I just can't believe you're actually here."

"It's okay, isn't it?"

"Are you kidding?" he said. "I feel like I've won the lottery."

She laughed.

"But, Allie, can I ask you something?" he asked.

She nodded and made a conscious effort to pay attention to
whatever he would say next. She wanted him so badly right now
that it was hard to concentrate on anything else.

"What happened? I mean, between the last time I saw you and tonight?"

"Nothing," she said, simply. "Nothing and everything."

He raised his eyebrows.

"I realized I was ready," she added.

He reached for her hand and held it up to the light.

"No wedding ring," he said quietly, running his fingers up and down her bare finger. She shivered. Even his most innocuous touch was enough to excite her.

"No wedding ring," she agreed. "I took it off tonight. For good."

"Are you sure about this?" he asked, giving her a penetrating look.

"Positive," she said. "I'll tell you all about it later. I promise. But I didn't come here to talk." Then, surprising herself, she went on, "At least not right away. There's something else I want to do first." And she kissed him again, just in case there was any doubt in his mind about what she meant.

He drew back again. Then he pulled her closer. "Now I *really* feel like I've won the lottery," he said, nuzzling her neck.

She laughed. "Does that mean you're going to invite me in?" she asked. They were still standing in the vestibule inside the front door of his cabin.

"Oh, yeah. Of course. I forgot," he said, hugging her tightly and planting a kiss on her forehead. "I'm sorry. I'm not being a very good host, am I?" He led her, by the hand, into the cabin's living room. There was a fire burning in the fireplace, she saw.

"Can I get you something to drink?" he asked.

"Sure. Whatever you're having."

He kissed her again and left the room. She wandered over to the fireplace, already missing him. When he came back, he handed her a glass of red wine, and she took a sip. It was delicious, but she wasn't really in the mood for it. If there was one thing she didn't need tonight, it was liquid courage.

She put her glass of wine down on the mantelpiece, and he took her in his arms again.

"The fire's a nice touch," she said, kissing his neck.

"Remember, I didn't know you were coming," he pointed out.

She smiled, and they kissed for a while. Bruce Springsteen played in the background, and a log occasionally cracked and popped in the fireplace.

Kissing Walker, Allie knew, was never an end in and of itself. The more they kissed, the more she wanted. Walker, apparently, felt the same way, because the next thing she knew, he'd placed a hand on either side of her waist and lifted her up. She wrapped her legs around his waist and tightened her grip around his neck, taking his tongue farther into her mouth.

Any self-consciousness she'd ever felt with him was gone now, completely melted away. Her only concern, in fact, as weeks of unwavering denial gave way to frantic desire, was that she couldn't hold him tightly enough, couldn't kiss him deeply enough, couldn't feel every single inch of his body against every single inch of her body.

She plucked, impatiently, at his shirt, then tugged with equal impatience at the waistband of his jeans. It seemed unfair, somehow, that his clothes wouldn't simply fall off like she needed them to. Taking them off, she realized, was going to be far too time-consuming.

"Allie," he murmured, breaking away from their kiss and speaking into the hollow of her neck. "Allie, should I get some . . . um, protection?"

Protection? she wondered. Oh, of course. *Protection.* It had been a long time since she'd had to worry about that.

"I forgot all about that," she admitted. "Can you . . . uh, take care of that?"

"Absolutely," he said.

"That'd be great," she said, pulling off his T-shirt and running her hands over his bare chest. *But it better be close by,* she added to herself. *Because if I have to wait much longer, I think I'll go crazy.*

"And, uh, as far as my history goes," he continued, obviously distracted by her hands moving greedily over his chest. "I haven't been with anyone recently. I saw my doctor, too, at the beginning of the summer, and everything was fine. I think, when I saw him, I was hoping against hope that something might happen between us, and I wanted to be ready." Running his lips along her earlobe, he added, "In retrospect, I think I might have been a little overconfident about the whole thing."

"Not *over*confident, it turns out. Just confident enough." Allie smiled, pulling him closer. "And as for my history, Walker, it's pretty simple. Just Gregg. No one before him. And no one after him, either."

Walker, surprised, pulled back slightly, and stared at her quizzically.

"Are you . . . are you saying that your husband was the only man you've ever been with?"

"Until now," Allie said, unbuttoning the button on his blue jeans and marveling that Walker didn't seem even slightly tired from holding her. "If it's not too presumptuous of me to assume we're going to make love tonight," she added, kissing his neck.

"It's not presumptuous," Walker said, in a qualifying tone. "But I'd be lying if I said I wasn't a little intimidated by the fact that you've only been with one other man. Someone you loved so much. It's a tough act to follow."

"Don't think of it that way," Allie said, stroking his cheek. But Walker looked suddenly indecisive. She knew he wasn't a man who typically suffered from a lack of confidence, not to mention paralyzing self-doubt. But she didn't want him to overthink this, either. And she knew only one way to distract him. Fortunately, it was a pretty good way.

So she tightened her legs around his waist and kissed him again, taking his whole tongue into her mouth and sucking on it. Hard. He groaned and moved his hands down over her blue jeans back pockets, squeezing gently. Now it was her turn to groan.

He knelt down and laid her on the thick, soft living room rug in front of the fireplace, sliding his hands up under her sweater. "I was going to take you upstairs to my bedroom," he said. "But I can see now we're never going to make it that far."

CHAPTER 23

You are so beautiful," Walker said, wonderingly, propping himself up on one elbow and looking down at Allie. They were still lying on the living room rug, in front of the fireplace, and he was watching the way the fire's shadows danced over her bare skin.

Allie started to disagree, but he silenced her with a kiss.

When he finally stopped kissing her, he looked at her skin in the firelight again and mused out loud, "What do you do to make your skin so beautiful? Dip yourself in liquid gold every morning?"

"That's exactly what I do," Allie said, a smile playing on her lips. "Every morning, as soon as I'm done brushing my teeth." She groped for the sheepskin throw that she had pulled off the couch at some point during their lovemaking and wrapped it securely around her naked body.

Walker watched her, amused. "It's a little late for that kind of modesty, isn't it? Especially since the last two hours have given me such a . . . um, *complete* knowledge of your body. And Allie?

Trust me when I say that body should never be covered up again. Not if you can possibly help it."

Allie smiled but refused to relinquish the throw. "Are you suggesting that I stop wearing clothes?"

"Only when you're alone with me," Walker said, running his fingers through her honey-colored hair. "Because as much as I think Butternut's citizens would enjoy seeing you naked, I'm too selfish to share you with them."

Allie's lips parted and her hazel eyes darkened, and Walker knew, instinctively, he could easily coax that sheepskin throw away from her now. But at the moment, as improbable as it seemed, his desire to talk to her was even stronger than his desire to make love to her again.

"Allie," he asked now, still stroking her gold-highlighted hair, "was tonight different than you thought it would be? Or didn't you think about what it would be like? Between us, I mean."

"Oh, I thought about it," she said, with a rueful smile. "Lately, to the exclusion of almost everything else in my life."

He shook his head in surprise. So it had been that way for her, too?

"What about you?" she asked, almost shyly. "Did you think about it, too?"

"You have no idea," he said, with a sigh.

"How close did tonight come to what you'd imagined?"

"Oh, I missed by a mile," he said. He stopped stroking her hair and ran a single finger down her throat to the hollow at its base. She shivered. "My imagination failed me," he continued. "I knew making love to you would be amazing. But I didn't know it would be *that* amazing."

She reached up to touch him now, stroking his cheek with

the back of her hand. "I couldn't say it any better than that," she admitted.

"There's only one thing I'd change," he said, his finger leaving the hollow of her neck and traveling down to where a hint of her cleavage was still visible above the throw. She squirmed a little with some combination of desire and impatience, but she didn't loosen her grip on it. Now it was her turn to want to talk.

"What would you change?" she asked.

"Well, when I imagined it, I always imagined carrying you up to my bedroom and making love to you in my bed. The way you deserve to be made love to."

"Well, I'm not sorry it happened here," she said, patting the rug beside her. "We couldn't wait, that's all. Besides, anyone can make love in a bed. That doesn't require a lot of imagination."

He smiled. Maybe she had a point there. There'd certainly been no shortage of imagination in their lovemaking tonight.

"Besides," she said, glancing around the living room. "This room is very romantic. In a north woods kind of a way. Sort of masculine and seductive at the same time."

Walker frowned. "You mean, like a bachelor pad?"

"No, I didn't mean that—" Allie started to say, with a little shake of her head. But Walker interrupted her.

"Look, it's important to me that you know something, okay?"

"Okay," Allie said.

"With the exception of my ex-wife, who lived here for four and a half months, I've never brought another woman here before tonight. I know you didn't ask, but I need you to know that. There was a woman I used to see, occasionally, in Minneapolis, but I haven't seen her since I met you that day at Pearl's. I called her after that and told her I couldn't see her anymore. Not in *that* way, anyway. And since that was basically our whole relationship . . ." His voice trailed off.

"Walker, it's okay," Allie said gently. "I know you're not some womanizer, if that's what you're concerned about. If you were, the gossip mill in Butternut would be running overtime. And you don't owe me any kind of explanation, either. Not for anything that happened before tonight. I'm sorry if I put you on the defensive." She reached up and kissed him lightly on his lips. "I didn't mean to."

He felt his tensed body relax. "You didn't put me on the defensive," he assured her. "I wanted you to know this isn't something I do all the time. This is different. *You're* different."

"You don't think I can tell that by the way you made love to me?" Allie asked softly, still stroking his cheek.

"God, I hope so," Walker said, bending down to kiss her.

After a moment, Allie broke away from him, then asked with a mischievous smile. "Remember what you said about making love to me in a real bed?"

He nodded.

"Well, it's not too late. You can take me up to your room now." She peeled the sheepskin throw away from her body and flung it casually aside.

Walker swallowed. She looked so beautiful that it almost hurt to look at her.

"I would take you there," he said, his voice thick with desire. "But I think we missed our window of opportunity again."

His hand reached down and cupped one of her breasts, which was golden in the firelight, except for the pink, puckered nipple, which hardened immediately under the caressing touch of his fingers.

"The problem with going upstairs," he said slowly, savoring the anticipation of making love to her almost as much as he knew he would savor the actual sensation of it, "is that it would take at least sixty seconds to get to my bedroom. And I can't wait that long. Not anymore."

"There's no reason why you should wait that long," she said, pulling him to her and initiating another round of lovemaking, the intensity of which left them both exhausted and exhilarated at the same time.

They did eventually make it up the stairs to Walker's bedroom. By then, the fire in the fireplace had burned down to a mound of glowing embers, and the sky was taking on the pale pink shades of early morning.

"It's so peaceful," Allie said softly, looking out at the mist-shrouded lake from Walker's bedroom window. She had the sheepskin throw wrapped around her again, and her tangled hair hung loose on her bare shoulders.

"Come to bed," Walker said, wrapping his arms around her from behind and kissing her neck in what he knew was an especially sensitive place for her.

Allie sighed, and it sounded to him like a perfect mixture of contentment and desire. She left the window and followed Walker to bed. There, they made love again, marveling at the delicious feel of the cool sheets against their bare skin.

Just as the sun was rising, Allie fell asleep. Walker knew he wouldn't be able to sleep, so instead he watched her sleep. She looked so young, he thought, her face relaxed in sleep, her honey-colored hair charmingly tumbled around on the pillow.

But in her own way, he knew, she was very mature. Far more mature than he was. Not only had she experienced more loss in her life than he had, but she'd had to assume more responsibility, too. Managing a successful business, as he'd done, was one thing. But being single-handedly responsible for a child? That was another thing.

He felt a stab of guilt then, thinking about how tired she'd be today. He could go back to sleep when she left. She'd have a whole day ahead of her with an energetic five-year-old.

So he resisted the urge to do what he wanted to do now—which was to run a finger down the inside of one of her thighs. The gesture, he knew, would wake her up immediately. And lead to more lovemaking. He had never been with a woman before whose body was so immediately responsive to his own touch. It was incredibly flattering. And deeply arousing.

He swallowed, hard, trying to rein in his own desire. They'd already made love four times, but he was still hungry for her. She'd reawakened his inner sixteen-year-old and brought him back to a time in his life when his sexual needs were seemingly inexhaustible and indefatigable.

But she needed to sleep. When she did wake up, there would be enough time to make love again. So he settled back on the pillows, closed his eyes, and listened to the steady rhythm of her breathing. He felt, too, the delicious warmth emanating off her naked body.

He lay that way until he felt a new sensation. An unfamiliar sensation. It started with a quickening of his pulse and was followed by a nameless feeling that settled in his ribs. It was a tightness, a squeezing sensation, that made him feel as if his breath were being forced out of him. He wondered, for one wild moment, if there could be something physically wrong with him. Was he having a heart attack? Or a stroke? But neither one was likely. He was thirty-five years old, and, as far as he knew, in perfect health.

It was more likely that whatever he was feeling was psychosomatic. The physical manifestation of some feeling he'd gotten good at ignoring. Or denying. Or keeping at a safe distance.

And that emotion, he knew, was fear.

He'd been afraid before, of course. Nobody could live thirty-five years without being afraid. But there were different kinds of fear, obviously.

He thought about Allie's late husband, fighting a war half a world away, under attack by enemy combatants. That was a special kind of fear, reserved for people brave enough to put themselves in almost impossibly dangerous situations. He'd never felt that kind of fear before.

But he'd felt other kinds of fear. Once, when he and his brother were teenagers, they'd taken an aluminum canoe out on a lake on an overcast summer afternoon and gotten caught in an electrical storm. He'd felt fear then. He'd felt it again, a few winters ago, driving up here late one night. His truck had skidded out on an icy road, and he'd narrowly missed hitting a tree. And then, last spring, he'd been hiking in the woods at dusk, and he'd accidentally gotten between a mother bear and her two cubs. He'd thought, for a second, that she was going to charge him, and he'd been afraid.

But watching Allie now, he realized he'd never been afraid like this before. Lightning, an icy road, an irritable bear—none of them had even come close to making him this afraid. Because now, for the first time in his life, he was in love. And it was terrifying.

Then again, for the first time in a long time, he was thinking clearly. Lying here, watching Allie sleep, he knew exactly what he needed to do. He just didn't know if he was brave enough to do it.

CHAPTER 24

"Allie, you look different," Sara Gage said thoughtfully, study-ing her across the desk in the back office of the Pine Cone Gallery. Sara was at the computer, and Allie was waiting for in-structions on hanging a new collection of watercolor paintings by a local artist Sara had recently discovered.

"Different *how*?" Allie asked, warily. It was Monday morning, and even though a whole day had passed since she'd left Walker's cabin on Sunday morning, she still felt somehow marked by their time together. Not just inwardly, but outwardly, too.

"Oh, I don't know," Sara said, frowning. "But you're absolutely glowing. Like you got a facial or something."

Or something. Something in this case being twelve uninter-rupted hours of mind-blowing sex with Walker Ford. Still, Allie was starting to wonder if the "glow" everyone kept commenting on was ever going to wear off.

But to Sara she said, lightly, "I *wish* I'd gotten a facial. But as far as I know, that's one perk Butternut doesn't offer." She added, unconvincingly, "It's too bad, really." But what was *really* too bad was how difficult it had been for her to function since their night together. Even the simplest things—like spreading butter on toast, or making a bed, or brushing her teeth—seemed to require a longer attention span than she was capable of.

The problem was, she was constantly revisiting that night. Replaying it in her mind down to the last detail. And there were *plenty* of details, each one seemingly more delicious than the last.

She started to remember one now, then realized that Sara was staring at her again, not even bothering to hide her curiosity. Allie stared back at her, her mind a complete blank. Had Sara asked her something? She had no idea, but she resolved to try to stop thinking about Walker Ford all the time. She could do that, couldn't she? She'd set the bar low to begin with. She'd just try to go for a minute without thinking about him. She immediately thought about him again. Maybe a minute was too long, she decided. Thirty seconds was probably more realistic.

"Did you want to discuss how you'd like me to hang those watercolors?" she asked Sara now, hoping to reach the thirty-second mark.

"The paintings?" Sara asked absent-mindedly, in a way that made Allie wonder if her inability to concentrate was contagious.

"The new watercolors?" Allie prompted.

"Oh, right," Sara said. "We'll get to that. But we have another fifteen minutes before the gallery opens, and I thought, since you've been working here for a month, now might be a good time for an employee review."

"Right now?" Allie asked, worriedly. She didn't know if she could pay attention long enough for them to have this conversation.

But Sara misunderstood her concerned expression. "Oh, Allie," she said quickly, "I don't want you to think I'm not happy with your work, because I am. Trust me. Receipts are up twenty percent from a month ago, and I know you're the one who deserves the credit for that."

Allie started to protest, but Sara waved her objections away. "No, it's true," she said. "As much as it pains me to admit it, you're a better saleswoman than I am. Our customers like you. And more important, they trust you. They don't feel like you just want them to buy something for the sake of buying something. They feel like you want them to be happy with their purchase."

"But I do," Allie said, without thinking.

"I know you do," Sara said, smiling. "You can't fake that kind of sincerity, Allie. And while sincerity isn't always a plus in the retail industry, it is in a place like this, where most of our business comes from repeat customers. So it goes without saying I'm very happy to have you here. But what about you? Are you happy working here?"

"Absolutely," Allie said, relieved. That question, at least, was easy to answer.

"Good," Sara said, with a satisfied nod. "I know the money's not great. But I am planning on giving you an end-of-season bonus, based on our profits. And, money aside, I want you to think of working at the Pine Cone Gallery as an investment in your future. I mean, don't get me wrong. I love owning it. But I'm not going to want to own it forever." She sighed, taking a sip of tea from the mug on her desk. "It's a lot of work, and my husband's tired of the Minnesota winters. And honestly, Allie, I think I'd be willing to consider selling if I could find the right buyer. You know, someone who cared about it, and the artists who show their work here, as much as I do. Someone like you," she finished, pointedly.

"Me?" Allie asked, surprised.

"Why not?" Sara said. "You obviously love art. You have a good eye for what will sell. You're a good saleswoman. And I think you'd be good, too, at cultivating relationships with the artists whose work we represent. It can be the most challenging part of the business, but it can also be the most rewarding."

Allie nodded, intrigued. "It's not something I have any experience doing, though," she confessed.

"Not yet," Sara said. "But we could easily change that. Tomorrow I'm going to an artist's studio near Ely to meet with a woman who makes exquisite hand-pounded gold jewelry. I saw her work at a crafts show last spring, and I've been thinking about selling it here since then. Would you like to come with me?"

"I'd love to come," Allie said, honestly. "It sounds fascinating. And thank you for thinking about my future. Sometimes," she added, "it's more than even I can do."

"Good," Sara said, smiling. "Now, is there anything else we need to discuss before we open?"

"No," Allie said, starting to stand up. And then she caught herself. "Yes, actually," she said, forcing herself to sit down again. "I was wondering . . ." She paused, searching for the right words. She didn't want to seem unprofessional. Especially after the conversation they'd just had. "I was wondering," she began again, "if I could have Wednesday off. If it's too late, if you already have plans, that's fine. I know I'm springing this on you."

But Sara only shrugged. "Of course," she said. "If you need a personal day, take one."

"I don't need a *personal* day," Allie said carefully, not wanting to misrepresent herself. "I wanted to take Wednesday off so I could go on a date."

"A date?" Sara asked, raising her eyebrows in surprise.

After a moment, she said quietly, "I wasn't aware that you were dating yet."

"Neither was I," Allie confessed. "I mean, it's still pretty new."

Sara smiled sympathetically, then said, "No, that's fine. Take Wednesday off. God knows you've earned it. But if it's not too personal, do you mind if I ask who you're going on a date with?"

"Oh, no, it's not too personal," Allie said, thinking that it *was* a little personal but realizing that if she and Walker were going to date, she was going to have to get used to people knowing about it. Not to mention talking about it.

So she looked Sara straight in the eye. "It's Walker Ford," she said, then somewhat unnecessarily she added, "From the boat-yard." If she'd learned anything this summer, it was that everybody in Butternut already knew everybody else.

"Walker Ford?" Sara repeated, her eyebrows shooting up in surprise. And then she seemed to recover herself. "I'm sorry," she said, quickly. "I don't mean to seem rude. I'm not surprised he's dating *you*. I'm surprised he's dating *anyone*. I thought he was sort of off the market."

"Well, like I said, it's all very new," Allie said vaguely, dodging the question of Walker's past availability. "It's not a big deal or anything." *Liar. It's a very big deal. For you, anyway.* "I wouldn't ask for Wednesday off," she continued, "but Wyatt will be at day camp, and it's simpler that way." She still hadn't decided how to broach the topic of her and Walker with Wyatt. After all, Wyatt thought of Walker as his fishing buddy, not someone his mother was romantically involved with.

"Of course," Sara said, nodding. "I'm just curious, though. Where are you going on your date?"

"We're going on a picnic," Allie said. "We're taking Walker's boat out to one of the islands in Butternut Lake. Red Rock Island, I think."

"Well, that sounds very nice," Sara said, wistfully. "I can't remember the last time my husband and I went on a picnic."

Allie didn't know what to say to this, so she smiled politely and excused herself to open the gallery. *There. That wasn't too painful,* she told herself about her conversation with Sara. The painful part, apparently, would come now. Because as nervous as she was about seeing Walker again, she honestly didn't know if she could wait two days to do it. It would be pure torture. Pure, sweet torture.

Forty-eight hours later, Allie was waiting at the end of her dock, watching Walker's powerboat glide smoothly over the surface of the lake in her direction. She was sitting down, her bare feet dangling over the side of the dock, barely skimming the surface of the water. She knew she'd have to stand up before Walker docked his boat, but at the moment, she didn't trust herself to do that. Her knees were shaking so violently she wasn't sure they could support her weight.

She didn't know if she was excited, nervous, or just plain crazy. She did know she hadn't been herself this morning. When she'd come back from dropping Wyatt off at day camp, for instance, she'd ignored the unmade beds, the breakfast dishes in the sink, and the loads of laundry waiting to go into the washing machine. Instead, she'd taken a bubble bath, something she rarely did at night, let alone in the middle of the morning. Then, after toweling off and drying her hair, she'd started trying on clothes for the picnic. Which was a little silly, really, considering that a T-shirt, shorts, and sneakers were the only sensible choice for the outing they were going on.

But the truth was, she didn't want to wear something sensible.

She wanted to wear something . . . something *romantic*. And practicality be damned. Which it was, in the end. Because the outfit she chose—a pale yellow cotton sundress, and no shoes—was hardly appropriate for an afternoon she'd spend climbing in and out of a boat, and hiking up and down the side of a rocky island.

Now, with Walker's boat only a hundred yards away, she held up her hand to shield her eyes from the glare off the water and felt her heart contract as she got her first good look at him since saying good-bye to him the morning after their lovemaking. *He looks amazing,* she thought. *He is amazing.* Her knees shook harder.

He waved to her now, and she waved back. Then she willed her rubbery legs to stand up so she could help him dock the boat.

"Hi," he said, almost shyly, as he maneuvered the boat parallel to the dock and reached out a hand to stabilize it against the dock's bumper.

"Hi," she said, and her voice sounded a little squeaky. There was still the problem with her knees, too.

He reached a hand up to her then and she took it, using it to help her keep her balance as she stepped down into the boat.

"Do you have everything you need?" he asked, looking at her a little quizzically.

Allie blushed. He was thinking, of course, about how completely unprepared she looked for a day on the lake. No hat or sunglasses. No bathing suit or beach towel. No bottled water, or sunscreen, or insect repellent. None of these, she realized, had even made her short list. Because the only things she'd thought to bring today was herself, and her little yellow sundress.

If Walker thought it was strange, though, he didn't say so. He just pushed his boat off from the dock and headed it out into the middle of the lake.

"Nice day for a picnic, huh?" he asked, his eyes brushing over her in that way they had. As if he could see right through the thin material of her dress.

"It's perfect," Allie agreed, feeling the warmth of the sun on her shoulders. She'd been afraid, actually, it would be cool. All the locals said they were going to have an early fall. And yesterday she'd spotted a tree across the lake whose upper branches were already beginning to turn a fiery shade of red. But today? Today was perfect. Warm, sunny, and slightly hazy, with a soft, luxuriant breeze that was more like a caress than a breeze.

"By the way," Walker said, taking her hand with the hand that wasn't on the boat's steering wheel, "you look amazing. Like summer itself."

"Thank you," Allie said, brushing back some hair that had worked itself loose from the French braid she'd braided it into.

"Do you . . . uh, recognize this boat?" he asked now, his eyes alight with anticipation.

Allie studied it, then frowned. "Is this . . . is this the boat I bought?"

Walker nodded, looking pleased. "What do you think?"

"I think," she said slowly, still examining it. "I think it looks really different than it did when I test-drove it with Cliff."

"Well, I gave it a few upgrades," Walker admitted.

"A few?" Allie asked.

He nodded. "I replaced the engine. I thought you and Wyatt might need more power. And I had the seats reupholstered, too. I thought the orange was a little tacky. The blue-and-white stripe seemed more like you, somehow."

"It's beautiful," she admitted, admiring the boat's big, shiny engine and crisp, blue-and-white-striped seat cushions. "But, Walker, tell me, honestly. Did you make *any* money on this boat by the time you were done 'upgrading' it?"

"Oh, I definitely came out ahead," he said, pulling her closer to him.

"Mmmm," Allie said, nuzzling his neck, enjoying the clean, masculine smell of him. "I hope you don't do all your business this way, Mr. Ford," she said, teasingly. "Because it sounds like a good way to run your boatyard right into the ground."

"Don't worry," he said, sliding the boat's gear shift into neutral and putting both his arms around her. "I have a very short list of customers who get preferential treatment."

They kissed for a little while, until Allie sensed, even through the thick fog of their desire, that they should probably stop while they still could. She broke away, a little breathlessly.

"What's wrong?" Walker asked, still holding her.

"We're out in the open," Allie said, gesturing to the lake around them. She was surprised to see that during their kiss the boat had drifted into the middle of the bay. "Anybody could see us," she added, placing a conciliatory kiss on his cheek.

"Anybody *could* see us," Walker pointed out, toying with the neckline of her sundress. "If there was anybody *to* see us." That was true, Allie thought. Except for some loons swimming near the boat, the bay was deserted.

Walker reached over and turned the boat's ignition off. Then he pressed a button on the dashboard. There was a whooshing sound, followed by a soft thud.

"What are you doing?" Allie asked, even though she thought she already knew. Her heart beat faster, if that was even possible.

"I put the anchor down," Walker said, reaching over and picking up a blanket that was sitting on one of the boat's seats, next to a large cooler.

"Why?" Allie asked, in almost a whisper.

"Because we're staying here for now," he said, spreading the blanket out in the bottom of the boat.

"Yes, I got that," she said. "But why?"

"Because," he said, turning back to her and taking her face between his hands. "Because I can't wait a second longer to make love to you." And he kissed her. A slow, simmering kiss that Allie thought might take her sundress right off.

"Walker," she said finally, getting enough of a grip on herself to pull away from him. "Are you crazy? We can't make love in broad daylight, in the middle of the lake."

But he looked unperturbed. "Give me one reason why not," he said, sitting down on the blanket and tugging her, gently, down beside him.

"I can give you a hundred reasons why not," she murmured, as he kissed her neck in that particularly maddening way he had and eased her down so that she was lying beside him. "For one thing, we're in public. For another thing, just because there's no one here now doesn't mean there won't be five minutes from now. And for another thing . . ." But she stopped when he started kissing her neck again. She knew it was hopeless to even try to formulate another sentence.

She watched now as Walker sat up and knelt in front of her, slowly sliding his hands up the skirt of her sundress.

"First of all," he said, picking up their conversation again, "it's a weekday. There's not going to be a lot of traffic on the lake. And if there is a boat in the bay, we'll hear its engine."

"What about canoes?" she objected, though not very strenuously. He was delicately stroking the inside of her thighs now, and it was all she could do not to squirm with anticipation.

"Canoes tend to stay close to shore," he murmured, reaching up and running a finger under the waistband of her underwear. She sucked in a breath, then watched, fascinated, as he slid the other hand up and, pulling gently, eased her underwear down over her thighs with tantalizing slowness.

"This is crazy," she said softly, as an unexpected breeze rocked the boat. She squinted at Walker, his silhouette black against the bright sun at his back.

"It's pretty crazy," he agreed, mildly. "But it's no crazier than anything else I've done since I met you."

Allie willed herself to breathe while he slid her underwear down to her ankles, and, pulling them off, tossed them aside.

"By the way," he said, stroking the insides of her thighs again and making Allie want him so badly that she was afraid she would cry out. "When I first saw that dress, I thought it was a little impractical for the afternoon we had planned. But then I realized something. You were thinking ahead when you put it on. Because now, I only have to take off one article of your clothing to make love to you."

Allie's breath caught on his words, and, after an internal struggle that lasted less than one second, she closed her eyes and gave herself over to the moment.

Later that evening, standing in front of her bathroom mirror, she was shocked by her transformation. Her hair was hopelessly tangled, the tip of her nose was sunburned, and her lips—she leaned closer to the mirror, studying them carefully—looked swollen. *Was it even possible,* she wondered, *to kiss so hard, and for so long, that your lips actually swelled up?* She had a guilty feeling that it was.

Well, there was nothing she could do about it now, she thought, dropping the towel she had wrapped around her and turning on the shower. She had exactly half an hour before Wyatt was due back from Jax and Jeremy's house, where he'd gone after day camp, and she was determined to look at least halfway presentable by then. She stepped into the shower, and stood under the nozzle, wincing slightly when the hot water touched her sunburned shoulders. Then she massaged shampoo through her hair and tried to think about ordinary things. Mundane things. Like the fact that she needed to buy more stamps. Or the fact that the refrigerator was overdue for a cleaning.

What she tried *not* to think about was the afternoon she'd spent with Walker. Not that it hadn't been amazing. It had been. After they'd made love that first time, there'd been more talking, more drifting, more lovemaking. And then, when they'd both gotten hot, there'd been a trip to a secluded cove where they'd skinny-dipped off a small, sandy beach. The skinny-dipping, of course, had led to more lovemaking. Which had led to more drifting and more talking. Which had started the whole cycle over again.

She turned off the shower now, stepped out onto the bath mat, and toweled herself off. She dressed quickly, in blue jeans and a T-shirt, and combed out her wet hair, pulling it back into a ponytail. Then she hurriedly did the things she'd left undone that morning, washing the breakfast dishes, making the beds, and putting in a load of laundry. Finally, she made herself a cup of chamomile tea—on the grounds that drinking it would make her feel calmer—and took it out on the twilit porch to wait for Jeremy and Wyatt.

She hadn't been sitting there for very long when she heard the crunch of tires on gravel and saw a pickup truck coming up the driveway. It pulled up in front of the cabin, and Allie saw, with surprise, that Jeremy wasn't driving it. Jax was. She frowned as her heavily pregnant friend slid out of the driver's seat and came around to the other side of the pickup.

"Jax," Allie protested, coming down the cabin's steps, "you said Jeremy would drive Wyatt home. Otherwise, I never would have agreed to this."

But Jax held a finger to her lips and opened the back door of the pickup. Wyatt, strapped into a car seat, was sound asleep.

"I'm sorry," Jax said softly. "I tried to keep him awake on the drive here. But I think a whole day of being Jade's best friend has practically done him in."

Allie laughed, in spite of herself. "I can see that," she said.

"He's really dirty, too," Jax added, apologetically, reaching to lift Wyatt out of the car seat. "I made him wash his hands and face before we left, but they were playing capture the flag before dinner and—"

"Jax? Are you crazy?" Allie interrupted her. "You're not carrying Wyatt into the house. He's way too heavy for you right now."

Jax shrugged unconcernedly, but she let Allie lift him out of his car seat and carry him inside. Allie took him straight to his bedroom, pulled the covers back on his bed, and laid him down on it. As she took off his shoes and socks, she tried not to think about the fine layer of dirt covering him. *No harm done,* she thought. Tomorrow morning, he would go straight into the bathtub and his sheets straight into the washing machine.

She pulled the covers over him, kissed him on his cheek, and turned off his bedside table lamp. When she came back into the living room, she found Jax sitting on the couch, tiny but for her enormous belly.

"Jax," she said sternly, "you shouldn't have driven him home."

But Jax held up a hand to stop her. "Allie, it's okay. I *wanted* to drive Wyatt home. I needed to think, and driving, for some reason, always helps me think more clearly."

Allie looked at Jax closely and realized that she looked tired. Tired and something else. Anxious, Allie decided.

"Jax, is everything okay?" she asked, sitting down beside her.

"With me? Of course?" Jax said, with a quick smile. "I'm just at the point in my pregnancy where I'm starting to feel like a beached whale."

Allie smiled, halfheartedly. But she didn't feel reassured. Typically, a pregnant Jax exuded good health. As if pregnancy agreed with her. Which, of course, it did. But tonight, there was a strained quality about her. Fatigue around her eyes. Worry lines on her forehead.

"I remember the last few weeks of my pregnancy with Wyatt," Allie said, squeezing Jax's little hand. "They were not pleasant. But, Jax? Promise me, no more driving alone at night, okay? I mean, you're what, eight and a half months pregnant now? You could go into labor at any time."

Again, Jax waved away her concern. "I have long labors, Allie. Freakishly long. Even with Jade, my third child, I was having contractions for a couple of days before she was born. Trust me, when I do go into labor, I'll have plenty of time to get to a hospital."

Allie nodded. But privately, she didn't feel reassured. She wasn't an expert on childbirth, but she knew that each labor and delivery was unique. Could Jax really predict what this one would be like?

"So are you going to tell me how the picnic today was?" Jax asked.

"The picnic?" Allie echoed, stalling for time. She was still composing her thoughts about it.

"You and Walker did go on a picnic today, didn't you?" Jax asked, amused.

"Yes, we did," Allie said, flushing hotly. She saw a mental snapshot of the two of them from earlier in the day. They were fresh from their skinny-dip, naked, lying on a blanket they'd spread on a bed of dry pine needles, in a little clearing near the sandy cove where they'd anchored the boat. She could still feel the warm sun dappling their skin, still smell the clean, dry pine needle scent. Still hear the soft, but urgent murmuring of their lovemaking.

"And . . ." Jax prompted. "How was it? The picnic, I mean."

"It was really nice," Allie said, suddenly examining her fingernails with interest.

Jax laughed. "You are a lousy liar, Allie Beckett," she said.

"I know," Allie said, blushing harder and glancing up, briefly. "I *am* a lousy liar. The picnic was pretty amazing, actually."

"And I'm guessing you're not referring to Caroline's potato salad?" Jax said, her blue eyes dancing mischievously.

Allie shook her head, feeling guilty again. She knew that Caroline had insisted on packing the picnic that Walker had brought for them, but it had sat virtually untouched all afternoon. Not once had either of them even remembered that it was there.

"But seriously, Allie," Jax said, her tone gentle, "all teasing aside. You look . . . you look different."

"You mean, like I've had a facial?" Allie asked, amused.

"No," Jax said, shaking her head. "Not exactly. What I meant by looking different was . . . you look happy."

Allie, whose eyes had strayed back down to her fingernails, looked up again. Jax was smiling at her, her face, though still tired looking, suffused with its own happiness. *She's happy because I'm happy,* Allie realized. And then, without warning, she felt her eyes tearing up. She was so lucky to have Jax for a friend. How had she ever managed without her all these years?

"Allie," Jax asked now, "are you in love with him?"

"In love?" Allie repeated, bemused. "I don't know about *in love*. I think *in lust* is more like it."

"Well, that's usually where love starts," Jax said, smiling.

Allie thought about that. Was it true? It had certainly been true with her and Gregg. Before there had been love between them, there had been pure chemistry. And when it came to Walker, who knew? Maybe their admittedly powerful attraction would lead to love, too. Maybe, on her part, it already had. But that was crazy, wasn't it?

Jax sighed, a tired sigh, and it interrupted Allie's thoughts.

"Oh, Jax, I'm sorry," Allie said. "I haven't asked you if you want anything to drink. Water, maybe? Or chamomile tea?"

But Jax shook her head. "No, I'm fine. But I better be getting home. Otherwise, Jeremy will worry." She hoisted herself off the couch, and Allie walked her out to her pickup.

"You're sure everything's okay?" Allie asked, again. She couldn't shake the feeling that something was wrong with Jax.

"Absolutely," Jax said. She started to open the door to her pickup, then stopped and turned to Allie. "It's just . . . it's just that I have to do something I don't want to do."

"So don't do it," Allie said, automatically. "I mean, you have the perfect excuse for not doing *anything* you don't want to do. You're about to have a baby. Ask Jeremy to do it for you."

"I can't," Jax said, shaking her head. "This is something I have to do alone."

Allie frowned. She didn't like the way that sounded. "Are you sure I can't help you? I mean, if nothing else, I could listen to you if you want to talk about it."

Jax hesitated. "It's tempting," she admitted. "But you've done enough, Allie. Just by being here tonight."

"You'll let me know if you change your mind?" Allie asked, as Jax got into her truck.

"I promise," Jax said, turning on the ignition.

She started to drive away, then stopped, and leaned out the window. "By the way, Allie. Just for the record, your skin *does* look amazing."

Allie laughed and watched her friend drive away. But she didn't go back inside the cabin yet. Instead, she sat down on the front steps, and, as the night fell around her, she thought about Jax. About whether or not she should have pushed her harder on letting Allie help her. Of course, there was no guarantee that she *could* help her. But still, something about Jax had unsettled her. Enough so that she couldn't shake that uncomfortable feeling for the rest of the night.

The next morning, though, Allie and Wyatt bumped into Jax at the grocery store, and Allie decided she'd been wrong to be so worried about her. She looked fine. Better than fine, really. She looked like herself. And Allie chalked up their conversation the night before to Jax's feeling tired. Or momentarily overwhelmed. She'd said she needed to do something she didn't want to do. But who among us, Allie wondered, never has to do something we don't want to do? That was just life, wasn't it? And Jax's life, she reminded herself, was pretty damned perfect. At least as far as Allie could tell.

CHAPTER 25

M iss Jax?"

"Frankie?" Jax said, surprised. And a little miffed. She hadn't expected anyone else she knew to be at the Mosquito Inn tonight. Except, of course, for Bobby. And he was fifteen minutes late already. She'd been sitting there, tucked into a booth, watching the front door and trying to look innocuous. Or as innocuous as a woman who was eight and a half months pregnant could look in a dive bar at nine o'clock on a Thursday night.

"Miss Jax, what are you doing here?" Frankie asked.

"The same thing you're doing here," Jax said, evasively, sipping her Coke.

"*I'm* playing pool," Frankie said, frowning. He indicated the pool cue he was holding in his right hand.

"Well, I'm meeting an old friend for a drink," Jax said. *An old friend who's blackmailing me. An old friend who I've been having murderous fantasies about.*

"This isn't a good place to meet a friend for a drink," Frankie said.

"You're here," Jax said, a little defensively.

Frankie shrugged his gigantic shoulders. "I come here some-times, to shoot pool," he said. "But this is no place for a lady like you, Miss Jax. Especially since you're . . . you know . . ." His voice trailed off.

"Pregnant?" Jax supplied, amused in spite of herself.

He nodded, embarrassed.

For all his outward toughness, Frankie, she knew, was very shy.

"Don't worry, Frankie," she said, glancing nervously at the door. "I'll be in and out before you know it."

But Frankie didn't budge. "Where's Jeremy?" he asked.

She sipped her Coke again, trying to stay calm. This was one problem she hadn't foreseen. "Jeremy's at his weekly poker game," she said. "And Caroline, bless her heart, has offered to stay with the girls for a couple of hours." *And unlike you, she didn't ask any questions,* she thought irritably. But she immediately felt guilty. Frankie wasn't prying. He was just being protective of her.

He wavered a little now. "Okay. I'll leave you alone. But when your friend gets here, you two should find someplace else to go. I mean, right now, it's pretty quiet here." He looked around at a mostly subdued crowd. "But later in the night, it gets a little . . . unpredictable."

"Look, don't worry about me," she said, keeping one eye on the door. "Believe it or not, I've been to places like this before. I know how to handle myself in them, okay?" And that part, at least, was true. It was why she was having such a visceral reaction to being here now. The smell of stale beer, the clink of glasses, the crack of pool balls knocking together. She'd spent way too much time in places like this when she was a child. When she was a child raising two drunk parents.

"I'll see you later, Frankie," she said, pointedly.

He nodded reluctantly and retreated to the back of the bar, where the pool tables were. *Thank God Bobby was late,* she thought, glancing at the door again. It had spared her the embarrassment of having to introduce him and Frankie to each other. Although part of her would have loved to have seen the expression on Bobby's face when he met someone as big, and as tough, as Frankie. Because for all his swagger, Bobby, she knew, was a coward.

She reached into her purse now, took out an unmarked envelope, and set it down on the table in front of her. It looked innocuous there, but what was inside of it, she knew, might one day cost her marriage, and maybe even her family. She opened the flap on the envelope and took out the check inside of it. It was made out to cash, for ten thousand dollars.

She'd transferred the money between accounts that morning. It hadn't come from their checking account or their savings account. It had come from a third account. An account they'd set up after Joy was born, at a time in their lives when they were barely making ends meet themselves. But they'd had a dream then, just the same. They'd wanted to save enough money to send Joy, and any other children they might have, to college.

Jax, of course, hadn't gone to college. Jeremy had gone, but he'd worked his way through and graduated with student loans they'd only just recently finished paying off. They'd both wanted their children to be able to go to their state university full-time, without having to wait tables, and they wanted them to graduate free and clear, without owing any money.

That sounded simple enough, at least on the face of it. But saving the money for their daughters' educations was more difficult than they'd ever imagined it would be. Life, they soon discovered, was full of emergencies, big and small. A new roof for the hardware store. A new transmission for Jeremy's truck. A new septic system for their house. The list went on.

Still, the college account grew slowly. Incrementally. Until, this last spring, it had reached the ten-thousand-dollar mark. They both knew that wasn't enough to pay Joy's way through college, let alone that of her younger sister's. But it was a start. And they were determined to do better in the future. After all, Jax knew how to economize. She'd been doing it all her life.

Which was why this morning's decision to transfer the money from the college savings account into their checking account, and to write a check for the same amount, had been such a wrenching decision for her. She hated the thought of giving that hard-earned money to someone as undeserving as Bobby. But even more, she hated the thought of Jeremy finding out about it.

The one thing that gave her hope that he might not find out right away was that it was Jax, with her head for numbers, who was responsible for both their personal finances and the hardware store's finances. She paid the bills, and the taxes, and made all the deposits, withdrawals, and transfers between accounts. And Jeremy rarely, if ever, monitored those accounts. But he had access to all the information, and it was only a matter of time before he stumbled on the fact that Jax had emptied the college fund.

Jax's plan, such as it was, was to somehow replace the missing money before that happened. How she would do that, of course, was anybody's guess. She didn't have another ten thousand dollars lying around. And she didn't know anyone else who did, either. But maybe, she reasoned, if she was very careful with their family's finances, and diverted as much money as possible back into that account, she could eventually build it back up again before Jeremy found out. It wasn't a very realistic plan, she knew. But right now, it was the only plan she had.

"Hey, baby," Bobby said, startling her as he slid into the booth across from her. She'd been so lost in her own thoughts, she'd forgotten to watch the door.

She looked at him now, warily, and was surprised to see how much prison had changed him. And not for the better, either. Outwardly, he looked more or less the same. He was a little thinner. His hair a little longer. But it was on the inside she knew the real changes had taken place. She could see it in the way he hunched protectively over the beer he'd brought to the table with him. And in the way his eyes shifted constantly around the room, as if trying to assess the threat level from every direction.

"Hi, Bobby," she said, neutrally. "You're looking well," she lied, hoping to keep things on a friendly footing.

"You're looking fat," he shot back, after giving her the once-over.

"I'm pregnant," she said, gritting her teeth.

"Jeez," he said, taking a long pull on his beer. "How many kids will that make?"

"Four," Jax said, hating him.

But the response didn't get a reaction out of him. He wasn't interested enough in her to care how many children she had, Jax realized. Instead, he looked around the room again, and Jax found herself doing the same. She was relieved to discover that nobody seemed to be paying any attention to them. She looked back at Bobby and watched in distaste as he swigged his beer and then set the empty bottle down hard on the table.

"What're you drinking?" he asked, standing up.

"Coke," Jax said distractedly, pushing her glass across the table to him.

"Jack and Coke?"

"A Jack Daniel's and Coke?" Jax clarified. "For God's sake, Bobby, I'm pregnant."

He shrugged, disinterested. "Whatever," he said.

"I'd like a *Coke-a-Cola,* if you're getting another round," she said, glaring at him.

"Fine," he said. But instead of going to the bar, he stood there, a little awkwardly. "Uh, I'm going to need some money," he said.

Jax sighed, reached into her wallet, and handed him some bills. He was back a few minutes later with their drinks.

"Is that for me?" he asked, eyeing the envelope.

Jax nodded and slid it across the table to him. "The check's in there. It's made out to cash, in the amount we discussed." She forced herself to sound calm and dispassionate. *This is a business transaction,* she reminded herself.

Bobby took a long draw on his beer bottle and glanced around the bar again. Then he picked up the envelope, slid the check out, and gave a low, long whistle.

She watched him, marveling that it was even possible to hate anyone as much as she hated him.

"This should set me up nicely here," he said, putting the check in his wallet.

Jax stared at him blankly.

"What's the matter?" Bobby asked, his eyes narrowing.

Jax gave herself a little shake. She'd probably just misunderstood him. "Nothing. You just made it sound like you were planning to stay here. In Butternut."

He drained the rest of his beer and smiled at her maliciously. "I am. Is that a problem?"

"Yes, it's a problem," she said, feeling a little tremor of panic. "It's a problem because our agreement was that after I gave you the money, you'd leave Butternut. Remember?"

"Did I say I'd leave?" he said, leaning forward across the table. "Because if I did, I've changed my mind. Now that I've got some cash, I want to hang around here for a while. Keep an eye on my daughter. Make sure she's being raised properly."

Jax felt the color drain out of her face.

"That's right," he said, nodding. "I want to meet my daughter."

"You can't," Jax said, her panic mounting. "You can't see her. She's not here. We sent her away for the summer. She won't be back for . . . for a long time," she finished.

"You know, I don't believe you, Jax," Bobby said, obviously annoyed. "I think you're lying. I think you're trying to keep me away from my daughter. But you can't do that, Jax."

I can damn well try, Jax thought, anger rising in her. And the anger, she decided, was better than the panic. It cleared her head.

"You promised me you wouldn't have any involvement in her life," she said, through clenched teeth.

"Promises are made to be broken," he said, with a shrug. "Besides, I might run out of money sometime. And even though you're crying poor now, I think there's more where this came from."

Before all those words were even out of Bobby's mouth, Jax felt the baby twist around inside of her. It was such a sudden, painful movement that she thought for a moment she might scream. But she didn't. Instead, she grabbed the edge of the table in front of her. Which was a good thing, since it steadied her when she felt the room tilt, precipitously, to one side. She heard the sounds in the bar—the hum of conversation, the tinkling of the jukebox, the slap of the screen door closing—

fade into a distant murmur, as a cold, prickly sweat broke out all over her body. Then, a wave of nausea rolled over her like a steamroller. She was either going to faint or throw up now, she thought, but either way, it wouldn't be pretty.

Somewhere, at the edge of her consciousness, she heard a voice. A familiar voice.

"Miss Jax, are you okay? What's the matter?" And then the same voice, "What the hell did you do to her?"

It was Frankie, she realized with relief, as his massive face swam into view. He was kneeling beside the booth, shaking her shoulders gently. "Jax? What's wrong? Should I call an ambulance?"

"No, no ambulance," Jax said woozily. "I'm fine, really."

"Well, you don't look fine," Frankie said doubtfully. "You," he said, apparently to Bobby. "Get her a glass of water and some napkins. *Now.*"

For once, apparently, Bobby did what he was told to do, because when Frankie spoke again he addressed only her.

"Miss Jax, you don't look good. Your skin . . . it's almost gray. Please let me call an ambulance, or take you to the hospital myself."

"No. Please don't, Frankie. I'll be all right. I promise." She took a deep, shaky breath. She did feel a little better. She didn't think she was going to faint or throw up anymore. But the panic? The panic was still there, thrumming through her veins. And as soon as she thought about what Bobby had said, it came rushing back.

Bobby returned from the bar then and set a glass of ice water and a stack of cocktail napkins down on the table in front of Jax. He slid back in across from her again and glanced, resentfully, at Frankie.

"I didn't do nothing to her," he muttered, under his breath.

But Frankie ignored him. He dipped a few of the cocktail napkins in the ice water and handed them to Jax.

"Put these on your forehead," he instructed her. She did, and their cool dampness made her feel better still.

"Thanks, Frankie," she said softly, dabbing her face with the wet napkins.

He stood up and turned his attention to Bobby. "I think it's time for you to clear out," he said quietly. And Jax heard the menace in his voice.

"We're not done here," Bobby said, irritably. "Jax and I still have some things we need to talk about."

"Oh, you're done here, all right," Frankie said. "You can walk out or I can carry you out, but either way, you're leaving now."

"This is none of your business," Bobby whined.

"Yes, it is. Miss Jax is a friend of mine, and you're obviously upsetting her. Now let's go."

Jax looked over at Bobby, wondering if he was going to try to fight Frankie. She was half hoping he would. There was no question in her mind of who would win that fight.

But Bobby was mean, not stupid. He leaned across the table. "I'll see you later," he said to Jax, in a way that made it seem as if he were spitting each word out at her. And then he slid out of the booth and walked out of the bar.

"I'll be right back," Frankie said to Jax, lumbering after him.

Jax's first thought, after they left, was that she should leave, too. The only problem was, she didn't trust her legs to work yet. Her second thought was that she'd made a terrible mistake. She'd risked her marriage and lost ten thousand dollars, all for nothing. Bobby wasn't going to keep his end of the bargain. He'd never intended to keep it. And Jax was stuck with him. He'd never leave now. Why should he when there was always the possibility that he might get more money out of her?

She started to cry now, quietly at first, and then louder. She didn't care if anyone noticed her or not. What difference did it make? Her life, as she knew it, was over. It would never be the same again.

She was sobbing, miserably and uncontrollably, when Frankie came back five minutes later.

"He's gone," he said darkly, barely managing to wedge himself into the other side of the booth.

She nodded, without looking up, and mopped her face with the already wet cocktail napkin.

"Miss Jax," Frankie said, "I thought you should know. I didn't just tell him to leave the bar. I told him to leave Butternut, too. I told him to leave, and not come back."

Jax looked up at Frankie in surprise. "You did?"

Frankie nodded. "He was threatening you. Wasn't he?"

"Yes," she said. Because what was the point in lying anymore?

"I thought so," Frankie said. "Anyway, I had a little talk with him. I can be pretty persuasive when I need to be." He spoke with a ghost of a smile.

Jax sighed and unceremoniously blew her nose into a cocktail napkin. "Thank you, Frankie," she said. "For trying to help, I mean. But Bobby has no intention of leaving here. He has . . . other plans." At the thought of what those plans might be, another sob escaped her.

"No, Miss Jax. Listen," Frankie said, leaning forward. "He's leaving. And he's not coming back."

Jax looked back up at him again and shook her head, sadly.

"Frankie, I don't know what Bobby told you. But he'll be back. He's not done with me, or my family, yet."

"Oh, he's done all right," Frankie said, confidently. "Trust me."

Jax sighed, and suddenly she felt so tired now that it was all she could do not to put her head down on the table and go to sleep. She opened her mouth to explain to Frankie, again, that he was wrong. But she couldn't. She didn't have the energy.

Frankie, though, saw the skepticism in her expression. He leaned across the table and said, in a soft but urgent tone, "Miss Jax, I told Bobby to clear out tonight. I told him if I ever saw him in Butternut again, I would kill him. Plain and simple."

"Frankie, why would you say that?" Jax asked, genuinely surprised. She knew there were people who were intimidated by Frankie's size. But she had never been one of them. She'd known, intuitively, that whatever his past, he was the gentlest of men.

"I said that because I meant it," he said, his eyes narrowing with resolve.

"Frankie"—she shook her head—"you wouldn't really kill him, would you?"

"Yes, I would. I've done it before," he said, quietly. "Killed a man, I mean. And Bobby knows that. We did time in the same prison. I told Bobby I'd do it again in a heartbeat if he didn't leave you alone. And he believed me. Trust me, Miss Jax. I saw it in his face."

"You killed a man?" Jax asked, disregarding the rest of what he'd said.

"I did," Frankie said.

"Why?" she asked, saying the first thing that came to her mind.

"The 'why' is not important," he said, with a wave of his enormous hand.

"It is to me," Jax said.

He frowned, thinking it over. "Okay," he said, finally. "I'll tell you what happened. But it stays here, in this booth, all right? Not even Miss Caroline knows this."

She nodded and then hiccuped loudly.

He smiled and pushed her Coke closer to her. She sipped it, obediently.

"I grew up in this family that was . . . kind of crazy, I guess," he said, with a sigh, his enormous shoulders hunching over. "My dad skipped out on us. My mom did her best, but honestly, Miss Jax, even her best wasn't very good. She always had some boyfriend around. And most of them, well, they weren't exactly the kind of guys who'd toss a baseball around with me, if you know what I mean."

Jax knew what he meant.

"Anyway," he continued, "one of Mom's boyfriends liked to knock my little sister and me around. When I got bigger, of course, that wasn't a problem. But by then, I guess, the damage had been done. Because when my sister got married, *way* too young, she married a guy just like my mom's boyfriend. He was a real hothead. He'd have a bad day at work, or whatever, and he'd come home and, you know, blow off steam by . . ." He looked away, struggling with the memory.

Jax reached across the table and tried, ineffectually, to hold his enormous hand in her own small one. "It's okay, Frankie. I get it," she whispered.

"Anyway," he said, "it made me crazy, the way he treated her. There wasn't a lot that I loved in this world, but I loved her. She was a sweet little thing. Believe it or not, even with me for a brother, she wasn't much bigger than you, Miss Jax. And I . . . I couldn't stand to see her living that way. So I came over one night to have a talk with her husband. He'd been drinking. And we started fighting. I was stronger than he was, but he had a knife. I didn't see it until it was too late. He was going to use it on me so I . . ." His voice trailed off.

"But, Frankie, that was self-defense, wasn't it? Why did you still go to prison?"

"Well, the DA saw it differently, I guess," he said with a shrug.

"Oh, Frankie," Jax said, her eyes filling with tears again. "I'm sorry. It seems so unfair. But, Frankie, it still doesn't explain why you'd threaten to kill Bobby."

He thought about it for a moment and she could see that he was struggling, again, to translate his thoughts into words. He wasn't much of a talker, Frankie. Or at least he hadn't been before tonight.

"I guess I'd kill Bobby to protect you," he said finally, after a long silence. "You and Jeremy. And the girls, of course. All of you, you helped me," he said, simply. "When I came to Butternut, straight from prison, Miss Caroline and your family, you all took a chance on me, and I've never forgotten it. I never will forget it."

"Frankie, we didn't do that much," Jax protested.

"You did *plenty* for me," Frankie said. "When Miss Caroline gave me that job, I had nowhere to live. Nobody wanted to rent to an ex-con, but Jeremy helped me find that apartment over the Laundromat. He even cosigned the lease."

Jax nodded thoughtfully. She remembered Jeremy doing that, but it hadn't surprised her. That was just the kind of person he was.

"Then, after I moved in," Frankie continued, "it turned out the apartment needed a lot of work, but I didn't have any money saved yet. Jeremy helped me again. He gave me a line of credit at the hardware store, and I got what I needed and I did the improvements myself. I know you haven't been there, Miss Jax, but it's real nice now. Cozy, I think you'd call it."

Jax smiled at his choice of words. She had known that Jeremy had helped Frankie then, too. "But, Frankie," she said now, "you paid the money back. You don't owe us anything. Not anymore."

"It isn't that I *owe* you anything," he said, carefully. "It's that people like you, you're good people, that's all. And maybe, in your life, you've seen mostly good people, too. But, Miss Jax, from where I've sat, I've seen mostly bad. Or maybe just too damaged to be good anymore. Anyway, it's what makes me want to protect someone like you and your family. You're kind. Sweet. Innocent-like. And I want you to stay that way."

But Jax's mind had caught on the word *innocent.* Her eyes dropped to the table. "I don't know how innocent I am," she said softly. "The truth's a lot more complicated than that."

But Frankie disagreed. "I don't mean I think you're perfect, Miss Jax. Everyone makes mistakes. But like Miss Caroline always says, everyone deserves a second chance. Or most people." His eyes darkened, and Jax knew he was referring to Bobby.

She sighed now, taking another tiny sip of her Coke. She'd stopped crying, at least in part because Frankie had distracted her by telling her about his own life. Now, inevitably, though, her thoughts returned to her own situation.

"Frankie, do you really think Bobby will stay away from here now?"

"I know he will," he said calmly.

"And if he doesn't?"

"You let me worry about that. But for now, Miss Jax, I need to walk you to your car. Things are already starting to go south around here."

Jax glanced around, suddenly aware of some commotion at the bar. She'd been oblivious to her surroundings, but now she realized how much more crowded the place had gotten. How much rowdier, too.

"Come on, I'll take you out through the kitchen," Frankie said. "The owner here's a friend of mine."

Frankie cleared a path for her, and Jax followed him, obediently, through the kitchen and out into the parking lot. Then he walked her to her pickup.

"Thanks, Frankie," she said, reaching up to hug him. It wasn't easy. Her arms couldn't even come close to spanning his girth, but she did her best. And he patted her awkwardly on the back with one of his huge hands.

"Frankie?" she said, thinking of something. She stood back and looked up at him. "Whatever happened to your sister?"

"I don't know," he said, looking down. "After what happened, she never spoke to me again. She said she'd loved her husband. Go figure, huh?" He tried to smile, but Jax saw he couldn't.

Jax closed her eyes, just for a second. It seemed to her, sometimes, that there was altogether too much pain in the world.

"Hey, it's okay," Frankie said, seeing her expression. "Things didn't work out too badly. I did my time, and I learned how to cook while I was doing it. And my sister? Maybe she figured things out. Who knows? Maybe she even met a nice guy."

"I hope so," Jax said, hugging him again.

But as they were hugging, Jax felt another one of the false contractions she'd been having lately. This one, though, was stronger than the others. So strong it momentarily took her breath away. It felt amazingly close to the real thing.

She sucked in a little breath, and Frankie looked down at her with concern.

"It's the baby," Jax explained, running a hand over her belly. "She's just making her presence known."

Frankie nodded, doubtfully. "You two better be getting home," he said, opening the front door of her pickup for her. She climbed in and let him close it behind her. And then, looking at her, Frankie grinned, his first true smile of the night.

"Now go home to those beautiful little girls," he said cheerfully. "And give them each a kiss good night."

"I'll do that," Jax said, gratefully, starting up the truck. And she did.

CHAPTER 26

But the next night, less than twenty-four hours after she'd left the Mosquito Inn, Jax was back in her pickup again. This time, though, she drove out to Butternut Lake.

"*Jax?*" Allie said to herself, standing at the kitchen window and holding a just-washed dinner dish in her hands. She put the dish in the dish rack, wiped her hands on a hand towel, and hurried out to meet her just as Jax was sliding awkwardly out of her truck.

"Jax," she said, reprovingly, and she would have said more, but something about Jax's demeanor stopped her. Maybe it was the way her shoulders were set, or the way her jaw was clenched. But whatever it was, Jax looked determined. Absolutely determined. And not at all like a woman paying a casual social call. She looked like a woman on a mission.

"Jax? What is it?" Allie asked, swallowing the lecture she'd planned on giving her again. The one about not driving alone, at night, in the country, at this stage of her pregnancy.

"I've been trying to reach you all day," Jax said, "but your phone was busy and—"

"Oh, it's been off the hook," Allie explained. "I just noticed it a little while ago. Wyatt must have knocked it over while he was playing."

"Well, I tried your cell phone, too," Jax said. "But it went straight to voice mail." Allie frowned, wondering if she'd forgotten to charge it again. It was something she knew she had to get back into the habit of doing.

But Jax interrupted this thought. "Is Wyatt still awake?" she asked.

"No," Allie said, shaking her head. "He needs to be asleep every night by eight thirty. It's the only way I can stay sane." She paused, waiting for Jax to say something. But Jax only nodded. She looked uncomfortable. More than uncomfortable, really. She looked like she was in pain.

"Jax, can I get you something? A glass of water, maybe?"

"Okay."

"Come on inside," Allie said, feeling a first flicker of anxiety.

Jax followed her up the cabin's steps, but when they reached the front porch she said, "If you don't mind, Allie, I think I'll wait out here." She lowered herself down onto the top step, then, and there was something about the way she did it—slowly, laboriously—that made Allie feel doubly uncomfortable. Jax—even a very pregnant Jax—was usually so light on her feet. So spry. She made pregnancy, even during the hot summer months, look easy. *But not tonight,* Allie thought. Tonight, Jax was making it look hard.

"I'll be right back," Allie said, hurrying into the cabin and pouring Jax a glass of water at the kitchen sink. As she did so, she tried to reassure herself. Well, of course Jax was tired. And uncomfortable. She was eight and a half months pregnant, for God's sake. Even the easiest pregnancies, Allie reminded herself, are difficult in the last weeks. And Jax—no matter how easy she made marriage, and pregnancy, and motherhood look—was, in the end, only human.

"Here you go," she said, coming back out onto the porch and handing Jax a glass of water.

Allie sat down beside her and watched while Jax took a tentative sip from the glass. It was only then that she noticed, under the porch light, that Jax's face was unnaturally pale, and covered, even on this warm night, with a sheen of perspiration.

"Jax? Are you going to tell me what you're doing here?" she asked, some internal alarm sounding in her brain.

Jax nodded. But what she said next took Allie completely by surprise.

"When was the last time you spoke to Walker?"

"Walker?" Allie echoed. "Not since the picnic on Wednesday. Today's Friday, so two days ago. Why?"

But Jax didn't answer. She was sipping her water again.

"Why, Jax, do you think that's strange?" Allie asked, her voice sounding small in the quiet night. "That he hasn't called me, I mean?"

But Jax answered this question with another question. "Did he tell you, the day of the picnic, that he was planning on having a visitor?" she asked, putting her glass of water down, a little unsteadily, on the top step between them.

"A visitor?" Allie repeated, surprised. "No. I don't think so. Why? What's going on?" she asked. Whatever impatience she was beginning to feel with Jax was tempered by her concern at Jax's appearance. She really did not look well.

Jax took a shaky breath now, then said, "This morning after the girls left for day camp, I went over to Pearl's. Caroline was busy, so I sat down at the counter, and I was drinking a cup of tea when this woman came in and sat down on the stool next to mine. Allie, I swear, when I turned to look at her, and realized who she was, I was so surprised, I almost spit out my tea."

"Who was she?" Allie asked, curious, but, at the same time, puzzled. Had Jax come all the way out here to tell her about some mystery woman?

Jax took another nervous sip of her water. "It was Caitlin. Walker's ex-wife."

Allie just stared at her.

"I know. It didn't make sense to me, either," Jax said, rushing on. "Nobody's even seen her here, in town, since she and Walker split up. At first, I thought maybe she was just passing through. Or meeting Walker for a cup of coffee. You know, ex-spouses trying to be civil, that kind of thing. But when I struck up a conversation with her, she told me she was going to be visiting Walker. And when I asked her for how long, she said she didn't know yet. She said it was going to be an 'open-ended' stay. Those were her exact words, actually." Jax shot Allie a worried look.

"That's strange," Allie murmured. But she didn't know what was stranger. Walker's ex-wife visiting him. Or Walker not telling her his ex-wife was visiting him.

"It *is* strange," Jax agreed. "But it's true, Allie. She's there right now. Her car is parked in his driveway."

Allie frowned. She was having difficulty processing what Jax was saying. But then something occurred to her. "Jax," she asked, "how do you know her car is parked in his driveway?"

Jax looked guilty. Then embarrassed. "When I passed his cabin, on my way here, I took a little detour. I drove down his driveway—not all the way down—just far enough down for me to see her car."

"You were spying on him?" Allie asked, incredulously.

"Sort of," Jax said, in a voice barely above a whisper.

"Why?"

"Because I needed to know. I needed to know because if she was there, and you didn't know, I wanted you to hear it from me. I mean, I didn't want you to call him and have her answer the phone. Or go over there and have her answer the door."

When Allie didn't say anything, she continued. "You were so happy the night after the picnic," she said. "I'd never seen you that way before. You seemed so . . . so in love with him. I didn't want you to get hurt. Or if you *did* get hurt, I wanted to try to minimize the hurt somehow."

Allie nodded, distractedly, still trying to make sense of all this. "Jax," she said, finally, "let's not jump to conclusions. There may be a perfectly reasonable explanation for all this." But even as she said these words, she didn't really believe them. If there were a perfectly reasonable explanation, why hadn't Walker already given it to her?

"You're right," Jax said, nodding vigorously. "I'm sure everything's fine." She gave Allie's hand a reassuring squeeze, and Allie was surprised at how cold and clammy Jax's hand felt on this warm night.

"Jax, what's wrong?" Allie asked, suddenly, as she watched a spasm of pain travel across Jax's face.

Jax started to answer her, then gave a little, strangled cry. Her hands flew protectively to her belly. "It's the baby," she said, a little breathlessly.

"Is she . . . is she okay?" Allie asked, her mouth suddenly dry.

"Oh, she's okay," Jax said, reaching her hands around to awkwardly massage her own lower back. "She's just letting me know she's on her way, that's all."

"On her way?" Allie repeated, uncomprehendingly.

"I'm in labor, Allie," Jax said, matter-of-factly. She stopped rubbing her back long enough to finish the water in her glass. "This baby's coming. Pretty soon, I think."

Allie just stared at her. She'd heard her. She just didn't believe her.

"Allie, it's okay," Jax said, seeing the expression on her face. "I've done this before, remember? Three times, in fact."

"Was that a contraction?" Allie asked.

"That was a contraction," Jax agreed, rubbing her lower back again. "Last night, I was at a bar with Frankie, and I felt something I think now might have been a very early contraction. But, obviously, I didn't take it seriously."

Allie stared at her, then said the first thing that came to her mind. "You were at a bar with Frankie last night?"

"Not drinking," Jax said quickly. "Just talking. It sounds strange, but—"

"Never mind about that now," Allie said, impatiently. "It doesn't matter. What matters is that you just had your first contraction, right?"

"Actually," Jax said, a little sheepishly. "That wasn't my first contraction. I've been having them for a while."

"*A while?*" Allie said. "How long is 'a while'?"

"Since before I decided to drive out here. But at that point, the contractions were still pretty far apart, and, well . . . I was worried about you."

Allie considered this. "Jax, you drove out here, even though you knew you were in labor, because you were worried about *me*?" she asked, incredulously.

Jax nodded. "I know, it sounds a little crazy. But I was sure

I'd have enough time to come out here and then get back before . . ." She trailed off, her face contorting in pain again. When the moment passed, she continued, "With my last pregnancies, I had long labors. And I mean *long*. With all three girls, my contractions started a couple of *days* before I had to get to the hospital. But this time"—she shook her head—"this time things are moving a lot faster."

"Oh, Jax," Allie said, reaching out to rub her lower back for her. "You're coming out here, like this, is quite possibly the nicest, but also the stupidest thing anyone has ever done for me."

"Thanks, I think," Jax said, with a little laugh, once the pain had subsided.

"Listen, I'll call Jeremy," Allie said, springing into action. "He's a fast driver, right? Faster than me, anyway. Even with the drive out here, he'll get you to the hospital in less time than I could."

But Jax shook her head. "Jeremy's in St. Paul. He left this morning. His cousin was in a motorcycle accident there yesterday."

"Jeremy left this close to your due date?" Allie asked, stunned.

"He was only going to be away for tonight," Jax said. "And we both thought there'd be plenty of time for him to drive back if I went into labor."

"Okay," Allie said, willing herself to be calm. "Jeremy's not here. But I am. I'll wake up Wyatt, put him in the backseat of the car, and drive you to the hospital myself."

"Allie, there isn't time. I'm sorry. The hospital's thirty minutes away from here. And, from the feel of things, I haven't got thirty minutes."

"Jax, I thought you said you had long labors."

"I *used* to have long labors. Now, apparently, I have *short* labors. Because this isn't like the others, Allie. This baby is coming fast. Much faster than I ever thought possible. The contractions are really close together now."

"Oh, Jax, you shouldn't have driven out here," Allie said, dismayed.

"I know. But I'm here now," she answered. "And there are probably worse places to have a baby."

Allie blinked at her, uncomprehendingly.

"Allie, I'm sorry," Jax said, her jaw clenched in obvious pain. "This wasn't the plan. I would never have willingly put you in this position. I was so sure I'd have more time."

"Jax, you're not saying you're going to have the baby here, are you?" Allie asked, as Jax's words finally cut through the fog that had descended around her brain.

"I'm not sure I have any choice," Jax said, with a little shake of her head. "But, Allie, look at it this way. Women used to have babies at home all the time. Other mothers would help them. You could help me. I mean, you've had a baby before, right?"

"*In a hospital, Jax,*" Allie said, sounding slightly hysterical, even to herself. "I had a baby in a hospital. Not in some backwoods cabin."

"Okay, but you know what it's like," Jax said, encouragingly. "It's not that hard."

"Jax, are we talking about the same thing?" Allie asked, dumbfounded. "Because let me tell you, having a baby was, bar none, the hardest thing I've ever done. And I didn't have a natural childbirth, either. I got to the hospital as soon as was humanly possible and I *begged* them to give me the drugs."

Jax laughed. Although how she could laugh at a time like this was beyond Allie.

"Okay," Jax conceded. "Having a baby is a *little* hard. I'll grant you that. But we don't have to do this alone, Allie. Call 911. It'll connect you to the Butternut Volunteer Fire Department. They have an ambulance, so they can get here quickly. And they're all trained paramedics, too, so they'll know how to deliver a baby. They're good guys. Trust me. I went to high school with half of them."

"I'll call right now," Allie said, heading for the telephone in the kitchen. Having something concrete to do, she knew, would help keep the panic at bay for a moment. She picked up the phone, dialed 911, and spoke to the emergency dispatcher. When she hung up, she went back to Jax.

"They're coming," she said, the relief audible in her voice. "Do you think you can wait until they get here?"

Jax nodded, her face tight with pain. Another contraction.

"We need to start timing these," Allie said, checking her watch. "But, Jax, do you think you'd be more comfortable inside?"

Jax shook her head. "I like it out here on the porch," she said. "I can see the stars from here."

"The stars?" Allie said, looking up into the night sky. It was inky black tonight, with a million pinpoints of light in it. She was amazed that Jax had even noticed.

"Okay," Allie said, sitting down beside her and reaching out to rub her lower back again. "We'll stay out here. But is there anything else I can do while we wait for the ambulance to get here?" she asked, keeping an eye on her watch so she'd be ready when the next contraction came. "Can I bring you another glass of water?"

Jax's body suddenly tensed with pain. Allie looked at her watch. Three minutes. She closed her eyes and said a silent prayer. *Please let that ambulance get here before that baby's born. There are a lot of things I know I can do. But bringing a baby into this world is not one of them.*

"You know what you can do for me, Allie?" Jax said, when the contraction had ended. "You can call Jeremy on his cell phone. I'll give you the number. But try not to scare him, okay? He'll have a long drive ahead of him tonight, and I don't want him to get in an accident. Also, I left my neighbor, Sally Ann, with the girls. You're going to need to call her at my house and let her know I'm going to be late."

That's an understatement, Allie thought. But she called Jeremy and Sally Ann, and, for both of them, she did her best impression of being calm. Jeremy, though, was anything but calm when Allie explained the situation to him. He was furious at himself for being so far away and worried sick about Jax.

So Allie reassured him and put Jax on the phone, but only for a minute. She could see it was a strain on Jax to speak normally.

After she said good-bye to Jeremy, Jax got up and paced up and down the length of the front porch, pausing occasionally to lean against the wall of the cabin, her eyes closed in some combination of pain and concentration. Allie continued to time her contractions and waited, anxiously, for the ambulance to come. In the end, it took only twenty minutes for it to get there. But to Allie, it felt like a lifetime.

She watched while it pulled into the driveway, and three firemen-paramedics spilled out.

"Hey, Jax," one of them said cheerfully, "we hear you're going to have a baby."

"It would appear that way," Jax said, sagging against the cabin wall.

"Hi, I'm Jed," he said, coming up the cabin's front steps and shaking Allie's hand. He was tall, broad shouldered, and very muscular. Allie thought about what Jax had said about going to high school with half the volunteer firemen. This one, Jed, looked like he'd been a linebacker on the football team.

"How far apart are her contractions?" he asked Allie now, glancing over at Jax. Judging from a little wail that escaped her, then, she seemed to be in the middle of a particularly intense one.

"Two minutes," Allie said. "Maybe less."

"Okay," he said calmly, assessing the situation. "I don't think there's going to be time to get to the hospital. Even if we *can* speed the whole way there. I think this baby is going to be born right here."

Allie nodded weakly. "I was afraid of that."

"It's nothing to be afraid of," he said, briskly. "Trust me, we've delivered many babies. One just recently. But we are going to need a place to set up. A bedroom, maybe?"

"Of course," Allie said, reassured by his confidence. "My son's asleep in his room. But you can have mine. I'll show you where it is."

"Good. Also, if you have any extra sheets and towels, now would be a good time to get those out for us."

"Absolutely," Allie said.

She showed Jed her bedroom, then brought him a stack of sheets and towels, and a cotton nightgown for Jax that was the closest thing she owned to a hospital gown.

Jax seemed reluctant to come inside, but Jed persuaded her, gently, to come into Allie's bedroom. He needed to examine her, he explained, so that they'd know how her labor was progressing.

While he did that, Allie went to check on Wyatt, her heart pounding. *What if the labor wasn't progressing normally,* she wondered. *What if the baby wasn't okay?* But she couldn't think about that now. So instead she straightened Wyatt's disheveled covers, marveling, for the thousandth time, at his ability to sleep through anything.

After she left his room, she searched, desperately, for something to do. Something that would be helpful to Jax. Something short of actually being in that room with her. Because Jax was definitely better off without her. She was such a nervous wreck that Jax would probably end up coaching *her* through the delivery.

Finally, she hit on an idea. *Ice chips.* She'd sucked on those while she was in labor with Wyatt. She went to the kitchen and emptied all the ice cube trays into a large plastic bag. Then she put it on the kitchen counter and started whacking it with a meat tenderizer, breaking the cubes into little shards of ice.

She'd made at least a pound of ice chips by the time Jed walked into the kitchen.

"What are you doing?" he asked.

"I'm making ice chips for Jax," Allie explained, continuing to thwack the bag of ice.

"She hasn't asked for ice chips," Jed said. "But she is asking for you."

"For me?" Allie asked, stopping the meat tenderizer in midswing.

He nodded. "She's doing really well, by the way. Her water just broke, and she's nine centimeters dilated. But she's going to be ready to start pushing soon, and she'd like you to be there with her."

But Allie shook her head, helplessly. "I'm sorry. I know it's cowardly. But I can't go in there. I just can't." Her voice cracked, and, to stop herself from crying, she went back to hitting the ice cubes.

"Hey, what's wrong?" Jed asked her, in between her whacking the ice cubes.

"What's wrong?" Allie repeated, putting down the meat tenderizer. "What's wrong? Jax is having a baby in the next room, for God's sake."

"That's right," he said, calmly. "And everything's going to be fine. So why are you in here, and not in there?"

She paused, slightly out of breath from her exertions. "Because I'm terrified," she said.

"Terrified of what?"

"Terrified of . . ." She stopped. It was hard to put this nameless fear into words. It made it feel too real. Too . . . *possible*. "I'm terrified of something happening to Jax. Or the baby. Or both of them," she said, her voice breaking. "And I couldn't stand it if it did. I've already lost someone once in my life that I loved. I can't lose anyone else right now. I just can't."

"Hey, we're not going to lose anyone here," Jed said, his friendly brown eyes looking into her own. "Jax is as strong as an ox. A *small* ox, maybe. But still, an ox. And the baby's fine. We have her hooked up to a fetal monitor and—"

"You have a fetal monitor?" Allie asked in surprise.

"That's right. We're not complete amateurs here," he said, good-naturedly. "Her heartbeat is really strong, by the way. But Jax, tough as she is, is in a lot of pain. And an epidural, unfortunately, is not in our bag of tricks. So forget about those ice chips"—he gave her an encouraging smile—"and get in there."

Allie wavered, then reached deep inside herself for something she hadn't even known was there anymore. "Okay, let's go," she said, suddenly, putting the meat tenderizer down. Jed smiled and led her to her bedroom. There, she brushed past the other paramedics to Jax, who was sitting on the edge of Allie's bed, rocking back and forth a little, her eyes half closed.

"Jax?" Allie said, taking her hand.

"You're here," Jax said, opening her eyes. She exhaled slowly, the relief palpable on her face.

"I'm here," Allie said, squeezing her hand.

CHAPTER 27

S he is *so* beautiful," Allie murmured, using the crumpled
tissue in her hand to wipe a tear out of the corner of her eye.
She couldn't remember the last time she'd cried this much. Okay,
she *could* remember the last time she'd cried this much. But the
circumstances tonight couldn't be more different. These weren't
tears of sorrow. They were tears of joy. Joy and relief.

"She *is* beautiful, isn't she?" Jax agreed, beaming with pride.
Jax was lying, propped up by pillows, on Allie's bed, wearing another nightgown Allie had helped her change into when Jed had
finally persuaded her to let go of the baby long enough for him
to examine her.

Now, though, the baby was back in Jax's arms, swaddled in a
faded blue bath towel and nothing else. Her name was Jenna, Jax
had announced, and as of this moment, she was not quite one
hour old. But even so, she seemed to Allie to be an unusually
alert baby. And an unusually beautiful one, too.

"She's one of the few newborns I've ever seen who doesn't
look like an overripe tomato," Allie confessed to Jax. "You know,
bright red and wrinkled all over."

Jax laughed and snuggled Jenna more securely against her. "Well, naturally, I'm a little biased. I think she's perfect. And you know what else, Allie? I think she may be the first one of my daughters who actually looks more like Jeremy than me. What do you think?"

"She does look like him," Allie agreed, leaning closer and studying Jenna's light brown eyes and dandelion soft brown hair. "But it's only fair, Jax, that one of your children looks like Jeremy. The other three are carbon copies of you."

"Oh, I'm glad she looks like him," Jax said fervently. "I'm absolutely thrilled."

Allie drew back, surprised by the strength of emotion in her voice. But then it occurred to her how exhausted Jax must be. She knew how exhausted *she* was, and she'd only *coached* Jax through the delivery.

On closer inspection, though, Allie had to admit that Jax didn't look exhausted. In fact, she looked absolutely radiant. Radiant and relaxed. Leave it to Jax to go through natural childbirth and look as if she'd been to a day spa.

There was a light tap on the door to Allie's room now and Jed stuck his head in. "How's everybody doing?" he asked.

"We're fine," Jax said, smiling. "Is it time to go?"

He nodded. "The stretcher's ready. And I spoke to the hospital. They're expecting us." The plan was to take Jax and Jenna to the hospital to be examined, and for Jeremy to meet them there.

"Any chance we can skip the stretcher?" Jax asked, hopefully. "I'm perfectly capable of walking."

"Sorry, Jax, those are the rules," Jed said, before ducking out again.

Jax rolled her eyes, but then turned her attention back to Jenna, tucking her towel more closely around her. And the expression on Jax's face as she looked down at her daughter was one of such pure love that Allie felt more tears welling up in her eyes. She sighed, resignedly, and plucked a few more tissues out of the box on the bedside table.

A few minutes later, Jed and the other two paramedics appeared in the doorway with the stretcher.

"Time to go, Jax," Jed said. "And Allie? We'll try not to wake up your son as we're leaving."

Allie laughed through her tears. "Honestly, if Jax's labor didn't wake him up, I don't think anything will."

"Amazing," Jed said, with a shake of his head.

"It *is* amazing," Allie agreed. "But I think he's going to be disappointed when he wakes up this morning and discovers he missed all the excitement."

Allie was right about that.

She waited until they were both sitting at the breakfast table before she told him. She'd wanted him to get at least half a bowl of cornflakes into his stomach before she broke the news. Wyatt, not surprisingly, was incredulous.

"Jax's baby was born here last night?" he repeated. "In our cabin?"

"In our cabin," Allie said, with a tired smile. She *still* had not been to sleep. She'd known it was pointless after Jax left to even try. She was still feeling the incredible rush of emotion, and excitement, from Jenna's birth. So she'd sat on the living room couch, leafing aimlessly through a book. Then, at dawn, she'd taken a cup of coffee out on the front porch and watched the sunrise.

"Why didn't you wake me up?" Wyatt asked, crestfallen. "I could have helped."

Allie suppressed a smile. "The firemen had everything under control," she assured him.

"Firemen?" he repeated, eyes widening.

Allie sighed inwardly. Now Wyatt would never forgive her. Missing a baby's birth was one thing. Missing real live firemen on his doorstep was another.

"Well, they were *volunteer* firemen," she said quickly. "Butternut isn't big enough to have a full-time fire department. So they have people who have other jobs during the day but can be firemen in an emergency."

"Did they have a truck?" he asked, putting another heaping spoonful of cornflakes into his mouth.

"No, no truck. Not last night," Allie said, relieved that she could answer that honestly. She didn't think it was necessary to mention that they'd had an ambulance instead. Ambulances ranked just slightly below fire trucks in Wyatt's estimation.

"But the real reason I didn't wake you up last night," she said, "was because I wanted you to be well rested for today. You're going to have a special visitor later this morning."

"Who?" he asked, gulping orange juice.

"Caroline," Allie said. "She called this morning and asked if she could come over for a while and play with you while I took a nap."

Wyatt's whole face lit up. Then he considered something. "Is Frankie coming, too?"

"No, Frankie's not coming," Allie said. "Somebody needs to stay at Pearl's and feed all those hungry customers," she explained.

Wyatt nodded thoughtfully. That seemed fair to him. He went back to eating his cereal, only to remember something once his mouth was full of cornflakes again.

"Did you know Frankie can crush a soda can against his head?" he asked Allie.

"No, sweetie," Allie said, the corners of her mouth lifting in an almost imperceptible smile. "But I believe it. And don't talk with your mouth full," she added, gently.

By the time Caroline arrived, Wyatt was practically dizzy with excitement.

"Caroline!" he shouted, flinging himself into her arms as soon as she got out of her car. "Jax's baby was born here last night. Right in my mom's bedroom. And it didn't even wake me up!"

Caroline laughed, hugging him back. "I know," she said. "I heard all about it. It was the talk of Pearl's this morning."

"There were real firemen and everything," Wyatt explained, following her up the porch steps where Allie was waiting. "Well, they were *half* firemen," he qualified. "They didn't have a fire engine."

"Not even *half* a fire engine?" Caroline asked, glancing at Allie in amusement.

But Wyatt ignored the question. "I'm going to get changed into my bathing suit," he announced, breathlessly, before disappearing into the cabin.

"Bathing suit? Are we going swimming?" Caroline asked, sitting down on the top step beside Allie.

Allie shook her head. "Oh no. Wyatt has much bigger plans for you. You're going to be catching tadpoles."

Caroline raised her eyebrows. "Tadpoles?"

"Catching tadpoles is his new calling in life. That, and digging up worms. Between the two of them, it's basically a full-time job. But you don't have to help him if you don't want to," she added, quickly. "He'd probably be just as happy having you watch him catch tadpoles."

"Are you kidding? I wouldn't miss it for the world," Caroline said, slipping off her sandals and rolling up her blue jeans.

But when she looked back up at Allie, her expression was suddenly serious. And even, Allie thought, a little angry.

"Do you mind telling me something?" she asked, tightly.

"Of course not," Allie replied, surprised by Caroline's sudden change of mood.

"What on earth was Jax thinking, driving alone out here last night, with that baby about to drop?"

"She *wasn't* thinking," Allie said, feeling guilty. "At least not about herself. She was thinking about me. About whether or not I'd heard about . . ." Her voice trailed off.

Caroline sighed. "That is so like Jax," she said, finally, with a mixture of affection and exasperation.

"I know," Allie agreed, unhappily. "And I feel terrible about it, Caroline. I really do. I mean, what if something had gone wrong last night? I never would have forgiven myself."

"Allie," Caroline said, "even if you'd known Jax was planning on coming out here last night, there wouldn't have been anything you could have done to stop her. She's as stubborn as a mule. Always has been. Always will be. And what's more"—Caroline put an arm around Allie's shoulder—"nothing *did* go wrong. Everything worked out all right, thanks to you. Once you realized Jax was in labor, you stepped up, and took charge."

"Ha!" Allie snorted. "I was a complete coward. I would have hidden in the kitchen all night if one of the paramedics hadn't given me a talking-to about how much Jax needed me."

"Well, maybe you needed a little encouragement." Caroline smiled. "Who wouldn't have, under the circumstances? The important thing is that you were there when it mattered. That's what counts."

"Maybe," Allie said. But she appreciated Caroline's loyalty.

Whatever she did, Allie knew, Caroline, and Jax, too, would always see the best in her.

"Listen, I'll take over now," Caroline said. "And you, I hope, will take a nap. A *long* nap."

"I'll try," Allie promised, starting to stand up. But Caroline grabbed her hand.

"Allie? One more thing. Don't believe everything you hear. About Walker, I mean. I'm sure Caitlin is here for a reason. A *good* reason. I trust Walker. I really do. After all, you don't pour a man's coffee for three years without learning *something* about him."

"I haven't given it a lot of thought," Allie said, honestly. And, amazingly, it was true. As soon as she'd realized Jax was in labor last night, she'd forced the thought of Walker Ford and his ex-wife out of her mind. The only thing that mattered, she'd told herself, was that Jax and the baby were safe. Everything else could wait.

After everyone had left that morning, she hadn't let herself think about him then, either. It seemed wrong, somehow, to be preoccupied by her own problems. They were so insignificant when compared to the birth of a child.

Now, of course, it would be harder. With Jax and the baby in good hands, and Caroline watching Wyatt, it was going to take some effort not to think about Walker. Not to mention his house-guest.

Caroline started to say something else just then, but Wyatt came barreling back out on to the front porch, wearing his favorite red bathing suit.

"Are you ready, Caroline?" he asked, jumping up and down.

"As ready as I'll ever be," Caroline said, winking at Allie.

Wyatt took Caroline's hand and tugged impatiently on it as she followed him down the cabin's front steps. "Don't worry, Caroline," he said, earnestly. "I'll teach you how to catch tadpoles. It's easy. You can even have your own bucket for them, if you want. That way you can take them home with you."

"That would be very nice," Caroline said, swinging Wyatt's hand.

Allie smiled, a little wearily, as she went back into the cabin.

But a moment later, she heard Caroline calling to her through the screen door. "Allie," she said, "I think you might have to postpone that nap. You have a visitor."

Allie came back out on the porch in time to see Walker's pickup roll into view. In an instant, her tiredness fell away from her. But it was almost immediately replaced by a stomach-churning dread. Suddenly, she felt certain she knew why Walker was here. But she forced herself to come down the steps and walk out to his truck to meet him.

Caroline tried to coax Wyatt down to the lake with her, but once he realized it was Walker, he ran up to him.

"Walker! You're here, too," he said, beaming at him and then back at Caroline, who'd come up beside him and taken his hand. He looked as if he could not believe his luck.

"Hey, buddy," Walker said, looking genuinely pleased to see Wyatt.

But Allie shot him a warning look. If he was here to break things off with her—and she felt sure that he was—she didn't want him making promises to Wyatt he couldn't keep.

"Do you want to catch tadpoles with us?" Wyatt asked. But Walker, taking his cue from Allie, seemed suddenly noncommittal. "Maybe some other time," he said. "Today I'm here to talk to your mom, okay?"

"Okay," Wyatt said. "But my mom's really tired," he warned.

"She helped Jax have a baby last night. Caroline said she's supposed to take a nap."

"Hello, Walker," Caroline said, now. And despite defending Walker only moments ago, there was a coolness to her tone that Allie had never heard before. Walker, she saw, noticed it, too.

"Hi, Caroline," he said, a little uneasily.

And then to Wyatt he said, "Listen, you'd better catch those tadpoles. They won't wait all day, you know. And don't worry about your mom. I know she's tired. I won't keep her long."

Wyatt nodded happily and let Caroline lead him away.

"Hi," Walker said to Allie, his blue eyes serious. "Is it okay if we talk now? I tried to get ahold of you yesterday, but I couldn't. Your line was busy. And your cell—"

"I know," Allie said, sighing inwardly. She'd forgotten to charge her cell phone. What a day for her to be out of reach, she thought. First Jax, and then Walker . . .

"Anyway, judging from what I heard in town this morning," he said, "you've had your hands full here. And if you'd rather I come back later, after you've had a chance to get some rest, that's fine."

But Allie shook her head. "No, now is as good a time as any," she said, walking back toward the cabin. And she meant it. Whatever Walker had come to say, she knew, wouldn't be any easier to hear later.

"Would you like an iced tea?" she asked, pushing the cabin's screen door open.

"Sure," he said. He followed her into the kitchen and sat down at the table. She poured their iced teas from the pitcher in the refrigerator and sat down across from him. It was hard not to think about another night in this kitchen. A night when he'd kissed her, passionately, just a few feet from where they were now sitting awkwardly.

He put some sugar in his iced tea. She fiddled with a lemon wedge in hers. But he didn't say anything.

Finally, she got impatient. "Look, Walker, we both know why you're here."

"We do?" he asked, surprised.

"Yes, we do. And since you can't seem to tell me, I'll make it easy for you. You're here because you don't . . . you don't want to see me anymore." *There,* she'd said it, never mind how much hearing herself say it had hurt.

"*What?* No," Walker said, obviously blindsided. "Why would I not want to see you anymore?"

"Because your ex-wife is back in your life."

He frowned. "You mean back in my life *to stay?*"

She shrugged, a tiny shrug.

"Allie," he said, "you've got it all wrong. That is *not* why I'm here. First of all, my ex-wife and I have been separated for over two years. And we've been divorced for over a year. We are *not* reconciling. That's not why she's here." He shook his head, looking less surprised now than disappointed. "You know, Allie," he added, "I wish, instead of listening to the Butternut rumor mill, you'd just picked up the phone and asked me why she was here."

Allie's cheeks flushed with anger. "And I wish you'd told me she was coming. Instead of leaving me to rely on the Butternut rumor mill for my information."

"Okay, that's fair," Walker said, calmly. "And I would have told you she was coming, if I'd known ahead of time."

"You mean, she just dropped by?"

"Yes, she did," he said. "And believe me, I was as surprised as you are." He added quickly, "She's not staying with me, by the way. She's staying at the White Pines resort. She drove over there last night after we had dinner."

After Jax saw her car in your driveway, Allie thought, tracing the pattern in the tablecloth with her fingertip.

"Look," he said, after a short silence. "My ex-wife—her name is Caitlin—isn't here because we're reconciling. She's here because we have some loose ends we need to tie up."

"Loose ends?" she echoed.

He sighed. "It's complicated. It turns out we haven't quite finished what we started."

"So you still care about her?" Allie asked, surprised by how hard the words were to say.

"Yes, I do—though not in the way you mean. But I realized, Allie, that I can't start things with you until I've ended things with her."

"I thought that was the point of getting a divorce, Walker. You ended things with someone."

"Well, divorce doesn't always bring closure. Or it didn't for us, anyway."

Allie felt impatient again. She needed him to get to the point. "Walker, why are you here, exactly?"

"I'm here to ask for more time," he said, quietly. "I'm here to ask if we can . . . put things on hold until I can figure this out. Not that long ago, Allie, you needed more time, too," he added gently.

Allie took a deep breath and closed her eyes. She had needed more time. But this was different, wasn't it? And, suddenly, she knew what she needed to do. What she needed to say. "No," she said, opening her eyes.

"No what?"

"No, Walker, I'm sorry. You can't have more time. You can't have more time because it's over between us."

He looked stunned. "Allie, that's *not* what I want," he said.

"Well, maybe it's not about what *you* want, Walker," she said, studying the tablecloth with renewed interest and trying to ignore the hot, prickly sensation of tears building up in her eyes. "Maybe it's about what *I* want, too. And I want it to be over. *Now.* I knew, from the morning we met at Pearl's, that it would be a mistake for us to get involved with each other. I should have listened to myself, Walker. I shouldn't have gotten caught up in the moment. Because I was right. It was a mistake."

"I don't believe that. And I don't think you believe it either."

"You're wrong," Allie said, but her voice quavered slightly when she said it.

"So that night we spent together, that was mistake? And that day on the boat? That was a mistake, too?" he asked, his blue eyes dark with anger.

"Yes," she said, lifting her chin stubbornly. "They may not have felt like mistakes at the time. But in retrospect, I think they were."

There was a burst of laughter from down at the lake, and Allie got up and walked over to the kitchen window. If she craned her neck, she could glimpse Caroline and Wyatt through the trees, splashing in the water at the lake's edge.

Walker got up and joined her at the window. He watched for a moment, too, then asked, quietly, "Allie, where is this coming from?"

Allie looked at him, then back out the window. When she spoke again, her voice was mercifully calm, betraying none of the emotional turmoil she felt inside. "Walker, I don't expect you to understand. You're not a father. But that little boy down there? He's my whole world. And I'm his whole world. Because except for a few other people—Caroline, Frankie, Jax's daughter, Jade—I'm it for him here. He's already had one parent taken away from him. So I've got to be here for him. Every day. All day long. It takes a lot of energy. Physical and emotional. But I have to have that energy. I have to be present in his life. Fully present. I can't spend my time waiting for you and your ex-wife to find closure. Or hoping that you and I can have a relationship of our own one day. I can't put my life on hold, Walker. Wyatt deserves better than that. And you know what? I deserve better than that, too. And now," she said, turning to him, "I need you to go. I really do need to get some rest."

Walker stared at her, wordlessly, frustration and sadness mingling in his face. Then he shook his head and started to say something, but changed his mind. He left the kitchen, left the cabin, and drove away.

Allie turned and watched out the other kitchen window as his truck disappeared down the driveway. Then she turned back to the window in front of her and found Wyatt's red bathing suit through the trees. A single, hot tear slid down her cheek. But that was the only one she allowed herself. She'd cried enough for one day.

Later that night, as she was putting calamine lotion on Wyatt's many mosquito bites, she looked for a way to broach the subject of Walker Ford with him. Wyatt needed to know that their Sunday morning fishing trips had ended. But she wanted to break it to him gently, in language he could understand. That meant skipping the part about her relationship with Walker. Or rather, her *former* relationship with Walker.

"You missed one," Wyatt said, interrupting her thoughts. He pointed to a mosquito bite on his elbow and Allie patted it with a calamine-soaked cotton ball.

Wyatt gave her a grateful smile. Allie thought he looked especially adorable. He was sitting on the edge of the bathtub, clean and sweet smelling after his bath, and wearing his favorite pair of pajamas, sky blue with a pattern of puffy white clouds on them.

"Is that all of them?" she asked, examining his arms.

Wyatt nodded.

"You know, Wyatt," she said, screwing the lid back on the calamine lotion, "this is the same stuff my mother put on me and my mother's mother put on her."

"Same bottle, too?" Wyatt asked, fascinated.

She chuckled. "No, not the same bottle. But it still looks exactly the same. And it still works as well, too."

"But it's pink," he objected, examining the splotches of it on his arms and legs.

Allie tried not to smile. "No, I wouldn't say it was pink. I'd say it was more of a *peachy* color." She tossed the cotton ball into the wastebasket and put the calamine lotion back into the medicine cabinet.

"All right, big boy," she said. "Time for bed."

"But I haven't finished my train tracks yet," Wyatt said, giving her a beseeching look.

Allie sighed. "Five minutes," she said sternly, following him into the living room, where he was adding a new spur to his railroad.

She sat down on the couch, watching him as he worked. When it had been more than five minutes, she gently interrupted him.

"Wyatt, honey?"

"Yes," he said, not looking up. He was lying on his stomach, level with the train track, frowning in concentration as he put a bridge together.

"Wyatt, I spoke to Walker Ford today. He said he's going to be really busy at the boatyard, and he's not going to be able to take you fishing anymore on Sunday mornings."

Wyatt paused and looked up.

"Not even sometimes?" he asked, his face still hopeful.

"Not even sometimes," Allie echoed, something catching in her throat. "But you know, Wyatt, we have our own boat now. I can take you fishing anytime. Or we could fish right off the end of our dock. I may not be as good at it as Walker is, but I know all the basics. We could still have fun together."

"Maybe," Wyatt said, going back to working on his train tracks. There would be no tears, Allie realized with relief. Just lingering disappointment. Which, in its own way, was almost as bad as tears.

The five minutes Allie had told Wyatt he could play for turned into ten. And then fifteen. She knew it was past his bedtime, but something was nagging at her. Something that had been at the edge of her consciousness all day.

"Wyatt," she said, tentatively, "do you still miss Eden Prairie?"

He shrugged. He was running an exploratory train around his system of tracks now, and Allie could tell he wasn't really listening to her.

She tried again. "I mean, do you miss our old neighborhood? And our old friends? You know, like Teddy?"

Wyatt gave a little sigh that was almost comical in its irritation. Like an old man who'd been interrupted while reading the newspaper.

"Sometimes I miss them," he said, glancing up from the train tracks.

"Because I was thinking . . ." *I was thinking that moving here may have been a mistake, after all.* But that's not what she said to Wyatt. What she said to Wyatt was, "I was thinking that we could move back to Eden Prairie. We couldn't have our old house back, of course. We already sold that. But we could rent an apartment there. I could find a job. And you could start kindergarten."

Wyatt stopped pushing the train around the tracks and looked up. She had his full attention now.

"We could still keep the cabin, you know," she said quickly. "Maybe come up here for a couple of weeks in the summer and see our friends. We just wouldn't live here all the time anymore."

"But I *like* living here all the time," Walker said, a frown creasing his smooth little forehead.

"Why?" Allie asked, knowing that if what he said had anything to do with Walker Ford, it would only strengthen her inclination to leave. Walker was not part of the picture anymore. For her or for Wyatt.

At first, Wyatt didn't say anything. He just looked around the living room. And Allie's eyes followed his as he did. Trying to see what he saw. It looked very different than it had on their first night here, almost three months ago. Between her and Johnny Miller, their handyman, they'd cleaned, painted, buffed, and polished every single inch of the cabin, inside and out. It had been hard work. But it had paid off. This room, for instance, had a soft, warm glow to it, and it looked not only lived in but well cared for, too. Maybe even *loved,* she realized with surprise.

"Wyatt," she persisted, "*why* do you want to stay here?"

He looked thoughtful. "Because it's home," he said finally. Decisively. And he went back to playing with his train set.

CHAPTER 28

So . . . you're staying?" Jax repeated, not trusting herself to believe what Allie had just said.

"We're staying," Allie agreed, with a rueful smile.

"Allie, that's the best news I've heard in a long time," Jax said, almost light-headed with relief. It had only been three months since Allie and Wyatt had moved to Butternut, but already it was impossible to imagine life here without them.

"I'd like to propose a toast, then," Jax said, giddily, raising her can of Coke. "To Allie and Wyatt staying in Butternut."

"I'll drink to that," Caroline said, and the three of them clinked their soda cans together.

It was nighttime, and they were sitting at Jax's kitchen table, eating the pizza that Allie and Caroline had brought over for dinner. Joy, Josie, Jade, and Wyatt had finished dinner already and were watching a movie in the living room. Jenna, now two weeks old, was sleeping in her crib upstairs, her baby monitor flickering on the table in front of Jax.

"Jax," Caroline said now, with mock disapproval, "you didn't really think Allie was going to leave because of some *man,* did you? I mean, if a woman left Butternut every time a relationship didn't work out, this town wouldn't have any women in it."

"No, of course I didn't think that," Jax said quickly. "I was just worried that after spending the summer here, she might decide Butternut was too dull for her, that's all."

"Dull?" Allie repeated, her eyes widening in disbelief. "Which part of it was dull, Jax? Wyatt and I fleeing our cabin during the tornado watch? Or your unplanned home birth, in *my* home?"

Jax laughed. The girl had a point.

"No, really," Allie said, her hazel eyes suddenly serious. "When Wyatt said this was our home, I realized he was right. It *is* our home. We could live in a hundred places, and not find one that felt as much like home as Butternut does, or as that tumbledown old cabin does. What happened between me and Walker isn't going to make it feel any *less* like home, for me or for Wyatt. Besides, things are really getting interesting at work. Sara's started taking me with her to some of the artists' studios, and she's going to let me start managing some of our relationships with them."

"Allie, that's wonderful," Caroline said, beaming at her.

"But there is one glitch in this whole plan to stay," Allie said, breaking off a piece of one of the chocolate chip cookies she'd baked for Jax. "I didn't realize when I told Walker that I didn't want to see him anymore that it would be impossible not to see him anymore in a town the size of Butternut."

"Do you see him often?" Caroline asked, popping open another can of soda.

Allie sighed. "All the time. At the gas station, at the grocery store, at the bank." She ticked the places off on her fingers. "The question is, where haven't I seen him?"

"That's all right," Caroline said. "You'll get used to it." But she didn't sound convinced.

"Maybe," Allie conceded. "But in the meantime, it's damned awkward. And the strange thing is, while I'm trying to ignore him, he's just staring at me. Like he's trying to get my attention. And then, at the grocery store the other day, he started to approach me. Of course, I just hightailed it out of there. But it was almost as if there was something he wanted to say to me."

"Maybe there *was* something he wanted to say to you," Jax interjected.

Allie shrugged. "I think he said it all, don't you?"

"What he said, Allie, was that he needed more time," Caroline pointed out. "He never said he didn't care about you."

Allie frowned, still picking at her cookie. "No, he never said he didn't care about me. And I think he *does* care, in his way. But he's not ready to have a serious relationship. And you know what?" she asked, looking at both of them in turn. "I'm not sure I'm ready to have one either."

"Is this about you feeling guilty?" Caroline asked.

"Yes. Yes and no," Allie said. "During that time we were together I was so caught up in the moment that I . . . I didn't think about Gregg as much as I should have."

"I didn't realize there were guidelines about that," Caroline said, gently.

"There aren't. But sometimes I wish there were. I mean, how do you fall in love with someone, while still remembering how much you loved—how much you *still* love—someone else?" Allie asked. But the infant monitor chose that moment to crackle to life. The three of them listened. There was a faint rustling, a tiny whimper, then silence.

"Close call," Caroline said, as she stood up and started to clear the table. Allie helped her.

"This is the longest she's ever slept," Jax said, glancing at her watch. "Six hours."

"Six hours is amazing for a two-week-old," Allie said, encouragingly, stacking the dirty dishes at the table. "I think she's going to be a really good sleeper."

"Maybe," Jax said, frowning. But she wasn't thinking about infant sleep cycles. She was thinking about why Jeremy hadn't come home yet tonight. He'd called earlier and told Jade to tell her he'd be home late. But it wasn't like him not to ask to speak to her directly. And it wasn't like him, either, to stay out late. Especially when they had a newborn at home.

As if reading Jax's mind, Caroline asked, "Where's Jeremy, hon?"

"Oh, he's working late," she said vaguely. "He'll be home soon." She started to put the leftover pizza away.

"Oh no you don't," Caroline scolded, whisking the pizza box away from her. "We're doing all the work tonight. Even if you make it harder for us by refusing to get a dishwasher."

"I like hand washing dishes," Jax said. But still, she didn't try to help them as they washed them for her. Being taken care of didn't come naturally to her. But tonight, she was too preoccupied by Jeremy's absence to object. Too unsettled by what it might mean. And too frightened to consider the question very closely.

"Something wrong, Jax?" Allie asked, drying a dish.

"No," Jax said quickly, shaking her head. "I'm fine."

But Allie didn't believe her. She put the plate she'd finished drying in the cupboard, hung up the dish towel, and came over to sit next to her at the kitchen table.

"I wonder," she asked Jax. "Does bringing home a new baby

get easier every time? Or does it always feel like you're doing it for the first time?"

"A little bit of both," Jax admitted. And then, much to her surprise, she started to cry.

"Oh, Jax," Allie said, giving her a hug. Caroline stopped wiping down the counter and came over to comfort her, too.

"I'm fine, really," Jax protested. "Just a little emotional."

"Of course you are," Allie said, reassuringly. "How could you not be? It's overwhelming, isn't it? Especially the sleep deprivation." She gave a little shudder, obviously remembering Wyatt's infancy.

"And the hormones," Caroline chimed in. "When I brought Daisy home from the hospital, I cried if anyone so much as said 'boo' to me."

Jax tried to smile as she mopped at her tears with the tissue Caroline had helpfully provided for her. But she knew it wasn't sleep deprivation. Or hormones. It was fear. Plain and simple. Fear that Jeremy's absence had something to do with him finding out about the money missing from the college savings account.

"I don't deserve you, either of you," Jax said gratefully, hugging them both, one after the other.

"Of course you do," Allie said, just as Wyatt appeared in the kitchen doorway.

"Mom, the movie's over," he said, rubbing his eyes sleepily.

"Already?" Allie asked. "Didn't we just put it in the DVD player?"

But he shook his head. "No, it's really over. Do you want to know what happened? I can tell you the whole movie."

"Oh, definitely," Allie assured him. "But let's save it for the drive home, okay?"

She smiled apologetically at Jax. "Are you okay?" she asked.

"We don't have to leave now. We can wait until Jeremy gets back." Caroline nodded her agreement.

"No, absolutely not," Jax said. "You both have work tomorrow, remember? And I'm much better now that I've had a good cry."

There was a flurry of activity, as Jax said good-bye to Allie, Wyatt, and Caroline and supervised the girls' bedtime routines. By some miracle, all three of them went to bed without complaint or incident.

Afterward, Jax checked on Jenna. She was still asleep, her breathing regular, and Jax adjusted her cotton blanket and left the room, closing the door silently behind her.

Then she went downstairs to the living room and waited. And waited. *And waited.* It was nine thirty. Then ten o'clock. Then ten thirty. *Where is he?* she wondered, with a rising sense of panic. *And why hasn't he called?*

Finally, a little before eleven, as a light rain started to fall, she heard a car pull up in front of the house. Someone got out of it, and it drove away. She listened to the footsteps crunching up the gravel walkway. Then she got up from the couch and looked out through the living room window.

It was Jeremy. But he seemed . . . *different.* Unsteady on his feet. Was he ill? she wondered, hurrying to open the front door for him.

"Jeremy? Are you okay?" she asked.

He stopped on the doorstep, listing slightly to one side. "I'm fine," he said, thickly, as he brushed past her on his way into the house. She cringed, reflexively, as she caught the scent of whiskey on him.

"Jeremy, are you drunk?" she asked, not trusting her powers of observation. She closed the door behind him and followed him into the living room, where he lowered himself, clumsily, into one of the armchairs. She sat down on the couch, careful to keep her distance from him. She felt as if she didn't know this Jeremy. She felt like he was a stranger to her.

Maybe that was because she'd never once, in all their years together, seen Jeremy drunk. Unlike Jax, who was a teetotaler, he did drink occasionally. A glass of champagne at their wedding. A beer at his poker games. But he never drank too much. He'd told Jax, once, it was because he'd decided, early on, that being drunk the night before wasn't worth the price of the hangover the next morning. But she had another theory about why he never crossed that line. It was out of respect for Jax. And the havoc that alcohol had wreaked in her life.

"What's wrong, Jax?" Jeremy asked, looking at her a little blearily.

"Nothing's wrong," Jax said tightly, looking away. "It's just that being drunk doesn't suit you," she said, finally.

There was a long silence. "Doesn't suit me, huh?" he asked, with uncharacteristic sarcasm. "Well, you know what doesn't suit you, Jax? Being a liar doesn't suit you."

Jax jerked her head up and looked at him, too surprised to say anything.

"Oh, don't act like you don't know what I'm talking about."

"I don't," Jax said, when she finally found her voice again. And it was true. To a point. There had been so many lies—not lies she'd told him, exactly, so much as truths she hadn't told him—that she didn't know which one he was referring to.

"Did you really think I wouldn't notice the missing money, Jax?" Jeremy asked now. "Ten thousand dollars is a lot of money to overlook, don't you think?"

She felt all the air rush out of her body at once. But when she could suck in a little breath, she whispered, "I knew you'd find out about it eventually. If I couldn't replace it first."

"Replace it?" he repeated, mockingly. Jax flinched. He'd never spoken to her in that tone of voice before. He'd never spoken to *anyone* in that tone of voice before, as far as she knew.

"And how were you going to replace it, exactly," he continued. "Who do you know who would lend you ten thousand dollars?"

"Nobody," she breathed, shakily. "I don't know anyone who could lend me that much money. But I had a plan . . ." Her voice trailed off. It was a lousy plan, and she knew it.

"A plan?" Jeremy mocked again. "You mean, like robbing a bank? Or was it robbing a liquor store, Jax?"

Jax's head jerked up again. So he knew. He'd made the connection. But how?

Jeremy watched the understanding register on her face, then shook his head. His anger seemed to have dissipated. But in its place was sadness. And the sadness, Jax decided, was worse than the anger. "If you wanted to throw that money away, Jax, why didn't you just do it?" he said now. "I could have forgiven you for that. But giving it to Bobby Lewis? Jax, what were you thinking?"

Jax's mind was racing. What did Jeremy know? And what didn't he know?

And Jeremy, seeing the expression on her face, laughed. A bitter laugh. "Jax, if I weren't so angry at you right now, I would almost—*almost*—feel sorry for you," he said. "Because it's making you crazy, isn't it? Trying to stay one step ahead of me. Trying to figure out where your plan went wrong."

Jax swallowed hard. But she didn't say anything. She couldn't. She was too terrified to speak.

"Well, I'll tell you where your plan went wrong," Jeremy said, with an almost eerie calmness. "It went wrong right from the very beginning, Jax. Because that's when you forgot how hard it is to keep secrets in Butternut. Big secrets. Little secrets. They all come out eventually in this town."

Jax was still trying to breathe normally. Trying, really, to breathe at all.

"And you know what, Jax?" he continued. "When I found out about your secrets—and your lies—I was willing to forgive you. Right up until today, I was defending you to myself. And then I had to make a deposit at the bank. I know ordinarily you'd handle that, but you were up with the baby last night, so I thought I'd give you a break and do it myself. Imagine my surprise when I saw John Quarterman and he mentioned your withdrawal. I didn't believe him at first. I had to see the account statement with my own eyes."

"But how . . ." Jax muttered, still not understanding how he'd put the two together.

"I knew Bobby had gotten out of prison, Jax," Jeremy said, understanding. "I knew he'd been here a couple of weeks ago. So it wasn't that difficult to put the two together."

He leaned forward now, resting his elbows on his knees and putting his head in his hands. He looked broken, almost. Defeated. And Jax's heart went out to him.

Sadness welled up inside her. *I'm sorry,* she thought. *I'm so sorry.* But she didn't trust her voice to speak the words.

"Why'd you do it, Jax?" he asked now, quietly, not looking up at her. "Why'd you give him the money?"

Again, she didn't speak.

He looked back up at her, sighed, and looked away. "Look, I know *why* you did it," he said, finally. "He was blackmailing you. But why did you *let* him blackmail you? Why didn't you come to me, Jax? Why didn't you tell me about it?"

She tried to swallow past the lump in her throat. Her eyes burned with tears. "I was trying to protect you," she said, softly.

"Protect me from what?" he asked, slumping back in his chair.

"From the truth," she said, simply. And it felt good, for once, to be honest. Whatever the consequences might be.

"Jax," Jeremy said, "I know the truth. I've always known the truth."

Jax looked at him now, questioningly. Were they talking about the same thing? she wondered. But she didn't see how they could be.

But Jeremy nodded. "Yes, Jax, *that* truth," he said, staring straight at her, his slightly bloodshot eyes suddenly coming into focus. "I know Bobby is Joy's father. I knew it the day she was born. I knew it the day you told me you were pregnant."

Jax stared at him uncomprehendingly. Her brain tried, and failed, to process what he'd said.

"Oh, for God's sake, Jax," he said, impatiently. "That first night, at the Fourth of July picnic, I heard you'd been seeing Bobby Lewis. That probably should have been the tip-off, right then and there, for me to stay away from you. Don't you think?"

Jax flinched. It was the first time she'd ever known Jeremy to say something cruel.

"But you know what, Jax? I couldn't stay away from you. I just couldn't. And I thought I had everything under control. Until the end of the night, when we were under that rowboat at the lake. And you seduced me, Jax, didn't you? Not that it was that difficult to do. I was in way over my head by then. I wanted you so badly. You were so innocent, and so knowing, at the same time. It was a pretty irresistible combination. For me, anyway."

Jax sat still, willing herself to listen, even though inside she was still reeling from shock.

"I told myself, that night, 'be careful.' 'Watch your step,'" Jeremy continued. "I knew you had an ulterior motive. And I thought I knew what it was, too. Because the only reason you'd be so casual about not using birth control was if you didn't care if you got pregnant. Or if you were already pregnant. I wasn't an idiot, even then. I knew about paternity tests. I knew I couldn't be held responsible for a child I hadn't fathered. I thought I was prepared for any contingency. But you know what, Jax?"

She shook her head. She didn't know. She didn't know *any-thing* anymore.

"There was one contingency I wasn't prepared for. And that was falling in love with you. Because by the time you told me you were pregnant, a couple of weeks later, I didn't care any-more who the father was. I figured raising another man's child was a small price to pay for spending the rest of my life with you. And then, when Joy was born, I realized it didn't matter whose child she was. I couldn't have loved her any more if she had been mine."

He looked at Jax, his face suddenly softened by some memory. Maybe the memory of the first time he'd held Joy.

"Don't get me wrong," he went on. "I wasn't sorry when Bobby Lewis went to prison. I didn't really want him hanging around, making trouble for us. And I was relieved, too, that Joy looked so much like you. I mean, I would have loved her all the same if she'd been the spitting image of that man. But still . . ."

"You knew?" Jax said, softly, wonderingly, still trying to un-derstand what he was telling her. "You knew that whole time? Why . . . why didn't you tell me you knew?"

"Why?" Jeremy asked, his head back in his hands. "I don't know. Now, of course, I wish I had. But at the time, I guess, it seemed so important to you that I *not* know. And I was worried, too, that if I told you I knew, you'd always be looking for signs that I didn't love Joy as much as I loved our other girls. Which I did. Which I *do*. I love her every bit as much as I love them."

"I know that," Jax said, her throat tightening. And it was true. She *did* know that. In retrospect, there had not been the least bit of difference in the way Jeremy had treated the girls over the years. But knowing that now only made her pain more acute. Because it only made her love him all the more, even as she knew she was about to lose him.

Now Jeremy sighed, heavily, and said, "Look, Jax, I don't want to leave you this way. But I can't stay, either. Not after what happened. I can forgive you for not telling me about Bobby being Joy's father. But this? I can't forgive you for this."

"Why not?" Jax asked, desperately fighting against what she knew now was inevitable. "Why is this so much worse?"

"Because you lied to me again," he said, an edge of anger returning to his voice. "And you took something that belonged to us—all six of us—and you threw it away. And not only that, Jax, but you didn't trust me enough to tell me the truth. Not in all the years of our marriage. And not now, either. Instead, you just kept lying. And hiding. And keeping secrets. And I can't stand it anymore, Jax. I can't live this way."

He rubbed his eyes, impatiently, and Jax realized, with surprise, that he was crying. Tonight was a night of firsts. The first time she'd ever seen Jeremy drunk. And the first time she'd ever seen him cry.

She took a deep breath now, working to keep the tears at bay. "Jeremy, you don't *have* to live this way anymore," she said. "You know the truth now. All of it. And I'll never lie to you again." Even as she said it, though, she knew it was too late. Way too late.

He said as much, too, by the way he looked at her, anger and pity mingling in his expression. "I hope you're not naive enough to think, Jax, that we've seen the last of Bobby Lewis," he said, ignoring her plea. "Because that's the problem with blackmail. It doesn't end with the payoff. Even if you tell him I know about Joy, it won't matter. Then he'll just threaten to have Joy take a DNA test. And while you and I both know he doesn't have any real interest in being Joy's father, the courts won't know that. So we'll probably pay him off again. Anything to keep him away from her, right?"

"Wrong," Jax said, shaking her head vehemently. "He's not coming back. He left town after I gave him the check. I haven't seen or heard from him since."

"Oh, give him time. He'll be back," Jeremy predicted, disgustedly.

"No, I'm positive he won't be," Jax said. "I'd stake my life on it."

Jeremy looked at her with curiosity. Then concern. "What'd you tell him, Jax?" he asked, a frown creasing his brow.

"I didn't tell him anything," she said. "But Frankie did. He was there the night I met Bobby, at the Mosquito Inn, and he knew Bobby was threatening me. So he walked him out to his truck. He told Bobby to leave and never come back. He told him if he ever did come back, he'd kill him. Just like that." Jax snapped her fingers. "And he meant it, too, Jeremy. Frankie's killed a man before, in self-defense. And he told me he'd do it again. To protect me. To protect *us*, actually, is what he said."

She'd hoped telling him this might bring Jeremy some relief. But she was disappointed. He didn't look relieved. He only looked angrier than he had been before.

"That's great," he said. "I'm thrilled to know that another man is fighting my battles for me. I mean, come on, Jax, don't you see? That was *my* conversation to have with Bobby. Not Frankie's.

And if you'd told me ahead of time you were meeting him, I could have come with you that night. We could have settled this with him together."

Then, suddenly, Jeremy sagged back in the armchair. He didn't look drunk anymore. He just looked exhausted. And it tore at Jax's heart.

She stood up and walked over to him, with the wild idea that she could help him somehow. Comfort him. Reassure him. Never mind the fact that she wasn't doing very well herself. She was trembling all over. And the tears she'd been trying to hold back were streaming down her face.

But as she approached him, Jeremy held up a hand.

"No, Jax. Don't," he said. "Don't make this any harder than it needs to be. I'm just going to throw some things into a suitcase and go. I won't drive. I'll call a friend to pick me up. Someone, hopefully, who'll let me sleep on their couch until I can find something more . . . permanent." He tripped a little over the word *permanent*.

But Jax heard it, just the same. And it sent an ice-cold jolt of fear through her whole body. But then, as it had in the past, the fear brought a new clarity with it, and with that clarity came a decision. She couldn't undo her past mistakes. But at least she could make the present a little easier for him. After all, he'd done nothing wrong. He had loved her, and Joy, despite knowing that Joy was Bobby's child. Why should he be punished? She was the one who'd gotten them to where they were now. She was the one who should leave.

"I'll leave, Jeremy," she said, a surreal sense of calm settling over her. "You stay here with the girls. They love you. They need you."

"Jax, I can't take care of Jenna," he said, in disbelief. "*And* three more children. *And* run a business."

"No, I'll take Jenna with me," Jax explained. "The girls will be starting school on Tuesday. And after school, Joy can be in charge. You'd be amazed at how responsible she's become this summer. She can help with homework, and dinner, and bedtime."

Jax thought about everything she would miss, the routine things she'd always taken so much pleasure in, and she had to choke back another sob. She felt fresh anguish knowing that her lies, her omissions, had, and would, cause the people she loved the most to suffer. And although she believed she was the one who should leave, the realization of what she was about to lose was almost too painful to contemplate.

Jeremy looked skeptical. "And where will you and Jenna go?" he asked.

We'll go to the only person I know who'd take in a mother and her two-week-old infant, Jax thought. "We'll go to Caroline's," she said. "And the girls can come visit me there every day after school." She willed herself, again, to be calm. She owed that much to Jeremy. She'd leave quickly and quietly. Without making a scene. Without any self-serving speeches, pleas for forgiveness, or ugly hysterics.

She stood and walked, mechanically, up the stairs to their bedroom. She took down a suitcase from the top shelf in the closet, put it on her bed, and started dumping her clothes into it. Then she carried the suitcase into Jenna's room and threw some of her stuff into it, too. It wasn't a great packing job. She'd have to come back some time, when Jeremy wasn't home. But she remembered the most important things for Jenna for the short run—diapers, wipes, and a dozen or so cotton onesies.

When she was done, she zippered the suitcase shut, carried it down to her pickup, and tossed it onto the front passenger seat. Then she unbuckled Jenna's car seat from the backseat and carried it upstairs. As she lifted her out of her crib and placed her gently into it, Jenna stirred, but she didn't wake up. Jax strapped her in and carried her downstairs. Jeremy was still sitting in the living room when she passed him on her way to the front door. He didn't look up.

Tears momentarily blurred her eyes as she fastened Jenna's car seat into the backseat. But she held them back as she drove the short distance to Pearl's, parked on the street in front of the coffee shop, and, lugging Jenna's car seat and her suitcase with her, rang the doorbell to Caroline's apartment.

"Jax?" Caroline said in surprise when she opened the door. In one quick glance, she took it all in. The baby. The suitcase. And the shell-shocked expression on Jax's face. "What is it, honey? What's wrong?"

"Everything," Jax whispered. "Everything's wrong."

"Oh, honey," Caroline said, sadly, taking the suitcase from Jax and leading her inside. "Come on in. You can tell me all about it upstairs."

And Jax did tell her all about it. From the beginning. And then she told her that the one thing she'd always been afraid would happen, had happened. She'd lost Jeremy. Probably forever.

CHAPTER 29

I t's showtime," Walker murmured, as he looked through the glass door of the Pine Cone Gallery and scanned the room, impatiently, for Allie. She was there, in the back right corner, standing in front of a painting, deep in conversation with a middle-aged woman. A customer, obviously, Walker thought, and he felt a fleeting jealousy of this person for being able to command Allie's undivided attention.

But when he pushed open the door and Allie heard the jangle of little bells attached to it, she glanced over at him. For a moment, anticipating another customer, the expression on her face was one of polite curiosity. But when she realized it was Walker, her pretty, smooth forehead creased in a frown, and she folded her arms grimly across her chest, angling her body away from the front of the gallery and Walker.

So she was just going to ignore him, Walker realized. Again. That was the pattern they'd fallen into since their talk in her kitchen that afternoon. She ignored him. And he let her ignore him.

Well, not today, Walker vowed. Today that was going to

change. Because he wasn't here as a jilted boyfriend. He was here as a customer. And, if she was as professional as he suspected she was, she was going to have to acknowledge him. Even if it took her all day to do it.

Fifteen minutes later, he was beginning to think it *would* take her all day to do it. She was still standing with the same woman, still examining the same painting. Walker, pretending to study a ceramic vase nearby, was eavesdropping on them. The woman loved the watercolor they were looking at, or claimed to, anyway, but she was worried about whether or not it would match the new slipcover on her sofa. *Ridiculous,* Walker thought. Who bought art to match their couch? And how could Allie tolerate people like this all day, anyway? It was an affront to her dignity, he decided. And while *she* might have to put up with it, *he* didn't have to.

So he wandered over to them, feigning casualness, until he was in front of the same painting as they were. It was a watercolor. A view of a lake's shoreline. A lake that looked remarkably like Butternut Lake. Walker liked it. And at five hundred dollars, it seemed reasonably priced to him.

"Nice painting," he said, edging closer. "Is that Butternut Lake?"

The woman with the new slipcover looked at him, a little nervously. She was obviously waiting for Allie to say something to him. But Allie pointedly ignored him.

He edged closer still. He was less than an arm's-length distance, now, from both of them. The woman took a step back and looked at Allie. "Do you want to help this customer?" she asked, frowning.

Allie's jaw clenched. She still wouldn't look at him. "Mr. Ford can see I'm busy right now," she said, to the customer, not to Walker. "He can come back another time."

"Actually, he can't," Walker said, stubbornly. "He needs to talk to you now."

"But I'm busy now," Allie said, still pretending to study the painting. "I would think even Mr. Ford could see that."

"I can see that," Walker said. "But I'm not leaving until you talk to me. Or at least agree to a time and a place to talk to me."

The customer, surprised, took another step back. She looked from Walker to Allie, waiting to see what would happen next.

Allie finally looked at Walker. "You have one minute," she said, in a clipped tone. She gestured for him to follow her to another corner of the gallery.

"*What are you doing here?*" she hissed at him, when they got there.

"Isn't it obvious?" he asked, leveling his gaze at her. "I'm here to see you."

"But this isn't the time," she said, coloring. "Or the place. I'm working." Walker tried to focus on her words, but he felt an unaccountable confusion descending over him. It was strange how she had that effect on him. No one else ever had.

Still, it was understandable. Today, for example, she looked particularly fetching. She was dressed in a tailored blouse, a pencil skirt, and low-heeled pumps, and her hair was pulled back and knotted loosely at the back of her neck. A pair of earrings dangled from her earlobes, and the faintest hint of perfume—jasmine?—clung to the air around her.

He'd never seen this side of her before. The working side. He wondered, briefly, if he found it more appealing than the side of her he already knew. The tank top, denim shorts, flip-flop side of her. But he decided he didn't. When it came to Allie, both sides of her were equally lovely. And equally irresistible.

"Walker?" she said now, her impatience growing. "I *said* I'm working."

"Look, I know that," he said, trying to focus. "And I tried to wait, but that woman is never going to make up her mind. I mean, it's a five-hundred-dollar painting. Why is she treating it like the most important decision she's ever made?"

Judging from the expression on Allie's face, though, he'd said the wrong thing. "Five hundred dollars is a lot of money," she snapped. "For *some* people, anyway."

"Okay, you're right. I didn't mean to imply that it wasn't. I just can't help but feel that that woman is wasting your time."

"As opposed to you, for instance?" Allie asked, raising her eyebrows.

Ouch, Walker thought. But he refused to be discouraged. "Look, I'll leave now, if you agree to meet me later."

"And if I don't?" Allie asked.

Walker hadn't considered this possibility. "Well, then, I'm staying," he said simply.

"You can't be serious?"

"What choice do I have, Allie? When I call you, it goes to voice mail. And when I see you, in public, you practically break your neck trying to get away from me." She didn't disagree.

"Look, just give me fifteen minutes. That's all I'll ask for. If you'll just hear me out, I promise you'll never have to speak to me again. Unless, of course, you want to." He gave her what he hoped was his most winning smile. But she didn't smile back. Then again, she didn't say no, either.

"Fine," she said, after thinking it over. "I'll talk to you as soon as that woman leaves. And you'll have exactly fifteen minutes."

But before he could answer her, he realized the woman who'd

been looking at the painting was heading for the front door. Allie noticed it, too.

"I'm sorry," Allie said, leaving Walker and approaching her. "I needed to speak to Mr. Ford. Do you have any more questions about the painting?"

The woman shook her head. "I don't think I'm ready to commit to it yet," she said, a little reproachfully. She didn't like the fact that Allie had abandoned her, Walker saw. "Maybe I'll come back the next time I'm in Butternut."

"We'd love to see you then," Allie said, smoothly. "In the meantime, would you like me to get you some information on the artist?"

"Sure," the woman said, pausing at the front door. She glanced warily at Walker. It didn't take a genius to see she'd heard at least part of his heated conversation with Allie.

While Allie was retrieving the artist's bio from behind the gallery's counter, Walker had an epiphany. He whipped out his wallet.

"Ms . . . um, I'm sorry, I didn't catch your name," he said, approaching the woman.

"I didn't tell you my name," she said, frowning.

"Oh, that's right," Walker said, flashing a smile at her. "We weren't introduced, were we?"

"No," she said. She was a little standoffish. But she was also a little intrigued. "My name is Anne Sanford."

"Well, Anne Sanford," Walker said, sliding his credit card out of his wallet. "This is your lucky day. Because I'm going to buy that painting. But not for me. I'm going to buy it for you."

"Why . . . why would you do that?" she stammered.

"Why wouldn't I?" Walker asked, smiling at her again and hoping that he still had a little of his old charm left. Apparently, he did, because she blushed and smiled, a little uncertainly, back at him.

Allie walked over to them now, simultaneously handing Anne Sanford a glossy brochure and glaring at Walker. "Mr. Ford," she said, coolly, "it's a nice gesture, really. But it's not necessary. If Ms. Sanford decides she'd like the painting, she can always come back and buy it for herself."

"But Ms. Sanford won't have to do that," Walker said breezily, pressing his credit card into Allie's hand. "Because Ms. Sanford—Anne—is leaving with the painting today. Isn't that right, Anne?" he asked, smiling at her again.

"I . . . I guess so," she said, smiling at Walker. Her reserve had completely melted. She looked like a schoolgirl who'd just been asked to a dance.

"Well, you heard her," Walker said to Allie, with a wink.

She gave him a withering look and went to ring up the painting. After Walker had carried the painting, wrapped in brown paper, out to Anne's car, and said his good-byes to her, he came back into the gallery.

He found Allie seething with anger.

"What's wrong?" he asked. "You sold the painting, didn't you?"

"I sold the painting to *you*," Allie pointed out. "I wanted to sell it to *her*."

"What's the difference?" Walker asked, walking over to the counter where Allie was straightening things out.

"The difference is something I would think you, as a businessman, would understand. I'm not just trying to sell a painting to her, Walker. I'm trying to build a relationship with her. So that the next time she's here—and there will be a next time, because her sister owns a cabin up here—she'll come back and buy something else."

Walker blew a breath out. He felt, quite literally, deflated. "Look, I'm sorry," he said. "I probably shouldn't have done that. But, Allie, I'm desperate. I need to talk to you. And I figured if I came in here, you wouldn't be able to get rid of me as easily as you get rid of me every place else in town."

"You were right about that," Allie said, with a ghost of a smile, her anger subsiding a little. She sat down on a high stool behind the counter, took out a brown paper bag, and slid out a sandwich, wrapped in waxed paper. "If it's okay with you," she said, unwrapping the sandwich, "I'm going to have my lunch while we talk." Then she corrected herself, saying, "While *you* talk."

"You haven't had lunch yet?" he asked, glancing at his watch. It was two thirty.

"I've been busy," she said, picking up the sandwich.

"Then let me take you out," he said, quickly. "I mean, I'm sure that sandwich is fine, if you made it. But, honestly, it just looks . . . it looks a little sad."

Allie looked at the sandwich, sighed, and put it down. "It *does* look a little sad," she admitted, stuffing it and the waxed paper back into the brown paper bag.

"Let me take you to Pearl's, then," he said, feeling a twinge of hope. "The BLT's on special today. Can someone else be here? For a little while?"

"I can close for half an hour. Sara doesn't mind if I do that when I'm alone here. But it needs to be quick," she added, still not meeting his eyes.

Allie put a BACK SOON sign in the window, locked the door, and followed Walker across the street to Pearl's. The lunch rush was over, and, except for a few stragglers, most of the tables were free.

Caroline was there, of course, leaning on the counter, and talking to Jax, who was sitting on one of the swivel seats, holding her baby. Walker, glancing over, marveled at how tiny the baby was. How old would she be now, he wondered. A month? He couldn't imagine how anyone could be brave enough to hold something that looked so small, and so vulnerable.

But Jax looked perfectly comfortable, holding Jenna upright on her chest so that Jenna's cheek rested on her shoulder. She waved to Allie, but when she saw she was with Walker, she politely looked away. Caroline was reserved, too. She came over, took their orders—two lemonades and two BLTs—and immediately retreated.

"How's Jax doing?" Walker asked, quietly, glancing over at her again.

Allie shrugged, noncommittally. "She's fine," she said.

"She left her husband and three of her children and she's fine?" Walker asked, skeptically.

"She's sees the older girls here every day," Allie said, with a little frown. "But the rest of it . . . it's complicated."

"I'll bet it is. I saw Jeremy at the hardware store yesterday," he said, after Caroline had brought both of them a lemonade. "He looked terrible. Like he hasn't slept in days. I was afraid he was going to fall asleep right there in the power tool aisle." Walker didn't tell her that he'd sympathized with Jeremy, then. He hadn't been sleeping all that well himself lately.

"I don't know how Jeremy's doing," Allie admitted. "But Jax is a survivor," she said, loyally. "One way or another, she'll come through this. But this isn't what you brought me here to talk about, is it?" she asked, sipping her lemonade.

"No," Walker said, glancing around nervously. He knew he

was running out of time. But he didn't want there to be any inter-
ruptions when he told her what he'd come to tell her. He decided
to wait until their orders came.

"How's Wyatt doing?" he asked, instead, really wanting to
know.

Allie's face softened instantly. "He just started kindergarten,"
she said, proudly. "And he loves it. He thinks his teacher, Ms.
Conover, looks like a princess. And, of course, he loves having
a best friend, Jade, who's in the first grade. That definitely gives
him bragging rights on the playground."

Walker smiled. "Bragging rights are important. And a teacher
who looks like a princess? That's definitely a bonus." He chuckled, some of his nervousness fading. "But what about fishing?" he
asked. "Have you taken him fishing recently?"

"No," Allie said, with a little shake of her head. "I've tried. But
I'm a poor substitute for you, apparently. Wyatt said . . ." But she
stopped midsentence. "Never mind," she amended, quickly.

But Walker understood. And if Wyatt missed their early morning fishing trips, he knew exactly how he felt. He missed them,
too. He hadn't been fishing, in fact, since the last time he'd gone
with Wyatt. It felt wrong, somehow, to go without him.

Caroline brought their sandwiches over, and when Walker
looked up, a few minutes later, she'd disappeared, along with Jax
and the baby, and the few other customers who'd been lingering
over their lunches. They had the place all to themselves, he realized. No more excuses for him to stall, then.

"Look," he said, his nervousness returning as he fidgeted with
his napkin. "I'm not very good at talking. That's why I like fishing, I guess. No talking necessary. But I need you to understand
why I acted the way I did. So just hear me out, okay? And try
to keep an open mind. I just . . . I just really need you to listen."

"I'm listening," Allie said, her face unreadable.

So he took a deep breath and started, without any preamble. He began with the day that Caitlin had come to his office at the boatyard and told him she was pregnant. The day he'd proposed to her. And then he moved on to the long, lonely months that followed, the two of them living together, as man and wife, but also, it turned out, as perfect strangers.

He was careful not to shift the blame on to Caitlin. In fact, he accepted all of it himself. He could have been honest with Caitlin when he'd realized their marriage was a mistake, he admitted to Allie. But instead, he'd ignored her and buried himself in his work. It was easier than telling Caitlin the truth, he said. But it was also more cowardly.

When he reached the part about Caitlin's not being able to feel the baby move anymore, he stumbled a little. This was new to him, this openness. He'd never talked about these things with anyone before. Not even his brother, Reid, who'd had to fill in most of the blanks on his own. But he kept going. There was no turning back now. Not when the stakes were this high.

So he told her about taking Caitlin to the hospital. About the news they'd gotten there. About her plans to leave him as soon as she was released. And about his convincing her to come home with him and give their marriage another try, even though, he'd realized later, he had no intention of trying again himself. And, finally, he told her about Caitlin's leaving, in the early hours of that snowy January morning.

He'd been looking down at his paper napkin—which he'd by now systematically shredded—but he stole a glance at Allie, half expecting her to look appalled by his insensitivity. Or disgusted by his selfishness. But she didn't look either of those things. She just looked sad.

"That was the last time I saw her," he said, reaching for another napkin from the napkin dispenser. "Until she came up here a month ago. And I might not have seen her again, Allie, if it hadn't been for you."

"Me?" she said, surprised.

"You," he nodded. "Because the morning after we spent the night together, I realized two things. The first was that I needed to see Caitlin again. I knew, then, my relationship with her wasn't over yet. It was over on paper. But that was all."

Allie frowned, not understanding.

"I don't mean that I still cared about her in that way," he said, quickly. "In a romantic way. But I cared about her as a person. And I owed her an apology, Allie. A *big* apology.

"As it turned out, though, I had no idea how to get in touch with her. Probably because she didn't *want* me to be able to get in touch with her. I finally tracked her down through a friend of hers, though, and I asked her if I could come down to Minneapolis to see her. But, instead, she came up here. I didn't know she was coming, Allie. I would have told you if I had. But she explained to me later that she didn't call ahead because she didn't know until she pulled into my driveway whether or not she'd be able to go through with it. *That's* how angry she still was."

He watched, now, while Allie looked down at her BLT and prodded it gently with one finger. But she didn't eat it.

"Anyway," Walker went on, "she stayed at the White Pines for a couple days, and we spent some time together. I'm not going to lie. It was a little tense at first. But we talked. We talked more than we did when we were actually married to each other. She told me that she'd gotten engaged." He brightened at the memory of how happy Caitlin had been whenever she'd mentioned her fiancé. "And I told her that I was sorry. And that . . . that I still blame myself for her losing the baby."

"Walker," Allie said, shaking her head. But he kept talking. "No, it's true, Allie. I do. Her doctor made some speech about how 'these things happen, and we don't necessarily know why.' But would it have happened if she hadn't been so miserable? Honestly, I have my doubts about that. I think I always will.

"But, still, it was good for us to see each other. Good for us to finally end our marriage, in a way our divorce never could. I think, I *know*, she's let go of some of the anger she felt at me. And I got to give her something I had that belonged to her. Nothing valuable. Just something she'd left behind." He shook his head, remembering the nightgown that, for a time, had taken up residence on the top shelf of his hall closet.

"But, Allie?" he went on, returning to the task at hand. "I realized something else that morning, lying in bed with you, watching you sleep . . ." He saw her color, slightly, at the intimate image his words evoked. "I realized that I was terrified. Terrified of the fact that I was in love with you," he said, looking steadily at her.

Her hazel eyes widened in surprise, and her golden skin flushed an even warmer pink. She definitely had not expected a declaration of love with her lunch order, Walker decided.

"It's true," he said, simply. "Not only that, but it was a first for me. I've never been in love before. And it scared the hell out of me. For a minute, I panicked. I thought I was having a heart attack." He chuckled at the memory. "Before then, I guess, I thought of falling in love as something that happened to other people, but not to me. I wasn't stupid enough to do that. But looking at you—and you looked beautiful, by the way—I was so filled with love for you. And I realized that you were it, Allie. And I thought, 'God help me, because I'm done for now.'"

Walker went on. "The simplest thing to do would have been to tell you how I felt. But that would have required more courage than I actually had. And when Caitlin came, I used that as an excuse to try to buy some time. I didn't realize you'd react that way, Allie, and tell me to get lost for good." He was still chagrined at the memory.

"I don't think those were my exact words," Allie murmured, with the closest thing to a smile he'd seen from her that afternoon.

"No," he agreed, "you were too polite to say that. But if you had said it, it probably wouldn't have been any less than I deserved."

He smiled at Allie now, marveling at how pretty she looked in the slats of light coming in through the coffee shop's half-closed blinds. A strand of hair had worked itself loose from the knot at the nape of her neck, he saw, and it was all he could do not to reach over and brush it off her cheek.

"Walker," she said, suddenly, straightening up in her chair, "I appreciate your honesty. I do. I know it couldn't have been easy for you to tell me everything you've told me. But I don't see how it changes anything. Between you and me, I mean."

He started in surprise. "Allie, it changes *everything*," he said.

But she looked doubtful. "I don't know that it does. I mean, it sounds like you've been able to gain some perspective on your past. And that's a good thing. But as far as I know, you're still the same man who panicked the morning after he spent the night with me. What makes you think you've changed? And what makes you think you won't panic again the next time? If there is a next time."

If. He didn't like the sound of that word.

"Look, Allie, I *was* that man. But I'm not that man anymore. I love you. And loving you, it's given me a courage I didn't even know I had. Maybe that's what love does to people. I don't know. I guess my learning curve is still pretty high."

But she shook her head. "Walker, how do you know this is love? How do you know it's not just some kind of infatuation?"

"I've considered that," he admitted. "Especially since this all feels new to me. The not being able to sleep. Or eat. Or concentrate at work. Or do anything, really, besides think about you. But I don't think it's just an adolescent crush, Allie. I think it's gone way beyond that. I think—or I like to think—that I'm capable of more now. I like to think I'm capable of loving you."

She thought for a second. "So that feeling you felt that morning, after we spent the night together, that fear, it's gone?" she asked.

He shrugged. "There's a little left, I guess. But mostly, that old fear has been replaced by a new fear. A fear of you not being part of my life."

She looked down and bit her lower lip. "I don't know," she said finally, softly. "I just don't know."

"What don't you know?" he asked. He was staring, involuntarily, at the hollow at the base of her neck. Remembering all the kisses he'd lavished on it. And all the pleasure he'd elicited from her by doing so. But sitting across the table from her now, it was as if there was an invisible wall separating them from each other. She was so close to him now, so tantalizingly close, but he couldn't reach out and touch her. Couldn't touch her neck. Couldn't even touch the pretty fingers of her suntanned hand resting lightly on the table. He swallowed some lemonade. *This is torture,* he thought. With no apparent end in sight.

"Walker, I'm sorry. But I don't know if I trust you," she said now, speaking so quietly that he had to lean forward to hear her. "And not just for my sake. But for Wyatt's sake, too. Because if it doesn't work out again, Walker, I'm not the only one who is going to get hurt. He's going to get hurt, too."

"I know that," he said quickly. "And I know I must seem like a poor risk to you. But, Allie, I can't prove to you that I've changed unless you *let* me prove it to you."

"So I'm just supposed to take some gigantic leap of faith?" she asked, doubtfully.

"Exactly," he said. "That's exactly what you're supposed to do."

"I . . . I need time to think," she said, finally. "I can't give you an answer right now."

Walker nodded. "Take as much time as you need. And, Allie, if you decide it's a no, that you don't want to try again, then I'll spare you the awkwardness of having to run into me in line at the grocery store anymore."

"What do you mean?"

"My brother, Reid, wants me to move back to Minneapolis. He's been trying to persuade me to do it all summer. He says the Butternut Boatyard doesn't need me there full-time anymore, and he's right. It doesn't. Cliff, our GM here, is more than ca-pable of running it by himself."

"And if we did decide to try again?" she asked, frowning.

"I'd stay here, with you and Wyatt, and run the Butternut Boatyard. And Cliff would move to Minneapolis and be Reid's right-hand man. That's my preference, obviously. But if I can't have you, then I don't want this," he said, gesturing around him.

"But you love your cabin," she objected. "And you love the lake."

"I do," he admitted. "But they won't mean anything without you and Wyatt in my life."

"Walker," she murmured. "This is a lot to take in."

"I know it is. I don't want to rush you, Allie. Take your time. And when you've made up your mind, call me. Or come over. Any time of the day or night."

He smiled, remembering the last time she'd come over. And the night of lovemaking it had led to. She saw that smile and frowned. She knew what he was remembering.

"Walker? Whatever happens, you know it's not just about you and me, right? It's about you, and me and Wyatt."

"I wouldn't have it any other way," he said, immediately. "He's an amazing little boy." *And I miss him,* he almost added. *I miss him like crazy.*

He watched her glance at her watch and saw the surprise register on her face. He glanced, guiltily, at his own watch. Had they really been sitting here for that long? She needed to get back to the gallery.

She reached into her handbag and took out her wallet, but Walker intercepted her.

"I'll take care of it," he said. "I'm sorry I kept you so long."

She said a quick, preoccupied good-bye and was gone.

Walker exhaled, slowly. He'd done everything he could do. He'd said his piece. It was out of his hands now. And whatever decision she made, he'd have to respect it. Live by it. The best that he could.

He left some bills on the table. Then glanced across at her plate. She hadn't taken a single bite of her sandwich. He sighed and wondered if he should have Caroline wrap it up so he could drop it off at the gallery. But he decided against it. He didn't know if she ever wanted to see him again or not.

CHAPTER 30

Caroline rang the front doorbell again, but this time she left her finger on it. She knew somebody was home. Lights were blazing from all the windows. And, from somewhere inside the house, she could hear the repetitive thudding of rock music. She wasn't leaving until somebody—*anybody*—opened this door.

Finally, after five minutes, she heard a voice. An exasperated voice.

"All right, knock it off. I'm coming, damn it."

The door opened, and there was Jeremy, looking thoroughly irritated. And thoroughly disheveled. He was wearing a dirty T-shirt and an old pair of jeans. His hair was uncombed, he had at least a three days' growth of razor stubble on his face, and his brown eyes were shadowed with fatigue.

"Oh, Jeremy," Caroline said sadly. "You look like hell."

"That's sweet of you to say," he growled, sarcastically. Caroline frowned. It wasn't in Jeremy's nature to be sarcastic. In fact, before his separation from Jax, he'd been unfailingly good-natured, not to mention polite. It was amazing, really, how much one person could change, and in how little time they could change, under the right circumstances. Or, in Jeremy's case, under the wrong circumstances.

"Are you going to ask me in?" Caroline asked coolly, when he made no move to do so.

He shrugged. "I assume you're here on some errand for Jax?"

"Actually, Jeremy, Jax doesn't know I'm here. But, yes, now that you mention it, I am here on her behalf."

"Well, I have nothing to say on that subject," he said, starting to close the door on her.

"Jeremy, don't you dare close this door in my face," Caroline said, warningly.

He looked at her defiantly, then lost his nerve. He looked down at the floor and sighed. A defeated sigh. "Fine, suit yourself," he said, opening the door wider.

Caroline came into the house and followed him into the living room. She looked around the room, speechless. The place was in a shambles. There were clothes, books, toys, and DVDs strewn everywhere, and dirty dishes were stacked on every surface.

"Jeremy, what happened here?" she asked, appalled, as she righted a large potted plant that had been tipped over, spilling dirt onto the living room rug.

"Three little girls happened here," he said, with an indifferent shrug.

And one presumably adult man, she wanted to say, but didn't.

"I'd ask you to sit down," he said, "but as you can see, there's nowhere to sit down."

Caroline nodded, frowning. The two armchairs had been dragged together and draped with blankets in some attempt at building a fort. And the couch, she saw, with surprise, was made up like a bed, though it was so rumpled she wondered how anyone could sleep on it. Staring at it now, something occurred to her.

When her husband had left her, it had been too painful to sleep alone in her suddenly too-big bed, so she'd slept on the couch instead. She wondered, sadly, if Jeremy was doing the same thing now.

She heard a commotion from upstairs now, angry, childish shrieking, followed by a door slamming.

"That's Joy and Josie fighting," Jeremy offered, glancing in the direction of the stairs. "That's all they do now. I don't know how Jax ever got them to stop."

"They're still awake?" Caroline asked in surprise.

He nodded, and even in his surly mood he had the decency to look embarrassed.

"Jeremy, it's almost eleven o'clock," she objected. "It's way past their bedtime. Especially on a school night."

"I can't get them to go to sleep," he admitted. "They miss Jax. And the good-night phone calls don't seem to be helping."

Caroline winced. She'd heard these phone calls, or Jax's side of them, anyway. They were pathetic things. Jax saying good night to each of her daughters in turn, while she tried, valiantly, not to cry.

"Jeremy," she said, something occurring to her. "What exactly do the girls think is going on here? With you and Jax, I mean?"

"They think Mommy and the baby are staying with you because Mommy needs some rest," he said.

Caroline sighed. "And how long do they think this arrangement is going to continue?"

"I have no idea," he said, still not looking at her.

She edged over to the couch and sat down, gingerly, on the

edge of it. "We need to talk," she said, gesturing to the couch beside her.

"We *are* talking," Jeremy pointed out.

"No, I mean *really* talk," Caroline said.

"I have nothing to say," Jeremy said sullenly. He didn't sit down next to her on the couch. But he did pull one of the armchairs over and sit, noncommittally, on the arm of it.

"Well, even if you have nothing to say for yourself," she said, not bothering to keep the irritation out of her voice, "I assume you'd like to know how your wife and daughter are doing."

"I don't need to ask. I know they're being well taken care of by you."

Yes, but you should be the one taking care of them, she almost said. But she caught herself.

"As a matter of fact," she said, "I *am* doing my best to make them comfortable. But there are certain things I can't do. I can't, for instance, persuade Jax to stop crying. All she does, Jeremy, all day long, is cry and nurse that baby. At the very least, I'd say, she's in serious danger of dehydration."

She smiled, trying to inject a little humor into the conversation, but Jeremy only said, wearily, "Get to the point, Caroline."

"The point," she said, "is that I want you to ask Jax to come home. Where she belongs. Because you and I both know that no matter how angry or how hurt you are, it's the right thing to do."

"Caroline, I told you. I'm not having this conversation," Jeremy said, starting to stand up.

"Well, at least have the decency to hear me out then," she said, sharply.

He sighed and sat back down.

"Jeremy, how much do you know about Jax's childhood?" she asked, changing tack.

He shrugged. "Jax doesn't like to talk about it. But I assume it wasn't exactly the whole white picket fence thing."

"That's an understatement," Caroline said. "But I'm going to tell you a little more about it."

"Don't bother, Caroline. Because if you think the fact that her parents were both drunks excuses what she did, I disagree."

"It doesn't *excuse* it," Caroline said, carefully. "But it might *explain* it. Do you know, for instance, that when Jax's parents got drunk, they used to fight with each other. I mean *really* fight. Physical stuff? And that when they fought, she would hide in a closet. She was generally safe in there. The only problem was, as she got older, the fighting got worse. That was when she started walking over to Pearl's. Which, I should point out, was a three-mile walk for her. She did it at all hours of the day and night, too. During the day, my parents would give her breakfast or lunch. And they'd give her something to do around the place and pay her a little money for doing it. They liked her, of course. You couldn't *not* like Jax. But mainly, I think, they felt sorry for her."

Jeremy still sat stony faced, not looking at her. But Caroline kept talking. "When Jax would come at night, my dad would let her sleep in the storage room. He'd bring down a blanket and pillow for her, and she'd sleep right on top of those enormous bags of flour he kept stacked in there. Then he'd wake her up early, when he came down to start the coffee, so she had enough time to walk home and get changed for school.

"One night, I remember so clearly. It was in the dead of winter. It must have been twenty degrees below zero. And Jax showed up at around two o'clock in the morning. She was freezing. She'd walked the whole way there through the snow. My mother brought her right up to the apartment and put her to bed.

She must have put five blankets on top of her. But it was almost morning before she got her to stop shivering."

"Okay, I get it," Jeremy snapped, finally shaken out of his torpor. "She had a lousy childhood. But, Caroline, it still doesn't explain why she did what she did. She lied to me. Every day of our marriage. And I let her lie, it's true. But I never expected this to happen. She took our money—money that we worked so hard to save—and gave it away. *Threw* it away, really. And she didn't tell me. She played me for the fool I was, I guess. But I'm not going to be that fool anymore."

Caroline shook her head, thinking, desperately, *he's got this all wrong*. But she knew there must be some way to get through to him.

"Jeremy," she said suddenly. "Did Jax ever tell you why she didn't want a dishwasher?"

He looked at her and frowned. "Caroline, I really don't see what that has to do with anything."

But she persisted. "Did Jax ever tell you why she didn't want a dishwasher?"

He shook his head, impatiently. "I don't know. She said she liked doing dishes."

"*Nobody* likes doing dishes," Caroline said. "Jax did them for a special reason. She told me about it once. She didn't tell you, probably, because she didn't want to burden you with how un- happy her childhood was. But I was here one day, after you two had gotten married and moved into this house. And I was sitting in your kitchen, watching Jax hand wash the breakfast dishes. I wanted to help her. But she wouldn't let me. And I said, 'Well, you're going to have a dishwasher put in, aren't you?' And she said no. And she told me that when she was a child, her family didn't have any dishes. None at all. It wasn't because they were poor, though money was scarce, of course. They didn't have any dishes because her parents would always break them when they fought with each other. So eventually, I guess, someone had the brilliant idea of just not replacing them anymore. So they ate off paper plates, or napkins, or nothing at all, I guess.

"And she told me that morning, in your kitchen, that every time she washed a dish, she was going to think about how lucky she was to have them. And how lucky she was to have you, too—"

"*Stop it,*" Jeremy beseeched, holding his hands up in surrender. "I can't take it anymore, Caroline. You think I don't still love her? You think it doesn't hurt me to hear this? But it doesn't undo what she already did."

"No, it doesn't," she agreed. "Nothing can do that. But, Jeremy, don't you see why Jax gave Bobby that ten thousand dollars? Don't you see what she was trying to protect? She was trying to protect all the things she thought about every time she washed the dishes. Was it right for her to give him that money? Probably not. Should she have told you about it? Probably. But Jeremy, in Jax's mind, she didn't have a choice. She thought if she gave him the money, he would leave you all alone, and you could get back to being what you are. A family who loves each other.

"I know ten thousand dollars is a lot of money," she continued, a little breathlessly. "And I know she knows that, too. But I don't think she put a price on what you had together, Jeremy. To her, I think, what you had was priceless. She gave Bobby Lewis ten thousand dollars. But Jeremy, honestly, I think she would have given him ten *million* dollars if she'd had it."

She stopped, her heart pounding, and waited. There was nothing more she could say. She knew that. The rest was up to Jeremy.

For a long time, he sat there, motionless, in the armchair. And then he leaned over, his elbows on his knees, and buried his face in his hands. Caroline thought he was going to cry. But he didn't. Although when he spoke again, he sounded so miserable that he might as well have been crying.

"What am I supposed to do now?"

"Now?" Caroline repeated, her mind racing. "You're supposed to come with me," she said, decisively. "Ask Joy to watch the younger girls. Come back with me. And bring your wife and daughter home, where they belong." She held her breath. But she exhaled when she saw him nod.

"I'll talk to Joy," he said. Then he pushed himself out of the armchair and headed up the stairs.

Less than fifteen minutes later, Caroline unlocked the front door to her apartment. Jax, she saw, was sitting on the couch in the living room, nursing the baby. She looked up when Caroline came in and tried to smile. Then she saw Jeremy behind Caroline.

"Jeremy?" she said softly, questioningly.

He nodded and, hesitantly, sat down next to her on the couch.

He reached out then and stroked Jenna's fuzzy head, barely visible above the top of her baby blanket.

"What are you doing here?" Jax asked. She looked both hopeful and afraid at the same time.

"I came to bring you two home," Jeremy said, his voice catching, as he gathered them both up in his arms.

"I need to do some things downstairs," Caroline said quickly, but neither of them paid any attention to her. Jax started sobbing, uncontrollably, this time with happiness. And by the time she closed the apartment door behind her, Caroline thought Jeremy might be crying a few tears of his own.

Don't you start crying, too, she told herself as she went downstairs. But she could already feel her tear glands going into overdrive. Maybe it was okay to have a good cry, she thought, letting herself into the coffee shop, if it was about someone else's life. And it wasn't a sad cry, but a happy cry. She started to walk over to the coffee machines behind the counter, but she stopped, midstride, when she passed the cash register. Then she hesitated and, opening it, lifted out the bill drawer and took out Buster Caine's business card. She studied it for a moment, but only a moment. Time was of the essence here. Too much time and she'd lose her nerve.

She walked over to the phone, picked it up, and dialed. He answered on the third ring.

"Hello?"

"Buster? Hi. It's Caroline. Caroline from the coffee shop?"

There was a pause. Then he said, amused, "I remember you, Caroline."

"Is it too late for me to call?"

"No, it's fine. I'm still awake. What can I do for you?"

"You can take me up in your plane," she answered, immediately.

There was another pause.

"I mean, if the offer still holds," she said, quickly.

"It still holds."

"Oh, okay. So what's a good time for you?"

"Well, that depends. What time do you close tomorrow?"

"Three thirty."

"Should I come by then?"

"Yes. And Buster?"

"Yes?"

"I'm really looking forward to this."

"Well, then, that makes two of us, Caroline."

CHAPTER 31

On a cool night in September, Allie sat on her front porch steps and tried to stop her knees from shaking. They were doing that thing again, the thing they'd done the day of her and Walker's picnic. She watched them now, trembling violently, resisting any effort on her part to still them. She wrapped her arms around them and pulled them up to her chest, resting her chin on them. They kept shaking. It was as if they had a mind of their own. As if they knew something she didn't.

Which was ridiculous, really. Because all she was doing here tonight was waiting for Walker to come over for an after-dinner cup of coffee. There was something she needed to discuss with him, obviously. Something important. But they were both grown-ups. Both rational people. And this evening would reflect that. There was no reason for her knees to be shaking uncontrollably.

She glanced at her watch. Eight fifty-five. If he was on time—and she had a feeling he would be—he'd be there in five minutes. But at that exact moment she heard his pickup rumbling up the driveway, heard the spit of gravel flying out from beneath the tires. The truck's headlights swung into view, briefly illuminating her as they traveled across the porch, then settling on a stand of birch trees that fringed the lake's shore. Walker cut the engine, and the birch trees jumped back into darkness. He got out of the truck and came around to the porch side of it.

"*Stop it*," Allie whispered, to her still-shaking knees.

"Hey," Walker said, raising a hand in greeting as he came up the steps.

"Hi," Allie said, standing up, and praying that her wobbly knees wouldn't buckle under her.

"Is Wyatt around?"

"Asleep," Allie said. "But he put up a good fight before he agreed to go to bed."

Walker smiled. "I would expect no less of him."

"I thought we'd have coffee out here," she said, gesturing to the porch. "But it's a little chilly with the wind off the lake. So maybe we should have it in the living room, instead." She'd forgotten how early fall came this far north. Already, she could feel the days getting shorter. Shorter and colder. This morning, in fact, when she'd left to drive Wyatt to school, they'd been able to see their breath in the air.

"It's a little chilly," Walker agreed, following her into the cabin. "But then again, today's September twentieth. The last day of summer. So maybe it's fitting that it should feel a little bit like winter."

The last day of summer, Allie thought, going into the kitchen to turn on the coffeepot. She'd forgotten all about that. Was it possible that she and Wyatt had only lived here for one summer? She remembered back to their first night. The cabin had been a wreck, with its listing front porch and the sputtering brown water that had come out of the faucets.

But, in truth, she and Wyatt hadn't been doing much better than the cabin. Outwardly, of course, they'd looked all right. But inside, they'd both been hurting. Badly.

She came into the living room now and perched, nervously, on the edge of the couch. Walker, who'd been standing around, unsure of what to do, sat down next to her, careful to keep a respectful distance between them.

She hesitated, trying to find the words to say what she wanted to say, but it was Walker who spoke first.

"I heard you and Wyatt were away."

"We were. For a long weekend." A long weekend in the truest sense of the word. They'd gone back to Eden Prairie and stayed with friends. She'd cleared out their storage area and given away most of Gregg's things. A few, she'd saved for Wyatt. A battered hockey stick Gregg had cherished. A guitar he'd played in a garage band in high school. A faded University of Minnesota sweatshirt. These things might not mean anything to Wyatt yet, but someday, she hoped, they would.

They'd also done something else while they were back in the Twin Cities' area. They'd visited Gregg's gravesite and left a picture there that Wyatt had drawn for him. It was a bright crayon drawing of Allie and Wyatt, standing in front of the cabin. Above them was a blue sky, with puffy white clouds and a smiling yellow sun in it. Wyatt had said he hoped Gregg would like it, and Allie had said that she knew he would.

But she didn't tell any of this to Walker. Not yet, anyway. There was something else she needed to say first. But it was harder than she'd known it would be. So instead, she stalled. "Do you want some coffee?" she asked, glancing away. "It's ready."

He nodded, distractedly, as if he hadn't really heard her.

She got up and went to the kitchen, filled two cups with coffee, and stirred half-and-half into both. When she came back to the living room, though, Walker wasn't sitting on the couch anymore. He was standing in front of the fireplace, staring at the new painting hanging above it.

"Is that . . . ?" he asked, mystified, pointing to the painting.

"It is," she said, handing him his cup of coffee. "It's the view of your dock, from my dock. Do you like it?"

He looked at her, uncomprehendingly, and looked back at the painting.

"Remember the painting you bought for that woman at the Pine Cone Gallery?" Allie said. "It's by the same artist. I really like his work, and I knew he's set a lot of his paintings here, on Butternut Lake. So I commissioned it from him. It's big, so it took him a few days of working on it, painting nonstop. He drove over here and worked on it while Wyatt and I were back in Eden Prairie. It was waiting for us when we came back."

"Why that view?" Walker asked.

"I don't know." Allie shrugged. "Maybe because I spent half of my waking hours staring at it this summer. But you know, Walker," she said, smiling, "if things don't work out between us this time, I'm going to be stuck with an awfully big reminder of you."

"So . . ." He stared at her, waiting for some additional explanation.

"So . . . I thought about what you said at Pearl's that day and I decided I want to take that leap of faith. With you, Walker. With us, I mean. I want to try again."

"Try again as in 'you and me'?"

She nodded. "If that's what you still want, too," she said.

"If that's what I still want?" he repeated, disbelievingly. "Allie, are you kidding? I've never wanted anything more. But I didn't think *you* wanted it. At least not anymore. So I was trying to prepare myself for the worst. Before I came here tonight, I felt like I was on my way to face a firing squad."

She laughed. Come to think of it, he had seemed uncharacteristically tense tonight. "So, we're going to do this? Try this, I mean?" she asked him.

"We'd be crazy not to," he said, smiling at her. And that smile practically made her swoon. He reached for her coffee cup then and put it down on the mantelpiece with his. And then he pulled her into his arms, and his lips found hers. "We need to celebrate," he said, between kisses. "Forget the coffee. Do you have any champagne?"

"Champagne, no," Allie said. "Apple juice, maybe."

"Apple juice isn't going to do it," he said, kissing her neck in that way she loved. "But there are other ways we could celebrate."

Allie's knees wobbled warningly, but there was something she wanted to say to Walker before it was too late.

"We'll celebrate," she said, shivering with desire. "I promise. But there are a few ground rules I want to establish, first."

"Right now?"

"Right now," she said. After all, if the past was any guide, her self-control with Walker wouldn't last much longer.

He stopped kissing her neck, but he left his arms around her. "Okay, shoot."

"Let's sit down," she suggested, gently disentangling herself from him. He followed her to the couch and they sat facing each other.

"Walker, Gregg was a good husband," she said, without any preamble.

"I know that," Walker said, automatically. If he was surprised at her choice of subjects, he didn't show it.

"And a good father," she added.

"I know that, too."

"I'm not going to forget about him, Walker. And, if I have my way, Wyatt's not going to forget about him, either."

"I don't want either of you to forget about him," Walker said, simply.

She nodded. She believed him. "I owe it to Gregg to remember him, and I owe it to myself and to Wyatt, too. I won't let his life not matter, Walker. But I know now that I need to live my life at the same time. And I want it to be a happy life. For a long time, I didn't want it to be happy. I thought it was my responsibility, in a way, to grieve for Gregg. Full-time. Like a job, almost. But anyone who knew Gregg knows that's not what he would have wanted for me. And I don't want it for me, either. Not anymore. But it's going to be a balancing act for me, at first, anyway. Keeping Gregg's memory alive. And allowing myself to be happy."

For a long moment, Walker looked at her thoughtfully, considering what she'd said. But when he spoke, he seemed to choose the exact words Allie needed to hear. "There's no reason you can't do both," he said. "Remember Gregg. And be happy. Especially since when you were with Gregg, you were happy. And while I didn't know Gregg, I'll help you and Wyatt in any way I can to keep his memory a part of your lives. I mean, it's no more, and no less, than any of us deserves. To be remembered, with love, by the people we loved. The people who loved us."

Allie nodded, close to tears. But she felt a sense of relief, too. She took a deep breath, and as she exhaled she felt the tension drain out of her body.

"Thank you," she said, inching closer to him.

"There's nothing to thank me for," he said, reaching out and taking her hand. "But now, I have something I want to say, too."

She raised her eyebrows.

"As I said, I never knew Gregg," he began. "But I feel like I owe him a debt, just the same. Because the two people he left behind are both very special people. And I feel like taking good care of them is the least I can do for him. So I'm going to love you two, and protect you, and never, ever hurt you. And while making promises is still pretty new to me, Allie, this is one promise I intend to keep."

Allie swallowed past a lump in her throat. "Walker, can I ask you a favor?"

"Anything," he said. And she knew he meant it. There was nothing this man wouldn't do for her now.

"Could you . . . could you just hold me?" she asked.

"I think so," Walker said, taking her in his arms. "I mean, I'll try," he amended, nuzzling her neck again. "I'll try like hell to *just* hold you. But, Allie, I have to warn you. I've spent so much time thinking about you—thinking about us, together—that I don't know if I can *just* hold you."

"Well, try, anyway," Allie said, snuggling deeper into his arms.

And Walker did try, for a little while. But inevitably, it seemed, they started kissing again, and, in short order, Walker had eased her down beside him on the couch and was unbuttoning her blouse.

"Oh, my knees were so right," Allie murmured, watching him.

"What did you say?" he asked, looking up from the button he'd just undone.

"I said 'we can't do this here,'" she amended quickly. "Wyatt's sleeping in the next room."

"You mean I can't kiss you?"

"It's not the kissing I'm worried about."

"So you're afraid we'll wake up Wyatt?" he clarified.

She nodded.

"The same Wyatt who slept through several hours of violent thunderstorms at my cabin and slept through a baby being born at yours? I think he can sleep through a little lovemaking, don't you?"

"A little?" she asked, only half joking.

"Okay, *a lot*," he admitted.

She laughed, but relented. "All right, but you have to leave before he wakes up in the morning. I don't want to spring this on him. We have to find the right way to tell him."

"Absolutely," Walker agreed. But he didn't go back to the buttons on her blouse. Instead, he picked her up, carried her into her bedroom, closed the door, and laid her down on her bed. There, they undressed each other, slowly, savoring every moment, and made love to each other with so much tenderness that it brought tears to Allie's eyes.

Later, as they lay in each other's arms, Walker saw one of those tears glistening on her cheek. "You're crying," he said in surprise, propping himself up on one elbow and brushing the tear gently away with his fingers. "What's wrong?"

"Nothing," she said, honestly. She touched his face, clouded as it was by concern for her. "Nothing's wrong. I'm just so happy. I don't think I could be any happier."

"Not even a little?" he asked, kissing her playfully.

"I don't think so," she said, kissing him back.

"You sure about that?" he asked again, running a tantalizing finger down her bare stomach.

"Okay. Maybe I could be a *little* happier," she conceded, pulling him back down beside her.

About the author

About the book

Insights,
Interviews
& More . . .

Meet Mary McNear

Amelia Kennedy

MARY MCNEAR is a writer living in San Francisco with her husband, two teenage children, and a high-strung minuscule white dog named Macaroon. She writes her novels in a local doughnut shop, where she sips Diet Pepsi, observes the hubbub of neighborhood life, and tries to resist the constant temptation of freshly made doughnuts. She bases her novels on a lifetime of summers spent in a small town on a lake in the northern Midwest. ∾

Author Essay

THE STORY OF ALLIE AND WYATT started to take shape in my mind a few years ago when I was watching a TV news story about a local National Guard unit that had been deployed to Afghanistan. In the piece they interviewed the young widow of one of its members, who also had a young son, and she looked absolutely stunned by what had happened to her husband. And I remembered thinking that when her husband joined the National Guard it had probably never occurred to either of them that one day he would be fighting a war half a world away.

The story was heartbreaking to me, especially since my own children were still young at the time, and I couldn't imagine my husband not being a part of our lives. I wondered how this family would go on, how they could even begin to rebuild their lives. Hopefully, everyone would rally around them, relatives would come stay with them, neighbors would bring them casseroles, and the son's school would have a fund-raiser. But then what? What about when all the others had gone back to their own lives? They'd be on their own again, wouldn't they?

And then I remembered something a friend of mine who'd lost her husband suddenly had once told me. She'd said that in some ways the beginning was easier. This period was scary and shocking and incredibly lonely, but everyone knew, or could at least imagine, how difficult it was for her. Later on ▶

3

was when it got harder. Not because all of them went back to their own lives, but because everyone seemed to be saying to her, in so many words, "So when are you going to get back to *your* own life?"

This was especially true of my friend because she was still young, as were her children. Several people—well-meaning, obviously, but misguided—actually said to her: "You're lucky you're still young. You can get married again and give your children another father. You can even have more children if you want to." And when she pointed out that she wasn't ready to move on yet, some of these same people seemed impatient with her.

Maybe, I thought as I considered that mother on television, the hardest part would come later for her, as it had for my friend. Or maybe the situation would just be hard in a different way. A new way. And that was when I started thinking about a mother and son who had been through a similar experience. How would they move on? And what if they weren't ready to do so when everyone else wanted them to? How might they handle this in their own time and in their own way? What would it take them, what does it take anyone, really, to start over again?

I chose to explore that question through the eyes of Allie, a young widow whose National Guardsman husband has died in Afghanistan, and Wyatt, her five-year-old son. I decided that at the beginning of the novel they would relocate from suburban Minneapolis to a fishing cabin in northern Minnesota that has been in their family for several generations. That cabin and the lake it is on are both intimately familiar to me; I spent my childhood summers in and on their real-life counterparts. My great-grandfather built my family's cabin in the Upper Midwest during the Depression, and while it has since been divided among countless aunts, uncles, nieces, nephews, and cousins, I still spend a couple of weeks there every summer with my mom, my sisters, and our children. Because no single family owns the cabin and maintenance and upkeep are dealt with by "committee," the place can sometimes look a little neglected. But the torn rug that people have been tripping over for years and the sliding screen door on the back porch that hasn't worked properly since the Eisenhower administration have also become part of the place's charm. In a world of granite kitchen countertops and megapixel flat-screen TVs, our cabin looks exactly like what it is: an uncomplicated, quiet place to spend a few weeks every summer remembering what it is we loved about these woods and this lake when we were children.

Once I had the idea of setting the novel on this lake, which I renamed Butternut Lake, the look and feel of the town of Butternut began to take shape in my mind. I didn't model this town on the town nearest to our summer cabin, though, because that town is too small! At about five hundred people, that town is less than half the size of the fictional Butternut. So instead I drew inspiration from the many other small towns in that area, an area where northern Michigan, northern Minnesota, and northern Wisconsin converge. We're often told that the American small town is in decline, but these communities would seem to counter this statement. And so, too, I decided, would Butternut, with its thriving businesses, shops, and restaurants. Well, *restaurant*. Because when you have a coffee shop as good as Pearl's, you don't need any other place to eat!

As the town of Butternut came into focus for me, its residents did, too. And here again I looked to models in the real world. The people who live in the Upper Midwest are different in many ways from their neighbors farther to the south and west. Maybe it's their proximity to Canada, a stone's throw away, or maybe it's the long winters or the short growing season, but the people who live in this part of the country tend to be reserved, especially with outsiders. This reserve shouldn't be confused with unfriendliness, though, because once it gives way you discover that they have a real warmth and generosity of spirit that informs almost everything they do. I knew the characters in Butternut would have those same qualities, but like Allie would also have their own challenges to overcome, their own mistakes to grapple with, and their own complicated relationships to sort out.

Once I got to this point in the process I was ready to take Allie and Wyatt, plunk them down into their family's old cabin, and stand back and let the lake, the town, and the people work ▶

Author Essay *(continued)*

their magic on a mother and son desperately in need of some. At the same time, though, I tried to keep one thought front and center in my mind: starting over after any kind of tragedy is one of the hardest, loneliest, and scariest things any of us will ever have to do. And those who've had to do it in the past or are doing it right now are the real heroes among us.

Q&A with
Mary McNear

How did you start writing?

Ever since I can remember, I've been making up stories, though I haven't always put them down on paper. As a child, I used to invent characters and intricate plots and then bully other children—usually my younger sister, younger cousins, or younger neighbors— into listening to them. As I got older, though, I decided that I wasn't brave enough to be a writer—something I believed it took a special kind of courage to be. So instead, after I graduated from college I went to graduate school and tried not to think about writing anymore. I wasn't entirely successful, though. For one thing, I kept making up stories—though I didn't make anyone listen to them anymore—and I was assaulted with frequent and painful reminders of what it was I really wanted to be doing. Bookstores, libraries, airport newsstands—the world was filled with evidence of other people writing the kind of fiction I wanted to write, namely women's fiction. Not surprisingly, I tried to avoid reading it myself. (I read a lot of mysteries, which I love, but which I've never actually wanted to write myself!)

But when I was in my early thirties and completing a PhD program, our son—who was three at the time—was diagnosed with autism. To say that this news was life-changing doesn't quite begin to cover it. But as I reordered ▶

my expectations and priorities, one of them refused to budge. I wanted to write novels. And I figured if our son was brave enough every day to confront a world that often felt incomprehensible and overwhelming, then I sure as hell could be brave enough to put pen to paper. So when I dropped out of graduate school and gave myself over to raising a child with special needs, I did something else, too. I made myself write for an hour a day. This was much harder than it sounds, especially since our daughter was born six months after our son's diagnosis. But I wrote for that hour even if it came, as it often did, at six o'clock in the morning or at twelve o'clock at night. I'm pretty sure it was that hour every day that kept me sane during those years.

Our son, by the way, graduated from high school this year. He's a bright, gentle, sweet young man. And the descendant of my first novel, which I started fifteen years ago in the waiting room of the speech therapist's office, is now being published!

Is Up at Butternut Lake *your first novel?*

It's my first novel to be published, but it's not the first novel I've written. There were *many* novels before this one, but if I have a strength as a writer I hope that it's honesty, and I knew the first several novels were not publishable. I didn't get discouraged because I also knew they were getting better. Writing, of course, is a famously nonlinear undertaking, and yet what surprised me the most about the books I wrote was that every single one of them was better than the one before it. Finally I knew I was getting close—really close. And Kimberly Whalen, who would become my agent, agreed. In fact, she said if I submitted my next novel to her, she'd read it and perhaps we could discuss representation. So I wrote it, she loved it, and the rest . . . well, the rest is this novel, *Up at Butternut Lake.*

How long did it take to write?

Up at Butternut Lake took a year to write and another year to edit. Originally it was twenty-five thousand words longer than it is now, but my agent, Kimberly Whalen, thought it needed to be shorter—and she was right. So I set about the humbling process of cutting supporting characters and subplots that, of course, I was very attached to. The upside, though, was that the editing process made me consider what was absolutely essential to the story I wanted to tell. It was hard, but it made the book much stronger.

What do you feel is the central theme of the novel?

Well, in one way or another, all of the other characters in the novel come face-to-face with their pasts, whether ▶

it's to take responsibility for mistakes they've made, grieve for losses they've endured, or overcome old fears that are now holding them back. Jax, for instance, has to meet head-on a series of bad decisions she made before her marriage to Jeremy—decisions threatening to tear apart the family she loves. Walker must acknowledge his unresolved feelings of guilt and pain over his marriage to Caitlin and the baby they lost. And Caroline must conquer her fear of taking risks and having a relationship, a fear developed over years of being a single working mother. Even Frankie must carve out a life for himself, despite the years he lost to jail. The death of a loved one, deception, a failed marriage, the darker parts of our past—all of these things can threaten the present and overshadow the future unless we confront them head-on. I wanted to write about how this process unfolds for the different characters in the novel.

In the novel you write about two women, Allie and Caroline, who are single mothers, each with one child. You also explore the friendships between Allie, Jax, and Caroline. Why did you choose to write about these three women?

I was interested in writing about how the friendships between these three women would evolve naturally in a small community. Allie, the one who has only recently returned to Butternut, is the one who brings them together as a group of friends. But they all have a common past in this town, and they all have children. These women understand that parenting—single parenting in particular—can be hard and lonely. Allie has to make big decisions without a partner to consult. Caroline's daughter has recently left for college, so Caroline has to come to terms with this life change without a partner to ameliorate her sense of loss. And while Jax has a husband, the secrets she has kept mean that in many ways she's had to navigate the experience of parenting alone. I wanted to write about the challenges of motherhood, but also about how friendships with other women can bring humor and insight to these challenges. Finally, I wanted to consider the role of friendship in our lives more generally. It isn't just single mothers who rely on friendships to get them through the day—it's all of us. You need friends who support you and make you laugh, but as Allie, Caroline, and Jax discover, you also want friends who can nudge you gently when you make mistakes or get off track.

In your bio you mention you write your books in a doughnut shop. Why is this a good setting for you?

One of the reasons I write in a doughnut shop is because writing can be lonely, and this way I'm always surrounded by people. But I also write there because I'm a world-class eavesdropper. I've ▶

actually used some of the dialogue I've heard there in my novels!

What made you want to write books with romance in them?

I thought about that recently when our daughter, who's in high school, invited a group of her girlfriends over to our house to get ready for a dance. None of them has a boyfriend, and all of them, it turned out, spent most of that night dancing with one another. But no matter. This was clearly beside the point. Because the point, as they were discovering that night while they gave one another manicures and wobbled around in unfamiliar high heels, was the sense they shared that *something might happen* at the dance. What it was they didn't know, but the possibility of it hung in the air that night more palpably than the Nicki Minaj perfume my daughter insisted on spritzing over everyone.

It doesn't matter what age we are. We remember that emotion. And even better, we still feel it! Not when we're getting ready for a dance, maybe. But at other moments that sense that something might happen finds and surprises us. I tried to capture that feeling—that jittery, scary, but mostly delicious feeling—when I wrote about Allie's falling in love with Walker. Because the next best thing to feeling something yourself is reading about someone else feeling it.

Where do you get story ideas?

As I said above, I got the idea for Allie
and Wyatt's story line watching the
news. But I look for ideas every summer
when I go back to the Midwest. Except
for my summers there, I've lived in the
city all my life, so I have an outsider's
fascination with small-town life. When
we go into the town five miles from
our cabin, I like hanging out at the little
coffee shop or in the tiny public library,
which is housed in a converted log cabin.
I think about all the things the people
who live there know about one another,
but I also think about all the things
they don't know about one another.
The things they *don't* know about one
another are intriguing, and are often
the subjects of my novels! ∽

Discussion Questions

1. Allie is torn between grieving for her deceased husband, Gregg, and falling in love with Walker. Is there an acceptable amount of time to grieve for a loved one? Must Allie stop grieving in order to move forward in her life?

2. Allie abruptly ends the relationship with Walker after Caitlin shows up at his house. She tells Walker she needs to protect Wyatt from the uncertainties of their relationship. Does she do the right thing? Is she simply protecting Wyatt? Or is there more to it than that? Is her reaction unreasonable?

3. After living in the cabin on Butternut Lake for only a couple of months, Wyatt tells Allie it feels like "home." What makes a place "home"? Does time have anything to do with it?

4. Why does Allie owe it to Gregg to remember him? How does Allie balance remembering Gregg and enjoying her new life with Walker?

5. Jax deceives Jeremy twice. First she fails to tell him that Joy is Bobby's daughter. Later she doesn't tell him that she's withdrawn ten thousand dollars to pay off Bobby. Is a lie of omission—especially a big one—just as reprehensible as an outright lie?

6. Bobby's appearance in town is an opportunity for Jax to come clean

and tell Jeremy the truth. But she doesn't. Does Jax believe that Jeremy will no longer love her if he knows the truth? How does Jax underestimate Jeremy's love for her? And how might her own unhappy childhood have compelled her to deceive him?

7. Jeremy knows from the beginning that Joy is not his daughter. Should he have told Jax when Joy was born that he knew the truth but loved them both anyway? By not doing so, was he complicit in Jax's deception?

8. What does Caitlin's nightgown symbolize for Walker? Is his inability to send the nightgown back to Caitlin or just throw it out a sign that there is unfinished business between them?

9. When Caitlin tells Walker that she's pregnant, he admits he's not really father material. He then remembers his troubled relationship with his own father. To what extent does your relationship with your own parents influence your capacity for parenting?

10. It's clear that Walker doesn't love Caitlin when she arrives at the boatyard to tell him she's pregnant. In fact, he acknowledges to himself that they have very little in common. So does he do the right thing when he asks her to marry him? Is he just postponing the inevitable? And to what extent is Walker responsible for the marriage not working? ▶

Discussion Questions *(continued)*

11. When Caitlin miscarries, both she and Walker grieve over the loss of their child. How does each express this loss? And how is this loss different than the death of Allie's husband?

12. Caroline helps to bring Jax and Jeremy back together, she encourages Allie to give Walker a chance, and she hires Frankie when no one else would. What role does she play in the novel?

13. Daisy is aware that her mother is lonely and prods her to join a book club or go on a date. But, as Caroline realizes, she has lost the ability to take risks. Why would being a single working parent make Caroline risk averse?

14. Despite the fact that Frankie killed a man in self-defense, he takes on the role of protector several times. Who are the people he protects in the novel? ∽

Don't miss the next book by your favorite author. Sign up now for AuthorTracker by visiting www.AuthorTracker.com.